PURSUED

BY
TRACY WOLFF

MILLS & BOON

Published in Great Britain 2015
by Mills & Boon, an imprint of Harlequin (UK) Limited,
Eton House, 18-24 Paradise Road, Richmond, Surrey, TW9 1SR

© 2015 Tracy L. Deebs-Elkenaney

ISBN: 978-0-263-25280-4

51-1015

Harlequin (UK) Limited's policy is to use papers that are natural, renewable and recyclable products and made from wood grown in sustainable forests. The logging and manufacturing processes conform to the legal environmental regulations of the country of origin.

Printed and bound in Spain
by CPI, Barcelon

Tracy Wolff collects books, English degrees and lipsticks, and has been known to forget where—and sometimes who—she is when immersed in a great novel. At six, she wrote her first short story—something with a rainbow and a prince—and at seven, she ventured into the wonderful world of girls' lit with her first Judy Blume novel. By ten, she'd read everything in the young-adult and classics sections of her local bookstore, so in desperation her mum started her on romance novels. And from the first page of the first book, Tracy knew she'd found her lifelong love. Tracy lives in Texas with her husband and three sons, where she pens romance novels and teaches writing at her local community college.

One

He was the most beautiful man she'd ever seen.

Desi Maddox knew that sounded excessive, melodramatic even, considering she was standing in a room filled with beautiful people in even more beautiful clothes, but the longer she stood there staring at him, the more convinced she became. He. Was. Gorgeous. So gorgeous that for long seconds he blinded her to everything around her, even the glitter of gems and flash of high society that under normal circumstances would be impossible to ignore.

But these were far from normal circumstances. How could they be when his emerald gaze met hers over the sea of people stretching between them and her knees trembled. Actually trembled. Up until now, she'd always thought that was a cliché best saved for chick flicks and romance novels. But here she was in the middle of a crowded ballroom and all she could do was stand there as her heart raced, her palms grew damp and her knees actually trembled with the force of her reaction to a man she'd never seen before and more than likely would never see again.

Which was probably a good thing, and knowing she wouldn't see him again was exactly what she needed to remind herself why she was here among the best and brightest of San Diego's high society. Scoping out hot men was definitely not what her boss was paying her for.

More's the pity.

Shaking her head in an effort to clear it, Desi forced herself to glance away from his mesmerizing gaze. Forced herself to check out the rest of the fancy gala, and the fancier people, she was currently stuck in the middle of. And the people were fancy, some of the fanciest she'd ever seen. Even he—of their own volition, her eyes moved back to Tall, Dark and Much Too Handsome— was fancy, in his five-thousand-dollar tuxedo and the flashing diamonds on his cuff links. She couldn't hope to compare.

Not that she wanted to. This was *so* not her scene, and once she'd paid her dues, her boss would recognize that fact and move her somewhere else. Somewhere where she could actually make a difference to the world. After all, what did it matter if the wife of the mayor of San Diego was wearing Manolos or Louboutins on her dainty, pampered feet?

It mattered too much, she told herself wryly as she looked around the crowded ballroom. To a lot of people, it mattered too much. Which was why, on her next sweep of the room, she made herself take her time, made herself study—and identify—each face that passed by. As she did, she didn't know whether to be pleased or horrified that she recognized nearly every person there. It was her job, after all, and it was nice to know that the hours she'd spent poring over old newspaper articles and photos hadn't gone to waste.

After all, unlike the rest of the people here, her role wasn't to drink champagne and drop a lot of money on the charity auction. No, her role, her *job*, was to stay on guard and pay attention to what everyone else was doing so she could write all about it when she got home. If she was lucky—if she kept her eyes open and her mouth shut—and the stars actually aligned, someone would say or do something really scandalous or important and she'd have the chance to write about that instead of the food, the wine and whatever designer was currently "it" among Southern California's social elite.

And if she wasn't lucky, well then she still had to pay attention. Still needed to record who was dating whom and who had made a fashion faux pas and who hadn't…

And yes, her job as the society-page reporter for the local paper really was as boring as it sounded. She tried not to let herself dwell on the fact that she'd spent four years at Columbia's School of Journalism only to end up here. Her father would be *so* proud of her—that is, if he hadn't been killed six months ago while embedded with troops in the Middle East.

A waiter passed by with a tray full of champagne flutes, and she reached out and snagged one of the halffull glasses. Drained it in one long—and hopefully elegant—sip. Then blocked her father's death and disapproval from her mind. She needed to focus on the job at hand. Currently, that job was reporting on this ridiculous affair.

To do her job, though, she needed to blend in with her surroundings. Not that she had much of a chance of actually doing that with her department-store dress and clearance shoes, but she could try. At least until her boss saw the light and took her off this godforsaken beat to put her on something a little more important. And more interesting, she thought, barely smothering yet another yawn as she overheard her fifth conversation of the night about liposuction.

Wanting to free up her hands, she turned to place her glass on the empty tray of yet another passing waiter. As she did, though, her eyes once again met dark green ones. And this time, the man they belonged to was only a couple of feet from her instead of halfway across the crowded ballroom.

She didn't know whether to run or rejoice.

In the end, she did neither. Instead, she just stared—stupefied—up into his too-gorgeous face and tried to think of something to say that wouldn't make her sound like a total moron. It didn't work. Her usually quick mind was a total blank, suddenly filled with nothing but images of him. High cheekbones. Shaggy black hair that fell over his forehead. Wickedly gleaming emerald eyes. Sensuous mouth turned up in a wide, charming smile. Broad shoulders. Lean hips. And tall, so tall that she was forced to look up despite the fact that she stood close to six feet in her four-inch heels.

The word *beautiful* really didn't do him justice. Neither did any other word she could think of at the moment. For a second, she was assailed by the fear that she might actually be drooling over the man, something that had never happened before in her twenty-three years of existence. Then again—she reached a discreet hand up to her chin to double-check and nearly sighed in relief when she found it still dry—she'd never seen a man like this up close before.

Hell, whom was she kidding? she asked herself as

her knees trembled for the second time that night. She'd never seen a man like this before ever, in real life or in pictures. And yet, here he was, standing right in front of her, his right hand holding a glass of champagne that he was quite obviously extending toward her.

"You look thirsty," he said, and—of course—his voice matched the rest of him. Deep and dark and wickedly amused. *So* wickedly amused. Suddenly her knees weren't all that was trembling. Her hand, as it reached for the glass of champagne, was shaking, as well.

What was wrong with her?

Besides the fact that her libido had obviously overpowered her brain? she asked herself viciously. But as she stood there, watching him watch her, she figured she'd better find a way to get her brain functioning again. Because the man obviously wasn't going anywhere until he got a response…even if she had no idea how she was supposed to respond to his observation that she was thirsty…

Eventually, though, her brain, and her sense of humor, kicked in. Thank God. "Funny, I was just thinking the same thing about you." It wasn't the wittiest comeback, but it would do.

"Were you?" His mouth curved in a crooked grin that did something strange to her stomach. "Well, you wouldn't be wrong." Then he lifted his own glass of champagne to his lips and took a deep drink. She watched, mesmerized, for long seconds before she managed to shake herself out of it. Jeez! How far gone was she that even watching him swallow was turning her on? Maybe she should just walk away now and cut her losses while she still could.

Even as the thought came to her, she knew she wouldn't do it. Partly because she wasn't sure her knees would hold her if she tried to walk away and partly…

partly because in that moment there was nowhere she'd rather be than right there, smiling up at this charming, beautiful man—and having him smile back at her.

"I'm Nic, by the way," he said, after he'd watched her take a slow, steadying drink from her own glass.

"I'm Desi." She held out her hand. He took it, but instead of shaking her hand as she'd expected, he just held it as he gently stroked his thumb across her palm.

The touch was so soft, so intimate, so not what she'd been expecting, that for long seconds she didn't know what to do. What to say. A tiny voice inside her whispered for her to let go, to step back, to walk away from the attraction that was holding them in thrall. But it was drowned out by the heat, the attraction, the *sizzle* that arced between them like lightning.

"Would you like to dance, Desi?" he asked, taking the glass from her other hand and depositing it on a passing tray.

She should say no. She had a million things to do here tonight and none of those things involved getting swept onto the dance floor by some hot, rich guy who had probably forgotten more about seduction than she'd ever known. But even as the thought occurred to her, even knowing that she might very well get burned before the night was over, she nodded. Then she let him lead her gently toward the center of the room. Playing with fire was a cliché for a reason.

The band was playing a slow song—of course it was—and he pulled her into his arms, started to move her across the crowded floor. He held her closer than was necessary or expected for a first dance between strangers. One hand on her lower back, his fingers curving over the soft swell of her hip. His other hand continuing to hold, continuing to stroke, her own. His hard, strong chest brushing against her own with each step they took. His thighs doing the same.

Deep inside, Desi felt herself melting. Felt herself falling a little more under his spell. She knew it was stupid, ridiculous, *insane*, but for the first time in her life, she didn't care. She didn't care if it was a bad idea to let him touch her. Didn't care if she'd regret it later. Didn't care, even, if she ended up getting in trouble at work because she'd spent time with Nic that she should have spent trying to pry quotes out of the local celebrities. Which, if she stopped to think about it, didn't make sense at all. She was a woman who lived to work, who was dying to make a name for herself as a journalist. The fact that she would put that at risk for a man she'd just met was absurd.

She wasn't that girl, had never been—and never wanted to be—*that girl*. And yet, here she was, moving closer instead of back. Arching forward so that her breasts and her thighs brushed more firmly against him, instead of walking away. Surrendering instead of putting up a fight.

The gleam in Nic's eyes as he looked down at her was as obvious as his rock-hard pelvis pressing against her own. Instead of offending her, it aroused her. Instead of making her scurry for cover, it made her clamor for more.

One night never hurt anyone, after all. And neither did one kiss. Or at least that was her story for this evening and she was sticking to it.

Which was why, after taking a deep breath, she tightened her hand where it rested against the back of his neck and pulled him forward. Pulled him down, down, down, until their bodies were meshed together and his lips met hers.

Two

She was delicious. It was the only thing Nic Durand could think as his lips met those of the beautiful blonde in his arms. Desi, she'd said her name was, he remembered as he fought to keep from getting completely lost in the feel of her soft hands on his neck and her lush body pressed so tightly against his own.

It was a lot harder not to get lost than it should have been. A lot harder than it had ever been. He'd met—and charmed—a lot of women in his life, but never had he been so affected by one. Never had he come so close to forgetting who and where he was when he was with one—even one as gorgeous, and amusing, as Desi. But here he was, attending his first charity gala since he and his brother had moved the headquarters of their diamond company to San Diego earlier that year, and all he could think about was getting his hands and mouth all over a woman he'd just met.

As second in command of Bijoux, he was in charge of marketing, advertising and public relations. It was his job to come to these ridiculous galas, his job to schmooze and donate pieces to the silent auction in an effort to continue building the philanthropic reputation of the business he and his brother, Marc, had poured their hearts and souls into ever since they'd taken over more than a decade before. The fact that he'd rather just give all that money straight to charity meant nothing. After all, experience had proved that buying seats at boring, trumped-up galas like this one always earned his company good PR. And good PR was the name of the game, especially when you were one of the new kids. And not just any new kid, but one determined to shake up the old system and make things happen. It was the best way to gain access. He'd come here tonight with an agenda—people to meet, business to do—but all it had taken was one look at Desi, one conversation with her, one feel of her pressed against him while dancing, to make all of that fly out the window.

And he didn't give a damn.

It was odd. Crazy, even. But he wasn't going to fight it, he decided as he slid his hand down her spine to rest against her lower back. Not when a simple kiss with her was hotter and more exciting than anything he'd done with any other woman.

With that thought in mind, he put a little pressure on her back, pressed her forward…and more tightly against him. She moaned a little at the contact, her mouth opening with the sound, and he took instant advantage by licking his way across the little dip in her upper lip, then across the soft fullness of her lower one. She gasped a little, her hands sliding up to clutch at his tuxedo shirt. It was all the invitation he needed.

Delving inside her then, he swept his tongue along her own. Once, twice, then again and again. Teasing, touching, *tasting* her. Learning her flavors...and her secrets.

Despite her sharp cool looks—all platinum-blond hair and ice-blue eyes, striking cheekbones and long, slender body—Desi was heat and spice. Cinnamon and cloves, overlaid by just a hint of the crisp, sweet champagne they had shared. The warmth of her seduced him, drew him in—drew him under—until all he could think of, all he could want, was her.

Sliding his other hand into her hair, he tangled his fingers in the silky strands and tugged gently. Her head tilted back in response, giving him better access to her mouth. And he took it without a thought to anything but how much he wanted her.

Sucking her lower lip between his teeth, he bit down gently, then soothed the small hurt with his tongue before once again licking inside her mouth. This time, he slid his tongue along her upper lip, toyed gently with the sensitive skin then delved deep into the recesses of her mouth.

Desi moaned, burrowing even closer as he licked his way across the roof of her mouth before tangling his tongue with hers. She tasted so good, felt so good, that he wanted nothing more than to stay right there forever.

But at that moment someone jostled him. The jolt broke the spell and he came back to himself slowly, became aware of their surroundings and the fact that he was about two seconds from undressing her in the middle of one of the most important social events of the Southern California season. He should be embarrassed, or at least shocked that he'd let things get so far out of hand. But he didn't care about that, didn't care about any of the people milling around them or what they must be thinking.

All he cared about was getting Desi out of there…and getting inside her as quickly as he possibly could.

Pulling away from her reluctantly, he forced himself to ignore her moan of protest—and the way it shot straight to his groin. It wasn't easy. Just as it wasn't easy to look away from her flushed cheeks, her swollen lip and slumberous eyes. But if he didn't, he would say to hell with social niceties and take her right here in the middle of the dance floor where everyone could see them. Where everyone could watch as he put his claim on her.

Just the thought—which was an admittedly odd one to have when he didn't know this woman at all—had him placing a hand on her lower back and escorting her through the bright crowds to the darkness of the balcony beyond the ballroom. As he did, he tried to ignore the looks they were getting. It wasn't easy, especially when he saw the way so many of the men were looking at them. Looking at her. Only the awareness that he was one small step away from growling and beating his chest like some kind of caveman kept him moving.

Desi went with him willingly, pliantly even, which soothed some of the strangely possessive feelings rocketing through him. But he'd barely gotten her outside— the door was still closing behind them—before she was on him. Her arms wrapping around his neck, her body wrapping itself around his own, her mouth desperately seeking his.

The same urgency was a fire inside him. A pounding drum in his bloodstream, a stroke of lightning that he couldn't shake. That he didn't want to shake.

All he wanted was her.

It was a shocking revelation, and a humbling one. He loved women, loved everything about them and always had. But this driving desire for Desi, this craving to have her any and every way he could, was something new. Something as unexpected as it was exciting.

Keeping his mouth on hers and his lips open so she could delve inside him the same way he had explored her, Nic turned them until her back was against the outside wall of the ballroom. She moaned softly as her bare skin came in contact with the building and he shifted back, so that he could slide an arm between her and the rough, cold stone.

"Please," she whimpered, pressing her pelvis against his as her hands clutched his shirt, pulling and tugging at it in a frantic need that mirrored his own.

To help her—and to get her hands on his bare skin faster—he pulled away slightly and ripped his shirt straight down in a practiced move that had the studs giving way to his impatience. Desi sighed then, her hands sliding beneath the parted fabric to caress his ribs, his back, his abdomen.

Her fingers felt so good—*she* felt so good—that for long seconds he did nothing but stand there, letting her explore him as he longed to explore her. But in the end, his need got the better of him and he took control, pulling the top of her dress down so he could see and touch and kiss her.

"Hey!" she protested breathlessly. "I wasn't done yet."

"I'm sorry," he told her as he gazed at the sun-kissed skin he had revealed. She wasn't wearing a bra, but then she didn't need one. Her breasts were small and high and perfect, tipped with pale pink nipples he was dying to taste. "I promise, you can touch me anywhere you want. Later. Right now, I have to—" His voice trailed off as he pressed hot, openmouthed kisses to her neck, her collarbone and the slope of her shoulder before moving on to her breasts.

Her skin was as soft and fragrant as he'd imagined it would be, and as he pulled her nipple into his mouth, as he circled her areola with his tongue and sucked just hard enough to have her crying out as she buried her hands in his hair, he felt as if he would die if he didn't have her. Soon.

"I need to be inside you," he growled against her breast.

"Yes," she gasped, her hands sliding from his hair to his shoulders, then down his chest to his waist, where she began fumbling with his belt buckle. "Now."

They were the two most beautiful words he'd ever heard.

He slipped a hand under the silky blue skirt of her dress, then slid his fingers up her thigh until he found her underwear—and more important, her sex. He traced the elastic leg of her panties for a few seconds, reveling in the feel of her. Soft. Wet. Hot. So hot that it took all his self-control not to plunge inside her right then.

Still, he couldn't resist slipping two fingers inside the lace.

Couldn't resist petting and stroking her until her knees buckled and she grabbed at him for support.

Couldn't resist slipping first one finger and then another into her tight, silky heat and pressing deep.

"Nic!" It was part command, part plea and in those moments he wanted—needed—nothing more than to give her what she was demanding of him. But first—

He ripped the fragile lace away from her body with one strong tug, then dropped to his knees in front of her.

"Oh, yes," she cried, her hands grabbing him as he lifted one of her legs over his shoulder and, in doing so, opened her completely to his eyes and hands and mouth. Then he leaned forward and blew a long, slow, steady stream of air right against her most sensitive spot.

She cried out then, a high-pitched strangled sound that made his own need skyrocket. But this wasn't just about him, wasn't some quick, anonymous screw. Not to him anyway. And though he didn't yet know what it was about Desi that intrigued him, he did know that he wanted to see her again. Did know that he wanted to get to know more about her than what color her nipples were or how hot and wet and tight she felt around his finger.

Although he was good with knowing all that, too. More than good, he admitted to himself as he worked his way across her flat stomach, kissing and licking and sucking every inch of her skin.

Her hands moved from his shoulders to his head, her fingers tangling in his hair with a sharpness that only turned him on more. Pleasure coursed through him and he groaned at the sensation before nipping sharply at her hip bone in retaliation.

She cried out again, wobbled a little, then grabbed on to him, her fingers digging into his shoulders as she fought to stay upright. Her obvious arousal fed his, and he gently bit her a second time. A third time. Then he laved the little stings and explored more of her soft, gorgeous skin. As he did, he couldn't help wondering if he'd left marks. If she would look in the mirror tomorrow and see tiny bruises on her hips, her stomach, her thighs, and think of him as he knew—even now—that he'd be thinking of her.

"Please, please, please," she whimpered in the sexiest mantra he'd ever heard. He laughed in response, then kissed his way back across her stomach, then lower, so that his tongue traced along the very edges of her sex.

She was shaking, her body and arms curving around him as much for support as to hold him to her. He loved the feel of her wrapped around him, loved the fact that she was as affected by what was happening between them as he was.

In answer to her silent pleas, he moved closer, pressed her legs apart a little more as he trailed his mouth lower. In response, she stroked her fingers down his face, rubbed the stubble on his jaw. She played with it for long seconds, and her fingers felt so good he felt his resolve crumble. He wanted to be inside her, *needed* to be inside her with a desperation that bordered on insanity.

But he wanted this more. It was a driving compulsion, this need to watch her while she came. To know what she looked like, sounded like, tasted like when he took her to the edge and then flung her over.

With that thought a beacon shining through his own dark and desperate need, he leaned forward and put his mouth on her. Then he nearly lost it as Desi pressed a hand against her mouth to muffle her scream.

She was in sensory overload, her every nerve popping with pleasure at the feel of Nic touching her. At the feel of his arm around her waist, his big, calloused hand kneading her backside. At the feel of his fingers still buried deep inside her. At the feel and sound and sight of his mouth moving against her sex.

It was so good, *so good*, that she couldn't stop herself from pressing back against the wall, against his hand, even as she tilted her hips forward to give him better access.

She was so close that it didn't take long to bring her right to the edge. She knew he was aware of how close she was. She could feel it in the tension of his shoulders and in the slow, careful way he caressed her. For a moment, just a moment, she wondered what he was waiting for, but then the insidious pleasure of what he was doing, the care he was taking, streaked through her. Intense, powerful, mind-numbing.

"Nic, I can't—"

"You can," he told her, his voice hoarse with his own restraint.

"I can't," she answered, the words broken and brittle and breathless. "I need—"

"I know what you need." He kissed her then, hot and openmouthed, making her knees tremble and her hands shake. Her whole body slammed into overload and she reached for him, her fingers tugging at his shirt, his hair, the bowtie hanging limply from his collar.

"Please, please, please," she muttered mindlessly as she arched against him. She needed more, needed him.

He cursed then, harsh and low, and the words felt hot against her skin. The sensation only added to the tension inside her until she couldn't think, couldn't see, couldn't breathe. All she could do was feel.

All she could do was crave.

And then he did it. He twisted his fingers inside her even as he swirled his tongue around her most sensitive spot and reached up with his free hand to pinch one of her nipples, hard.

The different sensations slammed Desi into overload. She careened straight over the edge into ecstasy, her body shuddering as pleasure swamped her, more intense and powerful and shattering than anything she had ever felt before.

"Nic!" Lost in the maelstrom, she cried out for him.

And he was there, his hands stroking her soothingly even as he took her higher and higher and higher. Even as he thrust her straight into the stars that shined so brilliantly above them.

When the pleasure broke, when she finally started

to come back to herself, Nic wouldn't allow it. Instead, he fumbled with the front of his tuxedo trousers as he shoved to his feet. Then he cupped his hands under her and lifted her right off her feet.

She was still pleasure drunk and more than a little dazed, but even so, her instincts kicked in. She wrapped her legs around his lean waist, her arms around his broad shoulders and pressed back against the wall for better leverage.

Then he was there between her thighs, blunt and hard and big. She had just come, but as he probed gently at her opening, Desi couldn't help but respond.

He had been so patient, so careful to ensure that she was satisfied, that she expected him to be impatient now. To be rough, hurried.

Instead, he took his time here, too. Leaning forward until his lips were right next to her ear, he whispered, "You're so damn beautiful." Then he pressed soft kisses to her cheek.

The words, combined with the feel of him right against the core of her body, took her arousal up another notch. "It's okay," she told him, arching her hips in an effort to encourage him. "I'm ready."

He groaned then, thrusting forward gently until he was buried halfway inside her. "Okay?" he ground out, and she felt him shaking from the effort it took to hold himself back.

Touched more than she wanted to be—certainly more than she'd expected to be from a torrid encounter with a stranger—she leaned into him. Pressed her mouth to his in a kiss as soft and gentle as his concern for her. "Please," she whispered against his lips. "I want to feel you inside me."

That whisper was all it took to snap his control like a twig—which she was exceptionally grateful for.

Nic thrust into her then, so hard that he slammed her back against the wall. But she was still wet, still turned-on, and more than ready for him. Pleasure crashed through her at the first stroke, coursing along her every nerve ending until her entire body felt lit up like the Fourth of July.

"Damn!" he growled, his fingers digging into her hips as he held her in place. "You feel good."

Again, she expected him to slam into her, even braced herself for it, but again he surprised her. He brushed kisses across her forehead, her cheeks, her lips as he waited for her to adjust to him. Only when she squirmed against him, trying to get closer, did he finally relent.

He began to move in slow, steady, powerful strokes that had her grasping at him as the need ratcheted up inside her. Soon—too soon—she was on the brink of coming again. But she didn't want to go over alone this time, didn't want to lose herself in the ecstasy without him.

Tightening her inner muscles in a long, slow caress, she did what she could to take him as high as he had taken her. She brushed her thumbs across his nipples, whispered how much she wanted him in his ear, lifted her hips to meet each of his thrusts. It must have worked, because he groaned, then began thrusting harder.

Then he was leaning forward, his mouth inches from hers. "Kiss me," he commanded, a scant moment before his lips slammed down on hers.

She did, pulling his lower lip between her teeth and nipping at him as he had done to her earlier. She wanted more of him, wanted all of him. Craved him until it was an inferno deep inside her.

She bit him again, a little harder this time, and the

shock of pain must have been what he was waiting for, because he came with a growl. She tore her mouth away from his, gasped for breath, but Nic wouldn't let her go. He followed her, his mouth ravenous on her own while the heat of his body seared hers wherever it touched. In moments, the pleasure swamped her, overwhelmed her, and she followed him over the edge, her body spinning wildly, gloriously, completely out of her control.

Three

When it was over, when she could breathe again and her scattered thoughts finally came back to her, Desi didn't know what to do. What to say. How to act.

There was a part of her that was shell-shocked. A part of her that couldn't believe she had just had sex with a stranger *in public*. And not just in public, but on the balcony outside a gala that she was supposed to be covering for work. If someone had told her an hour ago that before the night was over she'd be pressed up against the hotel's outside wall, her legs wrapped around Nic, whose last name she didn't even know, having just had the most intense orgasms of her life… Well, she wouldn't have called that person a liar. She would have called him or her a *damn* liar and then laughed herself silly.

But here she was. And the kicker was, she wasn't even sorry. How could she be when her body was so blissed out that she still wasn't sure her legs would be able to hold her when Nic decided to set her down? Which—thankfully—he hadn't yet made any move to do.

"You okay?" he asked after a minute, pressing his lips to her neck.

"I don't know. That was—" Her voice broke and she swallowed in an effort to get some moisture into her too-dry throat.

"Amazing," he said, kissing his way over her collarbone. "Incredible. Earth-shattering."

She giggled. It was a totally foreign sound to her, one Desi couldn't ever remember making in her adult life. She wasn't the giggling sort. Then again, she wasn't the one-night-stand, public-sex-against-a-building sort, either. And yet here she was, with absolutely no desire to move. And absolutely no regrets.

Nic lifted his head, gave her a mock frown that in no way reached the beautiful green eyes she could just barely make out in the shadows. "Are you saying that making love to me wasn't earth-shattering?"

He slipped a hand between them, circled his thumb around her. She gasped, arched against him. She knew exactly what he was doing, knew that he was teasing her, but she couldn't help it. Normally, she never let a man get the upper hand, but with Nic she couldn't help it. Everything about him appealed to her, drew a response from her that she had almost no control over. His sense of humor, the intelligence she could see in his eyes, the careful way he held and touched and kissed her. And, of course, the fact that he was the hottest man she had ever met certainly didn't hurt, either.

"I'm saying," she said, her voice more breathless than she would have liked, "that I very much enjoyed having sex with you."

"Sex, huh?" He rubbed a little harder, a little faster,

and shocks of electricity sparked through her. Just that easily, he made her ache. Made her want. Again.

"Nic," she whispered, cupping the back of his neck with her palm, even as her head fell back against the cool stucco wall.

"Desi." His voice was low, teasing, but she could hear the sudden thread of tension as clearly as she could feel him hardening once again within her.

"Don't play." Suddenly she was as needy, as desperate, as if she hadn't come at all.

He scraped his teeth along her jaw, bit lightly at the sensitive spot behind her ear. "I thought you liked it when I played." His breath was hot against her skin, the words a whisper that worked its way deep inside of her.

"You know what I mean." She clenched her core around him to underscore her words, took great delight in the sexy hiss the movement elicited from him. He closed his eyes, dropped his forehead against hers, and the hungry noise he made had her tightening her inner muscles again and again.

He cursed then, a harsh, sexy word that only ramped up her arousal more. From the moment he'd taken her out onto this balcony—hell, from the moment he'd kissed her on that dance floor—Nic had had the upper hand. She'd be lying if she said it didn't feel good to get a little of her own back. Especially when doing so was so incredibly pleasurable for both of them.

Nic's hand tightened on her behind as he lifted her nearly off him before letting her slowly sink back down. He did it a second time and then a third, all the while continuing to stroke her with his other hand. It took only a minute or two before ecstasy beckoned—brought even closer by his careless demonstration of strength—but just as she was about to go over the edge for the third time in less than an hour, he stilled.

"What's wrong?" She forced open her too-heavy lids, tried to focus on his face despite the urgent need lighting her up from the inside. "Why'd you stop?"

"Come home with me."

"What?" She was so far gone that her brain had trouble assimilating his words.

"Come home with me," he repeated, thrusting deep inside her for emphasis. She moaned despite herself, tried to arch against him and get that last bit of needed pressure. But he held her firmly, refused to let her move. Refused to let her come.

"Please," she gasped, her whole body shaking with the need for release. "I need—"

"I know what you need," he whispered, taking her mouth in a kiss that was somehow both hard and tender. "Say you'll go home with me and I'll let you come."

She bit his lip, not hard enough to draw blood but definitely hard enough to make him take notice. "Let me come," she countered breathlessly, "and maybe I'll go home with you."

He laughed then, a low, dark sound that sent shivers down her spine even as it made her entire body melt. "I want you in my bed."

She tightened around him yet again, taking great pleasure in the fact that he groaned deep in his throat. "You know what you need to do then."

"Is that a yes?" He stroked her once gently. Too gently, but she wasn't complaining as her nerve endings tingled.

"It's not a no."

He laughed again. "Damn, I like you, Desi."

"I certainly hope you do, considering what we've spent the last forty-five minutes doing." She had to bite her tongue, but somehow she managed to resist adding that she liked him, too. A lot. She hadn't been with that many men—only two before Nic—but neither of them had ever made her laugh. Not out of bed and certainly not while making love to her. Until him, until *now*, she hadn't even known that she'd been missing something.

He bent his head, licking his way over first one nipple and then the other. "Come home with me," he urged when she was even more of a trembling, needy mess, "and I'll spend the rest of the night showing you just how much I like you."

She didn't want to give in—not because she didn't like him, but because she did. Too much. And the last thing she needed right now was to fall for a sexy, charismatic rich guy who would break her heart if she let him.

And yet…and yet, like him, she wasn't quite ready for this night to end. Wasn't quite ready to walk away from Nic with his bright green eyes and ready smile, his quick wit and gentle hands. And she sure as hell wasn't ready to walk away from the pleasure he brought her so effortlessly.

"Please, Desi," he murmured against her cheek, and for the first time she heard the strain in his voice, felt it in the way he trembled against her. "I want you," he said. "If you just want it to be tonight, that's okay with me. But please—"

"Okay." In one desperate, vulnerable moment, she threw caution to the wind.

"Okay?"

"I'll come home with you."

His eyes shot up to hers. "You will?"

"I will." She grinned a little wickedly herself. "That is, if you make me come in the next sixty seconds." This might be her first—and probably her last—one-night stand, but that didn't mean she couldn't make the best of it…

"I thought you'd never ask." His answering smile was blinding, and it caught her right in the gut. Which probably would have made her nervous if her body hadn't been on a collision course with its third orgasm of the night.

Nic bent down and took her mouth with his. Less than thirty seconds later he was muffling her screams as she came and came and came.

His house was gorgeous. Worse, it was perfect. Which, she was growing desperately afraid, was simply a reflection of its owner. And while most women would jump at the shot to start something with a gorgeous, rich, *perfect* man, Desi wasn't most women. The thought of falling for Nic made her itch, so much so that she couldn't help casting a few surreptitious glances down at her bare legs to make sure she wasn't actually breaking out in hives.

Which was why it made absolutely no sense that she was sitting at the bar in the middle of Nic's (still didn't know his last name and still didn't want to) gorgeously designed arts-and-crafts kitchen at two in the morning, watching as he made her homemade blueberry pancakes. Simply because he'd asked what her favorite food was and that was what she had answered.

"So, what's your favorite TV show?" he questioned as he expertly flipped the first batch of pancakes. Watching him made her a little crazy, especially since all he had on was a pair of well-worn jeans. No man should be allowed to look that good outside the pages of a fashion magazine.

And no man should be able to make pancakes that perfect after three rounds of the best, most earth-shattering sex she had ever engaged in. It went against the laws of nature.

"Desi?" he prompted, casting a quick glance over his shoulder at her.

She tried to look as if she hadn't spent the past ten minutes ogling his perfectly defined back. Judging from the smirk on his face, she didn't succeed nearly as well as she'd hoped to.

So she cleared her throat and focused on answering his question as a means of distraction from the fact that she was more than a little afraid that she was turning into a sex addict. "I don't watch TV."

"What do you mean you don't watch TV?" He turned to stare at her incredulously. "*Everyone* watches TV."

She quirked a brow at him. "Not everyone. Obviously."

He named a few popular shows, but when she just shook her head, Nic sighed heavily. "Okay, fine. How about your favorite movie, then? Or do you not watch movies, either?"

"I watch movies. But it's hard to pick just one, isn't it?" She did her best to keep from smiling at his obvious frustration.

"Not necessarily."

"Oh, yeah? What's your favorite then?"

"Titanic."

It was her turn to stare at him incredulously. "You don't really mean that, right? You're just messing with me. You have to be."

"Why wouldn't I mean it?" He looked completely disgruntled now. "It's a fantastic movie. Love, passion, danger, excitement. What's not to like?"

"Oh, I don't know. Betrayal, maybe? Attempted suicide, attempted murder, poverty, *icebergs*, death. Not to mention the world's most infamous sinking ship." She paused as if considering. "You're right. What was I thinking? It's a barrel of laughs. Obviously."

He made a disgusted sound. "You're a real party pooper. Did anyone ever tell you that?"

"No."

"Well, then, let me be the first. You're a real party pooper."

"I'm a realist."

He snorted. "You're a nihilist."

She started to argue on general principle, but stopped before she could do more than utter a few incoherent sounds. After all, whom was she kidding? He was totally right. "Just call me Camus," she quipped with a shrug.

"Is that a movie?" he asked as he poured more batter on the griddle.

"Are you serious?" she demanded, watching him like a hawk as she tried to find some kind of tell to prove he was messing with her. But the look he sent her was utterly guileless. Not too guileless, mind you. Just guileless enough, as if he really had no idea what she was talking about.

Huh. Maybe he wasn't so perfect, after all. The thought made her inexplicably happy, though she refused to delve too deeply into why that was.

"Albert Camus was a French writer," she told him after a second.

"Oh." He shrugged. "Never heard of him."

That knowledge made her infinitely more relaxed. "Oh, well, a lot of people would say you weren't missing much."

"But not you."

"Maybe. Maybe not."

He grinned as he slid a plate piled high with perfect, golden, fluffy pancakes in front of her. "But you still didn't tell me what your favorite movie is."

"I told you I couldn't choose just one. Not all of us can wax poetic over a sinking boat, after all."

"More's the pity." He cast her a mischievous look that she immediately mistrusted. "But you know what? I think you're right. I don't think I can choose just one favorite movie. Now that I'm thinking about it, a few more come to mind."

"Oh yeah? Like what?"

"*The Stranger*, definitely. And maybe *The Guest*. And—"

"You suck!" she told him, breaking off a piece of pancake and throwing it at him. He caught it, of course. In his mouth. Without even trying. "Those are two of Albert Camus's most famous works."

"Are they?" he asked, his face a mask of complete and total innocence. "I had no idea."

She studied him closely, looking for his tell. He was lying to her, obviously, but the fact that she couldn't tell was odd. She could always tell—she prided herself on it. It's what made her such a good investigative journalist. And such a lousy society columnist.

The fact that he didn't seem to have a tell fascinated her. And made her very, very nervous all at the same time.

When she didn't say anything else, he nodded at her untouched plate. "Eat your pancakes before they get cold."

"Maybe I like cold pancakes."

"Do you?"

"I don't know. Do I?"

He didn't answer. Instead he grabbed the bottle of maple syrup and drizzled it over the top of her pancakes. Then he cut into them and lifted a forkful to her mouth.

He waited patiently for a few seconds, but when she just looked at him instead of taking the proffered bite, he rolled his eyes. "*My* pancakes don't taste good cold. Trust me."

Trust him. The idea was so ludicrous that she nearly laughed out loud. Only the knowledge that he definitely wouldn't get the joke kept her from making one wise-crack or another. But there was no way in hell she was *ever* going to trust *him*. Mr. Perfect. No, thank you. Been there, done that, still had the T-shirt as a not-so-pleasant memento.

Not that she was bitter or anything. Or sexist.

Because it wasn't that she didn't trust men. It was that she didn't trust *anybody*. Not when life had taught her over and over *and over* again that she couldn't count on anyone or anything. If she needed something, she could count on only herself to make it happen. Anyone else would just let her down.

Maybe it wasn't a great philosophy, and maybe—just maybe—it *was* a touch nihilistic. But it was *her* philoso-phy. She'd lived by it most of her life, and while it hadn't gotten her much—yet—it also hadn't cost her much since she'd adopted it. And in her mind, that was a win.

And yet, even understanding all that, she—inexplicably—leaned forward and let Nic feed her the bite of pancake. She had no idea why she did it, but it certainly wasn't because doing so made him look in-credibly happy. Not at all. Not even a little bit.

That was her story, and like her philosophy, she was sticking to it.

Which was why it was so strange when, after she finished chewing, Nic simply handed her the fork and went back to what he was doing without so much as backward glance. Was she the only one affected by th strange night of theirs?

It was a definite possibility, she told herself. He co

totally be the kind of guy who picked up a different
one-night stand at every party he went to. Which would
mean that tonight—hot sex and cool banter and delicious
pancakes—could be standard operating procedure for
him. Which was fine, she told herself, despite the sinking feeling in her stomach. One-night stands weren't SOP
for her—far from it—but that was what she'd expected,
what she'd wanted, when she'd come home with him.
Deciding in the middle of it that she wanted something
more wasn't okay, no matter how much pleasure he gave
her or how much she enjoyed sitting here, teasing him.

"So, favorite movie is off the table," he said, after he
poured another round of pancakes onto the griddle. "How
about favorite song?"

She forked up another bite of pancakes under his
watchful eye, took her time chewing it. "What's with all
the questions?" she asked after she finally swallowed it.

"What's with all the evasive answers?" he countered.

"I asked you first."

"Actually, if you think about it, I asked you first.
About your favorite song. And I'm still waiting."

"You are a persistent one," she said, narrowing her
eyes at him.

"I believe the word you're looking for is *charming*."
He crossed to the fridge, took out a bottle of champagne
and a quart of fresh-squeezed orange juice. "*Debonair*.
Maybe even…*sexy*?"

He wiggled his brows at her then, and it took every
ounce of concentration she had not to burst out laughing.
"Sexy, hmm. Maybe. And here I was thinking *humble*."

"Well, obviously. Being humble is what PR profes-
sionals the world over are known for."

"Is that what you are?" she asked, intrigued by the
rare glimpse into his real life. "A public relations guy?"

It would explain the gorgeous house and even more gorgeous artisan decorating scheme.

He shrugged. "In a manner of speaking."

"That isn't an answer."

He faked a surprised look as he slid a mimosa in front of her. "You don't actually think you're the only one who can dodge questions here, do you?"

She did laugh then. She couldn't help it. He really was the most charming and interesting man she had met in a very long time. Maybe ever.

She reached for the champagne flute he'd put in front of her and took a long sip. As she did, Nic took advantage of her preoccupation and grabbed her smartphone off the counter.

"What are you doing?" she demanded as he started pressing keys.

"Programming my number into it, so you can call me whenever you want."

"What makes you think I'm going to want to call you when tonight is over?"

He gave her what she guessed was his most unassuming look. "What makes you think you aren't?"

"Are we seriously going to spend the rest of the night asking each other questions and never getting any answers?"

"I don't know. Are we?"

She rolled her eyes in exasperation. But before she could say anything else, his phone started buzzing from where it sat next to the stove. He made no move to answer it.

"Aren't you going to get that?" she asked, partly because the reporter in her wanted to know who was calling him at two-thirty in the morning and partly because he was standing just a little too close to her. They weren't touching, but she could feel the heat emanating from his body, and it was making it impossible for her to think—and even more impossible for her to maintain the distance she was trying so desperately to cling to.

"It's just me, calling from your phone. So now I've got your number, too." He looked her in the eye when he said it and there was something in that look, something in his voice, that made her think he meant a lot more than the ten digits that made her phone ring.

Suddenly she was taking far too much effort not to squirm.

She didn't like the feeling any more than she liked the vulnerability that came with the knowledge that he could see more of her than she wanted him to. And so she did what she always did in situations like these—she went on the offensive. "What if I hadn't planned on giving you my number?"

He raised a brow. "You don't want me to have it?"

"That's not the point!"

"It's exactly the point."

"No, it—" She cut herself off. "You're a piece of work, you know that?"

"I have been told that a time or two." He paused, then said, "So I've got a proposition for you."

"Uh, no, thanks." She moved to stand up, but he pressed her back into the seat.

"You haven't even heard what I was going to say."

"Yeah, well, when a guy says those words to a girl he hardly knows, it usually ends with her chained in a basement somewhere while he maps out patterns to make a dress from her skin."

"Wow!" He cracked up. "Suspicious much?"

"I've seen *Silence of the Lambs*. I know how these things work."

"It appears that you do. But, sadly, I have no basement. And no handcuffs. And no deep-seated psychopathology, at least not that I know of. Also, I don't have a clue how to sew. So, you're probably safe."

"I'll be the judge of that." She eyed him with mock suspicion. "So what exactly is this proposition of yours?"

"That I keep your phone number, even though you aren't exactly overjoyed that I've got it. And I promise that I won't call you until you call me first. Fair?"

"What if I never call you?"

"Then I'll be very sad, but I promise I won't bother you with harassing phone calls. Deal?"

She thought about it for a moment, thought about whether or not she would ever want to talk to him again once this night was over. And decided, what the hell. She might as well leave the option open. If she didn't want to use it, well, then, he was giving her the perfect opportunity to walk away, no harm, no foul.

"Deal," she told him.

"Excellent." He smiled, then reached a hand up to rub the back of his neck. Involuntarily, her eyes were drawn to his very enticing six-pack and the V-cut that peeked out of the top of his low-slung jeans. She locked her jaw and, for the second time that night, tried not to drool.

She must not have been very successful, though, because his voice was amused a few seconds later when he asked, "See something you like?"

"I like you." The words were out before she had a clue she was going to say them. The second it registered that she'd actually spoken what she'd only planned to think, she clapped her hand over her mouth in horror.

She wanted to take them back, wanted to pretend she hadn't just screwed up everything by letting her tongue— and her emotions—get away from her. But it was too late. The words hung there in the air between them, like a bomb waiting to go off.

He didn't look horrified by her admission, though. Didn't look as if he was about to duck and cover in an effort to avoid the shrapnel from the bomb she had just dropped. In fact, Nic looked absolutely delighted, as though she'd given him a present…or the best orgasm of his life.

Which wasn't so far-fetched when she thought about it. He'd certainly done that for her, after all.

Before she could think of something—anything—to say that might work as damage control, he closed the small distance between them. He turned her stool around so that she was facing him, then moved closer still, until he was nestled between the V of her spread legs.

"I like you, too," he said, pressing a kiss to her forehead, then another one to her cheek and yet another one to her lips.

"Do you?" she asked, tilting her head back so he could skim his lips along the side of her neck.

"I do. And since we've established that you like me as well…" His hands went to the buttons of the too-big shirt she was wearing. His shirt, she thought dazedly as he slipped the first two buttons through their holes then gently skimmed his knuckles along the undersides of her breasts. "I think we should maybe head back to my bedroom and like each other some more."

"Like each other some more?" she repeated, trying to keep her voice steady despite the heat arcing through her like a lightning storm. "Is that what they're calling it these days?"

He laughed. "It's what I'm calling it. Sorry. I know it's not very romantic, but my brain pretty much stops working the second I touch you."

She was charmed by the admission despite herself. Determined to keep things light after the confession she'd had no intention of making, she told him, "I guess it's all right if your brain isn't working, as long as other parts of your anatomy are."

He quirked a brow at her. "The other parts of my anatomy are working just fine, thank you very much."

"Oh, yeah?" She ran a hand over his firm, hard chest. "Prove it."

His eyes darkened at the challenge and he grabbed her hips. Pulled her forward until she was balanced right on the edge of the seat and her sex was nestled right up against the hard ridge of his erection.

"Proof enough for you?" he whispered, his breath hot against her ear.

"I don't know. I think I might need a more detailed demonstration." She arched against him then, reveling in the groan he didn't even try to hold back.

"A more detailed demonstration, hmm?" He slid his hands under her and picked her up as if she weighed nothing. For the second time that night, Desi wound her arms and legs around him.

She clung to him like a limpet as he carried her out of the kitchen, through the family room and down the long hallway that led to his bedroom. She waited until he'd crossed over the threshold before she leaned forward and whispered in his ear, "'Need You Tonight.'"

"I need you, too," he said as he carried her over to the bed.

It was her turn to laugh. "I meant, that's my favorite song."

Something moved in his eyes—something wonderful and terrifying and so, so exhilarating. Then he was kissing her, his mouth slamming down on hers with the same desperation that was suddenly crashing through her.

And then they were falling onto the bed with him on top of her.

"What's *your* favorite song?" she managed to choke out as he finished unbuttoning her shirt, pressing kisses to each new bit of exposed skin. Her brain was going fast, her body taking over, but after all the back-and-forth, she wanted—needed—to know this one thing about him.

"I thought that was obvious," he said and she could feel him smile against her stomach. "Eric Clapton's 'Wonderful Tonight.'"

Four

Nic woke up alone. Which was unexpected. And which also really, really sucked.

Especially since it wasn't as if Desi was temporarily gone, like in the kitchen making coffee or the bathroom taking a shower. No, she had bugged out of his place and taken every last trace of her existence with her. She hadn't left a note, hadn't left a last name, hadn't left so much as a high-heeled glass slipper behind for him to go by.

She was *really* gone. So gone that if he didn't have scratches down his back from her nails, a bed that looked like a disaster zone, and—he glanced at his phone, just to make sure—her phone number in his contacts list, he might be tempted to think he'd imagined the whole damn thing.

But he hadn't imagined it. Desi was real. He had her number to prove it, he told himself as he stared at the

323 area code of his last missed call. Unfortunately, he also had a promise—not to use that phone number until she used his first.

Which, again, really, really sucked.

Because he liked her. He really, really liked her. More than should be possible considering he knew almost nothing about her—and what knowledge he did have, he'd gained from asking questions and pushing the issue until she very reluctantly responded.

Which, now that he thought about it, probably should have been his first clue that this wasn't going to go the way he'd wanted it to. Damn it, he really hated playing the fool.

A quick look at his bedside clock told him it was barely 7:00 a.m., and since he knew she'd been asleep in his bed at five, when he'd finally succumbed to exhaustion, he couldn't shake the idea that he had just missed her. That if only he had woken up a few minutes earlier, he would have caught her before she disappeared.

The thought made him crazy, especially since he'd planned on starting the morning the same way he'd spent most of the night. Deep inside Desi, watching her fall apart, as the defensive wall she'd built around herself crumbled one tiny brick at a time.

It seemed like a ridiculous plan now, considering he was alone in rapidly cooling sheets. After all, he'd known she was emotionally closed off—he would have had to be an idiot not to see the No Trespassing signs she had posted over pretty much every part of herself. And yet... and yet she'd opened up to him, over and over again through the night. Oh, not about big things such as who she was or why she had such a bleak outlook on people or even what her favorite movie was. But she'd let her guard down enough for him to catch glimpses of a lot of the mixed-up pieces that made her who she was.

He'd liked what he'd seen, a lot. Which was just one more reason this disappearing act of hers bothered him so much. For the first time in a very long time, he'd been looking forward to exploring her. To exploring *them* and finding out all the little things that made Desi tick.

For God's sake, he'd brought her to his *house*, which was something he did not normally do. At least not until he'd been on a few dates with a woman. And definitely not until he knew she was someone he wanted to get serious with.

Yet last night, on that balcony, he'd been adamant about convincing Desi to come home with him. True, part of that was because he'd really, really wanted to sleep with her again—the two times on the balcony hadn't been close to enough to exhaust the sexual chemistry between them. But that didn't explain why he'd been so determined to bring her home, to his house. They'd been at a hotel, for God's sake. How much easier would it have been to simply stop by the front desk and get a room for the night?

Instead, he'd brought her home. He'd made her blueberry pancakes and asked her questions and—when she had commented on various pieces of his furniture—had even thought about showing her his studio, which was pretty much the most sacred place in his house. He barely let his brother, Marc, in there, let alone anyone else.

But she didn't know any of that, a part of him rationalized. He'd thought he had made his interest clear to her last night, but maybe he hadn't. Maybe she'd thought she really was nothing more than a one-night stand to him. Maybe she'd thought he expected her to be gone when he woke up. After all, he hadn't said otherwise.

No, but he'd made a point of giving her his phone number, he told himself as he rolled out of bed and padded into the bathroom. Had made a point of getting hers. Surely that had given her a clue that he was interested in her.

Then again, maybe his interest—or lack thereof—wasn't the problem. Maybe hers was. She'd been pretty damn reluctant to answer even his most innocuous questions, and when she had answered, it was usually with a nonanswer. As if she was afraid of letting him too close, of letting him learn too much about her. Or maybe, more accurately, she didn't want him to get close to her.

Just the thought annoyed him. It had been a long time since he'd met a woman who really interested him. Who was smart and funny and also sexy as hell. So why was it that the first woman he did meet who interested him on all those fronts had gone running from him the first chance she'd gotten?

He turned on the shower, and while he was waiting for it to warm up, he took a long, hard look at himself in the mirror. As he did, he couldn't help wondering what it was Desi had seen when she'd looked at him. Had she seen his public persona, the easygoing, happy-go-lucky guy who was always up for a beer or a game of golf? The guy who didn't make waves and always had a joke at the ready?

Or had she seen deeper than that? Had she seen who he really was under all the polish and bull? He'd tried to show her a little bit of that guy last night, had thought—when he caught her looking at him as if she had a million questions—that maybe she had seen him. And if she had…if she had, was that who she had run away from? Not the man she'd picked up at the gala, but the one who lurked below his surface?

The idea grated. But it also lingered, long after he'd all but scrubbed himself raw in the shower in an effort to get rid of the warm-honey scent of her that had somehow embedded itself in his skin.

He was still poking at the wound, still turning it over in his mind, when he cruised into his brother's office an hour later.

"How was the gala?" Marc asked without looking up from where he was checking his first emails of the day.

"Enlightening," Nic answered, walking over to the window that made up one whole wall of the room. Beyond the company grounds were rocky cliffs and a small sandy beach. Beyond that was the endless Pacific. He watched the water for long minutes, saw the waves build out at sea, then crest, then roll harmlessly onto shore. It was winter, so the water was cold, but there were a few surfers out there, paddling on their boards as they waited for the next big wave.

For a second, he wanted to be out there with them. Wanted to be free, wanted—for just once in his life—to do whatever he wanted. To be whomever he wanted and to hell with the consequences.

But then Marc asked, "Enlightening how?" and the fantasy was shattered.

"What do you mean?" He turned to look at his brother.

Marc pushed back from his desk, then crossed the room to the small minifridge embedded in the bar. He grabbed a bottle of iced coffee for himself, then tossed Nic a pint of the fresh-squeezed orange juice he favored. He caught it neatly.

"When I asked you about the gala, you said it was enlightening. How so?" Marc came to stand next to him by the window, glancing out at the ocean before turning to Nic, an inquisitive look on his face.

Nic started to gloss over it, to focus on the people he'd met or the money he'd pledged from Bijoux. But Marc was his brother and his best friend, the only person he ever really opened up to. And so, before Nic even knew the words were there, he found himself saying, "I met a girl."

"You met a *girl*?"

"A woman," he corrected himself, thinking of Desi's lush curves and quick wit. "I met a woman."

"Do tell." Marc gestured to the chair opposite his desk, and though Nic had too much energy to really want to sit, he found himself doing so anyway. As usual.

"What's her name?" his brother asked.

"Desi."

"Desi…?"

"That's all. I don't have her last name."

"Well, that's sloppy on your part." Marc studied him closely. "Which is not an adjective I would usually use to describe you, so… This must be big."

"It's not big. It's not anything, really." And yet Nic really didn't like the way those words tasted in his mouth.

Marc laughed. "Of course not. Which is why you look like you swallowed a bug just saying that."

"Look, it's complicated."

"Dude, it's always complicated."

"Yeah, well, this time, it's really complicated." And so he told Marc the whole story, about how he'd fallen for Desi's looks at first sight and her startling quick wit almost as fast. About how he'd taken her home…and how he'd woken up alone.

"But you have her phone number, right?" Marc asked when Nic was finished with his tale of woe. "Please, tell me you were smart enough to get her number."

"Of course I was. But I was dumb enough to promise her I wouldn't call her until she called me."

Marc rolled his eyes. "All these years and have I really taught you nothing about how to woo a woman?"

"Considering you've spent the last six years licking your wounds from Isabella, I'd have to say that your own wooing skills are pretty lacking right now."

"I haven't been licking my wounds," Marc growled. "I've been busy running a multi-billion-dollar diamond corporation."

"Yeah, yeah, yeah. Call it whatever you like. Besides, I've been right here with you every step of the way, turning Bijoux into the second-largest responsibly sourced diamond corporation in the world."

"I know that—I wasn't implying otherwise. I was just saying I haven't had much time to woo anyone lately. Then again, neither have you. Maybe you're rusty."

Nic shot him a look. "I am not rusty, thank you very much." Sure, he preferred quality over quantity and always had, despite his playboy image in the press. But it wasn't as if he'd gone months without sex, for God's sake. His skills weren't rusty. At least, he didn't think they were.

God, what if that's why Desi had snuck out before he'd woken up? Because she'd thought he was bad in— No, no, no. That was one rabbit hole he was not going to fall down this morning. Because if he did…hell, if he did, he was afraid he'd never climb back out of it again.

"I'm not rusty," he said again, perhaps with more force than was absolutely necessary.

"I'm not saying you are." Marc held his hands up in mock surrender. "I'm just saying, if you have her phone number, why don't you use it?"

"I already told you—"

"I know. You can't call her until she calls you. But that doesn't mean you can't text her, right? Or did you make promises about that, too? And let me just say, if you did, you're stupider than you look."

"I didn't, actually," Nic answered as the wheels started turning in his brain. "I mean, I suppose an argument could be made about the spirit of the agreement—"

"Screw the spirit of the agreement. You like this woman, right?"

Nic thought of Desi's laugh, the way it filled a room and wrapped itself around him. Thought of her eyes, soft and pleasure dazed and welcoming. "Yeah," he told his brother hoarsely.

"So text her. Make her laugh. You're good at that. Then ask her out."

He nodded. Marc was right. Nic was good at that. He was usually really good at this whole dating thing. So what was it about Desi that threw him so completely off his game? He didn't know, but he figured it was important that she did. And he wanted to find out why he found her so fascinating. Why he'd spent the whole morning thinking about her when she'd made it fairly obvious that she didn't feel the same about him.

"Okay, yeah. I'll do that." He pushed to his feet, pulled his phone from his pocket. "Thanks, man."

Marc laughed. "I didn't mean now! It's barely eight in the morning. Besides, we're both due in a meeting that started five minutes ago."

"I'm not a total idiot, you know. I was just…thinking of what I wanted to say."

His brother came up behind him and clapped him on the back. "Wow, you really do have it bad."

Nic flipped him off as he led the way out of the office and down the hallway to the meeting room—after tucking his phone back in his pants. And if he spent the bulk of the meeting mentally composing a message to Desi, well, nobody needed to know that but him.

Five

"Desi, get in here. I've got a story for you," Malcolm Banks, her boss, called to her from across the newsroom.

"On my way," she answered, grabbing her tablet and heading toward the door with an enthusiasm she was far from feeling.

"Good luck," her friend Stephanie, a junior reporter for the fashion pages, mouthed to her. "Hope it's a good one!"

But Desi just shrugged. This was going to be another society story, she just knew it. She had, in fact, pretty much given up on getting a story of genuine worth anytime in the next decade or so. Because, despite her hard work generating and following up on numerous important story ideas over the past two months, Malcolm refused to give her a chance to write a story that really mattered.

He kept telling her she had to earn her way out of the society pages, and she kept trying. But she was beginning to think that she would be stuck there until she died. Or until Malcolm did, one or the other. Because there was no way she could get a job at another newspaper or magazine, not after she'd spent the past year and a half of her life covering parties and obituaries.

She didn't let her discontent show when she went into Malcolm's office. The only thing he hated more than whiners were salesmen, or so he said. And since local solicitors had long since learned their lesson about calling him—the hard way, but they'd learned it—she had no desire to be the low reporter on his totem pole. From what she'd seen in her time at the paper, bad things happened to those reporters…and she already had the crap assignments. She'd hate to see what would happen if she actually pissed off her boss.

It had taken her less than a minute to get to his office, but Malcolm was already engrossed in something else on the computer by the time she sat down in front of his desk. His distraction wasn't that unusual of an occurrence, so she settled in for a wait, patiently thumbing through her tablet as she did so. Seconds later, her phone buzzed with a text. Though she told herself not to get her hopes up, she couldn't stop herself from glancing at it, excitement welling up inside her at the possibility that it might be—

Nope. Not Nic. Just her friend and next-door neighbor, Serena, asking her to pick up some milk on the way home.

Her heart fell as she shoved the phone back in her pocket, despite the very stern talking-to that she gave herself. Of course it wasn't Nic. It hadn't been Nic in over three weeks. Which was fine. Better than fine. It was what she'd wanted, after all. Otherwise she would have answered one of the dozen text messages he'd sent her in the seven weeks since she'd snuck out of his house while he slept.

But she hadn't answered them, no matter what approach he'd taken. Funny, sweet, friendly, sexy. She'd read them all—over and over again—but hadn't been able to bring herself to answer them. Not because she didn't like him, but because she did. Not because she thought he was a jerk, but because she thought he was kind of…sweet. And goofy. And far too charming for her own peace of mind.

As she'd looked at those text messages, she could see herself falling for him, and she couldn't afford to do that. Couldn't afford to open herself up to him only to find out she was wrong. She'd been hurt doing that too many times before to risk it now. Or ever again.

"So, Desi," her boss finally began. "I have a story for you to write."

"Excellent," she answered with as much enthusiasm as she could muster, even while inside she was rolling her eyes. She could only imagine what he wanted this time. Probably gossip coverage of some socialite's garden party or something equally ridiculous.

"You know, for someone who's been begging to get out of the society pages for months, you certainly don't seem very excited about the opportunity."

It took a second for his words to sink in, but when they did she felt her whole body come to attention. Her gaze sharpened, her heart beat faster, and she leaned so far forward that she almost fell out of her chair. Even as she told herself to cool it—that she didn't even know what kind of story he was offering—her brain started racing with possibilities as excitement thrummed through her blood.

Malcolm must have seen the difference, because he laughed before saying, "Now there's the Desi I was expecting!" He nodded toward her tablet. "Ready to take notes?"

"Absolutely." If this was just some newly sadistic way for him to assign a high-society story to her, she swore she was going to kill him. And since she'd spent her off-hours moonlighting as the obituary writer for the past few months, she knew a bunch of ways to do it, too.

"So, I have a story for you. This morning, I got a tip about a business new to San Diego that might not be quite as legitimate as it seems on the surface."

Her mind started racing. Drugs. Guns. Mexican Mafia. She could practically feel herself champing at the bit to sink her teeth into whatever it was. She'd been trained in investigative journalism from a very early age by her father, one of the best reporters in the business. She could do this story. No, she *would* do this story.

"Diamonds," he told her after a brief pause that saw him turning back to his computer.

"Diamonds," she repeated. "Someone's using their business to smuggle diamonds?"

"I just sent the file I've begun assembling to your email," he told her as her tablet dinged to let her know she'd gotten mail. "It's got the basic information that the source gave me along with all of his contact info. I want you to get in touch with him, listen to his story the same way I did. Then I want you to do some digging. I want to know what's going on with this company, whether or not you think the accusations are true, and how you think it's happening."

"The diamond smuggling."

"I never said it was smuggling." He shot her a look. "Don't make assumptions. And look, I'm not just having you dig as an exercise. I really don't know if what this guy told me is true. If it is, it's a big damn deal. I just spent the last two hours researching these brothers, and if half of what this guy says turns out to be right, it's going to explode their whole damn lives. These guys have built their whole business on clean diamonds and—"

"Clean diamonds?" she asked, trying to wrap her head around the term. "Meaning not stolen?"

"*Clean* meaning responsibly sourced."

"Oh, of course. We're talking about conflict diamonds. Blood diamonds."

"Exactly."

"Bijoux." The name came to her easily, thanks to her time in the society pages. Much of San Diego's elite had been buzzing for the past few months about the fact that Marc Durand and his brother had come to town. They were big philanthropists and everyone wanted some of their money to support their pet charities—or themselves, for that matter.

She hadn't met either of the brothers yet. They'd been too busy setting up their business and their foundation to come to any of the galas she'd worked. Or if they had, she'd certainly never run into them. Which might be a good thing considering she was now going to be investigating them.

"Good," Malcolm told her with a satisfied nod.

"They're one of the biggest diamond corporations in the world right now, and you think they've been lying about where they get their diamonds."

"I don't know if they're lying or not, but your job is to figure out if they are. Right now, all I know is that somebody came to me and told me the brothers were pulling a fast one, masquerading as responsible diamond sourcers and then marking up the prices on conflict diamonds to ratchet up profits. I want to know if there's any truth to the story, and if there is, I want to know every single detail about it before we run this story and blow their whole business sky-high. You double-, triple- and quadruple-check this source and every other source you come across. Understand?"

"Absolutely." She opened up the file on her tablet, skimming over the information he'd sent her. Most of it was pretty sketchy, but she'd fix that soon enough. "When's the due date? And how many words do you want on this?"

Malcolm shook his head. "Let's just see how it goes. You find out if this is just some disgruntled ex-employee blowing smoke. If he is, the story goes away."

"And if he isn't?"

"If he isn't, we'll cross that bridge when we come to it. It will be a huge story and I'm thinking you'll probably need a partner to write it with you."

"I don't need a partner—" she started, but he held up a hand.

"Look, I know you're good. I know you're ready to show me what you've got. But you're still a rookie reporter and it doesn't matter how good you are, kid. There's no way I'm trusting a story this big to a snot-nosed society reporter."

"You're going to use me for the grunt work and then cut me out." She kept her voice calm when all she really wanted to do was curse. This could be her big break, and he was already talking about taking it away from her.

"I didn't say that. What I said was that I'm going to let you investigate and if you get something, I'm going to let you help write the biggest story of your career to date. If you want to write this story, if you want to see your byline front page above the fold, you need to give me something to work with. Show me what you got."

"Of course." She nodded calmly while inside she was

dancing. What he said made sense—and it was fair. She would investigate the hell out of this story, find out everything she could and even find out the angle she wanted to take. Maybe she'd even write the article and present it to him as a fait accompli. Then he would see what she could do and make an informed decision about how to proceed. And if she did this right—if she triple-checked her sources and dotted every i and crossed everything that even looked like a t—then he wouldn't have a choice. He'd have to move her out of the society pages and into news. Or at least into features.

This was what she'd been waiting for. Her big break. The story she'd been dying to tell.

"Got it?" Malcolm asked again.

Oh, she had it. God, did she ever. "Got it," she agreed.

"Good. Then go do your job. And don't forget, this is an extra assignment. You've still got your society-page duties—including that party tomorrow night. I'll cut down on you some, so you've got time to work on this on the clock, but you can't let the rest of your stories suffer for it."

"I won't."

He nodded, looking satisfied. Then, out of nowhere, he gestured wildly toward the door. "So go! Does it look like I've got time to stand around here chatting all damn day?"

"Right. I'm going." She quickly picked up her stuff, headed toward the door. But she stopped right before she crossed the threshold, turning back to look at him. "Thanks for giving me a shot. I won't let you down."

"I know you won't, kid. I knew the second I saw that picture that you would be perfect for the job."

"Picture?" she asked. "What picture?"

"The one of you and Nic Durand at the Children's

Hospital Gala in San Diego a few weeks ago. It was in the files under Bijoux when I went to look. Pretty dress, by the way."

She felt all the blood drain from her face as his words sunk in. "Me and Nic *Durand*?"

"Yeah. You look surprised. Didn't you get his name before you danced with him?"

Oh, God. Oh, God. Ohgod! Panic hit her like a freight train as she figured out that Nic—*her* Nic—was actually Nic Durand. But that was impossible. He'd said he was a PR guy. She remembered every second of the time she spent with him and she remembered, very clearly, him saying he worked in public relations. Then again, maybe he hadn't.

Something like that.

Those were his exact words when she'd asked him what he did. She'd leaped to the conclusion that he was a PR guy and he'd let her make the leap. More, he'd encouraged her to do it.

Typical, she told herself as she tried to tamp down the fury and the fear rocketing through her. He hadn't wanted her to know who he really was, hadn't wanted her to know how much money he was worth, just in case she decided to try to sink her claws into him. As if she'd ever do something like that. As if she would ever even consider sinking her claws into any man.

But figuring all this out now didn't make her current situation any less precarious. What was she supposed to do? Obviously, this was a very clear conflict of interest. She'd *slept* with Nic Durand, for God's sake. And then blown him off. And now she was supposed to investigate him? Fairly and impartially and with a very definite eye on the prize of becoming a reporter who did real stories as opposed to one who covered whose designer dress was actually an imitation?

How could she do it? How could she not do it, when she was standing in the middle of Malcolm's office and he was looking at her so expectantly? Maybe even paternally. She didn't want to disappoint him, but she also didn't know if she could do this. Didn't know if she could investigate Nic and his brother for something so despicable when—up until two minutes ago—there'd been a part of her that had longed to see him again for very nonbusiness reasons.

She must have been standing there trying to figure things out for longer than she'd thought, because Malcolm suddenly put a bracing hand on her shoulders. "Everything okay there, Desi?" he asked gruffly.

"Yes, of course," she lied. "Sorry, I was just thinking about what angle to take with my investigation."

"Well, I'd start by using the gala angle."

She looked at him blankly. "The gala angle?"

"Sure. You've already met him at least once, right?"

"Yes."

"Then call him up. Ask him for a tour of his business. Tell him you're writing a story about Bijoux since they're new to the area and set to become a major power player in Southern California. Men like that enjoy having their egos stroked."

"You want me to lie to him?" Was it possible for her to feel any sicker about this whole situation?

Malcolm glared at her sternly. "You're an investigative reporter, Maddox. You use whatever contacts you have to find out the truth. That's the way the job works."

"I know that, sir. It's just that—"

"Just what? I gave you this story because I figured you

already had an in with Nic Durand. Was I wrong about that? Should I give the story to someone else?"

He looked far from pleased at the prospect, and she knew if she followed her gut, if she told him yes he should give the story to someone else, he would do just that. And it would be a cold day in hell before she ever got another chance. She'd be writing obituaries and party gossip for as long as she worked for the *Los Angeles Times*. And maybe even longer.

"No, of course not," she told him, putting every ounce of conviction she could muster into her voice. Which wasn't much, if she was being honest, but at this point she would take what she could get.

"You don't sound too sure about that."

"I am sure. I've got this."

Malcolm finally nodded, satisfied. "Well, go get them, then. And don't forget to ask for help if you need it."

"I won't," she told him before making her way out of his office and back to her desk. As she did, her stomach pitched and rolled at the thought of the mess she had gotten herself into.

What was she supposed to do?

Then again, what could she do?

The questions echoed in her mind like a particularly terrifying mantra. But no matter how many times she asked them, no matter how many scenarios she ran through, she couldn't find a solution. She was going to have to investigate Nic Durand. And if he was guilty of what he was accused of…if he was guilty, she was going to have to write an article that exposed that guilt to the whole world.

The thought made her sick.

Because whatever his reasons for not telling her who he was—and she was forced to admit his omission could have been for any number of reasons besides him thinking she was a gold digger—after all, she hadn't exactly told him what she did for a living, either, had she?—he didn't deserve her using their connection, or whatever it was, to trick him into letting her inside Bijoux.

She had never used her body to get what she wanted, and she'd be damned if she'd use it now, even after the fact. No, she decided as she sat at her desk scrolling through the folder Malcolm had emailed her. If she had to do this investigation, then she would do it *her* way. Without involving Nic until she had no other choice in the matter. And when she'd reached that point, when she'd gathered as much information as she could on his company's diamond procurement, she would go to him. But she would do it the right way. She would be totally honest about who she was and what she wanted.

It was the only way she could do it, as far as she could tell. The only way she could write the story and also keep her integrity. Anything else was out of the question.

Satisfied with her decision—or at least as satisfied as she could be—she skimmed through the rest of the file before pulling out a yellow legal pad and making a list of every question she could think of pertaining to the investigation. It was just a start. She was sure she would come up with a bunch more as she delved into her research. But she needed to start somewhere, and this seemed as good a way to focus her research as any other.

Always start with the questions, her father used to tell her. How do you know what you're looking for if you don't even know what information you're missing? He'd said that to her a million times when she was young, back when he actually used to come home from his sojourns on the road. Back when he—when they—still had a home for him to come back to.

Shoving the unpleasant memories away, she dug into the story just as he'd taught her all those years ago. And soon she was so engrossed in her research that she forgot about everything else. It turned out the diamond trade was a fascinating—and brutal—world, one where human lives were often valued much less than the stones they mined.

She was so riveted by the stories that she didn't even notice Stephanie stopping by her desk until her friend put her hand on Desi's arm. Then she nearly jumped through the roof.

"I'm sorry!" Stephanie laughed when Desi had finally calmed down enough to take a breath. "I just wanted to see if you were ready to go to lunch."

"Oh, yeah. Of course. Give me five minutes to get all this in order, if that's okay."

"No problem. Looks like you got a decent story after all."

"Looks like. I hope I can do it justice."

"Of course you can! You'll be off the galas and into the news pages in no time."

"From your mouth to God's ears," Desi told her.

"Hush! Don't let Malcolm hear you say that. He'll think you're talking about him!"

They both laughed then, largely because Stephanie was right.

Desi closed her computer and locked up all of her paper research in her desk. It was early days yet, but it was never too early to be careful with her information. Another lesson her father had taught her before she'd hit her tenth birthday.

"Ready to go?" she asked after gathering her purse.

"Absolutely." But before she could step out from behind her desk, Stephanie leaned closer and whispered,

"Actually, I was hoping you had a tampon I could borrow. I always carry a couple in my purse, but for some reason I only had one today and there's no way I'll make it through the afternoon without an extra."

"Oh, right. Of course. I keep mine in my desk." Desi turned to open the drawer where she kept her personal stuff and pulled out the box of tampons she'd put in there weeks ago. But as she opened the box, it hit her that it was *un*opened. As in it had *never* been opened.

But that was impossible. She'd brought the box to work eight or nine weeks ago, when she'd used up the last of the old one. How could she have not had a period in the past nine weeks? And, more important, how could she not have noticed? She'd never had the most regular periods, despite being on the pill, but she'd never gone this long without one before, either. Alarm bells should have sounded at one point or another. They were definitely sounding now.

"Are you okay?" Stephanie asked as she reached out a hand to steady Desi's suddenly shaky form. "You've gone pale."

Desi didn't answer. She was too busy doing the math in her head. And then redoing it. And then redoing it again. But no matter how she looked at it, no matter how she counted, she should have had a period before now. Even worse, if she'd been close to her regular schedule last month, she would have been ovulating right about the time she and Nic had met.

Her knees gave way at the realization, and she probably would have fallen if Stephanie hadn't shoved the desk chair under Desi at the last second.

"Are you okay?" her friend asked again.

"I don't know." The words sounded hoarse as she forced them out of her too-tight throat. It wasn't possible. It just wasn't possible. She had been on the pill for years. And except for that first time on the balcony, she and Nic had used condoms. Which shouldn't have mattered in terms of pregnancy because she was on. The. Pill.

Except…except, she hadn't had a period. And—she took stock of her body, which felt totally normal except for the low-grade dizziness she'd been fighting for a few days—she had none of the signs that she would soon be getting a period. No cramps. No aching. No spotting. Nothing.

Nothing but dizziness. Nothing but a missed period. Nothing but—oh, God. Ohgodohgodohgod. For a second she thought she was actually going to have to put her head between her legs.

"Can you tell me what's wrong?" Stephanie asked, crouching down beside her. "Are you sick?"

Desi laughed a little hysterically then. "No, I'm not sick." And she wasn't, though she was very afraid that she was going to get sick if she didn't stave off this dizziness. And since the last thing she wanted to do was throw up in the middle of her office, she started breathing in through her nose and out through her mouth in the same steady rhythm she'd once seen a pregnant professor use.

It actually worked and in less than a minute she was feeling a lot steadier. At least physically. "Um, maybe you should go to lunch without me," she told Stephanie as she thrust the whole box of tampons at her. All she could think of was getting to the nearest drugstore and buying a pregnancy test. It would come back negative— of course it would come back negative because she was on the pill—but she needed to see the minus sign. Or the blank box. Or whatever the hell it was she was supposed to see, or not see, to prove to herself that she wasn't pregnant with Nic Durand's baby.

Except something in her wildly erratic behavior must have given her away—could it have been her death grip on the box of unopened tampons?—because Stephanie hauled her gently to her feet. Then whispered softly, "The convenience store on the corner should have a pregnancy test. If you'd like, I can run and get it for you."

Desi should have said she was fine, that she appreciated the offer but she could get the pregnancy test herself. Or better yet, she should have pretended that she had no idea what Stephanie was talking about. But the truth was, she was suddenly exhausted and shaky and terrified. So terrified. The last thing she wanted to do at that moment was to walk down the street and buy a damn pregnancy test that might change the course of the rest of her life.

And so she said yes to Stephanie's very kind offer. And then, after fumbling a twenty out of her wallet, she sat at her desk as her friend took off for the street as fast as her four-inch heels could carry her.

Desi didn't know how long Stephanie was gone, but she knew she didn't move, didn't think, barely even breathed in the time between when her friend left and when she returned, a small brown paper bag in her hand. How could Desi move when it felt as if her whole life hung in the balance?

"Go do it now," Stephanie urged as she handed over the bag. "It's better to know than not know."

Desi agreed, which was how she found herself alone in a bathroom stall, peeing on a small white stick. According to the directions, there'd be one line no matter what— pregnant or not pregnant. But if she was pregnant…

Except, she didn't have to wait five minutes. She didn't even have to wait one. By the time she had pulled her pants back up, there were two purple lines. Two very distinct purple lines.

She was pregnant with Nic Durand's baby, and she didn't have a clue what she was supposed to do about it.

Six

"Nic, there's a reporter on line two for you," his secretary said from where she was standing in the doorway to his office. "A Darlene Bloomburg from the *Los Angeles Times*."

He didn't bother glancing up from his laptop, where he was reviewing his marketing team's suggestions for Bijoux's winter ad campaigns. It was only July, but he wanted to ensure they made a huge splash with the holiday crowd. It was the next step in his plan to make Bijoux diamonds a household name. "Pass her over to Ollie," he suggested, referring to the head of Bijoux's public relations department. "She can get whatever she needs from him."

"I tried that," Katrina told him. "But she's determined to talk to you."

Something about the urgency in her voice snagged his attention, had him looking up from the proposed ad campaign and trying to figure out what he was missing. His secretary was a thirty-year veteran in her field, and totally unflappable most days, so the fact that she was standing in front of him, wringing her hands and biting her lip, didn't bode well for any of them.

"Is there something going on that I should know about?" he asked.

"I don't know. But I looked her up when she was so insistent, and she's the managing editor for the *Times*. Not the typical reporter we get calling us for a quote or some information on the diamond business."

"You think she's fact-checking an article about Bijoux?"

She nodded nervously. "I think she might be, yes."

"How come I didn't know the West Coast's largest paper was writing an article about us?"

"I don't know."

"Well, I'm going to find out. Tell the reporter—what's her name?"

"Darlene Bloomburg, sir."

"Tell Bloomburg that I'll be with her in a couple minutes. In the meantime, get Ollie in here, will you, please?"

"Right away, Nic."

Less than two minutes later, his PR director walked through the door, looking calm and collected despite the fact that he'd hightailed it over here from the other end of the floor.

"You know anything about this story?" Nic asked the other man.

Ollie shook his head. "No, nothing. But I'm sure it's nothing to worry about. Probably just a puff piece. We are in the middle of wedding season, after all."

"Maybe." But something felt off to Nic about that answer. Managing editors didn't usually need to fact-check fluff pieces. They had copy editors for stuff like that. "Let's just find out, shall we?" He reached for the phone and put it on speaker.

"This is Nic Durand."

"Hello, Mr. Durand. My name is Darlene Bloomburg and I'm managing editor of the *Los Angeles Times*."

"Please, call me Nic. It's nice to meet you, Darlene. What can I do for you?"

"I'm calling because we'll be running an article about Bijoux on the front page of Friday's edition and I wanted to check some facts as well as give you a chance to make a statement about the article's claims."

An alarm bell went off in his head and his eyes shot to Ollie, who looked as clueless as Nic felt. "You want me to make a statement."

"If you'd like to, yes."

"About what, may I ask?"

"About the fact that the *Times* has uncovered some credible information that proves Bijoux has been passing off conflict diamonds as conflict-free ones for several years."

The single alarm bell turned into a full-fledged five-alarm brigade. "That's impossible," he said. "What's your source?" Beside him, Ollie started turning red and making a stop gesture with his hands. Nic ignored him as the top of his own head threatened to blow off.

"What's impossible? That we've uncovered the evidence or—"

"That you think you can prove such a thing when it is blatantly untrue. I'm going to ask you again. What's your source?"

"It's the policy of the *Times* to never reveal a source. Am I correct in understanding that you dispute our findings, then?"

"Damn right I dispute them. Bijoux deals only in conflict-free diamonds and has for the ten years that Marc Durand and I have been in charge of this company. And it's Bijoux's policy to sue anyone who commits libel by printing otherwise."

"I see. Do you have any proof to back up your claims that your diamonds are conflict-free?"

"Are you serious with this? You're the one accusing me of lying and cheating and, more importantly, of buying diamonds from countries that allow the enslavement and murder of children as long as it results in gems for them to sell. I feel like you're the one who needs to provide the proof in this situation."

Next to him, Ollie changed from red to a very unbecoming shade of purple even as he waved his arms as if he was trying to attract the attention of a rescue plane. More to prevent his top PR guy from having a stroke in the middle of what promised to be the mother of all PR crises than because Nic wanted his help at that moment, Nic hit Mute on the phone and then asked, "What do you want me to say?"

"I want you to get the article," Ollie demanded. "There's no way they run that article without you seeing it first. Tell her—"

"I know what to tell her. You go get Hollister." He wanted Bijoux's head counsel in here, stat.

Nic unmuted the phone, this time hitting the button so hard that the entire device skidded a foot across his desk. Son of a bitch. He was going to get that article and then he was going to tear it—and the reporter who wrote it—apart with his bare hands. "I need to tell you, Darlene, that if you run that article as is, without giving me a chance to vet it first and debunk your obvious misinformation, you will be facing a lawsuit the likes of which the *Los Angeles Times* has never seen."

"Our information is good."

"Your information is wrong, that much I guarantee you."

"It comes from an insider at Bijoux. One who has proof that the company has systematically bought conflict diamonds and passed them off as conflict-free diamonds for at least seven of the last ten years."

"Let me get this straight. You're claiming that one of my people came to you and gave you information implicating us in not only buying conflict diamonds but then in conspiring to defraud consumers by claiming the gems are conflict-free."

"Essentially, yes, that is what the source has provided us proof of."

"And again, this came from one of our people?"

"That is correct."

"And you think you're going to run this article in three days."

"We *are* going to run this article in three days,"

Over his dead body they were. "Yeah, well, Darlene, that just isn't going to happen."

"With all due respect, Nic—"

"With all due respect, Darlene, you've been taken for a ride."

"The *Los Angeles Times* does not get taken for a ride, Mr. Durand. We triple-check our sources—"

"Well, you didn't in this case. This is the first time either Marc or myself has heard of these allegations, and in a situation like this, no one else is in a position to know more about our diamonds, and where they come from, than we do. I know where every single shipment comes from. Marc personally inspects every mine on a regular basis. The certification numbers on the stones come straight to us, and only our in-house diamond experts ever get near those numbers. All of our diamonds are conflict-free. All of them. Now, you are welcome to come in and tour our facilities and see all of the safeguards we have in place to ensure that what you're accusing us of doesn't happen. In the meantime, I'll be happy to courier over all of our PR materials so you can see where our diamonds really do come from."

"Our reporter tried to come for a tour on two separate occasions while she was researching this article. Both times she was turned away by your PR office."

He ground his teeth together, wondering what the hell Ollie had been thinking. Probably that he didn't have time to babysit a reporter on a puff piece, what with the sudden uptick in business and philanthropy—and the publicity both generated. But if she had told him what the story was about, there was no way Ollie would have turned her away. And no way this information wouldn't have been brought to Nic's attention a hell of a lot sooner than three days before the article was supposed to run.

Which, he figured, was exactly why the reporter hadn't told anyone the nature of the story she was writing. And now they were all paying for it…

"Your reporter's inability to explain her article idea to my PR department is not my fault."

"Of course not. But your PR department's secrecy and inability to deal with the community when necessary is not our fault, either."

He ground his teeth, counted to ten to keep from spewing onto her all the vitriol that was racing through his brain. When he could finally speak again without fear of telling the managing editor of the *Los Angeles Times* to go to hell and take her newspaper with her, he said,

"I'll courier over that information to you right away. In the meantime, you can email or fax a copy of that article to my office."

"We are under no obligation to do so, Mr. Durand." Her voice was firm, with absolutely no uncertainty whatsoever. Which seemed impossible to him considering the claims she was making—and the proof he had to refute them.

Who was her source? he wondered again. He went through a list of all the employees who had left recently and couldn't think of one who would do this—or who *could* do this. All of them had left on good terms, and not one of them had access to the kind of information that would convince the *Times* to run such a negative story. Largely because that information didn't exist, but still. If it did, no way any of them would have been able to access it.

"You may not be under any obligation, Darlene, but you're going to do it anyway. Because if you don't, my attorneys will be filing for injunctions today against your paper, you and the reporter who wrote this drivel. And if you run this article as is, without getting to the truth of the matter, I will sue you. By the time we're done, Bijoux will own the *Los Angeles Times* and all of your assets. Now, you have until eleven o'clock to provide me with a copy of that article. Or the Los Angeles civil court system will be hearing from us."

He hung up the phone without giving her the chance to say another word. He'd heard more than enough.

For long seconds, Nic could do nothing but stand there, staring into space and imagining the worst-case scenario if this thing went to print. Bijoux would lose everything it had gained under Marc and Nic's leadership. They'd be crucified in the press—and in the international human rights community. They'd be sued by God only knew how many consumer groups and diamond retailers. And they'd be investigated by numerous federal and international law agencies. Not to mention the fact that if any of that happened, it would break his brother's heart.

Which was why Nic was going to make sure that it didn't. He and Marc had worked too hard to build up this company after they'd taken it over ten years before. They'd faced their father's disapproval, their board's disapproval. Hell, even the industry had frowned on Marc and Nic's determination to use only responsibly sourced diamonds.

In the interim years, the industry had grown much more supportive of what he and his brother were doing—largely because of the growing interest from human rights groups in places like Sierra Leone and Liberia. New laws had been passed making trading in conflict diamonds illegal, but just because it was illegal didn't mean that less reputable companies didn't still buy up conflict diamonds. It only meant they did it in secret instead of on the open market as they used to.

He and Marc did not do that. They did not buy conflict diamonds. They didn't work with anyone who dealt in conflict diamonds. And they sure as hell didn't cover up their illegal activity by passing the diamonds off to consumers at a jacked-up price.

The accusation was absurd, completely and totally ludicrous. But that didn't matter. Once it was out there, once the general public got hold of it, Bijoux's brand would be annihilated and everything he and Marc had worked so hard for would be destroyed right along with it.

There was no way he would let that happen. Not to his brother, not to his employees and not to the family business he'd worked so many long, hard hours to develop.

If the *Los Angeles Times* really wanted to pick a fight with him, then it'd better come at him with everything it had. Because he was about to make it his life's mission to bring those bastards down.

"We have a problem."

His brother looked up as Nic blew right past Marc's assistant and entered his office with a slam of his door.

"What's going on?" Marc asked, looking faintly alarmed.

Operating on instinct, and rage, Nic slammed his hand down on the desk hard enough to rattle everything resting on top of it—including Marc's laptop and cup of coffee. Then watched as his brother grabbed the coffee and put it on the credenza behind him despite the obvious tension in the air. Such a Marc thing to do. Staying calm when Nic was still so furious he could barely think, let alone form coherent sentences.

When he turned back to face Nic, Marc was completely composed, but he figured that wasn't going to last long. His brother might be the cool one of the two of them, but he was even more ragingly protective of this business than Nic was. Once he heard what was going on, Marc would lose it as completely as Nic had.

"Tell me."

"I just got off the phone with a reporter from the *Los Angeles Times*. She's doing an exposé on Bijoux and wanted a comment before the article goes to print."

"An exposé? What the hell does she have to expose?" Marc stood up then and walked around the desk. "Between you and me, we're in charge of every aspect of this company. Nothing happens here that we don't know about, and we run a clean company."

"That's exactly what I told her." Nic shoved a hand

through his hair as he tried to make sense of the situation for what felt like the millionth time. They were good to their employees, treated them well. Gave them raises twice a year, bonuses once a year. Hell, they'd built a state-of-the-art facility on the edge of the ocean, one that provided everything from free health care to free day care and three meals a day for their employees.

He and Marc were invited to weddings, christenings, birthday parties…and they went, every time. Fostering a sense of community, of family, within the company was incredibly important to him—probably because he'd never had much of a family beyond his brother. The fact that someone would be so disgruntled, so angry, *so vengeful*, that the person would deliberately sabotage them like this…it made absolutely no sense.

"And?" Marc ground out the words. "What's she exposing?"

God, Nic didn't want to tell his brother this. Didn't want to see how devastated he was going to be at the accusation. Not when Marc had poured his heart and soul into making Bijoux not only a success, but also a company with a heart and a social conscience.

Still, it had to be done, and Nic might as well rip the bandage off as quickly, as cleanly as possible. "According to her, she's exposing the fact that we're pulling diamonds from conflict areas, certifying them as conflict-free and then passing them on to the consumer at the higher rate to maximize profits."

Marc's mouth actually dropped open, and for long seconds he did nothing but stare at Nic. "That's ridiculous," he finally sputtered.

"I know it's ridiculous! I told her as much. She says she has an unimpeachable source who has given her credible evidence."

"Who's the source?"

"She wouldn't tell me that." Nic fought the urge to slam his hand into the wall as frustration welled up in him all over again.

"Of course she wouldn't tell you that, because the source is bullshit. The whole story is bullshit. I know where every single shipment of diamonds comes from. I personally inspect every mine on a regular basis. The certification numbers come straight to me, and only our in-house diamond experts—experts whom I have hand-picked and trust implicitly—ever get near those numbers."

"I told her *all* of that. I invited her to come in and take a tour of our new facilities and see exactly how things work here at Bijoux."

"And what did she say?"

"She said she had tried to come for a tour, but PR had put her off. It's too late now. The story is slotted to run on Friday, and they really want a comment from us before it goes to print."

"Friday's in three days."

"I'm aware of that. It's why I'm here, freaking out."

"Screw that." Marc picked up his phone and dialed an in-house number. They both waited impatiently for the line to be picked up.

"Hollister Banks." The voice of their lead counsel came through the speakerphone. He was obviously out of his earlier meeting—and just as obviously hadn't yet gotten the urgent message Nic had left for him. He sounded far too cheerful.

"Hollister. This is Marc. I need you in my office now."

"Be there in five."

His brother didn't bother to say goodbye before hanging up and dialing another number. "Lisa Brown, how may I help you?"

Nic listened as Marc told their top diamond inspector the same thing he'd just told Hollister.

"But, Marc, I just got in a whole new shipment—"

"So put it in the vault and then get up here." The impatience in his voice must have gotten through to her, because Lisa didn't argue again. She agreed before quietly hanging up the phone.

It took Lisa and Hollister only a couple of minutes to get to Marc's office, and soon the four of them were gathered in the small sitting area to the left of his desk. No one said a word as Nic once again recounted his discussion with Darlene Bloomburg.

He got angrier and angrier as he told the story. By the end, he was literally shaking with rage. This was more than just his company they were screwing. It was his life, his brother's life, his employees' lives. If Bijoux went down for this—and he'd been in marketing long enough to know that if this story ran, they would absolutely take major hits no matter how untrue the accusations were—it'd be more than just Marc's and Nic's asses on the line. His employees would be under investigation and, if the hits were bad enough, also out of jobs. All because some ignorant reporter with a chip on her shoulder couldn't get her facts straight.

As he tried to channel his rage, he promised himself that if this story ran he would make it his life's mission to get that reporter fired. Hell, he'd get her fired even if it didn't run. She should have known better than to make this kind of mistake.

"Who's the source?" Marc asked Lisa after she and Hollister had absorbed the story—and its implications.

"Why are you asking me? I have no idea who would

make up a false claim like this and feed it to the *Times*. I'm sure it's none of our people."

"The reporter seemed pretty adamant that it was an insider. Someone who had the position and the access to prove what he or she is saying." It was the third time Nic had said those words, and they still felt disgusting in his mouth.

"But that's impossible. Because what the person is saying isn't *true*. The claims are preposterous," Lisa asserted. "Marc and I are the first and last in the chain of command when it comes to accepting and certifying the conflict-free diamonds. There's no way one of us would make a mistake like that—and we sure as hell wouldn't lie about the gems being conflict-free to make extra money. So even if someone messed with the diamonds between when I see them and when Marc does, he would catch it."

"Not to mention the fact that there are cameras everywhere, manned twenty-four/seven by security guards who get paid very well to make sure no one tampers with our stones." Everyone in the room knew that already, but Nic felt the need to add it anyway.

"What this person is saying just isn't possible," Lisa continued. "That's why Marc insists on being the last point of contact for the stones before we ship them out. He verifies the geology and the ID numbers associated with them."

"There is a way it would work," Marc interrupted, his voice a little weaker than usual. "If I were involved in the duplicity, it would explain everything."

"But you're not!" Nic said at the same time Lisa exclaimed, "That's absurd!"

Nic knew his brother almost as well as he knew himself, and if there was one thing he was certain of it was that Marc would never do anything to harm Bijoux. The two of them had worked too hard to get the company to where it was to let a little extra profit ruin everything. They already had more money than they could spend in three lifetimes. Why risk it all, especially in such a despicable way, for some extra cash?

People *died* mining conflict diamonds. Children were exploited, beaten, starved, worked nearly to death. No amount of extra profit was worth propagating such blatant human rights violations. No amount of money was worth the stain dealing in conflict diamonds would leave on his soul.

"Marc's making sense. It's what they'll argue," Hollister said, and though it was obvious by his tone that he disagreed, Nic could tell his ready agreement bothered Marc.

Not that Nic blamed Hollister. This was more than a company to them, more than profits and bottom lines. More even than diamonds. Their great-grandfather had started Bijoux in the early twentieth century and it had been run by a Durand ever since.

When Nic and Marc took it over, they'd had to act fast to repair the damage their father had done through years of neglect and disinterest. It wasn't that he'd wanted to run the company into the ground, but he'd always been more interested in the adventures—and the women— the Durand money could buy rather than the day-to-day work of being CEO.

Which was why Nic and his brother had worked so hard to rebuild things. For years, they'd put their lives into this company and in a decade had managed to take Bijoux from a floundering behemoth into the second-largest diamond distributor in the world. They'd brought it into the twenty-first century and had created a business model that would help those who couldn't help themselves and that wouldn't exploit those who needed protection most.

"I don't care what you have to do," Marc told Hollister after a long pause. "I want that story stopped. We've worked too hard to build this company into what it is to have another setback—especially one like this. The jewel theft six years ago hurt our reputation and nearly bankrupted us. This will destroy everything Nic and I have been trying to do. You know as well as I do, even if we prove the accusations false in court, the stigma will still be attached. Even if we get the *Los Angeles Times* to print a retraction, it won't matter. The damage will have already been done. I'm not having it. Not this time. Not about something like this."

His words echoed Nic's thoughts from earlier, and the similarity was eerie enough to make the situation really sink in. From the moment he'd heard about the article, he'd been operating under the assumption that they would find a way to stop it. But what if they didn't? What if it actually got printed? What if everything they'd worked so hard for actually went up in smoke?

What would they do then?

What would *he* do then?

Marc must have been thinking along the same lines, because there was a renewed urgency in his voice when he told Hollister, "Call the editor. Tell him the story is blatant bullshit and if he runs it I will sue their asses and tie them up in court for years to come. By the time I'm done, they won't have a computer to their name let alone a press to run the paper on."

"I'll do my best, but—"

"Do better than your best. Do whatever it takes to make it happen. If you have to, remind them that they can't afford to go against Bijoux in today's precarious print-media market. If they think they're going to do billions of dollars of damage to this company with a blatantly false story based on a source they won't reveal, and that I won't retaliate, then they are bigger fools than I'm already giving them credit for. You can assure them that if they don't provide me with definitive proof as to the truth of their claims, then I will make it my life's work to destroy everyone and everything involved in this story. And when you tell them that, make sure they understand I don't make idle threats."

"I'll lay it out for them. But Marc," Hollister cautioned, "if you're wrong and you've antagonized the largest newspaper on the West Coast—"

"I'm not wrong. We don't deal in blood diamonds. We will *never* deal in blood diamonds, and anyone who says differently is a damn liar."

"I already made those threats to the managing editor," Nic said after everyone absorbed Marc's words. "And while I agree they'll sound better coming from our lead counsel, we need to do more than threaten them. We need to prove to them that they're wrong."

"And how exactly are we going to do that?" Lisa asked. "If we don't know who they're getting information from, or even what that information is, how can we contradict them?"

"By hiring an expert in conflict diamonds." Hollister had obviously gotten with the program. "By taking him up to Canada where we get our stock, letting him examine the mines we pull from. And then bringing him back here and giving him access to anything and everything he wants. We don't have any secrets—at least not of the blood-diamond variety. So let's prove that."

"Yes, but getting an expert of that caliber on board could take weeks," Lisa protested. "There are barely a dozen people in the world with the credentials to sign off unquestioningly on our diamonds. Even if we pay twice the going rate, there's no guarantee that one of them will be available."

"But one is available." Nic glanced at his brother when he said it, knowing very well that Marc would not appreciate his suggestion. But desperate times called for desperate measures, and he would do anything—anything—to stop this from happening. Including dig up his brother's very painful past. "She lives right here in San Diego and teaches at GIA. She could totally do it."

Marc knew whom Nic was talking about, and he didn't take the suggestion well. Big shock there. Nic waited for him to say something, but when Marc did nothing but stand there silently, Nic couldn't help goading him. "Dude, you look like you swallowed a bug."

"I can't call Isa, Nic. She'd laugh in my face. Or she'd deliberately sabotage us just to get back at me. There's no way I can ask her to do this."

Nic rolled his eyes. "Weren't you the one saying we can't afford to screw around with this? Isa's here, she has the experience, and if you pay her well and get a sub to carry her classes, she's probably available. It doesn't get much better than that."

"You should give her a call," Hollister urged.

"Yeah, absolutely," agreed Lisa. "I'd forgotten about Isabella Moreno being here in San Diego. I've met her a few times and she's really lovely—we should totally get her. I can try to talk to her, if you'd like."

"No," Marc told Lisa harshly, after a few uncomfortable seconds passed. "I'll take care of getting her on board."

He didn't sound happy about it, but he looked resigned. And wary. Which was good enough for Nic. His brother was an arrogant bastard, but Bijoux meant everything to him. He'd get Isa on board, even if it meant he had to crawl to do it.

In the meantime, Nic would meet with Ollie and scour the article that should be in his inbox by now. If the worst case happened and this thing actually went to print, he wanted to be ready with the best damage control the industry had ever seen.

Seven

The next few days were excruciatingly slow as Nic waited for Isa's findings. He was sure Marc felt the same torture, but at least his brother was out in the world, actively working to save their company. He'd taken Isabella to Canada and now he was here, in the building with her, checking out their diamonds. Proving, unequivocally, once and for all, that whoever had given the *Times* its information had been wrong. All Nic was doing was sitting here, feeling as if he was fighting with both hands tied behind his back.

It wasn't a good feeling.

But then, how could it be when everything he'd worked for, everything Marc had worked for, could go up in smoke any minute? Simply because someone with a grudge had lied about them. Simply because some reporter had said so. It was infuriating.

Nic and Ollie had put together a damn good plan for

damage control over the past seventy-two hours, but Nic really hoped they'd never have to use it. Hollister had managed to get the article pushed back a few days, though not canceled, and now the only thing left to do was wait.

Wait for Isa to certify their diamonds as conflict-free.

Wait for the *Times* to decide what it would do about the article.

Wait for security to comb through the company files and find out the identity of the source.

Too bad he hated waiting with the passion of a thousand burning suns.

Yet, it seemed as if it was all he'd been doing lately. Even before this whole thing started. Ever since Nic had met Desi, really. He'd texted her a few times right after they'd been together, but she'd never responded. He'd dropped down to once a week after that because he hadn't wanted to harass her. He'd just wanted…her. If he hadn't, he would have given up after the second day.

But he hadn't given up. Instead, he'd waited seven weeks for her to respond to him and she never had. Not one returned text, not one phone call, nothing but total and complete radio silence. Which was why he'd finally given up on her, why he'd gone so far as to erase her number from his phone. He liked her a lot, but if she didn't feel the same way about him, he wasn't going to spend the next year moping around about the one who'd gotten away. Not when they'd spent less than twelve hours together total.

He'd thought if he shoved Desi out of his mind—and took her off his phone—he wouldn't have to think about her again.

Too bad it hadn't worked.

Determined to get her out of his mind once and for

all, he grabbed his laptop. Started fiddling with the winter marketing plans. He'd had a great idea about them when he'd been wandering his empty house at three that morning. He should probably write it down before it disappeared.

But he'd only just opened the advertising budget spreadsheet when the intercom on his desk buzzed with his brother's voice. The sound cut through Nic's not-so-pleasant thoughts, giving him the distraction he'd been looking for. "Come to my office, will you? I want to talk to you about something."

"Be right there," Nic answered, glad beyond measure that he finally had something to do. Sure, he had his normal workload, but none of that interested him right now. Nothing did, except putting this story to rest once and for all.

Grabbing his phone and his cup of coffee off his desk, he made his way to Marc's office. As Nic walked down the long corridor that separated their corner offices, people called out hellos from every door that he passed.

He returned the greetings as naturally as he could, but he could tell his staff knew something was wrong. There were a bunch of questioning looks, and even their greetings were more subdued than normal. Not that he blamed them. He hadn't exactly been his normal exuberant self lately, either. It was pretty hard to act as if everything was all right when he and his brother might very well be captaining a sinking ship. They'd already been hit by the iceberg. Now they just had to wait to see if they'd somehow manage to stay afloat.

"What's up?" he asked as he let himself into Marc's office.

"I want to talk about the December ad campaign. I

want to hit it harder, want to make sure we're everywhere we need to be."

"We will be, I promise."

"Still, I want to put more money toward the campaign. Another fifty million or so—"

"We don't need another fifty million—"

"You don't know that. You don't know what we'll need if—"

"I do know. And that's why we're retooling part of the campaign. There will still be the ads that focus on giving her diamonds, etc. But we'll also have ads about making the world a better place, bringing holiday cheer to those who have none—it'll have Bijoux's name on it, but there will be no mention of buying anything, no mention of gifts. Instead we'll focus on children in developing nations, with a particular emphasis on conflict diamonds and those who are forced to mine them."

"That's really smart, actually. I'm impressed."

"Don't sound so surprised. I do, occasionally, know what I'm doing, you know."

Marc snorted. "Well, let's not get all crazy now."

"Yeah, 'cause I'm the crazy one in the room."

"Excuse me? I will have you know that I am exceptionally sane."

"Yeah, that's what they all say, bro, right before they chop off an ear. Or some other more important body part."

"I assure you," Marc told him, completely deadpan, "I have no intention of chopping off *my* ear or anyone else's."

"Hey, don't knock it till you've tried it. Insanity might look good on you."

"But it already looks so good on you."

"I think you're confused. This isn't insanity, man. This is confidence."

Marc studied him for a second before shaking his head. "Nah. It's insanity."

Nic couldn't help it. He burst out laughing. It felt good to share a little banter with his brother, especially when things had been so tense lately. As he sank into a chair on the visitor's side of his brother's desk, he told himself it was a sign that things were looking up.

Harrison, one of the attorneys working their end of the situation and one of his closest friends at the company, walked in a couple of minutes later. He'd barely sat down before the door opened again and this time it was Isa who walked in, carrying a thick manila folder in her hand.

She grinned at all of them before perching on the corner of Marc's desk and sliding the folder across the dark cherrywood.

Mark looked at her inquisitively, at least until he opened it and saw what was written there. Then he broke out in a huge smile as he asked, "We got it?"

"You absolutely got it," Isa told him. "I didn't find one irregularity."

Adrenaline raced through Nic at the confirmation and he jumped out of his chair, pumped a fist in the air. "I knew it, baby!" he all but shouted. "I knew that reporter had a bad source." He gave Marc a second to look over the documentation she'd provided, then ripped the folder out of his hands and headed for the door.

"Hey, where are you going?" his brother called after him.

"To make a copy of this file. And then I'm going to go down to the *Los Angeles Times* myself and force-feed every single page of this to that jackal of a reporter. I hope she chokes on it."

"I feel obliged to warn you of the illegality of such actions." Harrison somehow managed to keep a straight face as he said it.

Nic flipped him off on his way out of the office. And though he wanted to celebrate with Marc and Isa and everyone else who had helped clear Bijoux of any wrongdoing, his job wasn't done yet. He needed to make sure the *Los Angeles Times*—and one particular reporter—got this information. And while he could, and would, have it emailed over, there was no way he was leaving this to the whims of someone's email habits. He was hand delivering this baby himself.

Besides, he really wanted to see D. E. Maddox's face when he plopped the report on her desk.

Since it was midmorning, the drive from their offices in north Carlsbad to the headquarters of the *Los Angeles Times* was less than an hour and a half. On the way, he plotted what he would say to Maddox and her managing editor. About a million expletives came to mind, but since he was a gentleman and not in the habit of cursing at women—even women who had nearly destroyed his family's business—he worked out a little speech instead. Short, pithy, to the point and—yes, he admitted it—more than a little smug. He might be a gentleman, but that didn't mean he shouldn't gloat a little. Especially about something like this.

He pulled into the parking lot exactly one hour and fourteen minutes after he left his office in Carlsbad—okay, maybe he'd sped a little, but he'd be lying if he said he wasn't anxious to get this whole thing over with and behind him. Behind Bijoux.

He figured he'd have to talk his way around a few security guards, maybe a receptionist or two, before he'd be able to get to either Maddox or Bloomburg. But it turned out that the huge compound that had once belonged exclusively to the *Los Angeles Times* now housed some kind of call center and a few other businesses that had nothing to do with the news. Which meant Nic waltzed right through the central lobby, where he checked the building's directory and got onto an elevator that took him straight to the newspaper's main floor.

He stepped off the elevator into a huge newsroom packed with desks. It was almost empty, which wasn't a surprise considering he'd arrived in the middle of the lunch hour. Except for a couple of stragglers, the few people who were there were huddled around a table at the front of the room, talking animatedly—probably about how to ruin the reputations of other businesses in the area. Which, okay, might be an unfair assessment, but he wasn't exactly feeling kindly toward the paper at the moment, or anyone who worked there.

There was still no receptionist to check in with, nobody to even give his name to. And while he knew security at Bijoux was over the top because of the nature of their business—and because they housed diamonds in their state-of-the-art vault—he admitted to being a little shocked at just how laissez-faire this place was about security.

Still, it worked in his favor, so he wasn't complaining. The paper had certainly had the element of surprise when it had contacted him less than a week ago. Now he was returning the favor. Neither Maddox nor Bloomburg would ever expect him to show up here. He'd find Maddox's desk and be waiting for her when she got back from lunch.

A big guy with a camera hanging around his neck finally stopped him when he was halfway through the room. But when Nic told him he had something to deliver to D. E. Maddox, the guy waved him toward a desk in the back corner. It was, surprisingly, one of only three desks in the cavernous space that actually had someone sitting at it.

Which was even more perfect. He'd prefer to confront Maddox and get this over with as quickly as possible.

As he approached, she had her back to him, which gave him a perfect view of what looked like miles of platinum blond hair. The sight tugged something inside of him, making him think of Desi and the night he'd spent with her hair fanned out on his pillow. He shoved the memory down—the last thing he needed right now was to be distracted by thoughts of her—but for some reason she just wouldn't leave his head. It was only when he got closer to the woman that he understood why that was.

As he approached her at an angle, he could see her profile clearly. Could see her high cheekbones and lush full lips. Could see her sun-kissed skin and the dimple low on her right cheek. Suddenly it didn't seem so far-fetched that she reminded him of the woman he had spent the past eighteen weeks trying to forget.

"Desi?" He hadn't meant to say her name out loud, hadn't meant to attract her attention until he'd had a second to deal with the shock of finding out that D. E. Maddox, hated reporter and company annihilator, was none other than the woman he'd taken home for one unforgettable night.

But she turned toward him as soon as he said her name, her eyes widening as she realized who it was standing only a few feet from her desk. He expected her to look guilty, or at the very least, apologetic. Instead, her eyes burned with a fury that made the anger in his own gut look like nothing.

"What are you doing here?" she demanded as she pushed to her feet. "Slumming it?"

Slumming it? He couldn't even figure out what she meant, let alone how he was supposed to respond to the bizarre accusation. How could he understand when he was still reeling from the realization that *Desi* had been investigating him for weeks? That she'd been right under his nose for the past few days and he hadn't had a clue?

"Well?" she asked, and it was the impatience in her voice that finally kick-started his brain into gear.

"I'm here to deliver this to D. E. Maddox," he said, brandishing the folder like the weapon it was. "But I have to admit I'm a little surprised to see *you* sitting at *her* desk."

"I don't know why you would be." She had the audacity to shrug. "It's not like you know anything about me."

"So you're really going to do this?" he demanded as the fury inside him kindled into ugly rage. "Pretend that nothing happened between us."

"Nothing did happen between us," she answered coolly. "At least, nothing important."

"So that night was what? A setup for this, then? A way for you to get to know your assignment before you ruined his business and his life?"

"I didn't ruin your life or your business. You did that all on your own when you decided to trade in conflict diamonds."

"I told your managing editor the other day and now I'm telling you. Bijoux does not deal in conflict diamonds." He dropped the folder on her desk. "I've got the proof that we don't right here."

She didn't even bother to glance down at the file. "And I have proof that you do."

"So show it to me."

"I'm not going to do that."

"Of course not. Who cares if you run a fake story as long as you get the attention you need, right?"

"I don't fake evidence," she said as she stood up and started around the desk. "And I didn't fake this story."

"Well, someone sure as hell faked evidence. Maybe it wasn't you. Maybe you're not inherently dishonest. Maybe you're just a sloppy reporter."

"Who do you think you are?" she demanded as she went toe-to-toe with him.

For a second—just a second—he was distracted by her flashing eyes and flushed skin. By her honeysuckle-and-vanilla scent. By her warmth. But then her words sank in and he found his temper flashing from dangerous to boiling point in the space of one breath and the next.

"Who do I *think* I am?" he repeated. "I don't think anything, sweetheart. I know exactly who I am. I'm the man whose career—and hundred-year-old family business—you set out to ruin on a whim. I'm the man you have accused of the vilest crimes and human rights violations imaginable. I'm the man you slept with to get a story and then dropped the moment you realized I wouldn't be useful to you."

"I didn't accuse you of anything you haven't done. And I didn't drop you. You dropped me."

He stared at her, speechless. For a moment, he honestly feared his head would explode. "Is that how you do it?" he wondered aloud. "Is that how you justify the lives you ruin? You just rewrite history to fit whatever version you need it to fit? You need a big story to break your career wide open? No problem. It's easy to manufacture evidence. You want to forget that you slept with me to get a story? That's easy. Just pretend I didn't text you for weeks trying to get you to talk to me." He threw his arms wide. "You've missed your calling, Desi. Oops, I mean D.E. You shouldn't be a journalist. You should be a fiction writer. You'd probably top the charts with your very first book."

She didn't answer him for long seconds. Instead she just stared at him with her jaw locked and her eyes as cold and blue as the Pacific in the middle of a midwinter temper tantrum.

"You don't know what you're talking about," she finally said.

"You know, you're going to call me a liar one time too many and then…"

"And then what?"

He was too stunned by her brazenness and her sheer lack of remorse to answer.

"That's what I thought," she sneered. "You've got nothing."

Rage exploded within him, mixed with disbelief and confusion and more attraction than he wanted to admit to, and Nic finally snapped. Taking a step forward, he crowded her against her desk before closing the last inches between them. But the second his body brushed against hers, he knew he'd made a mistake. Because with that first touch, the low-grade attraction that had hummed between them from the moment he'd said her name exploded into a conflagration of fiery want and desperate need.

He wasn't the only one affected. He could see Desi's awareness in her flushed skin. Could hear it in her ragged breathing and feel it in the not-quite-steady hands she pressed against his chest.

"What are you doing?" she whispered as he pressed even closer.

"I don't have a clue," he admitted.

"Then maybe you should stop."

"Maybe I should. But if you want me to do that, you probably shouldn't hold me quite so tightly." He glanced down to where she had tangled her fingers in his dress shirt.

She gasped then, started to pull back. But he didn't let her. Instead, he held her in place with one hand on her hip and the other between her shoulder blades.

Time stopped as they stood there, bodies locked together in a too-intimate bid for dominance—of the situation and each other. He didn't know what he was doing, didn't know what he was pushing for. All he knew was that part of him wanted to punish her for what she'd put him through but the other part of him wanted nothing more than to take her back to his house and make love to her until she screamed his name. Until she couldn't even think of defying him again.

They might have stayed there forever in their oddly intimate standoff, except just as Nic shifted to make sure she was comfortable, he felt a small but very definite kick against his abdomen.

"What was that?" he demanded, jumping back.

"That," she said, looking pointedly down at her gently rounded stomach, "is why I left you a voice mail."

Eight

She couldn't tell if Nic looked more stupefied or stupid as he gazed down at the firm curve of her stomach. "Close your mouth," she told him after a minute, "or you'll end up catching flies."

"You're pregnant?"

"Sure looks like it, doesn't it?" She didn't mean to be flippant, but come on. How long was he going to keep up this charade? After trying to get him on the phone three different times, she'd finally given up and broken the news to him in a voice mail. And she hadn't been delicate about the information, either. She'd told him, straight up, that she was pregnant and that she'd very much like it if he'd call her back.

Needless to say, he hadn't.

And now, here he was, looking completely shocked by her baby bump seconds after he'd accused her of falsifying evidence for her article. Which was total and complete bull. She'd double-, triple- and quadruple-checked everything in that article, so for him to come around here beating his chest and threatening her just because he didn't like what she'd found out…well, that wasn't exactly her problem, was it?

Except the longer he stood there, the more it began to feel as if it was totally her problem. And when the elevators started dinging, marking the return of most of the staff, she knew she had to get him somewhere more private. Standing in the middle of a room of reporters was not where they needed to hash this out—especially if she wanted to keep hidden the fact that he was the father of her unborn child.

"Come on," she said, making an executive decision to get them both out of there before things got even messier than they already were.

She grabbed his arm and propelled him toward the staircase situated in the left corner of the building. She'd get him outside to the back parking lot. Since the *Times'* staff had been cut down to a fraction of its former size, no one needed to park back there anymore.

He seemed to be somewhat recovered by the time they made it down the stairs and out of the building. Or at least recovered enough to ask, "It's mine?"

"Of course it's yours. Otherwise I wouldn't have felt the need to call you and leave you that voice mail."

"I swear, I didn't get the voice mail. If I had, I would have called you. I would have—" He broke off, shook his head. "So you're eighteen weeks along, then?"

"You came up with that number pretty quick," she told him, surprised that he remembered exactly when they'd met.

"I'm not the one who walked away."

"What's that supposed to mean?"

"It means, I wanted to see you again. I texted you numerous times trying to get you to respond. You're the one who chose not to."

He was right. She knew he was right, but still, she couldn't let it go. "If you were so interested in me, why didn't you call me back when I called you? Even if you didn't get the voice mail, you had to have seen that I called."

For the first time since he'd shown up in her office like some kind of avenging angel, he wouldn't look her in the eye. Which told her everything she needed to know even before he said, "I erased your number. If you called—"

"When I called," she corrected him.

"When you called," he conceded, "you would have come up as an unknown number."

Well, if that didn't tell her exactly where she stood with the man who was the father of her child, nothing else would. She'd spent weeks, months, obsessively rereading his texts while he'd simply erased her from his life.

Then again, that was about par for the course with her, wasn't it? Growing attached when she knew she shouldn't and then being shown, again and again, that she didn't matter at all.

"Right. Of course." She tried to sound flippant, but from the look on his face she wasn't carrying it off nearly as well as she'd hoped to. "That's fine. Perfect, really, just go back to that."

"Go back to what?"

"You living your life, me living mine and never the twain shall meet."

He looked at her as if she'd lost her mind. "I hate to break it to you, Desi, but the twain has already met. And it made a baby when it did."

"You say that like I'm supposed to be surprised by

the consequences of our one night together. I'm the one who's been carrying this kid for the last eighteen weeks. And I'm the one who's going to have to deal with it after it's born. So you can take all your 'we made a baby' crap and go back where you came from."

"You don't really think it's going to be that easy, do you?"

"I don't see why it has to be complicated. You go about living your life exactly as you always have and I'll figure out what to do about the baby."

"As we've already established, you're eighteen weeks along. Which means you've already decided what to do about the baby. And if you're not having an abortion—"

"I'm not! So you're out of luck on that front."

Nic made a low, angry sound deep in his throat, shoved a frustrated hand through his hair. "Are you being deliberately obtuse? I said it was obvious that you've made up your mind to have the baby and you read that as I want you to get an abortion? What's wrong with you?"

She nearly laughed. If she had a dollar for every time someone had asked her that question in her life…well, she wouldn't be working a crappy entry-level journalism job, that's for sure. "Look, I don't even know why we're having this discussion. It's not your problem—"

"Not my problem?" he squawked.

"Exactly. Not your problem. My job isn't great but it's got good benefits and my dad's life insurance left me pretty well off when he died. So you don't have to worry that I want something from you, because I don't. I know this is my baby and—"

"Your baby?"

She glared at him, totally exasperated by his continued interruptions when she was trying so hard to get through this conversation without crying. Since she'd gotten pregnant, the hormones had her emotions all over the place.

"You know, you're really beginning to sound like a parrot."

"And you're beginning to sound like a lunatic. That baby you're carrying is as much mine as it is yours and—"

"Really? As much yours as mine? Possession is nine-tenths of the law, Nic, and right now he's inside my body, so…" She gave a little shrug to underscore her meaning—and to irritate the hell out of him. Judging from the way he was suddenly grinding his teeth together, it was working.

"It's a he? You know it's a he already?"

She almost lied, almost told him she didn't know. From the time she'd found out about the baby, but particularly after she'd called Nic and not gotten a response, she'd begun to think of this baby as exclusively hers. Someone she could take care of, someone she could love. Someone who would never go to sleep wondering where she was or when he would see her again.

And now, Nic was here. Talking about the baby as if he was already invested in him or something. She didn't trust it…and she didn't trust Nic.

But lying about it just to hurt him wasn't right, either. And so she nodded, reluctantly. "Yes, it's a boy."

His eyes glazed over at the confirmation and, for long seconds, he seemed dazed. A little out of it.

"Wow. It just got real, you know? We're having a boy."

She really didn't like the sound of that. "*I'm* having a boy."

"Are we back to that? Seriously?" He looked so disappointed that it struck a chord deep inside her. Made her squirm a little uncomfortably under his scrutiny—and under the realization that here was a man who seemed to take his responsibilities seriously. A man who wouldn't just run away from his child at the first sign of trouble.

But how did she know that, really? He'd just found out she was pregnant, so of course he was interested. Of course he wanted to be involved. But that didn't mean he'd thought it through, didn't mean he wasn't going to balk once the truth settled in.

Just the thought had her backing up and cupping a protective hand over the soft swell of her baby. "Back to it? I don't think we ever left it," she told him. "This is *my* son."

"*Our* son."

"*My* son. He—"

"God." Nic ran a frustrated hand through his hair in a motion that was becoming familiar to her, even in the short time they'd spent together. "Why are you being so obstinate about this?" he exploded. "I don't get you. I really don't. First you don't answer me when I try to get in touch with you after our night together. Then you write that assassination article and try to ruin my family's company based on a bunch of lies. And now? Now you're trying to cut me out of our kid's life before he's even born. I don't get it. What did I ever do to you to make you hate me this much?"

"I don't hate you," she told him as guilt spread through her. She tried to cut it out, to nip it in the bud, but it wasn't so easy to do when he was looking at her as if she'd just ruined Santa Claus, the Easter Bunny and the Tooth Fairy all at the same time.

"Really? Because it sure seems like you do from where I'm sitting." He shook his head, then turned his back on her and started to walk away.

Her heart dropped. He was leaving already, giving up. Which was fine, she told herself. Better now than after the baby was born. Or after she'd come to depend on him.

But it turned out, he wasn't going far. Just to the fence a few yards away. She watched as he stood there for long seconds, head bowed and hands shoved in his pockets. The guilt burning inside her got a little harder to ignore.

"Look," she said, taking a few tentative steps in his direction. "Me writing that article has nothing to do with you."

He looked at her as if she was crazy. "You wrote an exposé about my family. You all but crucified my brother with the vicious lies of a source you won't stop protecting. It doesn't get any more 'about me' than that."

"They weren't lies."

He snorted. "Yeah. Keep telling yourself that. For a journalist, you sure don't seem to give a shit about truth."

Anger flashed through her, replacing the guilt. "You don't know anything about me!"

"Because you won't talk to me. Jesus, you're halfway done with your pregnancy and you didn't even tell me about it."

"I told you—"

"In a voice mail? In one lousy voice mail? Who does that?" He turned on her then, stalking toward her like the predator she was sure he was.

"I was pregnant with a stranger's baby! What else was I supposed to do?"

"You were supposed to answer my texts!" he roared. "You were supposed to talk to me about that bastard's accusations against Bijoux. You were supposed to get in my face about this pregnancy and make me hear you."

"That's not how I do things." She didn't beg for attention, not now, not anymore. And certainly not from a man who meant nothing to her.

"How? Reasonably? Honestly? Like an adult? Yeah, believe me, I'm getting that's not your way."

"Screw you!" Her own anger roared back to life. "You exploit children and consumers. You get rich off blood diamonds. You lie every day of your life. Who the hell are you to judge me?" She'd been so disappointed when the allegations had proved to be true, had been so hurt even though she'd known it was a ridiculous response. But he'd seemed like such a good guy that night at his house. Had seemed so perfect. To find out that he actually dealt with monsters just to turn a profit, just to go from a billionaire to a bigger billionaire…it had wounded her way more than it should have.

"You don't listen to anybody, do you?" he demanded incredulously. "You believe what you want and do your own thing and to hell with the consequences. To hell with the truth. How do you plan on being a news reporter with an attitude like that?"

His words were a slap across the face, a hit at the deepest, most sensitive part of her soul. "I *am* a news reporter."

"You're a child playing at being a grown-up." He shook his head, shoved his hands deep in his pockets as he took a steadying breath. "You know what? We're not getting anywhere with this. Why don't you go upstairs, read the file I gave you and talk to your managing editor, who's got a copy of it by now. Then figure out what you want to do and call me. We'll talk then."

"Yeah, right, I'll be sure to do that. Maybe I'll even leave a voice mail."

His face darkened and for a second it looked as if he was going to tell her off, once and for all. But in the end, he swallowed whatever obnoxious thing he'd thought of saying and simply told her, "Call me when you want to talk."

"I'm never going to want to talk to you."

"Well, that's too bad, isn't it? Because that's *my* baby you're carrying and I *will* be a part of his life. In fact, the only question from where I'm standing is, will you?"

The words were his parting shot and then he turned, walking away from her. Leaving her staring after him with her mouth open and fear clawing at her throat. She'd been around the block enough times to recognize a threat when she heard one.

For a second, she couldn't quite figure out how she'd gotten to this point. That morning, she'd woken up a soon-to-be single mother and she'd been okay with that. No, she'd been more than okay. She'd been happy with it. Fast-forward six hours, and the man who had fathered her child, a man she didn't even know, had just threatened to take that baby from her. And he was rich enough to do it.

"Hey!" she called, but he didn't turn around. Didn't so much as flinch to acknowledge that he heard her. "Nic!" She started after him, but before she could take more than two steps, her phone buzzed with a text. She glanced down at it, then froze when she saw Malcolm's words. "Bijoux article canceled. Source a hoax. See me ASAP."

Nine

Nic climbed into his car and roared out of the parking lot with no intention of stopping until he was several miles away from Desi Maddox and the *Los Angeles Times*. Running might be a juvenile reaction, but if he'd stood there arguing with her for much longer he would have said something he regretted. And since she was the mother of his child—*his child*—that didn't seem like the best course of action. For any of their sakes.

For once, LA traffic cooperated with him and as he sped through the streets he tried to calm down, tried to wrap his head around the fact that not only had he found Desi after all these months, but that he was also about to become a father. A *father*. The word reverberated in his head, the weight of it pressing in on him from all sides.

In a little less than five months, he would be a father. To a bouncing baby boy. And then what? He didn't know the first thing about parenting. How could he, when his own father had set such a shiningly bad example?

Then again, maybe Nic knew more than he thought. If he just did the opposite of everything his own father had done, he could probably win a father-of-the-year award.

He kept driving, sliding his Porsche in and out of traffic as he tried not to panic. It wasn't that he didn't want to parent his son, wasn't that he was afraid of the responsibility of it. Because he wasn't—no matter what Desi had concocted in her head about him being a soulless monster with a Peter Pan complex. That wasn't the case. He was more than willing to step up to the plate here, more than willing to take care of his child.

He was just terrified of screwing it up. Of making mistakes that hurt his kid the way his father had hurt him and Marc. He didn't want to do that. Didn't want to be the guy who let his family down over and over and over again.

Lost in thought, he cruised through a yellow light as it turned red. Horns blared at him from both sides of the cross-traffic, and he waved a hand in silent apology even as he decided he should probably pull over before he caused an accident.

Griffith Park and Observatory was only a couple of blocks ahead of him, so he angled his way through traffic, moving to the right lane so he could make the turn into the parking lot. But once there, he couldn't just sit. His thoughts were too momentous, too overwhelming. He needed to be doing something or he would be crushed under the weight of them.

He climbed out of the car and headed for the park. If nothing else, he could walk. Nothing like a shot of nature in the middle of a crowded city to help a guy clear his head.

But as he walked, things only got more muddled. Oh, not the fact that he was going to be a father to this baby.

That part he was crystal clear about. His kid, his responsibility.

But the rest of it…yeah, the rest of it was a hell of a lot murkier.

What kind of father would he be?

How would he avoid hurting his own child the way his dad had hurt him?

How would he get past the wall Desi had built around herself and get her to talk to him—and listen to him?

How were the two of them going to build some kind of secure family unit for their child when she seemed to hate him? When she believed the worst of him? When she wanted nothing to do with him?

He'd lived that life, caught between two parents who hated each other and used their children as weapons. There was no way he would let that happen to his kid. No way he would let his son grow up the same way he and Marc had.

But how was Nic going to stop it? How was he going to convince Desi that she could trust him not to hurt her or the baby? And speaking of trust, how the hell was *he* ever going to trust *her* again after everything she'd done?

He was willing to accept that she'd believed the wrong source, that she'd bought whatever ridiculous bill of goods had been sold to her. But she was an investigative journalist—albeit a green one judging from the lack of bylines he'd found when researching her. It was her job to dig for facts. Her job to talk to people on both sides of the issue as she tried to figure out who was telling the truth.

She hadn't done that. Despite the fact that they'd spent what he'd thought was a fairly spectacular night together, despite the fact that she was carrying the baby who in time would be heir to Bijoux, she'd had no problem writing an article that would have brought his family's company to its knees. And she hadn't even had the decency to give him a heads-up, let alone contact him to get his side of the story.

How much did she have to hate him to do something like that? And why? What had he done to her except give her seven orgasms—not that he'd been counting—and try to see her again? He'd liked her, really liked her…at least until she'd done all this.

As he walked, he went over the night they'd spent together, searching for something he could have done to set her off. She'd freaked out a little when he'd gotten her phone number, but they'd compromised. He'd played by the rules she set. And still she'd nearly destroyed him.

It didn't make sense.

"Daddy! Daddy! Push me higher!"

The high-pitched squeal got his attention, followed by the sound of deep male laughter. He glanced over toward the playscape, saw a man about his own age pushing a small boy on the swings. The kid was adorable, dark, wild curls and big brown eyes and the biggest smile Nic had ever seen.

"Faster, Daddy, faster!"

The man laughed again, then did as his son requested.

Nic didn't mean to stare, but he couldn't look away. They both looked so happy, the kid and the dad, who looked as if there was nowhere in the world he'd rather be.

Nic wasn't sure how long he stood there, but it was long enough to have the dad giving him a weird look. Great. He'd gone from human rights violator to park pervert in under an hour. It was shaping up to be one hell of a day.

"Sorry," he said, putting a little more distance between him and the kid. "I just found out I'm…um, expecting… an, uh, boy." What was wrong with him that he was tripping over his own tongue? That never happened to him. He was the guy who always had a joke or a story, the one who could put anyone at ease. And yet, here he was, trying to form a simple sentence about the fact that he, too, was going to be a father, and he ended up sounding like a blathering idiot.

But blathering idiot must be the language of fathers everywhere, because, somehow the guy got what Nic was saying. The suspicious look disappeared from his face, giving way to a grin that was a tad sympathetic. "You just found out you and your wife are expecting a boy?" he said.

Not quite, but it was close enough that Nic was willing to go with it. "Yeah. It's…"

"Intense," the other guy filled in.

"Yes. Exactly. Totally intense. I can't quite wrap my head around it yet."

"Daddy, higher!" the kid said again.

"Any higher and your mother will have my head," the guy responded. But Nic noticed that he pushed the boy a little bit harder, let him go a little bit higher. "Yeah, it's crazy. But it's great, too, you know. Because—" he nodded toward his son "—you get this awesome kid out of the deal."

"I can see. How old is he?"

"Just turned four."

"He's great."

The guy's chest puffed out a little. "He is, isn't he? A bit of a daredevil, always wanting to go faster or climb higher. He keeps us on our toes."

"I bet."

"Slower, Daddy!"

"Slower?" The man looked down at his son in surprise.

"I want to go on the slide now."

"Oh, sure." Nic watched as the man carefully stopped

the swing and helped his son off. "You want to go on that slide over there?" he asked, pointing to the largest one on the playscape.

"No. I want to do the big one. Over there." The kid pointed to a huge, curved slide obviously meant for older kids.

"Of course you do." The dad rolled his eyes, but he held out a hand for the kid and the boy took it. "Let's go." He glanced back at Nic as they started to walk away. "Hey, good luck with the baby."

"Thanks. I appreciate that."

"You'll need it. It's the craziest thing you'll ever do. But also the best."

And then he scooped his kid up onto his shoulders and took off running across the park while the little boy shrieked in delight.

Nic stood where he was for long seconds, staring after them until they reached the other playscape. Then as the kid climbed up the slide and his dad climbed up right behind him, Nic felt himself calm down. Everything was going to be fine. He might not know anything about parenting yet, but he had five months to learn the basics. And a lifetime to learn the rest of it.

Desi had better get on board. He was willing to take a backseat, willing to do things her way. As long as her way didn't involve cutting him out completely. Because she was carrying his kid—his son—and while he was willing to compromise, the one thing he wasn't willing to do was walk away. The sooner she accepted that, the better off they would all be.

How had she screwed up this badly? Desi stared at the evidence on the desk in front of her, sorted through it for what had to be the fiftieth time as she wrapped her mind around the fact that she had made a terrible mistake.

Nic had brought all kinds of documentation with him, including page after page of chemical analysis of the diamonds sold by Bijoux. Diamonds whose environmental coating and chemical thumbprint matched exactly those being dug up in Canadian diamond mines. Not African mines. Canadian. All of which were conflict-free and responsibly sourced.

That wasn't all the evidence Nic had brought, though it was certainly damning enough considering it was signed by one of the top conflict-diamond experts in the world. But he'd also brought affidavits from the foremen at each of the mines, explaining the amount of diamonds each mine yielded and how many pounds of diamonds had gone to Bijoux in the preceding three years. Amounts that matched Bijoux's certified goods received records.

He had done all his homework, had provided the paper with everything he could possibly need to debunk her story. And maybe she still wouldn't believe it no matter what he said—documents could be forged after all—except Malcolm had spent the past few days running her source to ground. After Darlene had spoken with Nic last week about the article and he had been so adamant about filing a libel claim if they published the information, Malcolm had wanted to triple-check her source.

Which she'd done herself after he'd given his information to Desi. But she must have missed something because early this morning Malcolm had talked with him. And had somehow managed to get from the man what she couldn't. An admission that he had forged the documents he'd given her—from Bijoux and from the two diamond mines in Africa—in order to make it look as if Marc and Nic Durand were dirty.

All of it, forged. All of it, lies. Pages and pages of forgeries that she had bought hook, line and sinker. Because she'd wanted the story to be real—had needed the story to be real so she could write the article and move her career away from dresses and into real news. And to hell with whether or not she wrecked the lives of two innocent men. To hell if she brought down an entire business—and an entire newspaper—with her mistakes. She'd needed to get the scoop.

How could she have been so stupid? So gullible? So anxious to get the information that she'd overlooked her source's tells. And now that she looked back on it, there had been many. She'd just been so caught up in getting the story and not disappointing Malcolm, in getting the truth—ha, wasn't that a joke—that she'd looked past them. She'd made excuses for them in her own mind.

The source was nervous.

The source was a little confused but once he calmed down, he sorted it out.

The source was doing a brave thing coming forward and blowing the whistle, but he was just an amateur. Of course he hadn't known exactly what she'd need for the story.

God, she was such a fool. And the worst kind of fool—the arrogant kind who refused to see, let alone admit, when she was wrong. Just thinking about what she'd said to Nic when he'd tried to hand her the documents… She'd had in her hands the proof that he was none of those things but she'd been too stubborn to look at it. Too stubborn to admit that maybe, just maybe, she'd been wrong.

And now, the story she'd worked so hard on was dead. Malcolm told her it wasn't her fault, told her Candace—the more experienced reporter he'd put on the case to work with her—had missed the same things she had. Which was true. Candace had.

But Candace hadn't spent the time on this story that Desi had.

Candace didn't know it the way she did.

Candace hadn't been trained at an early age by Alan Maddox, one of the best investigative journalists who had ever lived.

If Candace had made a mistake, it was in trusting Desi, who had assured her over and over again that the information they had was legit.

Which it wasn't. Not at all. Not even a little bit.

So now, here she was, back in the society pages—for a little while anyway. Malcolm assured her that her job wasn't in jeopardy, but with a screwup of this magnitude, how could it not be? If that story had run—if Malcolm and Darlene had been just a little less conscientious—the paper would be in really hot water right now. And Bijoux would be under siege from everyone from the press to human rights organizations to consumer groups to lawyers bringing civil suits on behalf of clients who'd purchased Bijoux diamonds…the horrors would have gone on and on.

And it would have been all her fault.

Yet Nic had still wanted to talk to her, had still wanted to listen to her. And in her utter and complete arrogance, she'd driven him away. Worse, she'd backed him into a corner where he thought that the only choice he had was to fight her—for his company and for their baby.

Nice job, Desi. Somehow she'd managed to mess her life up so royally, so completely, that she could not even begin to imagine how to fix it. She didn't even know if fixing it was possible.

But she also knew she had to try. She'd made this

mess, and while Malcolm was helping her clean it up on the professional level, she owed it to Nic, and their baby, to try to fix it on the personal front, as well.

Which meant she would have to call him. And explain the situation. And grovel—a lot. God. She closed her eyes, lowered her head to the desk. She hated groveling. She really, really, really hated groveling—especially when she was the one in the wrong.

But she was smart enough—and woman enough—to admit that she had brought it on herself. She was the one who hadn't listened to Nic and she was the one who was so wrapped up in her investigation, and the kind of man she'd thought he was, that she'd left one voice mail for him and then given up. Even though she was carrying his baby. And even though she'd known—though she would deny it to her dying day—that there was a good chance that after she'd ignored him for weeks that he wouldn't listen to any message she left.

Just because she knew what she needed to do didn't mean it was easy. Desi gave herself five minutes to sulk and then did what she had to do. She put on her big-girl panties and called Nic.

Ten

He brought her to one of his favorite restaurants in LA, a little trattoria in the heart of Beverly Hills. He liked it because the food was great and the owner's brother had worked for Bijoux for years, but he could tell the moment they walked into the place that he had definitely chosen wrong.

Though Desi didn't say anything, it was obvious that she was uncomfortable. He thought about ignoring her discomfort so as not to make it any worse, but they already had a lot of strikes against them. This dinner was supposed to be about finding some common ground, and if it would make her feel better to go someplace else, then he was more than willing to do that for her.

But when he asked if she'd feel more comfortable at one of the other restaurants on the street, she just shrugged and said, "This is fine."

"Are you sure? Because if you don't like Italian—"

"Everyone likes Italian food," she told him with a slightly exasperated roll of her eyes. "That's not the problem."

"Then what is?"

"This place is expensive."

"Don't worry about that. I asked you out—"

"I don't want your money. That's not why I called you tonight. And it's definitely not why I'm keeping the baby. I just want to say that up front and you need to believe me. I don't need or want you to take me to fancy restaurants and spend a lot on me."

"Believe me," he answered with a smirk, "I am well aware that you don't want my money, Desi. Otherwise you wouldn't have written an article guaranteed to cost me billions."

She flushed, and for the first time since they sat down, she refused to look him in the eye. "I know I already said it, but I'm really sorry about that. I wasn't out to get you. I just believed the wrong person and…" Her voice trailed off as she ducked her head.

He didn't like this new, humble version of her. Yes, ten hours ago he'd pretty much been out for D. E. Maddox's blood. But that was before he realized D. E. Maddox was also Desi. The woman he'd spent the most sensual, sexy, satisfying night of his life with. The woman who met him point for point with strength and attitude. The woman who, he now knew, was carrying his child.

"Look, why don't we just start over?" he told her, reaching across the table and resting his hand on top of hers.

"Start over?" She looked incredulous. "I'm nearly five months pregnant with your son. I think it's a little late to try starting over."

He laughed. "I don't mean that I want to walk up to

you in a bar and introduce myself to you while we pretend we don't know each other. I just mean, let's have a clean slate. Leave whatever's in the past in the past and deal with where we are now without any of the junk from before messing it up."

"You want us to just forget everything?"

"Why not?"

"Do you think we can do that?"

"Do you not?"

She laughed then. "Are we seriously back to this? Answering each other's questions with more questions?"

"Hey. I asked the first question—you've just been piling question on question after that."

"I'm pretty sure that's not how it happened." She eyed him skeptically. "But I'm willing to take the blame this time, as a peace offering."

He felt himself relax, really relax, for the first time in days. Desi was here with him, they were having a conversation that didn't involve sniping at each other—and that he hoped would, soon enough, also include real communication. Plus, his company was safe. At this exact moment in time, what else could he ask for?

After giving their order to the waiter—chicken picatta for him and angel-hair pasta for her—the two of them made small talk. About LA, about the weather, about a band they had both recently seen in concert. But as the meal went on, Nic grew increasingly frustrated. Not because he minded talking to Desi about that stuff—she was smart and funny and interesting, and if things were normal he'd be happy to spend the evening laughing and flirting with her over their dimly lit table.

But things weren't normal, and while he tended to be pretty easygoing about most things that didn't involve Bijoux, he wasn't okay with being easygoing about this.

Not when she was carrying his child. And not when they had so much to figure out.

By the time their meal had been cleared and he had ordered dessert—she had passed, but he hoped to tempt her with some lemon marscapone cheesecake—he was more than ready to talk about their son and what arrangements they were going to make for him.

Desi seemed to sense his mood, because she stopped right in the middle of the story she was telling and looked at him.

He didn't like the apprehension in her eyes, or the way her body tensed as if she was waiting for a blow. He'd spent his whole life charming women. The last thing he wanted was for the mother of his child—for Desi—to be afraid of him.

Reaching across the table, he slid his hand down her hair. She startled at his touch, but he didn't move his hand away. Instead he pushed an errant lock behind her ear. Then he skimmed a finger down the soft curve of her cheek.

Her eyes drifted shut at the first touch of his skin on hers and she swayed a little. Leaned her cheek into his hand. And, just that easily, the fire that had burned so hotly on the night they met reignited.

It had been eighteen weeks since he'd held her, eighteen weeks since he'd kissed his way across her shoulders and down the delicate curve of her spine. But he still remembered what she felt like against him, around him. Still remembered the way she moaned when he slipped inside her and the way she raked her fingers down his back when she came.

"Let me take you back to your place," he said, his voice hoarse with a desire he didn't even try to hide. "Let me make you feel good."

Her eyes flew open at his words, and in their depths he saw the same arousal he was feeling, the same need. But there was a reluctance there, too, that spoke of confusion and conflict, and he knew—no matter how much he wanted her—he couldn't have her. Not now. Not when things were still so unsettled between them.

So he pulled back, let his hand fall away from her cheek.

"I'm sorry," she said. "I've made such a mess of things."

She had, but he wasn't going to blame her for it. Not when he'd made his share of mistakes, too. He was the one who had erased her number from his phone. He was the one who hadn't been diligent about listening to his messages and had ended up missing the most important voice mail of his life.

"That's why we're starting over. No more messes to clean up, from either of us." Because his head was still a little cloudy with desire—and it wasn't the only part of his anatomy to feel that way—he leaned back in his chair and took a long sip of water while he tried to get his thoughts together.

"Look, I know you want to talk about the baby, but I'm not sure what to say about that yet. I've spent the last three months thinking I'm going to be doing this alone and now you're here and you want to be involved. That's great, but I need time to adjust."

"I get that. I do. And we've got time to figure everything out But I want you to know that you aren't in this alone anymore."

"I know."

"No, I don't think you do," he told her. "I don't just want to be a part of the baby's life after he's born. I want to start now. You're pregnant and, I don't know, pregnant women need things, right? If you do, I want to be there to help you out."

For long seconds, Desi didn't say anything. Which was fine, because she didn't reject his words outright. But the longer she kept him waiting, the more anxious he got. He'd already threatened her once today about the baby. He didn't want her to think he was doing it again.

But just as he opened his mouth to explain, she said, "I'm okay with that."

"You are?"

"You don't have to sound so surprised," she said with a laugh.

"I'm not. It's just… I was a real ass about the baby earlier and I'm sorry. I don't want you to think this is a part of what happened before because it's not."

"Hey, you're the one who keeps talking about a clean slate. I think that's supposed to work both ways, isn't it?"

"Yeah. I guess it is."

She nodded, then took a deep breath. Let it out slowly. "So, you want to be a part of the pregnancy?"

"Absolutely." He thought back to when he was in the park earlier, to the father and the son who'd been at the swings when he was walking by. He wanted that, more than he'd ever imagined possible, and he was going to do whatever he had to do to get it.

"Okay. I have a doctor's appointment next week. You could come to that if you want."

"I do want to. But I want more than that, as well."

"More?" She looked confused. "That's pretty much all there is at this point. A doctor's appointment once a month and then, when I'm closer to my due date, one every two weeks. And, I should probably warn you, they aren't very exciting appointments, you know? I pee on a stick, I listen to the baby's heartbeat—which, I admit, is the best part. Sometimes the doctor takes my blood. But that's it."

"It sounds pretty good to me."

"That's because you aren't the one getting stuck with needles," she told him.

"Well, thank God," he said, adding an exaggerated eye roll for effect. "I'm a crier."

"You know, I can see that about you," she said with a laugh. "You've got that look about you."

He lifted a brow at her. "I look like a crybaby?"

"You look…sensitive."

That startled a laugh out of him. "Well, I've got to say, that's the first time anyone's ever told me *that*."

"That's because you keep your sensitive side hidden behind all that charm."

She said it as a joke, but again, there was something about the look in her eye that told him she saw more than he wanted her to. More than he wanted *anyone* to. His whole life he'd been the joker, the charmer, the easygoing one who countered Marc's intensity. He'd been the one who defused their father's temper when things started to go bad and the one who stepped between him and Marc when things *did* go bad. And he did it all with a smile.

He'd spent years honing the persona, years perfecting it until everyone who knew him believed he was *that* guy. Hell, most of the time he believed it himself. The idea that Desi saw through the mask, that she saw what no one else had ever bothered to look for, rocked him to his core.

Which was the only excuse he had for what happened next.

From that moment in the park, when he'd decided definitively what he wanted, he'd been working toward this moment. Everything he'd done since then had been geared toward making Desi trust him, geared toward making her want to go along with his suggestion. He'd even had a plan about how to broach the idea.

But as he sat here, reeling from what should have been a simple throwaway observation but somehow wasn't, he wanted nothing so much as to change the subject. To get the focus off him. So he blurted out the first thing that came to mind, not caring—until it was too late—that doing so blew his whole plan sky high.

"I want you to move in with me," he told her straight out, not even bothering to cushion the blow.

"Move in with you?" She looked at him as if he was crazy. "You can't be serious."

"I'm totally serious."

"You aren't."

He waited until the waiter stopped by to freshen their waters and drop off dessert before he said, "I am." Then he reached over and forked up a bite of cheesecake and held it out to her.

She didn't take it right away. Instead, she studied him and studied the bite of cheesecake while the second hand wound its way around his watch.

"Maybe you are," she finally said, leaning forward to take the bite off his fork. "But you shouldn't be. We don't even know each other."

She'd gotten a tiny dab of whipped cream on his very favorite part of her upper lip and he wanted nothing more than to lean forward and lick it off. The only thing holding him back was the fact that he knew it wouldn't score him any points right now—and it sure as hell wouldn't help him convince her that he wasn't angling for a roommate-with-benefits relationship...

"But it makes perfect sense. What if something happens and you need me—"

"I didn't realize you were a doctor."

"That's not what I meant."

"No, but if I need you, I can call you." She held up her phone. "That's what these really nifty smartphones are for. That is, of course, provided you actually pick up this time."

She said it as if it was a joke, but there was an underlying bite to it that he'd have to be an idiot to miss. "Exactly my point. If we were living together, you wouldn't have to call me. I'd just be there."

She sighed heavily, then said, "Nic, look, I know this whole baby thing has thrown you for a loop today. Believe me, I get that. I've known for months and it still freaks me out. But that doesn't mean we have to do anything crazy. I understand that this is your gut reaction. But why don't you take a few days and really think about it. Make sure being involved is what you really want—"

"It is what I want. I'm not the kind of guy who runs from his responsibilities, Desi."

"But see, that shouldn't be why you decide to stick around. Only because the baby is your responsibility. You should be a part of his life because you want to be, not because you feel like you have to be."

"Now you're twisting my words. Of course I want to be a part of his life—"

"Just listen to me for a minute, okay?" It was her turn to reach across the table and put her hand on his. "You need to seriously think about this before you do anything rash. Because if you want out, it would be better if you walked away now rather than in four months or four years, when you decide you're bored."

"Why are you so sure I'm going to walk away?" he asked.

"Why are you so sure you're not?"

"And we're back to trading questions." He couldn't quite keep the frustration out of his voice.

"We are," she agreed with a small smile. "But they're important questions. And you didn't answer mine."

"Neither did you." He caught her gaze, held it, then refused to look away.

Desi blinked first, glancing up at the twinkling lights that lined the nearby windows. "I just think you need to think about things."

"I have thought about them."

"For a few *hours*!"

"Sometimes a few hours are all you need."

She rolled her eyes. "You're being completely irrational."

Her voice rose on the last couple of words, and that's when it hit him just how upset she was by this whole discussion. Oh, she was fronting, pretending she was amused and exasperated, but there was something else underneath it all. Something dark, and maybe a little afraid.

It was the fear that gave him pause, that had him sitting back in his chair, studying her as he tried to figure out what made her tick. He didn't have much luck, which was frustrating, but on this one small point, he would concede she was right. They didn't know each other, and until they did, he couldn't get a bead on her.

Which was only one more reason for them to move in together, he decided. Nothing broke down barriers like the forced intimacy of cohabitation. Instinct told him not to mention that to Desi, however, because it might send her running for the hills.

"What's it going to take," he asked, when the silence between them moved from uncomfortable to unbearable, "for you to agree to move in with me?"

"Nothing," she answered immediately. "Because it's not going to happen. Beyond all the reasons why two people who don't know each other shouldn't be moving in together, there are also the logistics. You live and work in San Diego. I live and work in LA. There's no way I'm driving three hours, in traffic, to work and home every day. It isn't going to happen."

"If that's your biggest objection, forget about it. We can totally fix it."

"How can we fix it? Even all your money isn't enough to make LA traffic move during rush hour."

"Maybe not, but there are other ways to get to work besides a car."

"Like what?"

"Like a helicopter." He drained his water glass in one long sip. "See, problem solved."

"Yes, but I don't have a helicopter."

"Maybe not, but I've got three."

"Look," she said, throwing her napkin down on the table and standing up. "We're done talking about this. I'm going to the bathroom and when I come back we need a new topic of conversation. Because if we don't, I'm out of here. And I can promise that neither the baby nor I will be pleased about looking for a bus stop in Beverly Hills."

Eleven

By the time she got back from the bathroom—where she'd had more than a few WTF moments—Nic had paid the bill and was waiting to escort her out to the car. He hadn't, however, come up with a new topic of conversation. Instead, he had a new twist on the old one.

"So," he said as he slid behind the wheel of a car that cost significantly more than she made in a year and started the engine, "I think I've found a solution."

"I didn't know we had a problem," she answered drily.

He ignored her. "You don't want to move in with me, so why don't I move in with you?"

She burst out laughing. She knew it was rude, especially when he looked so pleased with his suggestion, but she couldn't help it. The idea of a multibillionaire slumming it in her tiny fourth-story walk-up in Los Feliz was hilarious, especially considering the fact that his *pantry* was bigger than her whole apartment.

The look he gave her as he backed out of the parking space was decidedly disgruntled. "I don't see what's so funny."

"Really? You don't?"

"No."

She thought about enlightening him, but the truth was, he might actually have hit on the perfect solution for getting him off her back about this. He wouldn't last a day in her apartment, so why not let him move in? The first morning he couldn't get hot water or the air-conditioning went on the fritz, he'd be out of there. Billionaire playboys born with silver spoons in their mouths rarely knew how to rough it. Not that she'd met that many billionaire playboys—or even more than one, really—but she was certain her opinion would hold up.

"Okay, fine," she said as he pulled into traffic. "You can move in with me."

"Seriously?" He glanced over at her before fastening his eyes back on the road. "You mean it?"

"I do. If you're willing to move into my place—which, I'm warning you, is small—then who am I to tell you no? But we need to lay down some ground rules if we're going to do this."

His smile quickly turned perplexed. "Ground rules?"

"Yeah, like who gets the bathroom when and who does what chores and no sex. You know, the usual."

Now he was frowning and it was all she could do not to crack up again. It was wrong of her to be enjoying this so much, but she couldn't help it. After all the tension of the day, messing with him was a welcome relief.

"Do you have a problem with any of those rules?" she asked when she'd finally managed to choke down her mirth. The last thing she wanted him to know was how utterly and completely she expected this to fail.

"Well, you can have the bathroom whenever you want and I'll hire someone to do the cleaning and I'll do the rest of the chores. But the no-sex rule—I'm not really okay with that one, no."

"Oh." She kept her voice as innocent as possible. "That's kind of a deal breaker for me, to be honest."

"But we've already had sex. And—" he made a point of glancing at her stomach "—you're pregnant. So, I'm not really sure what the point would be of abstaining."

"The point is what I said back at the restaurant. I don't know you. And my one and only one-night stand excluded, I'm not in the habit of sleeping with men I don't know. So, yeah, it's a deal breaker."

"I'm your only one-night stand?"

She did laugh then, at the sheer ridiculousness of his response. "Seriously, that's what you got out of what I said? That you're my one and only?"

"No, I heard all of it. But that was definitely the most interesting part."

"Of course it was," she said with a snort. "You are such a guy."

He shot her an amused look. "I never claimed to be anything else, sweetheart."

"Don't call me that." The words were instantaneous and forceful, welling up from a place she hadn't thought of in years.

"What?" He looked mystified. "Sweetheart?"

"Yes, that. Don't *ever* call me that."

"Sure." He held up a placating hand. "I'm sorry. I didn't mean to upset you."

"You didn't upset me," she contradicted him.

He didn't respond, but the silence spoke louder than any words ever could. He knew she was lying, knew she'd had a strong and immediate reaction to that word. And still he wasn't calling her on it. She didn't know if that endeared him to her or just pissed her off.

It took a few minutes for the awkwardness to wear off, but Nic finally asked for directions to her apartment.

She kept her voice light and relaxed when she gave them, and eventually the last of the tension eased away. At least until he'd parked his car and started following her up the stairs to her apartment.

"Is there an elevator?" he asked after they'd started on the third flight.

"Nope," she answered cheerfully.

"That's going to be a problem for you the last couple months of your pregnancy, don't you think?" She could practically hear the wheels turning in his head as he tried to figure out how to use this to get her out of the apartment and into his house.

Not that she would let that happen.

"I already asked my doctor about it. She said it should be fine—exercise is good for me and the baby. She did warn that if I ended up having a C-section, I wouldn't be allowed to go up and down them the first few weeks, but at this point there's nothing to indicate I'll have anything but a normal delivery." She smiled at him blithely.

"So, there are early indicators that someone might need a C-section?"

"Yes, but I don't have any of them." She reached for his hand, squeezed it, as they finally made it to her door. "Relax, Nic. Everything's fine with my pregnancy so far. It's totally boring, which is a good thing, my doctor assures me."

He still didn't look convinced, but he let it go as she unlocked her apartment door. "Are you coming in?" she asked after she'd stepped into her three-foot-by-three-foot entryway.

"Do you want me to?" He watched her face closely as he waited for her answer. "You look pretty tired."

She felt pretty tired. The day had brought so many emotional highs and lows she felt as if she'd run a marathon—or maybe two. The exhaustion of her first trimester had disappeared a few weeks ago, but that didn't mean she wasn't tired at the end of every day. As Stephanie had told Desi the other day when she'd been caught napping in the break room, making another person was pretty hard work.

But she and Nic still had things to talk about—such as her ground rules and whether or not he really wanted to do this now that he'd seen just how small her apartment was. "It's fine," she told him, stepping back so he could enter.

He must have read the tiredness on her face, though, because he shook his head. "I think I'll get going. Let you get some rest." He pulled his phone out of his pocket, then looked a little shamefaced as he asked, "Can I get your number again? I promise not to erase it this time."

"I guess we'll just have to wait and see about that," she said.

She'd meant it as a joke, but his eyes shot to hers. He was deadly serious—deadly earnest—when he told her, "I'm not going anywhere, Desi."

Yeah, that's what they all said. And somehow it had never quite worked out that way for her. Oh, they all had a really good reason for why they had to leave—or why she had to—but the results were always the same. Her, alone, trying to pick up the pieces of a heart broken by too many people too many ways and too many times.

But she was done with that, she told herself as she rattled off her phone number. Done with opening herself up to someone only to watch the person walk away. So she'd give Nic a chance, she'd let him into this baby's life, but that was it. There was no way she would let herself depend on him. No way she would let him hurt her when he finally decided to walk away.

It had taken him eight weeks to erase her from his phone when she didn't answer his texts. Once the baby was born and everything got harder, how long would it take him to leave them both?

Not very long was her bet. Not very long, at all.

"Get some sleep," he told her after saving her number. "I'll call you tomorrow and we'll talk about the logistics of me moving in. I want to do it as soon as possible."

"How soon is that?" she asked warily.

"This coming weekend, if that's okay with you. I'd do it sooner, but I know you have work and the last thing I want to do is rock the boat for you at the paper."

She snorted. "Yeah, well, I think that boat has already been rocked pretty hard today." The memory made her wince even as it brought the guilt back. She'd almost ruined Nic and his brother, almost brought down their entire company, and yet here he was, telling her that he didn't want to disrupt her job. If things had been reversed, she'd probably be calling for his head on a silver platter, baby or no baby.

"I'm sorry," she told him. "An apology is not close to being enough when my carelessness nearly cost you and your family everything, but I don't know what else to say."

"Clean slate, remember?" He leaned over then and pressed a lingering kiss to her forehead. "We're starting over."

Were they? His gentle, platonic kiss somehow managed to send heat sizzling along her nerve endings. Because from where she stood, it felt as if they were picking up right where they'd left off eighteen weeks before.

It was an alarming idea, considering the close quarters they would be living in. And the no-sex rule she was serious about enforcing. Chemistry between them had never been a problem, and she knew if she let him back in her bed, getting rid of him would take a hell of a lot longer than it would otherwise. After all, how would they find out how incompatible they were in real life if they never actually got out of bed?

She knew this, understood it, even believed it wholeheartedly. And still her body swayed toward him, still she tilted her face up for a kiss that shouldn't happen. Still she longed to feel his hard, calloused hands brushing over her skin.

Nic's eyes darkened as she stared up into them. They turned the same green as the storm-tossed Atlantic, and she felt more of her resistance give way. If he kissed her right now...if he *touched* her, she wasn't sure she'd have the strength to say no.

But in the end, he did neither. Instead, he took a couple of steps back, until he was no longer in touching distance. He gave her a sweet smile—sweeter than anything she thought a guy like him was capable of—and said, "Go get some sleep. I'll call you in the morning and we'll get the details of my move worked out. We'll both feel better then."

She was glad he sounded certain, because suddenly she was anything but. Still, she nodded, gave him the best smile she could muster. "Yeah. We'll talk tomorrow."

They stood there for several long seconds more, neither of them taking the first move to break the new and tenuous connection between them. All she had to do was step back and close the door. All he had to do was turn and walk away. And still they silently watched each other. Silently imagined what might be coming next... for both of them.

Despite her best intentions, she felt herself softening toward him. Felt herself wondering if maybe he would stick around for a while—for the baby, of course, not for her.

But after everything she'd been through, after all the people she'd had to tell goodbye over the years, even thinking he might stay for the baby felt like a weakness. More, it felt like a betrayal.

And so she found the will to step back.

Found the will to whisper a soft good-night.

And somehow she even found the will to close the door in Nic's very handsome, very sexy, very sweet face.

By Sunday, Desi still wasn't over her moment of weakness. In fact, she'd spent the better part of the week berating herself for it even as she felt herself falling a little more under Nic's spell with each day that passed.

He'd called her twice a day, every day, just to check on her. He had a small basket of fresh fruit delivered to her doorstep each morning and a healthy, delicious dinner delivered each night. He even drove up from San Diego one day to meet her for lunch so he could check on her and the baby. And through it all, he had never voiced a word of dissension at the increasingly ridiculous rules she'd insisted on making up for their living arrangement.

The guy definitely had his eye on the endgame, and that wasn't going to do. Not when he was being so nice about it. And not when she felt as if she was one small step away from getting sucked into a vortex of need and want and emotional attachment.

Wasn't going to happen.

Which was why, on this fine Sunday morning in July, she stood in the middle of her very small kitchen watching her neighbor Serena direct her burly boyfriend and brother, telling them where in Desi's apartment they should put the French provincial sofa they were currently carrying. Not that it really mattered. The thing would dominate the room wherever they put it.

How could it not? It was huge and ugly and the most atrocious shade of hot pink she had ever seen. It was also curved and hard as a rock and would be absolutely miserable for Nic to sleep on. One night on the thing and his back would never be the same.

At another time, she might feel badly about conspiring to torture Nic while he was being so determinedly supportive, but desperate times called for desperate measures. He was moving in later that afternoon, and with the way her stupid pregnancy hormones were all out of whack, she didn't trust herself not to jump him. Or much worse, fall for him.

Which was why she'd begged Serena to let her borrow her friend's most prized piece of furniture. It would cost Desi a couple of hundred bucks and an entire day spent at the spa, but at this point, that seemed a small price to pay. Nic had to go and he had to go fast.

She would make those words her mantra and use them every time she felt her resolve weakening. Which lately seemed to be every time she saw Nic or heard his voice on the phone or even thought about him—which she was doing more and more lately.

Stupid pregnancy hormones.

By the time Nic showed up at her door with two suitcases and a laptop case filled with electronics, she was a wreck. Especially since she hadn't had anything to do but sit around and wait for him to appear.

Normally she spent Sunday mornings cleaning her apartment, but a cleaning service had shown up before she'd left for work on Thursday. When she'd tried to turn them away, thinking they'd gotten the apartment number wrong, they'd assured her that Nic had sent them. And that they'd be back every week to make sure her apartment was "spick-and-span." Their words, not hers.

When she'd tried to talk to Nic about it, to tell him she didn't need or want him to pay for a cleaning service, he'd told her it wasn't for her, it was for him. He was a total pig, he claimed, and he needed someone to clean up after him.

The fact that she could hear the laughter in his voice as he said it—and called him on it—didn't make him change his story. That was when she'd figured out what she'd only suspected when she'd gone home with him all those weeks ago—that she really had met her match.

"I cleared out half the closet for you," she told him as he made his way into the apartment. "I figured you could use that chest for stuff you didn't want to hang up." She pointed at the arts and crafts–style highboy she had found at a garage sale right out of college. She'd brought it home, stripped it and painted it a bright sunshiny yellow that she loved—and that, it turned out, clashed horribly with the hot pink French provincial sofa that now dominated her living area.

Normally she used the chest to hold her books, but for now they were in boxes under her bed. If she played her cards right, the books would be back where they belonged by Wednesday. Maybe sooner, if that couch was as uncomfortable to stretch out on as she imagined it would be.

"Thanks," he said with a smile that was way too sexy for her peace of mind. "I really appreciate that."

Guilt slithered through her, made her palms sweat and

her stomach swirl. But she shoved it back down, hard. Nic had to go and he had to go now. She repeated her mantra like the lifeline it was.

"Do you need help unpacking?" she asked, reaching for one of his suitcases.

"I've got it." He held the bag away from her. "Why don't you sit down and rest while I empty these suitcases, and then I'll take you to lunch."

"I'm pregnant, Nic, not an invalid."

"True, but I am neither pregnant nor an invalid, so I beat you." He pointed to the monstrosity of a sofa without so much as batting an eye. "Now, sit."

She did her best not to cringe. Why, oh why, had she not considered the fact that he would expect her to sit on that couch? Which wasn't as bad as lying on it, obviously, but was still not good.

"I actually prefer the bar stools," she said, gesturing to the three chairs that lined the overhanging counter on the outside edge of her kitchen.

As she turned away, she thought she heard him murmur, "I bet," under his breath, but when she whirled back to look at him, his smile was perfectly innocent.

Yeah, as if she was buying that.

After grabbing her laptop off her desk, she settled at the bar to put the finishing touches on an article about the charity ball benefiting the LA Zoo that she'd attended the night before. It was due by five, but getting it in early could only help her career. Though Malcolm didn't treat her any differently, she couldn't help feeling as if she was persona non grata in the newsroom.

Or maybe that was her own sense of guilt and responsibility. Stephanie—who'd been at the *Times* for nearly ten years—had assured her that all reporters screwed up sometimes. Maybe that was true. But how many of them screwed up on their first major assignment? When she'd asked Stephanie that, her friend had suddenly needed to make a phone call. Which told Desi everything she already knew.

She'd written the zoo story earlier because she'd thought it'd be hard to work with Nic in her apartment. After all, the place was only about seven hundred square feet, and he was big enough that it felt as if he took up most of it.

Yet, as he unpacked, he was as unobtrusive as a gorgeous, six-foot-four man could be. He didn't interrupt her, didn't ask her where he should put his belongings. He just did his thing and let her do hers. If she'd had a little more self-control and actually been able to stop herself from stealing glances at him every five seconds, she probably would have finished proofing her article a heck of a lot faster.

As it was, they finished their tasks at the same time, after which Nic insisted on taking her out to lunch to celebrate their new living arrangement. He plied her with *queso* and guacamole and deep-fried ice cream—which was nowhere near as disgusting as it sounded—then took her for a walk around Griffith Park. It was crowded because it was a weekend, but it was fun all the same.

She'd spent so much of her life alone—by circumstance when she was young and by choice after she reached adulthood—that it hadn't occurred to her how nice it could be to do things with someone else. How something as simple as a walk in the park became so much more fun when there was someone to share it with.

And when they finally made it back to her apartment and she saw what she'd missed earlier—three books on pregnancy and parenting that Nic had, if judging by the bookmark placement, been spending some serious time reading—it hit her that she might be in serious trouble.

Because for the first time since she'd decided to let Nic move in, she wasn't thinking about how to get rid of him. Instead, she was thinking of ways to make him stay.

Twelve

Nic had just finished shaving early Monday morning when Desi called to him from the kitchen. "Nic! Come here! Hurry up!"

The urgency in her tone struck fear into his heart, and he rushed out of the bathroom and through the bedroom without even stopping to grab a shirt. "Are you okay?" he called as he ran through her matchbox-sized apartment. "What's wrong?"

He got to the kitchen before she could answer, and he glanced around wildly, looking for some kind of threat. But there was nothing, only Desi leaning against the kitchen counter, her hand on her stomach and a huge smile on her face.

"Is something wrong with the baby?" he asked as he crossed the kitchen and stopped directly in front of her.

"He's kicking!"

It was so not what he'd expected her to say that it took

her words a few seconds to register. When they did, his gaze flew to her stomach. He'd felt that one small kick at her desk, but he'd been too surprised to appreciate it—or the fact that it happened on a regular basis. "He's kicking?"

"Yes." Rolling her eyes at his slowness, she pushed her clothes out of the way with one hand and grabbed his hand with the other. Then she brought his palm to her bare stomach and held it there.

For long moments, he didn't feel anything and he looked at Desi questioningly. But she just nodded her encouragement, her hand tightening on his. So he waited, heart pounding and breath held, to feel…something.

And then, there it was. A gentle bump against his palm.

"He kicked me!" he crowed with delight.

"Actually, I think he kicked me," she told him drily. "You're just collateral damage."

"Don't listen to your mother," he told the baby as he dropped to the ground at Desi's feet and leaned his mouth close to her gently rounded tummy. "She's just grumpy cuz she's not allowed coffee in the mornings anymore."

"Hey! Don't be calling me grumpy to the baby." Desi poked at his shoulder. "Or I won't tell you the next time he kicks."

"See, I told you she was grumpy. Mean, too." He smoothed his palm over her stomach, checking out the changes to her body since the last time he'd been this close to her. There weren't many yet, despite the fact that she was nearly halfway through her pregnancy. Just the added roundness to her tummy and the swelling of her breasts, both of which he found sexy as hell.

"You'd be mean, too, if you had to give up caffeine cold turkey."

"No doubt," he soothed, just as the baby kicked a second time.

"See! He got my hand again! I told you he was kicking me."

She snorted. "No offense, but *your* hand pretty much covers *my* entire stomach at this point."

He wasn't sure what it was that did it, but suddenly he was much less aware of the baby and much more aware of the fact that he was on his knees in front of Desi, his hand resting on the bare, silky skin of her stomach and his mouth inches away from her sex.

Once the realization set in, he couldn't stop himself from leaning forward slightly and breathing her in.

Desi stiffened against him and he froze, ready to apologize. But she didn't push him away. Instead, her hands came to rest on his shoulders, then slid slowly up his neck so that her fingers could tangle in his hair.

Desire shot through him at the first touch of her hands, and he leaned forward even more, until he closed the last scant inch between her stomach and his lips.

She groaned at his mouth on her skin, but again she didn't push him away. Instead she pulled him closer, her body arching against his as her fingers tightened in his hair. He'd read in one of the pregnancy manuals he'd picked up that women's hormones went crazy during pregnancy, which often caused a spike in their libido. If that was what was happening now, he didn't want to take advantage of it, even though his whole body ached with the need to touch her, to kiss her, to slide inside her welcoming heat and feel her clench around him.

But at the same time, he didn't want to leave her like this, either. He could feel her arousal in the way she was moving restlessly against him, could hear it in the soft sounds of distress she was making in the back of her throat. Could smell it in the sexy warmth of her skin.

"Let me make you feel good," he whispered against her skin as he skimmed his lips across her belly. "Just that. Nothing else."

"Yes," she said, her head falling back against the cabinet with a light thump. "Please, Nic. I need—"

He clamped a gentle hand over her mouth, not because he didn't want to hear the words of need pouring out, but because they were building his own arousal, making him hotter and harder than he'd been since the last time he'd had Desi's body pressed against his own. And no matter how much he wanted to make love to her right now, her words from the other night—her rules—were fresh in his head.

He didn't mind bending the rules to make her feel good, but until she told him otherwise, sex was off the table. Which would have sucked completely if he didn't at least get the benefit of watching Desi climax. She was so beautiful, so hot, so gorgeous when she came, and he'd missed seeing it more than he should have if all she'd been to him was a one-night stand.

But there was time enough to deal with that later, to try to figure out where they were going from here and how everything would end up. Right now…right now all he wanted was to get his mouth on Desi and to hear her call his name as she came.

With that thought in mind, he pressed soft kisses in a straight line up from her abdomen. When her tank top got in his way, he pulled it off with a growl and flung it over his shoulder. And there she was, soft, sun-kissed skin and full, heavy breasts. Dark pink nipples peeking between strands of long blond hair.

"Beautiful," he murmured as he looked up at her. "You're so damn beautiful, Desi."

She was looking back down at him, worrying her lower lip between her teeth. She blushed at his words, turned away, but he caught her chin in his hand and gently brought her gaze back down to his.

"Don't hide from me," he told her, underscoring his words with a soft bite to the underside of her breast.

She moaned, her eyes going blurry, and he almost lost it. Almost turned her around, bent her over the counter and took her as he'd dreamed of too many times in the past five months.

But that wasn't what she needed right now—wasn't what either of them needed—and so he tamped down the wildness inside himself and concentrated on her instead. Just her.

The changes in her body were more evident now that she was naked, her stomach round, her breasts full and swollen, her nipples bright pink and hard as rubies. She was still tan, golden, but for the first time he could see blue veins running beneath the delicate skin of her breasts.

They made her seem so fragile, so delicate, and he forced himself to be gentle as he cupped her breasts in his hands. She gasped, and he asked, "Are they sore?" before leaning in to trace the upper curves with his tongue. "The books say—"

"They're okay. A little sensitive, but if you're gentle—"

Her breath broke as he licked his way closer and closer to her nipple. Tiny, tender strokes of his tongue meant to both soothe and inflame. He took his time, was as slow and gentle as he knew how to be as he relearned her body after all the long months without her. He kissed and licked and lapped at her, learning every inch—every centimeter—of her breasts all over again.

It took only a couple of minutes before Desi was thrashing against him, her beautiful body trembling with need as she clutched at his back, his shoulders, his hair. He loved the way her hands felt on him, loved even more the way she responded to him. The way she held nothing back. The way she gave him everything.

He wanted to do that for her. Wanted to give *her* everything. Wanted to make her feel so good that even when this was over, even when she was away from him, she wouldn't remember all her reasons for why they shouldn't be together.

He wanted her to want him—to need him—the same way he needed her.

"Nic, please." She trembled against him, then bucked and arched as she tried to coax him into giving her what she wanted.

He laughed and pulled his mouth completely away, but stayed close enough that she could still feel his breath on her nipple. She moaned in response, grabbing his head in her hands and tangling her fingers in his hair as she tried to pull him back to her breast.

"Don't tease me," she pleaded.

"Baby, I haven't begun to tease you." He curled his tongue around her areola and sucked it into his mouth hard enough to have her gasping.

"Too much?" he asked, immediately softening the pressure. The last thing he wanted to do was hurt her.

"No! Please. I'm so close. I'm—" She broke off as he stripped her pajama pants down her legs and tossed them aside. "Take me," she said. "Please, Nic, I want to feel you."

"I'm right here," he told her, kissing his way down to

her firm, round stomach. The noises she was making, the things she was saying—they were revving him up, making it harder for him to be careful. Harder for him to take his time.

Even as he tried to calm down, his hands were rough when he parted her trembling thighs. She cried out and he soothed her with a kiss to the soft skin right above her navel. Then he pulled back and just looked at her for long seconds. "You're so beautiful, Desi. So damn beautiful." He stroked a finger right down the center of her.

As he did, he noticed a small tattoo on her inner thigh that hadn't been there five months before. He spread her legs wider so that he could get a better look.

"I like this," he murmured, leaning forward so his mouth brushed against the tattoo. "It's new."

"I got it on a trip I took to San Francisco, before I knew I was pregnant."

"It suits you." He nuzzled at the small tattoo, licked over it again and again. He moved on, skimming his lips over her hip bone and her abdomen as he stopped to explore each curve and freckle.

"I can't—Nic, I'm going to fall," Desi cried out, her hands clutching his shoulders.

"I won't let you." His mouth closed over her navel, and he fought to keep his tongue gentle as he probed her belly button and the soft skin of her belly. "I've got you, Desi. I promise. I've got you."

And then he was moving on, moving down, his lips skimming over the curve of her stomach, down the side of her hip. He made little forays under her hip bone, delicate touches and sharp little nips, all designed to make the fire burn hotter inside her.

And then he was there, right there, his mouth poised over her sex. She smelled delicious, like warm honey, and for long seconds he just knelt there, his cheek pressed against her as he tried to absorb her scent. He took a deep breath, then another and another, even as his thumbs stroked closer and closer to her slick, sexy folds.

With each slide of his thumb, Desi trembled more. With each press of his fingers into her hip, she took a shuddering breath. And when he moved forward, blowing one long, warm stream of air against her, she started to cry, her body spasming with even the lightest touch.

He was nearly as desperate as she was, his erection so hard he feared he might actually come in his pants like a teenager with his first girl. But this wasn't about him getting off, he reminded himself viciously. This was about giving Desi as much pleasure as her body could handle.

He wanted to savor her, wanted to push her higher than she'd ever gone before and then send her flying over the edge.

He knew he didn't have much longer, though, not with the way she was coming apart in his hands, her body so sensitive and responsive it humbled him even as it made him sweat.

"You're unbelievable," he muttered as he delivered one long, lingering lick along her sex. "So sexy, so gorgeously responsive, I could just—" He stopped talking as Desi screamed, her hands grabbing his hair. He kissed her a second time, then again and again, lingering each time on her most sensitive spot.

And then his name fell from her lips like a prayer as she hurtled over the edge of ecstasy. He held her while she came, stoking the flames higher and higher until she screamed silently, her hands holding him as if he was a lifeline. And when her body came back to earth, he held her still and murmured sweet nonsense words as he pressed gentle kisses to every part of her he could reach.

When she was lucid again—when she'd stopped trembling and her eyes grew a little more focused, a little less dazed—she sank to the ground beside him and started to unbuckle his belt. Though it cost him, he stopped her with a gentle hand over hers.

"Don't you want…?" She looked confused, and maybe even a little hurt, which was the last thing he was going for.

"Believe me, I want," he told her, pulling her into his lap and cuddling her against him. "But not now, when we still have so many things unsettled between us."

"I don't understand. I thought you wanted me. I thought—" She broke off, looking away.

"Don't do that, baby. Talk to me." Gently, he turned her face back to his. "What did you think?"

"I don't know, I just… I made the no-sex rule, but I thought that was more for you than for me. And now I'm the one taking advantage of you, and—"

He laughed. He couldn't help it. "Oh, honey, you can take advantage of me anytime you want."

She pouted up at him. "I'm trying to be serious here."

"I'm being serious. Believe me. Anytime you want." He lowered his mouth to hers, slow and lingering. But as he started slipping under her spell, he heard the beat of a helicopter's propeller closing in on the building.

He pulled away reluctantly and dropped one final kiss on her forehead before gently setting her on the floor next to him. "I have to go, baby. That's my ride."

"Your ride?" She looked confused.

"The helicopter that's about to land on the roof? It's for me."

Her mouth fell open and she stared at him out of huge, shocked eyes. "I didn't think you were serious about that."

"Are you kidding me? If you think I'm going to spend five hours in traffic every day when I could be spending them with you and the baby, you are sorely mistaken."

After giving her one more kiss—he couldn't resist—he climbed to his feet. Which was no easy task considering the pain he was in after spending the night on that ridiculous sofa of Desi's.

If he didn't know any better, he would think Desi had bought the thing for the sole purpose of making him as uncomfortable as possible. Except it wasn't as if furniture stores just had these things lying around. No way could she have gotten it there on such short notice. Which meant, unbelievably, that she actually liked the thing.

"I'll be home around seven," he told her after hustling into the bathroom and grabbing his shirt off the back of the door. He buttoned it up as he slipped his feet into his dress shoes, then grabbed his briefcase and headed for the door.

He changed course at the last second, detouring to the kitchen to drop another quick kiss on Desi's lips. "If I'm going to be late, I'll text you."

"I actually have a gala to cover tonight, so I won't be here when you get back."

"A gala? Where?"

"SeaWorld. It's for Save Our Oceans—a lot of Hollywood types are supposed to be there as well as the business elite."

"Save Our Oceans—that's a good cause." He raised a brow. "Want a date?"

"A date? You mean, you really want to come?"

"Well, the last gala we attended ended pretty well, I think. So, yes. I do want to go."

She laughed. "I'm not going to have sex with you on the balcony at SeaWorld."

"A guy can dream." He pulled open the front door. "I'll send the helicopter for you and we can meet up at the gala. Sound good?"

"Yeah, I guess."

He didn't like the uncertainty in her voice. "What's wrong?"

"Nothing, it's just… I've never been in a helicopter before."

"Oh, right. Would you rather drive? I can send a car for you—"

"I'm a big girl, Nic. I am more than capable of driving myself to San Diego. That's how I met you, after all."

"I've never once doubted your capabilities. I just thought I'd have a car bring you down, we could spend the night at my place and in the morning I'll fly with you back to LA. The first time you ride in a helicopter shouldn't be by yourself. There's no fun in that."

"But what about you? You're working in San Diego tomorrow, aren't you?"

"Yeah, but the helicopter has to fly back to San Diego anyway. I'll catch a ride."

She rolled her eyes. "You'll catch a ride?"

"Okay, fine, I'll make them give me a ride." He glanced down as his phone beeped with a text. The pilot telling him they were waiting for him—as if he hadn't heard the noise of the approach. "I've got to go," he told her, "before all your neighbors revolt. Does the plan sound good to you?"

"Yes, the plan works, Mr. CEO."

"I think you've got me confused with my brother. I'm CCO. It's a very different thing."

He ducked out before she decided to throw something

at him, and as he closed the door behind him, he couldn't
help thinking that Desi was right. It did sound good. And
so did everything else about their arrangement at the moment. Well, everything except that damn couch.

Thirteen

He'd sent a limo for her. An actual limousine, long and black with tinted windows and a driver in a full suit. And not one of those rental limousines, either—no, this limo belonged to Bijoux, and was at the disposal of the Durand brothers only. She knew that because she'd asked the driver, who had been more than happy to wax poetic about his employers.

Of course he had. Everyone *loved* Marc and Nic Durand. Everyone except her, she assured herself as she uneasily settled into the plush leather seats. She was woman enough to admit how wrong about them she'd been when she'd taken the word of a source who was more disgruntled employee than whistle-blower. She was even woman enough to admit that she liked Nic—he was pretty impossible *not* to like, after all, considering how kind and charming and supportive he was being.

But that didn't mean that she loved him. And it certainly didn't mean that she was on her way to falling *in love* with him. She barely knew the man after all.

And if that wasn't strictly true—if she knew his favorite color and how he liked to walk barefoot on the beach at midnight and that he gave huge amounts of his money away to those less fortunate and that he believed in standing up even when no one else would and that he liked his coffee with the teeniest drop of cream in it—well, that *really* wasn't *that* much to know about a person, was it? It certainly wasn't enough to make her fall in love with him when she had sworn she would never do that. With anyone. Ever.

Nic Durand could be as charming as he wanted to be, could do a million wonderful things for her and their child, and it still wouldn't matter, Desi assured herself. There was no way she would let any of that sway her from her course, no way she would let herself soften, let herself forget. No way she would let herself depend on him. Because that didn't work for her—it never had. Never would. The moment she started to believe someone cared about her, that the person wouldn't leave her— boom. That's exactly what happened.

So, no. There would be no falling for Nic, she told herself again as the limo made its way through the streets of LA before turning onto the freeway. Yes, he was living with her. Yes, they were incredibly sexually compatible, and yes, she was having his baby—but that was all there was. It was enough. More than enough. Trying for anything else would only end with one—or both— of them getting hurt.

The thought depressed her so much that she closed her eyes and willed herself not to think about it anymore. Nic had been living with her for only twenty-four hours, had been back in her life for only one week, yet the idea of him walking out of her life one day soon bothered her more than she would ever be comfortable with.

It had been a crazy day, and it wasn't long before the motion of the car had her drifting off to sleep. She'd planned on only dozing—wanting to be alert enough to answer if Nic texted her—but the next thing she knew, they were pulling into the massive SeaWorld parking lot. She reached for her phone and the directions she'd downloaded earlier on how to get to the pavilion, but the driver seemed to know exactly where he was going as he wound his way to the private entrance.

When they arrived, she thanked the driver profusely and tried to tip him, but of course he wouldn't take her money. Desi shook her head ruefully as she climbed out of the car. Having Nic around to take care of her was going to ruin her if she wasn't careful.

A glance at her phone showed she hadn't missed any texts from Nic, but then again, she'd made it to San Diego earlier than expected. She set her phone to recorder mode—which was one of the ways she kept track of who was talking to whom and what they were wearing while they were doing it—then followed the pathway up to the pavilion's main door.

Once she was checked in, she walked through the venue, scoping it out. She'd never been to a charity ball here before, and as she walked in the door, she was charmed to see the huge aquariums that surrounded the room on all sides. The decor was very much "under the sea," which was to be expected, considering the charity benefiting from the night's gala. The aquariums blended in beautifully.

She took quiet note of who was already there—not a lot of people yet whom her readers would be interested in—then made her way to the aquariums. She wanted to see the fish. She could imagine the beginning of her piece starting with the fish and expanding to the oceans and then the purpose of the gala. The society reporter before her used to focus exclusively on the glitterati, but Desi had gotten in the habit of giving her readers a little more of the atmosphere and charity angle before launching into the who's who.

So far her readers seemed to like it. Or, at least, they hadn't complained about it, so she'd take a win where she could get it.

Especially after her debacle with the Bijoux article. Her cheeks heated as she once again thought of how badly she'd messed up that whole thing. She'd spent much of last week going over her notes, trying to see where she'd gone wrong in vetting the source, but everything had checked out. Everything had seemed fine…right up until it had all fallen apart.

She still didn't understand how she had made such a terrible mistake.

Malcolm told her it was because her nose wasn't developed yet—he was always going on about how all the great investigative reporters had a nose for a story…and a nose for the truth. When she was little, before her mother had died and her father had bugged out for parts unknown, her dad used to say the same thing. But he'd told her she had that nose. That she was going to be a great reporter.

And though he'd disappointed her in a lot of different ways through the years, she'd never doubted him when it came to that. Probably because she hadn't wanted to doubt him. Hadn't wanted to acknowledge that the one tenuous thing that held them together was nothing but a lie.

As she stood staring at a particularly beautifully arranged aquarium—filled with orange clownfish and yellow-and-blue angelfish swimming amid bright pink, yellow-and-blue sea anemones—she was hit with the most awful thought yet. What if she didn't really want to be a reporter? What if she'd done all this—busted her butt at the top journalism school in the nation, worked her heart out to land the worst job at one of the most prestigious papers in the country—not because she actually wanted to be a journalist, but because she'd been so desperate to get her father's attention, to make him love her, that she'd made herself into a person she thought he would want?

It hadn't worked. Not that it was exactly a surprise—from the moment her mother had died, Desi had ceased to exist for her father. Then again, everything had ceased to exist except his job. He'd shuffled her from relative to relative, exhausting their hospitality while he chased stories overseas.

And where had that gotten them? He was dead and she was in the middle of this ballroom, taking notes about rich people and wondering if maybe her whole life up until this point had been a lie. Not exactly a stellar year for either of them, if she did say so herself.

Her soul-searching was cut off when a familiar male voice asked, "Sparkling water?"

She turned to see Nic, a glass of champagne in one hand and a glass of sparkling water in the other. He was dressed in a different tuxedo from the one he'd been wearing the night she met him, but he still looked absolutely gorgeous. Absolutely devastating. Or maybe it was just that she was devastated. She couldn't tell. All she knew was she wanted nothing more than to throw herself into his arms, burrow into his chest and pretend that everything was going to be okay.

"You look thirsty," he told her, holding out one of the glasses with a quirk of his eyebrow.

And because she knew he would take her mind off everything that was whirling in her brain—and because she knew a perfect setup when she saw one—she took the glass from him. Then she looked over the rim and delivered her line. "Funny, I was just about to say the same thing about you."

"Were you?" he asked with the crooked grin she had come to love. "Well, you wouldn't be wrong."

She went off script then, tapping his glass. "You should probably drink up, then."

"Oh, I intend to. In fact—" He paused suddenly, his eyes darkening to the mossy green shade she loved the most. "What's wrong?"

"Nothing at all," she lied. "Why?"

"Something is," he told her as he searched her face. He was frowning now, all levity replaced by concern.

How could he tell? she wondered a little wildly, even as she calmly met his gaze. She'd learned a long time ago to keep her emotions tucked deep inside, so deep that sometimes even she forgot they were there. So how did he know?

"I can see it," he said, and for one crazy moment she thought he had read her mind. But then she realized he was reacting to her denial…and the upset she obviously wasn't as good at hiding as she'd thought she was.

"Here." He cupped her cheek in his hand, rubbed his thumb gently over the skin just beyond the curve of her mouth. "Your dimple's gone. That only happens when you're upset."

No one had ever seen that before—not even her. She'd gone through most of her adult life thinking she was one of the very few people who didn't have a tell, thinking she had hidden herself deeply enough that there was nothing for anyone to see.

And then Nic had come along and blown that idea right out of the water when they'd barely known each other a week. How did he do it? How did he see her when she couldn't even see herself?

"Desi?" he urged, stepping closer. "What's wrong?"

"Nothing—"

"Don't do that. Don't pretend with me."

"I'm not. I swear." And to her astonishment, she wasn't. Because right then, in that moment, standing in his arms, she *was* okay. More okay than she'd been in a very long time. "It's just been a crazy day. But I'm good now."

She could tell from the look in his eyes that he understood what she hadn't been able to say—that being with him had made her okay—but he didn't push it. He didn't say anything at all. Instead, he dropped his glass of champagne on the tray of a passing waiter and pulled her into his arms.

"Is this the part where you ask me to dance?" she teased, more than ready to clear her head of painful thoughts.

"Actually, this is the part where I whisk you outside and ravish you." But contrary to his words, he swept her onto the almost empty dance floor, spinning her around to the beat of some old-time song she recognized but couldn't name.

"I thought I told you earlier that we weren't making love on the balcony this time."

He laughed, bending his head to drop a soft, sweet, *sexy* kiss on her shoulder. "Yes, but I checked. No balcony."

She laughed then, too—she couldn't help it. No matter how awful her mood was, Nic always found a way to make things better.

"So I'll take that as a yes?" he asked blithely.

"Take it as a maybe," she answered.

He quirked a brow. "*Maybe's* not *no*."

"No, it isn't." She held on while he twirled them around. "But it's not yes, ei—" She broke off midsentence, gasping and clinging to him as he suddenly lifted her up and spun her around.

"Let go," he said as he gently moved her away from his body. And though it went against every instinct she had, Desi did what he said for once. And then laughed her head off as he spun her all the way out before reeling her back in with a quick snap of his wrist.

She felt it happen right then—in the middle of the dance floor at a fancy gala that he belonged at and she certainly didn't. Desi felt herself slide headfirst into love with Nic Durand.

She spent the evening breaking all the rules. Instead of blending into the background and observing the wealthy and sometimes famous, she allowed herself to be introduced to them. To be drawn into conversations with them. Then again, it wasn't as if she had a choice.

Being Nic Durand's date meant being surrounded by people all the time. She wasn't the only one who loved him, after all. He might be new to Southern California's high society, but Nic had the kind of personality people gravitated to—and the billions of dollars at his disposal only added to his appeal. But even without the money, he was one of those guys everyone wanted to be friends with. Larger than life, funny as hell, handsome as all get out—and nice to boot. What was there not to love? God knew, she'd tried and look where it had gotten her.

Still, she couldn't quite believe that she was in the thick of things—wasn't sure that she wanted to be, if she was honest. When she'd agreed to taking him as her date, she'd kind of planned to still do the wallflower thing. Sure, she'd known he'd attract attention, but she thought that would only make it easier for her to blend in to the crowds.

But Nic wasn't okay with her blending in to the background. Actually, he wasn't okay with her being more than two feet from him all night. Not in a creepy, possessive kind of way that would have made her champ at the bit—and probably deck him before the night was over—but in the concerned, solicitous way that said he was looking out for her. And that he was proud to have her by his side.

And so she found herself making miles of mental notes about who was doing what with whom—and what they were wearing while they were doing it. Twice, she slipped away to ostensibly use the bathroom only to spend the time hiding in a corner and talking into her recorder as fast as she could.

Not that she was talking to these people under false pretenses—everyone Nic introduced her to was told she worked for the *Los Angeles Times* and was covering the party for their society pages. But the thing was, no one seemed to care. At least that she could tell, no one acted any differently toward her at all.

At least until she met Marc Durand.

From the moment she locked eyes with Nic's brother, she knew she was in trouble. And she couldn't even say that she didn't deserve it, because she totally did. He was the CEO of Bijoux, the man she had almost accused in print of lying, cheating, stealing and helping to fund the most egregious human rights violations. Was it any wonder he was looking at her as if he wanted to take her apart tiny piece by tiny piece? And then feed those tiny pieces to one of the sharks swimming in the tanks just beyond the pavilion?

Marc saw her and she saw Marc before Nic had a clue that anything was amiss. She tried to slip away before the eldest Durand could make a scene, but the moment she moved an inch farther away than Nic deemed acceptable, he turned to her with a frown. "Everything okay?" he asked.

She, who always had a snappy comeback, had no idea what she was supposed to say to that. And so she just shook her head, letting her eyes find Marc and his date, as they were trying to extricate themselves from the clutches of San Diego's mayor.

Nic followed her gaze, and sudden understanding flashed across his face. Then he pulled her in close, bending his head to whisper in her ear, "Everything's fine. Don't worry."

Don't worry? Easy for him to say.

He flashed Marc a grin, but Nic's older brother continued to glare at her. Which was fine, she told herself as she braced for the impending storm. She owed the man a serious apology—now was as good a time as any to get it over with. She just wished it didn't have to be in front of all these people. The humiliation of making the mistake was bad enough, but having all these people witness the fallout—people she had to work around regularly—was more than a little daunting.

Nic must not have figured that out, though, because after excusing them from a group of movie execs, he put a hand on her lower back and propelled her straight toward the center of the ballroom. Straight toward Marc.

"Hey, bro," Nic said when they reached the other

couple. He clapped Marc on the back before turning to Marc's date, a gorgeous redhead with kind eyes and stunning bone structure. "Isa, you look gorgeous tonight as always." Nic leaned down to kiss her cheek.

"I do what I can," she responded, hugging him warmly. "Keeping up with the Durand brothers isn't always easy."

"I think you've got that backward," Nic told her with a laugh. "You've certainly kept Marc on his toes through the years."

"Yeah, well, someone had to." She cast a teasing glance at the man in question, then slipped her hand into his and squeezed.

"Isn't that the truth?" He kept his hand on Desi's back as he turned to her. "Desi, this is my future sister-in-law, Isa. Isa, this is Desi." He said her name with a kind of reverence it didn't deserve, his voice soft and warm and open as he pulled her even closer into his side. It was the first clue she had—or, at least, the first one she paid attention to—that said his feelings might be as strong as hers. Panic raced through her at the thought, mingled with the discomfort she already felt upon meeting Marc. For a moment all she wanted was to find a place to hide.

But that wasn't fair—to Nic or to Marc and Isa. Desi had screwed up royally and it was time to finish paying the piper. Which was why, when Nic turned to introduce her to his brother, she made sure to meet Marc's eyes, though it was the last thing she wanted to do. He was as handsome as his brother, but in a much colder, more standoffish way. How did Isa avoid getting frostbite? Desi wondered as she held her hand out to him.

"It's nice to finally put a face with the name," Marc said, his blue eyes coolly assessing her as he shook her hand. "Nic's been talking about his Desi for months."

The words should have warmed her—God knew, she'd

spent much of the past five months thinking about Nic, too—but there was something in the way Marc said them that made the words sound like a condemnation instead of a simple observation.

Then again, in his mind, she'd seduced his brother, gotten pregnant, then disappeared only to write an exposé full of lies about his company. The surprise wasn't that he was insulting to her. The surprise was that he was speaking to her at all.

With that thought in mind, she took a deep breath and willed herself not to screw up what she was going to say next. Which was probably easier said than done, considering how nervous she was. And how badly she'd already messed up.

"Actually, I'm really glad we're getting this chance to meet," she told him.

"Are you, now?" He lifted a brow—it was obviously a family talent, one designed to make these two men even more devastatingly attractive. And infinitely more intimidating. "And why's that?"

His tone was polite, insouciant even, but—unlike his brother—he had a tell. It was a small one, but the way his lips tightened just a little when he looked at her told her how angry he was. Which was…fair enough.

"I want to apologize for all the trouble my article caused you," she told him. Beside her, she felt Nic stiffen, then move as if he wanted to say something. Without breaking eye contact with Marc, she put a restraining hand on Nic's hip, telling him without words that she was a big girl and needed to take care of this herself.

He didn't relax at all, but at least he didn't butt in, so she counted it as a win.

"I know that's not enough," she continued, keeping her voice steady despite Marc's laser-like gaze. "Just like

I know how much damage it would have done if that article had actually gone to print. I made a lot of mistakes when I was writing that article—including avoiding speaking with Nic early on because of what had happened between us—and I'm really sorry for what I put you both through."

"It's fine, Desi." Nic wrapped a protective arm around her shoulder. "Marc understands." This last was accompanied by a hard look at his brother, one that basically told Marc he'd better accept her apology or there would be hell to pay later.

She hated so much that she was a point of contention between the two brothers. They were close—she'd read that while she'd been researching her article and now, seeing them together, she knew it was true. And the fact that they were bristling at each other right now, because of her, made her a little sick.

"On the plus side," Isa said, trying to break the very obvious tension, "if you hadn't written that article, Marc and I probably wouldn't be together now. And neither would you and Nic. So, that's two good things that came out of it, right?"

"Absolutely," Nic said, and from the look on his face he actually meant it. Which seemed crazy to her after everything she'd put him through. But when he'd said clean slate, he'd really meant it. Which—again—made him a much better person than she'd ever imagined.

"That is a good point," Marc said, and he sounded friendlier than he had just a few moments before. But the tell was still there, the tightening of his lips, even when he was smiling, and she knew things weren't nearly as over as Nic wanted them to be.

Fourteen

It took only two hours for the situation to come to a head. In that time, she'd danced with Nic, recorded copious notes and even managed to make the rounds of the aquariums to see the ones she'd missed. She'd also let Nic talk her into bidding on a homemade wooden cradle for the baby, donated to the silent auction by a San Diego artisan.

It would fit really well in Nic's house, a traitorous little voice in the back of her head said. Not that she was seriously thinking of moving in with him or anything. Because she wasn't. Not yet and probably not ever. But the cradle was pretty and she would love to put her baby in it, so who cared where it went as long as it kept their son safe and happy.

"Would you like more water?" Nic asked as they finished a dance and he escorted her off the dance floor.

"Actually, I was hoping to cut in," Marc said smoothly

as he appeared from nowhere. "May I have this dance?" he asked her.

She knew she should say no, knew she should make some kind of excuse and get out of it. But there was a predatory light in his eyes that told her escape wouldn't be possible—not unless she wanted to cause more trouble between Nic and Marc, which was the absolute last thing she wanted.

Besides, she would have to deal with him some time—he was her baby's uncle, after all. She might as well hear him out, let him say everything he wanted to say to her right now, and then maybe they'd be able to move past it. If she was lucky.

"I was just going to get her some water, actually—" Nic started.

"I'd love to dance," she told Marc. Then she stood on her tiptoes to give Nic a quick kiss on the cheek. "The baby and I are perfectly hydrated. So stop worrying and dance with Isa."

Then she turned to Marc and let him sweep her onto the dance floor.

He was a surprisingly good dancer. He didn't have Nic's finesse, but then again, who did? And it wasn't as if he was trying to finesse her anyway. In fact, when she glanced up at him, it looked more as though he was trying to figure her out.

It was on their second turn around the floor that she said, "Let's just get it out of the way, okay?"

He glanced down at her, brows lifted in surprise. "I'm beginning to see what Nic likes about you."

"No, you aren't. You don't want your brother anywhere near me."

"Touché." He inclined his head. "Unfortunately, Nic doesn't share my sentiments. And since you're currently carrying the first heir to Bijoux, that isn't an option any-way."

"If that's the case, then what do you want?"

"And here I was just about to ask you that question." His eyes were hard.

"I don't want anything—"

"Everybody wants something, Desi. It's the nature of the beast. And I'd rather know your endgame now than find out about it the hard way, after you destroy my brother."

"That's not going to happen."

"You're damn right it isn't going to happen, because I'm not going to let it happen. So tell me what you're after and I'll make sure you get it, in exchange for—"

"In exchange for what?" Nic asked from where he was suddenly standing between them. "What do you think you're doing, Marc?" He kept his voice down and his body language relaxed so as not to draw attention to them, but his gaze was fierce and furious. So fierce and furious that she didn't know how his brother even man-aged to look him in the eye.

Marc did, though, and he was easily as livid as Nic. "I'm the one who should be asking you that question, shouldn't I? This woman nearly destroyed us and now you're playing house with her? I get that she's having your baby, but you're a lot stupider than I gave you credit for if you can't figure out that even that was a setup. I don't know what her endgame is yet, but you can't be so blinded by the sex that you don't know that there is one."

Nic's hands clenched into fists as he gave up any pre-tense of being relaxed. "You're going to want to shut up and back off, man."

"Nic, it's fine." She tried to get his attention. "Marc's just trying to protect you."

"Yeah, well, he's doing a lousy job of it," Nic told her as he moved to put his body between her and Marc.

"Or what? You'll punch me in the middle of a charity gala?" Marc challenged him. "Go ahead. That'd be great PR for Bijoux, huh? Or has a week with her made you forget everything we've worked so hard for?"

"I think you're the one who's forgotten—"

"Stop it, Nic!" she said, grabbing his arm. She would not be the cause of them having a fight in the middle of SeaWorld, for God's sake.

"Okay, that's enough, you two." Isa stepped in then, too, grabbing Marc's arm and pulling him back a few steps. "Tomorrow in the office is soon enough to talk about this. For now—" she shot Marc a look that told him she had had more than enough "—you can take me home."

"We're not done here," Nic told her.

"Yes, you are. We all are." The look Isa gave him was as pissed off as it was understanding. "Your brother needs a time-out."

"I'm not five," Marc told her.

"Then stop acting like you are," she answered sweetly as she pulled and prodded him until he gave in.

"We're going to talk tomorrow," he told Nic before turning away.

"Damn straight we are. And it'll be your turn to apologize to Desi."

"That's not necessary, Nic," she said as Marc and Isa walked away.

"It absolutely is. You're my—" Nic broke off, shoving a frustrated hand through his hair. "He doesn't get to talk to you like that."

There was a part of her that was desperate to know what he'd almost said, but another part knew it was better if she didn't know. Better if she didn't make what was between them—a baby—into more than it was, no matter how she felt about him.

"He's just trying to protect you, you know."

"Are we seriously having this conversation right now?" he asked as he escorted her off the dance floor. "He insulted you. Why are you defending him?"

"Because he's your brother. And he loves you. Of course he's suspicious of me—why wouldn't he be after the trouble I caused?"

Nic looked at her broodingly. "I'm not suspicious of you."

"Because you're an idiot."

"Hey!"

"Or maybe just the best person on the planet," she continued as if he hadn't interrupted her. "I haven't decided yet."

"Well, after we get back to the house, maybe I can find a way to help you make up your mind." His voice dropped several notches.

She gave him her best sultry look. "Maybe you can." But as she let him lead her out to the parking lot—and the limo that was magically sitting at the curb waiting for them—she couldn't forget Marc's words.

Any more than she could forget the look on his face when Nic had taken her side against his.

She couldn't do that. She couldn't be the one who divided the two of them. Couldn't be the one who broke up the most important relationship in Nic's life. She'd been alone. She knew how that felt, knew what it did to you deep inside. She wouldn't wish that on anyone, let alone Nic. Wonderful, fun, exciting, beautiful, kind Nic.

But she couldn't say that to him. How could she when

he was holding her and touching her and looking at her as if she'd hung the moon?

There was a part of her that wanted to wallow in it, that wanted to wrap his affection around herself and snuggle in for as long as it lasted.

What kind of person would that make her, though? It would end—of course it would end, because it always ended—and then where would he be? All alone. She couldn't do that to him. She wouldn't do that to him.

But that didn't mean she had to walk away yet. She could have this night, could have these last stolen moments with him before she had to give him up. It wasn't enough—wasn't close to being enough—but it was what she had. And she would make the best of it.

They didn't talk much during the ride. Instead, they sat close together in the back of the limo, hands touching, legs brushing. By the time the driver pulled the limo to a stop at the top of Nic's long driveway, Desi was practically vibrating with desire. With need. With a desperation that came as much from Nic himself as from knowing this would be their last time together.

The moment the front door closed behind them, Nic was on her. He whirled her around, pressed her back against the wall and then slammed his mouth down on hers. And then they were kissing, kissing, kissing, their mouths and tongues and bodies tangling together. She didn't know where she left off and he began.

It was a powerful thought, a humbling one, and it nearly broke her. How could it not when she imagined how it could have been between them. How it should have been.

His hands slid up her legs, fumbled with her underwear. But she knew if she let him touch her it would be all over. She would be lost in the maelstrom of pleasure he brought her every time he touched her.

And she wanted that—her body was screaming for it—but she wanted to pleasure him more. She wanted to take him as high as he took her and then watch him shatter with the ecstasy coursing through him.

Which was why she pushed him away.

"Desi?" He sounded confused and more than a little pleasure drugged. "What's wrong? Are you okay?"

She didn't answer him. Instead she put her hands on his shoulders and pushed, turning him—turning them—until he was the one with his back against the wall.

Once she had him where she wanted him, though, she took her time. If this was all she would have with him, she wanted to go slow, wanted it to last. Wanted it to be perfect.

She pulled his shirt from his pants, slowly worked the diamond studs through his buttonholes. Ran her hands over his smooth, hard chest and reveled in his groans, in the soft, sexy pleas falling from his lips as she undressed him completely.

And then she was on her knees in front of him, kissing and licking and stroking as he called out her name. The sound burrowed inside her, filled her up, filled her to bursting and her heart was so wide-open that she felt it break in two even as he fell apart around her.

Fifteen

Nic woke alone.

Again.

At first he couldn't believe that she was really gone—how could he after the night they'd had? She'd made love to him as if he was her everything, as if he was the only thing, and he'd tried to make love to her the same way. Tried to tell her with his actions what she wouldn't yet believe if he told her in words—that he was in love with her. That he wanted to spend the rest of his life making her, and the baby, as happy as she made him.

Telling himself that she was up before the alarm only so she could pack, he pulled on a pair of sweats and headed toward the kitchen to see if maybe she was making a cup of tea for herself. Or breakfast. Or—

Except the kitchen was empty. As was the rest of the house—he knew because, like an idiot, he checked every single room. She was in none of them. And he didn't know why.

She hadn't seemed angry at Marc last night. He'd been furious at his brother—was still furious—but she'd seemed strangely understanding. Had even urged Nic to get over his anger and talk to Marc about what he'd said, even though it was the last thing Nic wanted to do.

So why was she gone? Had he upset her somehow? Had he been too rough with his lovemaking? Had he hurt her? Just the thought made him sick to his stomach, and he headed back to his room to grab his phone and call her.

But when he picked it up, he saw that she had beaten him to the punch. There was a series of text messages from her that told him everything he needed to know.

I'm sorry, Nic. This isn't working. I thought I could do this, but I can't. I still plan to have the baby, and of course, you can have as large or small a part in his life as you would like. But the whole being-in-a-relationship, living-together thing…it just isn't for me. I'll have your stuff delivered to your office this week. My only request is that you don't contact me until I contact you. And I will, I promise. Just not for a little while. Thank you for everything.

Don't contact me.
Thank you for everything.
Don't contact me.
Thank you for everything.

He read the message over a dozen times. Two dozen times. Until he had it memorized so well that he didn't even need to look at it anymore and still it played in his head.

This isn't working.
Don't contact me.
Thank you for everything.

Shocked and devastated—more devastated than he had

any right to be considering how little time he'd known her—he sank down onto the edge of the bed with his head in his hands. And tried to figure out what the hell had happened. What he'd done wrong. How he'd spooked her.

He was a savvy businessman and an even savvier student of human nature—he had to be to do the job he did. And yet, this time, he had nothing. Yes, Marc had attacked her at the gala, but she was the one who had stopped Nic from defending her. She was the one who had defended Marc, for God's sake. And even after that, she hadn't seemed to hold it against Nic. Instead, she'd come home with him. She'd made love to him, had let him make love to her. And it had been everything their first night together had been, only more. Because this time they'd known it meant something.

Or at least, he'd *thought* it had meant something. Now, sitting here in an empty bed that still smelled of her, he wasn't sure it had meant anything at all.

Suddenly, he wasn't sure of anything when it came to Desi and him and the relationship he'd been trying so hard to build with her. For the baby's sake…and for his.

Because he loved this woman, loved her more than he'd ever loved anyone. And though a lot of people would say it was ridiculous to fall in love with someone so quickly, he knew that wasn't the case. Because he hadn't fallen in love with Desi over the past few days as they'd tried to figure out what to do with the baby.

He'd fallen in love with her that night, nineteen weeks ago, when he'd brought her home and made love to her as if his life depended on it. Because, it turned out, it did. It really did. The life he wanted, the life he was so desperate for—with her and him and their baby—did depend on it.

And he would have sworn she felt it, too. If not that first night, then certainly last night, when they'd made love again and again and again. When he'd whispered in her ear and kissed her rounded stomach and nearly cried with how right it had all felt. When he'd held her in his arms and talked about anything and everything, including their baby and the future that they shared.

Damn it, he couldn't have been that wrong. He couldn't have imagined the look on her face or the love in her voice or the aching tenderness of her touch. He couldn't have imagined all of that.

Which meant she hadn't answered all of his questions after all. Because the one thing she was missing, the one answer she hadn't given him, was why.

And as he sat there, smartphone clutched in his hand and his heart on the floor, he knew it was the only answer that mattered.

He got to her apartment—to their apartment—before she did.

As he bounded down the stairs from the roof, he prayed he wasn't too late. That she would talk to him, listen to him and give him a chance to somehow fix whatever had gone so terribly wrong.

He hit the apartment at a dead run, spent a good five minutes knocking on the door—and listening for sounds within—as he pleaded with her to let him in before it occurred to him that a helicopter was a lot faster than a car and that Desi hadn't even made it home yet.

Once that realization dawned, he'd stood there for long seconds trying to decide between respecting her wishes and waiting outside or going in and having the element of surprise on his side. It wasn't much of a debate—he needed every bit of help he could get.

He let himself into the apartment they'd managed to share successfully for only a short while. Because he couldn't just sit—especially not on Desi's hideously ugly and uncomfortable couch—he paced the apartment while he waited, going over the arguments he'd formulated in his head on the helicopter ride up. As he stood in her apartment, watching the sun rise over the City of Angels, he couldn't help thinking that none of the arguments were good enough.

He was desperately afraid that nothing was, that there would be no way to convince her that he wanted her, that he needed her. That he loved her.

He was still angsting over it, still trying to decide the best way to make his case, when the front door opened. And then she was there, in the foyer, staring at him with wide and exhausted eyes.

He stared back. He could do nothing else.

They stood like that for long seconds, staring at each other, a million unspoken words and thoughts and feelings arcing between them like a live wire.

And then she moved, breaking the connection between them as she dropped her overnight bag on the floor at her feet. "What are you doing here?" she asked.

"I came for you." It wasn't what he'd practiced, wasn't what he'd planned to say at all. But it was real and it was honest, which was all he had to give since she'd refused everything else.

She breathed out then, a long, slow thing that seemed to take more than air. It took her bones, her muscles, her very will, too, because the next thing he knew, she was slumped on the floor, sobbing into her knees.

He was across the apartment in a moment, dropping beside her and murmuring, "No, Desi, no. Baby, please don't cry. I'm sorry. Whatever it is I did, I'm so, so sorry."

That only made her cry harder. He didn't know if it was emotional or hormonal or a little bit of both, but it broke his heart to see her in so much pain. Nearly killed him to think that he had somehow been the cause of it. When he could take it no more, he ignored her hands pushing him away and pulled her into his lap.

"Don't—"

"Shh," he told her, one hand cupping her head while the other stroked her back. "Just relax and let me take care of you."

"I don't need you to take care of me," she said even as her hands came up to curl in his shirt.

"Believe me, I am well aware of that fact." He continued to rock her anyway. "But I need to hold you right now. Please, let me hold you."

She kept crying, but she didn't protest again. She just curled into a ball on his lap and sobbed into his chest. And sobbed. And sobbed. And sobbed.

When he could take it no more, when his heart was in danger of breaking wide open under the force of her sorrow, he bent his head. Brushed soft kisses over her temples and down her cheek. And pleaded, "Desi, please, tell me what's wrong. Let me help. Please, sweetheart—"

He broke off as she stiffened in his arms, flashed back to the last time he'd called her sweetheart and what her reaction had been. "I'm sorry—"

"Stop saying that," she told him as her tears died down. "None of this is your fault. It's mine."

"It's ours," he told her. "I'm doing something that's pushing you away, and whatever it is, I'm sorry for it. But please, Desi, you have to talk to me. You can't just walk away like we're nothing. You're carrying my baby—"

"I already said you could see the baby whenever you want."

"And I appreciate that. I do. But it's not just the baby I want."

"You don't mean that."

"I do mean it."

"You can't." She struggled against his hold, climbing off his lap the second he let her go.

He was up in a second, following her across the apartment—at least until she held up a hand and said, "Stop. Just…stop for a second, please."

"Yeah, okay." He froze in place. "Sure."

She laughed then, and somehow it was the saddest sound he'd ever heard. "Why do you have to be so perfect?" she asked.

"I'm not—"

"You are. I knew it that first night. Everything about you was so, so right for me, and it scared the hell out of me. It sent me running away from you as far and as fast as I could go. And it would have been okay. If you had just stayed gone, everything would have been all right. Instead you're here and you're breaking my heart—"

"I don't want to break your heart," he told her, crossing to her because he couldn't not touch her when he told her this. "And I don't want you to break mine. I love you. I'm in love with you, Desi, and I want to be with you. I want to marry you. Why is that so hard for you to understand?"

"Because no one ever has."

"Wanted to marry you?" He hoped not. He hated the very idea of her being close enough to another man to even entertain the idea.

"Loved me."

"That can't be true."

She bowed her head, wrapped her arms around her stomach in a move that was so obviously self-protective that it broke his heart. "It is true. No one has ever loved me. I mean, except my mother and she died when I was nine, so…it's been a while.

"My dad freaked out when she died. He couldn't handle it and he certainly couldn't handle me. He was a reporter, too. One of the best investigative journalists in the world. And the day after my mother's funeral, he parked me with my grieving grandparents and took off to find a war to cover.

"He came back a few months later, just in time to have a fight with my grandmother and take me off her hands. Not because he wanted anything to do with me, mind you, but to punish her for saying he was being a terrible dad. Two weeks later, he dumped me on his college roommate and his wife, and took off again. Six months later he showed back up because they were having their own kid and didn't want me around anymore. So he brought me to visit his sister and snuck out on her in the middle of the night.

"The night he left, I knew he was going to go. He called me sweetheart when I went up to bed. And I knew. He only ever called me sweetheart right before he left me. My aunt kept me for three months before she shipped me off to my mother's brother. And that's pretty much how it went until I graduated high school and left for college.

"And you know the worst part? At the gala last night, I realized I've done all this for him. I worked like a dog to get a degree in journalism from Columbia. I've spent two years writing ridiculous articles that I don't care about for the *Los Angeles Times*. I took the assignment on Bijoux, even knowing that I shouldn't have, and we all know how that turned out. I did it all, hoping that one day he'd be proud of me. That one day he would come back and see what I'd done and he'd tell me I'd done a good job." Her voice broke. "How pathetic is that? How ridiculous and pathetic am I?"

"You're not pathetic at all."

She snorted. "Yeah, right."

She wouldn't look at him. He wanted, so badly, to see her face, but she wouldn't lift her head. Wouldn't let him see.

Jesus. He didn't have a clue what he was supposed to say, how he could talk about this without sounding like a total douche. Sure, he'd had absentee parents—a father who cared more about screwing around with women half his age than he ever did about his family and a mother who cared more about status than she did about her husband screwing around on her—but through it all, Nic had always had a home. He always knew where he was going to be sleeping and what his routine would be like and whom he would see at school. And he'd always, always, had Marc. His brother might be a busybody with trust issues a mile wide, but he was a great big brother. He'd never once been anywhere but in Nic's corner.

Who had been in Desi's corner? he wondered as she put on the kettle for tea. Who'd had her back when she'd needed it most? The idea that there had been no one, that the woman he loved had essentially been on her own at the age of nine, wounded him on a visceral level.

"That's why you kept the baby. So you'd have someone to love you."

"Maybe." She shrugged as she put a tea bag in a cup. "I thought about having an abortion but I just…couldn't. And I could never give him up for adoption. I'd go crazy wondering if he was okay, if he was with someone who loved him or if he was just— " Her voice broke, but she swallowed. Tried again. "Or if he was just being tolerated. I can't stand the idea of him being anywhere he isn't loved."

Nic did cross to her then, did pull her into his arms and let his hands rest on her tummy. On their baby.

"That will never happen to him," he assured her. "We'll never *let* that happen to him. He will know every day of his life that he is loved. And so will you, if you'll trust me. If you'll let me love you. I'm not saying I won't make mistakes, as I'm pretty new to this serious-relationship thing, too. But I promise you, Desi, that if you let me, I will love you forever. I will be there when you wake up and I will be there when you fall asleep and I will be there all the times you need me in between."

"You don't know that."

"I do know it, Desi."

Another sob racked her body and she covered her mouth to silence the sound. "Don't say that," she said when she could speak again. "Don't say it if you don't mean it."

"I never say things I don't mean." He got in her face then, circled her upper arms with his hands and waited until she looked up at him. Until she looked him in the eye. "I love you," he told her. "I will love you tomorrow. I will love you next year. I will love you in twenty years if you'll let me. I will—"

She stopped him with a kiss, one that stole his breath and most of the brain cells in his head. Which was why, when she finally pulled back, all he could do was stare at her dumbly.

"You should be careful what you promise," she told him when they both finally caught their breath.

"I'm always careful with my promises," he answered. "Because I never break them."

"I know." She pressed a soft kiss to his lips. "I almost never make promises, either, because I don't believe in breaking them. But I'll make a promise to you, if you'll let me."

Let her? He nodded eagerly. Too eagerly if her muffled laugh was anything to go by. But he couldn't help it. He'd die to hear her tell him that she loved him. That she wanted him to be a part of her and the baby's lives.

"Then it's my turn to make a promise. And I promise you, Nic Durand, that I will love you for as long as I live. I will live with you in that great big house of yours by the ocean. I will laugh with you. I will raise children with you. And I will love you until I die."

Tears bloomed in his eyes, too, but when he reached for her, she held up a hand to stop him. "I'm not done yet."

She'd already told him everything he wanted to hear, so much more than he had imagined her conceding when he'd climbed in that helicopter to chase after her. But he just nodded, and waited for whatever else she had to say.

"Not only all of that, but I also promise to never, ever, *ever* write another article about you or your brother or your company as long as we both shall live."

He laughed then, because how could he not? He was getting everything he'd ever wanted, and all he had to do was fall in love with the most wonderful woman in the world. He kind of felt as if he'd cheated the system, and won. It was a beautiful feeling, one he would cherish for the rest of his life.

And as he swept her into his arms and carried her the twenty-two steps necessary to take her through the living room and into the bedroom, he did ask her for one more thing. A new couch.

He counted it as a sign that she loved him that she laughed only a little…and gave in with only a very little struggle.

* * * * *

"You leave me no choice, Princess."

Then he tipped her chin up and leaned forward. Anticipation pulsed through her veins. Every single second was an unnerving kind of torture. And finally, his mouth was on hers, his hand coming to wrap more firmly around her jaw, as if he couldn't get enough, as if he would devour her.

Long live the king!

She touched his face, and a groan erupted from his throat.

A whimpering, mewling sound came from hers. Mortification would have set in, if the king wasn't equally as needy.

After who knew how long, Juan Carlos placed his hands on both her shoulders and, she sensed, with great reluctance eased her away.

He leaned back against the seat, breathing hard. "I've never made love to a woman in a limo before, Princess. But it wouldn't take much to change that."

* * *

A Royal Temptation
is part of the series Dynasties:
The Montoros—One royal family must
choose between love and destiny!

A ROYAL
TEMPTATION

BY
CHARLENE SANDS

Published in Great Britain 2015
by Mills & Boon, an imprint of Harlequin (UK) Limited,
Eton House, 18-24 Paradise Road, Richmond, Surrey, TW9 1SR

© 2015 by Harlequin Books S.A.

Special thanks and acknowledgement are given to Charlene Sands for her contribution to the Dynasties: The Montoros series.

ISBN: 978-0-263-25280-4

51-1015

Harlequin (UK) Limited's policy is to use papers that are natural, renewable and recyclable products and made from wood grown in sustainable forests. The logging and manufacturing processes conform to the legal environmental regulations of the country of origin.

Printed and bound in Spain
by CPI, Barcelona

Charlene Sands is a *USA TODAY* bestselling author of more than thirty-five romance novels, writing sensual contemporary romances and stories of the Old West. Her books have been honored with a National Readers' Choice Award, a CataRomance Reviewers' Choice Award, and she's a double recipient of the Booksellers' Best Award. She belongs to the Orange County chapter and the Los Angeles chapter of RWA.

Charlene writes "hunky heroes with heart." She knows a little something about true romance—she married her high school sweetheart! When not writing, Charlene enjoys sunny Pacific beaches, great coffee, reading books from her favorite authors and spending time with her family. You can find her on Facebook and Twitter. Charlene loves to hear from her readers! You can write her at PO Box 4883, West Hills, CA 91308, USA, or sign up for her newsletter for fun blogs and ongoing contests at www.charlenesands.com.

To Allyson Pearlman, Robin Rose, Mary Hernandez and Pam Frendian. You're my crew, my Best Friends Forever. Your friendship puts lightness in my heart and a smile on my face every day. I am surrounded by the best and I love you dearly.

One

Juan Carlos Salazar II stood at the altar in Saint Lucia's Cathedral, holding his head high as he accepted the responsibility and honor of being crowned King Montoro of Alma. In a dreamlike state he went through the motions that would bring the monarchy back to what it had once been decades ago. He'd been orphaned at a young age and taken in by his uncle. Since then, he'd lived a life filled with determination and dignity. He'd always known great things would come to him if he worked hard and kept his focus. But king? Never in his life would he have guessed his own true destiny.

With the golden orb and blessed scepter in his hands, he saw the austere ceremony in the cathedral was coming to a close. Prime Minister Rivera had given a speech full of renewed hope for the country, the small set of islands off the coast of Spain that had been ravaged by the now overthrown dictatorship of the Tantaberras. Seventy years of oppression overturned by loyal citizens, who looked to Juan Carlos for the reinstatement of a monarchy that would capture their hearts and minds.

Archbishop Santiago placed the royal robe over Juan Carlos's shoulders. As he took his seat on the throne, the archbishop set the jeweled crown of Alma upon his head. All of the tradition, ritual and protocol of the coronation had been observed, and he was now King Montoro of

Alma, the true heir to the throne. He spoke an oath and vowed to be much more than a figurehead as he promised to restore order and hope to the country.

It was a monumental time in Alma's history and he was happy to have the support of his cousins, Gabriel, Rafe and Bella. They were smiling and nodding their approval from their seats, Bella with tears in her eyes. They'd all lived and thrived in the United States before this, and forgive him, but heaven knew Rafe and Gabriel, who were once thought to be first in line to the throne but had been disqualified for separate and unique reasons, were not cut out for the rigors and sacrifice of royal life. They were only too glad to see Juan Carlos accept the position of sovereign.

A woman seated several rows behind his cousins caught his attention. Deep cerulean-blue eyes, clear and large, stood out against her porcelain face and white-blond hair. She reminded him of a snow queen from a fairy tale in his youth. And as he was ushered down the aisle after the coronation their gazes locked for an instant and her one eyelid closed in a wink. Was it for him? His lips immediately quirked up at the notion and he forced the smile from his expression. Still, his heart did a little tumble as it had been doing all day, but this time it was the woman, and not the ceremony, that had caused the commotion.

The next hour passed, again in dreamlike wonder, as he was escorted out of the cathedral by Alma's finest royal guards, to be met with unrestrained jubilation all along the parade route. He sat atop a convertible car and waved with gloved hands, as they made their way toward the palace. And there, on the top steps of Alma's regal old-world palace, Juan Carlos began his first speech as king.

"Citizens of Alma, as your new king, I promise to honor the sovereignty of our nation, to always put the country first and to work alongside our parliament to restore our democracy. It is a vow I take with an open but steady heart and a determination to see that our freedoms are never threatened again."

Cheers went up. "Viva Juan Carlos!"

Juan Carlos waited until the crowd calmed to finish a speech that was interrupted three more times by applause.

He left the palace steps energized, instilled with the very same hope he saw in the eyes of his fellow countrymen. He was a foreigner, by all rights, an American, and yet, they'd accepted him and looked to him to help establish a newer, brighter Alma.

He would not let them down.

As austere as his day was, he took a moment to reflect on the coronation and picture the beautiful woman in the light blue chiffon gown, her eyes as vibrant as deep ocean waters. He'd searched for her during the procession, the parade and the speech that followed, only to be disappointed.

She'd been a diversion from the gravity of the day.

Winking at him had brought a smile to his lips.

Who was she?

And would she have his children?

"Do I need to call you Your Highness?" his cousin Rafe asked as he pumped Juan Carlos's hand. They stood off to the side in the palace's grand ballroom. The coronation gala was well underway and the orchestra played lively tunes. An array of fresh flowers decorated the arched entryways, aisles and tables.

"You mean, as opposed to Squirt, Idiot and Bonehead like when we were kids?"

"Hey, I wasn't that bad."

"You were a year older and that gave you bullying rights."

"Okay, guilty as charged. But now you can have me hung by the neck until dead."

"I could've done that to you back then, too."

"Ha, funny."

"Call me Juan Carlos or cuz, just like you do now. Your Highness comes into play only on formal occasions or royal business."

All amusement on his cousin's face disappeared. "Seriously, Juan Carlos, congratulations. The family is proud of you. You're the only one of the lot who was cut out for this. You are honoring our aunt Isabella's final wishes by restoring the monarchy."

Juan Carlos came to the throne quite by accident, after Bella discovered a secret cache of letters that revealed Rafe, Gabriel and Bella's late grandfather, Raphael Montoro II, was illegitimate and not the true heir to the throne. As such, neither of Juan Carlos's cousins would have been the rightful king. The former queen's indiscretion had been kept hidden all these years until her great-grandchildren had uncovered it.

"Thank you, cousin. I've thought about my grandmother these past few weeks and I think she would approve. It means a great deal to me." He sighed. "I hope to make a diff—" He caught a glimpse of a woman in blue and craned his neck to get a better look.

It was her. She was attending the gala. Only dignitaries, friends and family members along with the royal photographers and journalists had been invited to the party, two hundred strong.

"Hey," Rafe asked. "What are you stretching your neck to see?"

"She's here," he muttered, without shifting his gaze. She was standing near an archway leading to the foyer, looking to make an escape.

"Juan Carlos?"

"Oh, uh, I saw a woman at the coronation and I haven't stopped thinking about her."

"This I've got to see. Any woman who can take your

mind off a day as big as this has got to be something special. Where is she?"

"I'm not going to point. Just look for the most beautiful woman in the room and you'll find her."

"Emily is right there, talking to Bella."

"Spoken like a besotted newlywed. Okay, yes, Emily is gorgeous, now find a woman in blue who is not your wife."

"If you'd agreed to a formal receiving line, you'd have met her already."

He hadn't wanted a stiff, awkward line of people congratulating him. He'd make his way over to his guests and speak with them during the course of the evening. He'd vowed to be a king *of* the people and *for* the people and that started right now. "Do you see her?"

"Ah, I do see her now. Very blonde, nice body, great eyes."

"That's her. Do you know who she is?"

"No, but apparently she knows Alex and Maria Ramon. They just walked up to her and they appear friendly."

"Well, then, I think it's time I spoke with Alma's deputy prime minister of commerce and his wife, don't you?"

Juan Carlos moved swiftly across the ballroom and as he approached, Alex spotted him and smiled. "Your Highness." Juan Carlos nodded. It would take some time getting used to that greeting.

Maria, not one to stand on ceremony, hugged his neck. She and Alex had just married and postponed their honeymoon to attend the coronation. "I'm happy to see this day, Your Highness. You are just what Alma needs."

"Thank you, Maria."

As he made eye contact with the blonde woman, it felt as if something quick and sharp had pierced his body. Her eyes were large, shaped like perfect twin almonds, the sparkle in them as bright as any star. Mesmerized, he couldn't look away.

"And please, let me introduce you to Portia Lindstrom, Princess of Samforstand."

Princess?

She *could* have his children.

Juan Carlos offered her his hand and at the touch of her delicate palm, he once again felt that quick, sharp sensation. "Nice to meet you, Princess. I'm glad you could make the coronation. It's a good day for Alma, I hope."

"I'm sure it will be, Your Majesty. And please, call me Portia."

"I will," he said. "If you call me Juan Carlos."

A pink cast tinged her porcelain skin. "I couldn't."

"Why not?"

"Because, you're the king."

"I'll let you in on a secret. Up until a few months ago, I was living in Miami and running a rather large business conglomerate. I'm afraid I still have American ties and king is not in their vocabulary, unless we're talking about Elvis."

She smiled. "I live in America, too. I'm on the west coast right now. My family was from a tiny country near Scandinavia."

"Well, then, we have a lot in common. As you can see, Alma is not a large country, either."

Maria and Alex exchanged looks and excused themselves. He'd forgotten they were there. It was rude of him. But now, he was alone with Portia.

"You are a curiosity. You won't call me Juan Carlos, but yet you wink at me just as I am crowned king."

Portia froze. Surely the king didn't believe she'd actually winked at him. It was that darn nervous twitch of hers. It would have to happen at the exact moment she'd first made eye contact with him. She should be immune to royalty—she'd met enough princes and princesses in her twenty-eight years—but Juan Carlos Salazar seemed different, strikingly handsome and down to earth. Before she could explain about the wink, the orchestra began playing a lovely Latin waltz.

He bowed in old world fashion. "Princess Portia, I'd be honored if you danced with me."

"I'm afraid I don't waltz."

"Neither do I," he replied. "We can wing it and set a new trend."

She chuckled. He didn't act like the stuffed-shirt royals she'd met in the past, and when he took her hand and led her to the unoccupied dance floor, she didn't protest. He was a better dancer than he let on, and she glided across the floor with him, fully aware every set of eyes in the room were on them.

"We're the only ones out here," she whispered.

He grinned, flashing white teeth against golden-brown skin. He was tall and dashing and at the moment, charming her silly by staring into her eyes as if she was the only person who existed in the world. It was quite flattering.

"Don't worry. Other guests will join in after the king's first dance. It's tradition."

"Then I should be honored you picked me."

"After that wink, how could I not pick you?" He held her possessively and spoke with authority, as if he'd been king all of his life.

"It was a twitch. I had something in my eye."

"I choose to believe it was a wink."

"Yes, Your Highness."

He smiled again and moved her across the dance floor as if she were light as air.

When the dance ended, he didn't release her hand. "Will you take a walk with me?"

"You want to leave your own gala?"

He shrugged and didn't appear worried. "It's been a long, monumental day. I could use a little break."

Portia couldn't very well say no. And getting some fresh air did sound good. Because of her title, she'd been invited to the gala, and to refuse such a high honor would've been unheard of. Her mother and father's greatest wish, as her grandmother told it, was for her to remain true to her royal bloodlines, even while having a career and life of her own. So she juggled her time accordingly, to honor her deceased parents' wishes. She hadn't had enough time with them, but she'd hoped to make them proud. "Well, then, yes. I'll walk with you."

They strode off the dance floor in silence. His hand pressed to her back, he guided her toward a small back door and they ducked out to a deserted foyer. "There are private gardens just outside where we can sit."

He opened a door she was sure only royals were privy to, and a gust of cool autumn air hit her. Without a second's hesitation, Juan Carlos removed his tuxedo jacket and placed it around her shoulders. "Better?"

"Yes, thank you." She tugged the lapels closed and kept her hands there, away from the king's tempting grasp. His dark eyes were on her every move, and when he touched her, her pulse raced in a way it hadn't in a very long time.

He led her to grounds surrounded by lattices covered with vines. "Would you like to sit down?"

"Okay."

She sat on a delicately woven rattan love seat and he lowered down beside her, his six-foot presence looming large next to her. Aware of the solid breadth of his shoulders and the scent of his skin, she found the new king of Alma a little too appealing. "It's nice here. Quiet," she said. "You must be exhausted."

"Yes, but invigorated, too. If that makes any sense to you."

"It does. When I'm researching a piece of art for a client, I might work sixteen-hour days, but I always get excited when I locate it." His brows came together as if he were puzzled. "I'm an art advisor," she explained. "I help collectors build their collections."

"Impressive. And do you work in your country?"

"I'm based out of Los Angeles and New York. I don't spend any time in Samforstand."

"That's how it was for me. I worked out of Miami and New York, but now, Alma will be my permanent home. My duty is here and I will adjust. The country is beautiful, so it won't be a hardship."

"Excuse me, Your Highness," said a voice from behind the bench.

"Yes?" Juan Carlos turned around.

"I'm sorry to interrupt, but Chancellor Benoit has been called away and insists on saying his farewells to you personally. He is waiting in the antechamber."

"All right, thank you. Please tell the chancellor I will be in to see him shortly."

The man gave a curt nod and walked off.

"Well, looks like duty calls. I'm sorry." He rose and extended his hand. "Please save another dance for me tonight, Portia. There's more I want to learn about...*art advising*." He smiled.

Her heart hammered. She didn't know what to make of the cocoon-like hold he had on her. She'd only just met him and already he was wrapping himself around her thoughts with his silent compliments and easy ways. "I will."

She rose and he walked her back to the ballroom, depositing her exactly where he'd found her, beside Maria and Alex.

"I will be back," he said.

Portia's throat hitched and she nodded.

"Looks like the king is smitten." Maria kept her voice

low enough for only Portia's ears. She was sure Maria, a public relations expert and friend, had been instrumental in her receiving an invitation to the coronation and gala.

"He's being gracious, Maria."

Maria seemed to ignore her comment. "He's a good man."

"Perfect for Alma. But not for me." She was attracted to Juan Carlos. Any woman with blood running through her veins would be, but talk about high profile. You couldn't get much higher, and that's the last thing Portia needed in her life. It had taken her three years to climb out of the hole she'd dug for herself by getting involved with the Duke of Discourse, Travis Miles, LA's favorite talk show host.

Charming, debonair and controversial, he'd dragged her into his limelight from the start of their love affair to the bitter, heartbreaking end. Her career had suffered as the details of his neglect and wandering eye came into play. She'd almost lost all credibility with her clients. Luckily, she'd managed her way out of that situation, vowing to keep a low profile, stay in the small circle of the art world and not allow another high-profile charmer to get to her. And that included the king of Alma.

"I don't know about that," Maria said, matter-of-factly.

"I do," she said, convincing herself of that very thing. "I have an important meeting in Los Angeles with a client in a few days."

"A lot could happen in a few days, Portia."

But the conversation ended when a nice-looking gentleman approached, introduced himself as Alma's secretary of defense, and asked her to dance.

Portia accepted, and as she was being led to the dance floor, shot an over-the-shoulder glance at Maria.

Only to find Juan Carlos standing there, his gaze following her every movement.

He had indeed come back for her.

* * *

Gnashing his teeth, Juan Carlos ran a hand down his face to cover the tightness in his jaw. Princess Portia had danced nonstop with three men since he'd returned from seeing Chancellor Benoit off. Every time Juan Carlos thought to approach, he was interrupted or summoned into a conversation with a group of dignitaries. He couldn't fall short of his duties on his coronation day, yet the beautiful snow queen consumed his thoughts, and as he spoke with others, he kept one eye on Portia.

Finally free from conversations, he had an aide approach the orchestra and suggest that they take a five-minute break. The music died instantly and Juan Carlos strode over to the table where Portia had just taken a seat. "Hello again."

Those startling blue eyes lifted to him. "Hello."

"I'm happy to see you having a good time."

"I am," she said. "Would you like to sit down?"

"I have a better idea."

Her eyes twinkled. "Really? What would that be?"

He offered his hand again, hoping she'd take it. "Come with me and find out."

Her hesitation rattled his nerves. "Where?"

"Trust me and I'll show you."

She rose then, and as they walked out of the ballroom again with her hand in his, she watched him carefully. She had no reason not to trust him. He would never steer her wrong.

"In here," he said.

He tugged her into a spacious office and shut the door. It was black as coal at first, but the light of the full moon streamed in and his eyes adjusted so that he could make out Portia's silhouette. He took her gently into his arms and overwhelming sensations rushed through his body. Silently, with a look, she questioned his actions, but with his eyes he assured her she had nothing to fear. Then the orchestra began playing and as music piped into the room through the air ducts, he began to move her along to the beat. She tossed her head back and laughed. "You aren't serious."

He grinned. "It's the only way I can assure us not being interrupted again."

"You are resourceful, Your Highness. We have an entire dance floor all to ourselves."

"What would make it perfect would be if you'd call me Juan Carlos."

"But you've earned the right to be called king."

"Tonight, for now, think of me as a man, and not a king."

"I'll try, but you have to understand, after all the adoration, the photos and parades and galas in your honor, it's not easy for me."

He did understand, but pressed his reasoning a little further. "Think of it this way. How would you like it if everyone you knew called you Princess Portia?"

She gave it some thought and nodded. "I see your point."

He drew her inches closer, so that her sweet breaths touched his face, but he didn't dare do more. Though he wanted to crush her against him, feel her body sway with his, he couldn't rush her or scare her off. These feelings pulsed through him with near desperation. He'd never been so…besotted. Such an old-world word, but that's exactly how he felt.

"How long will you be in Alma?" he asked.

"I leave for the States in two days. I'm due back at work."

News he didn't want to hear. "Are you working with a client?"

"Yes, he's someone very influential and I'm thrilled to have the chance to meet with him for the first time. He's new to collecting, and I have an interview with him to see where his tastes lie."

"I see. It's a good opportunity for you. I would imagine being Princess Portia of Samforstand carries some weight in your line of work."

"I'll admit, using my royal heritage has helped me attain clients, but it's my expertise that has earned their trust."

"Trust is important," he said.

"You have the trust of the entire country right now."

"Yes," he said, sighing. "It's a big responsibility. I'm sure you take your responsibility seriously."

"I do. My reputation earns me that trust and I guard it like a mother would her child."

He smiled at the image gathering in his mind, of Portia, mother of his child.

Dios. He was in deep. How was it possible? He had known her less than a day.

And already, he was naming their first-born child.

Two

Stately and grand, Portia's hotel in Del Sol was just a short distance from the palace. The big bed in her room was cushy and comfy. The morning sunlight streamed in to warm her and the air was sweetened by a bouquet of roses, compliments of the hotel manager. It was all fit for a princess. Yet she hadn't slept well.

Last night, as Juan Carlos bid her farewell, he'd almost kissed her. She was sure he would have if they hadn't been surrounded by his guests. She'd thought about that non-kiss during the night. How would his lips feel against hers? Heavens, she hadn't had so much as a date with a man in almost a year, and it had been even longer since she was ravaged by a kiss. Which, she was sure, would have happened had they been alone.

She was thankful that he hadn't locked lips with her in front of the attendees at the gala. Yet, lightbulbs had flashed and pictures had been snapped of the two of them. It was last thing she needed and she'd dashed out as rapidly as Cinderella racing against the midnight hour.

When he'd asked her to join him for brunch this morning, she'd quickly agreed, despite her tingling nerves and fuzzy brain.

Her brunch "date" with the King of Montoro would happen precisely at ten o'clock and he'd promised they wouldn't be interrupted.

She heard the familiar Bruno Mars ringtone of her cell phone and grabbed it from the nightstand. Her assistant's name popped up on the screen and she smiled. From the very beginning, her assistant had been her closest friend. "Hello, Jasmine."

"Hi, Portia. I hope I didn't wake you?"

"No, not at all. I'm getting ready to have brunch. It's good to hear your voice."

"Did you survive the coronation?" Jasmine Farr never minced words. "I know you weren't thrilled about attending."

"Actually, it wasn't so bad." The newly named king was quite a man. "And it's my lot in life to attend these functions every so often."

"That's what you get for being a princess." She chuckled. "I saw some of the coronation on YouTube."

"That was fast."

"It always is. Anyway, I'm calling to tell you that Mr. Greenboro had to cancel your meeting this week. He's flying out of the country and won't be back for three months. He sends his apologies, of course, and he did reschedule. I hope it's okay that I took the liberty of making that appointment. I didn't think you'd want to let him get away."

"Oh, I'm disappointed. I'd set the entire week aside to work with him, but I'm glad you're on the ball and rescheduled with him. Text me that date and I'll mark it on my calendar."

"Will do. So, now you don't have to rush back. There's really nothing else going on this week."

"Right."

"You've worked hard these past few months and you've been meaning to pencil in a vacation. Seems like a perfect opportunity."

"It is beautiful here."

"From the pictures I'm seeing, the beaches are to die for. I wish I could join you. I'd come in an instant."

"Why don't you come? We could have spa days together."

"I can't. I'm flying to Maryland for my cousin's wedding at the end of the week. "

"I'd forgotten about that. Darn."

"But that doesn't mean you can't stay on. I can book you a villa suite in Playa del Onda. The beach resort is top notch. You'll get lots of R&R."

"Let me think about it. I'll get back to you later on today."

After she ended the call, she stripped off her pajamas and entered the shower. The pounding water rained down and woke her up to the possibility of an actual vacation: away from phones, away from the hectic pace of gallery openings, away from the pressures of making art selections for her obscenely rich or drastically eccentric clients. Her schedule was a busy one, and this did seem like a perfect opportunity to unwind.

When she was finished with her shower, she slipped into a white dress with red polka dots that belted at the waist, slid on navy patent leather shoes and tossed her hair up into a ponytail. She applied light makeup, including eyeliner and soft pink lip gloss.

The jewelry she chose was delicate: a thin strand of pearls around her neck and wrist. She fastened her watch on her left arm and noted the time. Juan Carlos was sending a car for her in ten minutes. She grabbed her purse and left the hotel room.

In the lobby, she was greeted by a uniformed driver who escorted her to an ink-black limousine. She played the role of princess well, but she would rather be wearing a pair of jeans and going to the local café for a bite of breakfast.

"Your Highness," the driver said, as he opened the door for her, "allow me."

She slid into the backseat and bumped legs with Juan Carlos. Her breath hitched in her throat. He took in her wide-eyed surprise and grinned. "Good morning, Portia."

"Excuse me, but I didn't expect you to come to pick me up."

Should she worry about the implications? This wasn't a date. At least, not in any real sense.

"It's a nice morning for a drive. After yesterday's events, I thought you might like to join me to see some of the city. I hope you don't mind, but I've changed our brunch plans for today."

He wore dark slacks and a casual white silk shirt, opened slightly at the collar. She glimpsed his tanned chest and gulped for air.

"Of course not."

"Great. You look very pretty this morning."

"Thank you." *And you look dynamic, powerful and gorgeous.*

He issued directions to the driver and they took off.

"How were your first twenty-four hours as king?" she asked.

He rubbed his chin, thinking for a second. "It's strange that I don't feel any different. I keep expecting a big transformation, but I'm just me."

She smiled at his earnest answer. "I thought it would be an adjustment for you. Every move you make now will be documented somehow." She glanced out the window, expecting to see photographers following the limo, snapping pictures. She'd had experience with her ex-boyfriend's fame and it had gotten old very fast. No one should be followed and photographed at every turn for entertainment's sake. "How did you escape the palace?"

He chuckled. "You make it seem like prison."

"No, no. I'm sorry. That's not what I meant."

"I know what you meant, Portia." Her name slid effortlessly from his lips. "There are some advantages to being king."

"Such as?" she probed.

"Such as, I didn't make my intentions known. No one expected me to take a drive this morning. No one questioned me. I had the car ready to pick you up, and then I merely slipped into the backseat before anyone at the palace got wind of it."

"You snuck out."

He laughed again and she joined in. "Okay, yes. I snuck out."

Speaking to him put her at ease and she settled back in her seat. "Do you have bodyguards?"

"Yes, they are following behind somewhere."

"You're not worried?"

He shook his head. "No. I'm not worried. And neither should you be."

"Okay, I'll trust you." She'd never traveled with bodyguards, but her situation was quite different. As an exiled princess, she'd grown up in America and never had what Juan Carlos now had: a citizenry eager to reinstate their monarchy. "But you must have dozens of dignitaries and family members waiting to speak with you at the palace."

"Which I will do later. But for now," he said, reaching for her hand, "I find being with you more important."

Juan Carlos held her hand during the tour of the city. He showed her sites of great historical significance and some trendy new hot spots that were cropping up. The rise of democracy was good for enterprise, he explained.

As he spoke, the tone of his deep and sincere voice brought a smile to her lips more times than she could count. It was intimate in a way, hearing the love he had for a country that was almost as new to him as it was to her. He kept her hand locked in his as if it was precious. As if he needed the connection. To hear him say that being with her was important did wonders for her ego.

Yet she only indulged him because nothing could possibly come of it. And because it had been a long time since she'd enjoyed a man's company so much.

Tomorrow, she would leave Del Sol.

The limo stopped at a tiny café off the main street of town. "I hear Matteo's is fantastic."

"You've never eaten here before?" she asked.

"No, I haven't. We'll experience it together. Do you mind?"

"I love adventure."

He nodded, a satisfied glimmer in his eyes. "I thought you might."

They exited the limo, which looked out of place on the backstreets of the royal city. Once inside, they were escorted to their table by the owner. He was sweating, nervous and fidgety. Juan Carlos clapped him on the back gently to reassure him. "Bring us your specials, Matteo. I hear they are the best in all of Del Sol."

"*Si, si.* I will be glad to serve you myself, Your Majesty."

Juan Carlos nodded. "Thank you."

Though the café walls showed signs of age, it was a clean, modest place. "Are you sure the food is good here?" she asked.

His brows gathered. "It comes highly recommended. Why?"

"We're the only ones seated."

Juan Carlos looked around the empty café. "My bodyguards. They called ahead to announce my arrival. I'll make it up to Matteo. I can't have him losing business on my account."

"I'm sure he'll be boasting that King Montoro of Alma dined in his café. His business will double by next week."

Juan Carlos sharpened his gaze on her. "I hadn't thought of that."

"You're new to this royal thing."

"Yes, I guess I am."

Just wait, she wanted to say. He was an intelligent man, from all she'd read about him. He managed the sizable personal accounts of the Montoros and had helped build a fortune for the family. He had wits and smarts, but nothing would prepare him for the limelight he'd just entered. He'd have to experience it himself, the good, the bad, the ugly. His life would be under a microscope now.

And she didn't want to be the amoeba next to him.

Coffee was served, along with fresh handmade tortillas, butter and a bowl of cut fruit. "Looks delicious," Juan Carlos said to Matteo.

"Please, is there anything else I can bring you while the meal is cooking?"

"This is perfect. Don't you agree, Portia?"

She nodded and smiled at the owner.

When Matteo left the room she continued to smile. "You're kind. He will always remember this day because you put him at ease."

Travis Miles had been kind, too, in the beginning.

"Now who is being kind?" he asked.

"I'm just speaking the truth. You'll impact a great many lives."

"In a positive way, I hope and pray."

"Kind," she repeated. "You care about the people in the country."

"Thank you." His incredibly warm brown eyes softened and her stomach did a little flip.

She buttered a tortilla, rolled it up and took a few bites. She sipped coffee and asked Juan Carlos a few pointed questions about his life to keep the conversation flowing and her mind off the fact that King Montoro was a hunk.

The meal was delivered with fanfare. Matteo and his staff put out the dishes in sweeping motions and finally left them to dine privately. The food was delicious. The main dish consisted of bits of sautéed pork topped with eggs and lathered with a creamy, mildly spicy sauce. There was also some type of sweet corn soufflé served inside the husks, as well as caramelized plantains. Every bite she took rewarded her taste buds. "Mmm…this is heavenly."

Juan Carlos nodded, his mouth full.

As he chewed, his gaze remained on her. He had warm, luxurious, intense eyes that didn't stray. Goose bumps rode up and down her arms. As far as men went, Juan Carlos had it all, except for one thing. His fatal flaw. He was king. And that meant after today, she couldn't see him again.

"So what are your plans for the rest of the day?" he asked.

"Oh, I'm, uh, going to…" She really didn't have any plans. Maybe do a little shopping. Check out the only art museum in the city. "I'll be packing."

"That can't take all day."

"I wouldn't think so."

"Would you consider having dinner with me?"

No. No. No. "I really shouldn't."

Juan Carlos leaned back in his seat, studying her. "Do you have a man in your life, Portia?"

Slowly, she shook her head. She felt a trap coming.

"No one? I find that hard to believe. Do you date?"

"Rarely. My career is demanding. And it's very important to me. I've worked hard to get where I am."

"Admirable. Are you working tonight?"

"No, but I…"

He grinned. "I'm only asking for a dinner date, Portia."

Her shoulders sagged an inch. A barely noticeable move,

but she felt the defeat all the way down to her toes. She couldn't insult the king. "Then, yes, I'll have dinner with you."

After the meal, Juan Carlos escorted her to the limo. She took a seat at the far window and he climbed in after her. To his credit, he didn't crowd her, leaving a modest amount of space between them. But as the car took off, he placed his hand over hers on the empty seat, and wild pings of awareness shot through her body.

Don't let him get to you, Portia.

He's not the man for you.

As the limo pulled up to the hotel, Juan Carlos spoke to the driver. "Give us a minute please, Roberto."

The driver's door opened and closed quietly. Silence filled the air and suddenly she did feel crowded, though Juan Carlos hadn't made a move toward her. "I cannot walk you to your door, Princess."

"I understand."

"Do you? Do you know how much I want to?" His eyes were down, gazing at her hand as his thumb worked circles over her fingers. Her nerves jumped, like kernels of corn popping in a fry pan, one right after the other. "I don't want to cause you any inconvenience."

"I...know."

He tugged her hand gently and she fell forward, closing the gap between them. His dark-fringed eyelids lifted; she was struck by all-consuming heat. He wasn't moving a muscle, but leaving it up to her. As if she had a choice now. As if she could deny him. His mesmerizing hunger was contagious; years of abstinence made her hungry, as well. Her gaze lowered to his mouth. Lord in heaven, she wanted his kiss.

She moistened her lips and his eyes drew down immediately. "You leave me no choice, Princess."

He used a finger to tilt her chin, and then bent his head

toward her. Anticipation pulsed through her veins. Every single second was an unnerving kind of torture. And finally, his mouth was on hers, his hand coming to wrap more firmly around her jaw, as if he couldn't get enough, as if he would devour her.

Long live the king!

Her tummy ached from goodness and she indulged like a miser finding a hidden supply of cash. She touched his face, his jaw steel under her fingertips, and a groan erupted from his throat.

A whimpering mewling sound came from hers. Mortification would have set in, if the king wasn't equally as needy. But there was no shame, just honesty, and it was, after all, the kiss to end all kisses. Juan Carlos didn't let up, not for a moment. His lips worked hers hard, then soft, then hard again. Under her dress, her nipples ached. She was pretty sure the king was experiencing the same agony, but farther south on his body.

She didn't know whose mouth opened first, or whether it was at the exact same instant, but suddenly she was being swept up and hollowed out, his tongue doing a thorough job of ravaging her. Any second now, she'd be out of her head with lust. But Juan Carlos placed his hands on her shoulders and, she sensed, with great reluctance, moved her away from him.

He leaned back against the seat, breathing hard. "I've never made love to a woman in a limo before, Princess. It wouldn't take much to change that," he said. He tried for amusement, tried to chuckle, but a serious tone had given away his innermost thoughts.

"It would be a first for me, too," she said, coming up for air.

A rumpled mess, she tried her best to straighten herself out before she exited the limo.

He pressed a button and the window rolled down. Roberto appeared by the car door. "See Princess Portia to her hotel room," Juan Carlos said calmly. He'd gotten his emotions in check already, while she was still a ravaged jumble of nerves.

Again, those warm brown eyes lit upon her. "I'll send a car to pick you up for dinner at seven."

She swallowed. "Maybe…we shouldn't," she squeaked.

"Are you afraid of me?" he asked, though his confident tone indicated that it wasn't even a concern.

She shook her head. "I'm leaving in the morning."

"And you love your job. Your career means a lot to you. Yes, that's clear."

He'd made her refusal seem silly. And it was. Nothing would happen unless she wanted it to happen. She already knew Juan Carlos was that type of man.

"I'll see you tonight," she said finally. When the driver opened the car door, she rushed out.

She hadn't exactly lied to him, had she?

She said she'd be gone, and he thought she meant back to the States. But she'd made up her mind to vacation on the shores of Alma, at least until the end of the week.

But he didn't need to know that.

After a late lunch, Juan Carlos had a meeting in the city with the prime minister and few of Alma's most trusted and prominent business leaders. He struggled to keep his mind on the topics at hand. The restoration of the entire country was a tall order. But every so often, his mind traveled to that place where Portia was in his arms. The image of her lips locked on his, their bodies pulsing to the same lusty rhythms, knocked him for a loop and sent his brain waves scrambling. She was, in his estimation, perfect. For him. For the country.

Wow. Where had that come from? Why was he thinking of her in terms of permanence? As a queen for Alma, for goodness' sake.

Because aside from the fact that his sensual response was like the national flag being hoisted to full mast every time he looked at her, there was no doubt in his mind that she could take a place by his side at the throne.

As a public figure, he was never alone much anymore, but that didn't mean he wasn't lonely. He hadn't had a serious relationship for years. His ambition had gotten in the way and sure, he'd had a few women in his life, but nothing serious. No one who'd made him feel like this.

Portia's face flashed in his mind, that porcelain skin, those ice-blue eyes, that haughty chin, that mouth that tasted like sweet sin. The snow queen had become important to him in a short time, and…

"Your Majesty? Juan Carlos, are you all right?"

"Huh? Oh, yeah, I'm fine." Prime Minister Rivera was giving him a strange look. "Just deep in thought."

They'd been talking about how to bring new enterprise to Alma and how the rise of the monarchy would bring in tourism. They needed to brand themselves as a free country and show the world that democracy reigned, that new visitors and new businesses were welcome to their stunning Atlantic shores.

"Actually, I have an idea as to how to draw more tourists," Juan Carlos said.

"Really?"

Alex Ramon's ears perked up. As the deputy prime minister of commerce, he was fully immersed in the issue. "Tell us your thoughts."

"It's been rumored in our family for years that our ancestors had stashed a considerable amount of artwork, sculptures and paintings on land that had fallen to ruin. Land that Tantaberra overlooked. Right before the family was deposed, they'd thought to hide the art so it wouldn't fall into the dictator's greedy hands."

Juan Carlos's mind was clicking fast. He didn't know how true those rumors were. He'd only heard the tales while growing up; Uncle Rafael had spoken of hidden treasures the way a master storyteller would about a pirate's bounty. It had all been exciting, the sort of thing that captured a little boy's imagination. But the rumors had held fast and true during his adulthood, and only recently, his cousin Bella had found a hidden cache of letters at one of the family's abandoned farms, letters that proved that he, a Salazar and not a Montoro, was the rightful heir to the throne.

"I have plans to visit the area myself and see what I can find. If it's true, and artwork is indeed on the property, think of the story. The art could be restored, and we could have a special showing or a series of showings to bring awareness to Alma."

"It's genius, Your Highness," Prime Minister Rivera said. Others around the board table agreed.

The meeting ran long and Juan Carlos didn't get back to the palace until six. He had just enough time to shower and dress for dinner. His pulse sped up as he thought of Portia again, of her sweetly exotic scent and the way she'd filled his body with pleasure when he was near her. She caused him to gasp and sweat and breathe hard. It wasn't ideal. She was a hard case. She didn't seem interested in him. And that worried him, because as far as he was concerned, she was The One.

He came down at precisely six forty-five and bumped into his new secretary at the base of the winding staircase, nearly knocking the clipboard out of her hands. "Oh, sorry, Your Highness." She was out of breath, as if she'd been running a marathon.

"My apologies," he said. "I've been preoccupied and didn't see you."

Alicia was redheaded, shapely and quite efficient. She wore glasses, but under those glasses were pretty, light green eyes. She'd taken on a lot, being a first hire, as there was much ground to cover. "Your seven o'clock appointment is here."

Warmth spread through his body at the mention of his dinner date. "Princess Portia?"

"Oh, uh. No, Your Highness. I'm sorry. I don't see Princess Portia on the books." She studied her clipboard, going over the names. "No, you have appointments every half hour for the next few hours. I penciled in a dinner break for you at nine."

"I thought those were on tomorrow night's schedule." Surely, he hadn't been mistaken, had he? Yet he had to take Alicia at her word. He'd already come to find that she rarely if ever made mistakes. He, on the other hand, had been hypnotized by a pair of deep ocean-blue eyes and was more than distracted.

"I can't possibly make all of those appointments." High-ranking officials and the heads of businesses along with their wives or husbands wanted to meet the new king. It was as simple as that. It was good for commerce to know the pillars of trade in Alma, so he'd agreed to a few evening appointments. Under normal circumstances, he'd rather cut off his right arm than cancel them, but he couldn't break a date with Portia. "See what you can do about cancelling them. Who was first on the schedule?"

"Mr. and Mrs. Rubino. The Rubinos are in the royal study. And your next appointment after that is already here, I'm afraid. They are notoriously early for every occasion, I'm told. They are waiting in the throne room."

He ran his hands through his hair. "Fine. I'll see them. But see what you can do about cancelling the rest."

"Yes, Your Highness. I'll do my best." She bit her lower lip, her eyes downcast. "Sorry for the confusion."

"Alicia?"

"Yes?"

"It's not your doing. I forgot about these appointments. We're all learning here. It's new to all of us."

She had ten years of experience running a duke's household in London, coordinating parties and events with dignitaries and the royal family. She hadn't much to learn. He was the one who had screwed up.

"Yes, Your Highness. I'll get on those cancellations right away."

Juan Carlos rubbed the back of his neck and headed to the study.

With luck, he could salvage the evening.

Portia had been stood up. She'd been delivered to the palace minutes before seven, only to be informed that the king had visitors and to please be patient and wait. She was shown to the dining room and shortly after, the palace chef himself had set dishes of appetizers on the table before her.

Candles were lit and soft music filtered into the room.

The only problem? Her date wasn't here. And she wasn't about to eat a thing until he showed. Call her stubborn.

It was after eight. She knew because her stomach refused to stop growling and finally, she'd glanced at her watch.

She'd already taken in the paintings on the walls, assessing them and noting that they weren't up to par with usual palatial art. Oh, they were lovely pieces, but from contemporary artists. Many of them were replicas of the real thing. It was a curiosity. The monarchy stretched way beyond the years of the dictatorship. There should be older, more authentic works on the walls. But this was only one room. Maybe for security reasons, the gallery held the most valuable pieces.

After wandering the dining hall, she picked a particular patch of space near the fireplace and began pacing.

She couldn't fault Juan Carlos. His secretary had taken the blame, explaining that she'd failed to remind the king of his visitors. She'd tried her best to cancel the meetings, but she was afraid she wasn't as successful as she'd hoped.

But the more Portia thought about it, the more pangs of anger replaced her patience.

How long would he keep her waiting?

Travis is in a meeting. He won't be available for hours. He'd like you to wait, though.

This isn't the same thing, she reminded herself. Her ex-boyfriend wasn't a king. Well, maybe the king of late-night television. And she'd fallen for him. He was funny and charming and kind. It was like a regular Cinderella story, the poor broke comedian hooks up with a real live princess. Travis was far from poor now, although he'd come from humble beginnings and the press loved their story and ate it up.

A new American fairy tale, they'd called it.

Travis had been on top of the world when they were together. Everyone loved him and thought he was worthy of a princess from an obscure little country. Only dating a supermodel would have given him more credibility.

And here she was, doing the same thing. Another American fairy tale, only this time with a real king.

Stupid of her.

Her nerves were jumpy and by the time eight-thirty rolled around, she was royally pissed.

Juan Carlos had twisted her arm to accept this dinner date, the way charming men did. He'd trapped her and then kissed her until every brain cell was lulled into capitulation. God, she'd been looking forward to being alone with him again. That kiss was good. Better than good. It was the best kiss she'd ever had. Not even Travis could kiss like that, and he'd been plenty experienced in that department.

"Sorry, so sorry, Portia."

She jumped. "Oh!" Juan Carlos entered the room, looking dashing in a dark buttoned-up suit but no tie. Another growl emitted from her stomach, this time not due to hunger.

"Did Alicia explain what happened? It was my fault. This is the first chance I've had to—"

"It's been over ninety minutes," was all she could think to say.

"I would've cancelled with you and sent you home, but this is your last night in Alma. Selfishly, I wanted to see you again."

Guilt rose like bile in her throat. She remained silent.

He glanced at the feast of food that had been put before her. "You didn't touch anything Chef prepared. You must be famished."

"I'm not hungry anymore, Your Majesty."

His lips pursed in disapproval.

She still couldn't bring herself to call him by his given name.

"You've been so patient. There's just one more meeting I have to get through. Will you wait?"

She shook her head. "Actually, I think I'd like to go."

"You're angry."

"No, I'm tired and, and…"

"Angry."

She didn't respond. "Will you have your driver take me back to the hotel?"

Juan Carlos closed his eyes briefly. "Yes, of course. I just assumed after we kissed, you'd… Never mind. You're right. I shouldn't have made you wait."

A man who admitted when he was wrong? How rare.

"Duty called. I'm afraid it always will."

That's how it had worked with Travis. The difference? Travis had been building his own personal dynasty, while Juan Carlos was trying to build one for his country. But that still left Portia with the same end result. She'd never be a top priority and while she liked Juan Carlos, she had vowed, after many disappointments with Travis, to never get herself in that situation again.

With that, she wished Juan Carlos a good evening, assured him she wasn't angry and put enough distance between them that he couldn't touch her, couldn't plant his delicious lips on hers again and make her change her mind.

Three

The beach at Playa del Onda was one of the most stunning Portia had ever visited. Warm sand squeezed between her toes as she sat on a lounge chair, reading a book. This morning she'd gotten up early and taken a long jog along the shoreline, the October sun warming her through and through. She'd met a lovely family of tourists and had breakfast with them at a terrace café that overlooked the Atlantic. But their two little children, aged five and three, reminded her that it would probably be a long time before she was blessed with motherhood.

Often, she thought of having a family. She'd been orphaned at a young age. Aside from her great-aunt Margreta, she had no other family. Her grandmother Joanna had died during Portia's sophomore year in college. But she had her work and it fulfilled her, and she had good friends. She wasn't complaining. Yet being here on this beautiful beach was not only relaxing, it was…lonely.

Face it, Portia. How many books can you read this week? How many hot stone spa treatments can you indulge in? How many solo dinners in your room can you enjoy?

It had been three days of torturous relaxation. And it didn't compute. How odd for her to realize while on a vacation in a beautiful locale that she wasn't made for inactivity. She liked to keep active, to busy herself with things that mattered. Yesterday, she'd given herself a mental slap.

You deserve this vacation, so shut up, sit back and enjoy yourself.

Today, the mental slaps weren't working. Her relaxation was even more forced. She fidgeted in her chair; the book in her hands no longer held her interest. Sunglasses shading her eyes, she watched others frolicking on the sand, tossing a Frisbee, their laughter drifting over to her, reminding her how lonely she was. How bored.

She wished Jasmine was here. They would've had a good time with shopping, spa dates and maybe a nightclub or two.

The Frisbee landed at her feet and a teenage boy trotted over and stopped abruptly, blasting sand onto her legs. "Excuse me," he said. He reached for the Frisbee slowly, eyeing her legs, then her bikini-clad body. "Want to play with us?" he asked.

He had Spanish good looks, dark hair, bronzed skin and a charming smile. He was sixteen tops, and she would've actually considered tossing the Frisbee around with him, if he hadn't been so blatant about ogling her breasts.

She was saved from refusing, when the concierge from the Villa Delgado approached. "Excuse me, Princess."

The boy blinked at her title, turned a lovely shade of cherry-blossom pink and bowed, before dashing off. She chuckled under her breath. Her royal status did have some advantages. "Yes," she said to the concierge, removing her sunglasses.

"You have a phone call at the desk. A woman named Jasmine. She says she works for you. Apparently, she hasn't been able to reach you on your cell phone."

"I left my cell in my room," she replied. She didn't want to be interrupted in her state of lonely boredom. Now she realized how silly that seemed. "Sorry you had to track me down."

"Not a problem, Princess Portia."

"Will you tell her that I'll call her as soon as I get to my room?"

"My pleasure," he said.

When he walked off, she gathered up her beach bag, hat and sunglasses and promptly made her way toward the villa. Her suite with its second-floor terrace came into view. It was really quite picturesque, the columns and archways suggesting old-world grace and style. Why couldn't she like being here more? Why wasn't she okay with being idle? Maybe things had changed with Jasmine. Maybe her friend would come join her, after all. Her hope in her throat, Portia hiked a little faster to reach her suite of rooms.

Once inside, she set her things down on the dining table and headed for the bedroom, where she was sure she'd left her phone. It was charging on her nightstand. She unhooked the charger, just as she heard a knock at the door.

She belted her cover-up a little tighter and moved to the door. With a gentle tug on the knob, the door opened and she came face to face with Juan Carlos Salazar. The king.

She blinked and a rush of heat rose up her neck. She trembled at the sight of him, *the gorgeous, unexpected, surprising* sight of him. The phone slipped slightly in her hand and she grabbed at it before it crashed onto the floor.

His eyes were on her, and those dark raised brows made her flush even hotter. With guilt. Piercing disappointment flickered in his eyes. She hadn't told him the absolute truth when she'd left Del Sol.

"Princess," he said.

"Your Majesty," she responded.

His lips twitched. "I see you've decided to stay on in Alma, after all."

"I, uh, yes." She didn't owe him an explanation. One heart-robbing kiss didn't give him that right. "My plans changed."

"Quite unexpectedly, I assume."

"Yes, that's right." The movement of two bodyguards caught her attention. They stayed back, at least five feet away, but she was certain they could hear every word. "Would you like to come in?"

His gaze dipped down to her bikini-clad body, covered only by a soft robe of silk that reached her thighs. "Yes."

She backed up a few steps and he nodded to his bodyguards and then entered. They stood face-to-face again, alone in her suite.

Despite her guilt and a sense of being caught red-handed, this was the most exciting thing that had happened to her in three days. But how did he find out where she was and what did he want from her?

Her cell phone buzzed and she looked down at the screen. A text was coming through from Jasmine. She hadn't had time to call her back yet. Quickly, she scanned the message.

Heads up. I might've made a mistake by giving King Montoro your location. He was charming and said it was a business thing. Apologizing in advance. Love you!

She lifted her lids to him. Okay, so he wasn't psychic. But he was thorough.

"It's good to see you again," he said.

Warmth swelled inside her like an overflowing river. He had too much of an effect on her.

"It's nice to see you, but I do admit, it's quite a surprise."

On this warm day, he was wearing dark trousers and a tan shirt, sleeves rolled up with his hands in his pockets, looking as casual and delicious as any man she'd ever met. Man, *not king*. But she couldn't forget who he was. "I have to admit, I was also surprised to learn you hadn't left the country."

"You were looking for me?"

"Yes, I spoke with your assistant. She's very nice, by the way, and she's loyal to you. But the fact is, I have something of a business venture for you. And after I told her a little about it, she was willing to let me get in touch with you."

His eyes skimmed over Portia's body. Another wave of heat shimmied down to her belly and she turned away from his hot, assessing stare. Man or king, he was dangerous. "Would you like to sit down?" She waved him over to a latte-colored leather chair by the window that faced the Atlantic. "Please give me a minute to change my clothes."

"Only if you have to."

There was a wicked twinkle in his eyes that tweaked something lusty and recently unleashed in her body. It made her run, not walk toward her bedroom. "I'll be a minute, Your Majesty," she called over her shoulder.

His chuckle followed her into her room.

She scrubbed her face clean of sunscreen and removed her hair fastener, combing the tangles away and then gathering the strands back up into a long ponytail. She put on a pair of white capris and an off-the-shoulder cornflower-blue blouse.

A hint of lip gloss, some shading to her eyelids and she was ready. And more than mildly curious as to what was so important that King Juan Carlos had come all the way here to seek her out. She gave a last glance in the mirror and nodded. She felt a little less vulnerable to the king's hungry eyes now.

Juan Carlos stood when Portia entered the room. His heart hammered in his chest at the sight of her. She didn't know it yet, but he was determined to possess her. Aside from his newfound reign over Alma and his duties here, she'd become the most important thing in his life.

In such a short time.

It wasn't rational. He had no explanation for it. He'd never experienced anything quite like this. When she'd left the palace the other night, remorse had plagued him and lingered for days. Was he pathetic? Or simply a man who knows what he wants.

She was perfect, his ideal woman. She was royal, beautiful, smart, but at the moment…quite unattainable.

"Princess," he said.

"Would you like something cold to drink?" she asked.

"No, thank you."

"Okay, then maybe we should sit down and you can tell me what this is all about."

She took a seat, her eyes widening as she waited for him to explain.

"It seems I might have need for your services."

"My services? As an art advisor?"

"Well, yes. In a way. It would be something quite adventurous. You did say you liked adventure, didn't you?"

"I do."

"Well, then, let me explain. I don't know how much you know about the history of Alma, but it's been rumored that right before my family fled the country, they hid artwork dating back before World War II on the grounds of their abandoned farm. It's very run-down and Tantaberra never went there, so it was the perfect hiding place. Now that I'm king, I want to find those treasured pieces belonging to the royal family. It would go a long way in helping the country heal and bring new hope to our people. Imagine what a find that would be."

"It would be monumental," she agreed. Fireworks lit in her eyes at the mention of hidden art.

Good. He had her attention.

"But I see that you're vacationing here, so maybe you'd be too busy to help me locate the treasure."

"You want my help in locating the artwork?"

"Yes, I would need someone to help me hunt for it, and then assess its value. You'd be able to look at something and determine if it's authentic, I would imagine."

"Yes, for the most part. It's what I do. But you plan on doing this by yourself?"

"I can donate a few days of my time, yes. I wouldn't want word to leak out about what I was doing. If I come up empty, or if there are other issues regarding the artwork we find, I would rather it not become public knowledge immediately. Bella and her husband had already begun renovations on the property but given the site's historical significance, they've agreed to allow me to take over and devote the full resources of the crown to the project. As we speak, there is a team working on the grounds, getting it ready for my arrival. So Princess Portia, would you consider helping me? Of course, you'd be paid for your time."

"So, this is a job offer?"

"Yes, I'm offering you a job and an adventure."

She smiled, leaning forward and placing her hands on her crossed knee. "Who else will be there?"

He gathered his brows. "No one but my bodyguards. As I said, I plan to do this discreetly."

"It's intriguing, Your Majesty. But the two us alone, all that time?"

"Is that a problem for you?" God only knew, it was a problem for him. How could he keep his hands off her? It would be a living hell, but not worse than having her living a continent away. A few days was all he was asking of her.

"Maybe. Answer one thing for me, please."

He extended his arms, palms up. "Anything."

"Do you have an ulterior motive in offering me this opportunity? And please don't make me spell it out."

He smiled. She'd made her point and he wouldn't do her a disservice by lying to her. "If you mean, do I value a few more days in your company, then yes. I suppose. But I do honestly have good reason to be asking this of you. You are an expert, are you not?"

"I am."

The sparkle in her eyes evaporated.

"What is it?"

She rose from her seat, and good manners had him rising, too. She walked behind the chair, putting distance between them, and leaned her elbows on the back, a battle raging in her eyes, on her face. "I'm not presuming anything here, but I do have to tell you where I stand. It's… it's complicated. Because I do like you."

Encouraging. He nodded.

"And that kiss we shared…well, it bordered on amazing."

He nodded again. She had something to say and he wanted to hear it.

Or maybe not.

"But the truth is, you're King Montoro of Alma. You're new to this king thing, but you'll find out how demanding a job it will be. And you'll be in the spotlight. All. The. Time."

"Does that worry you?"

"Yes. You see, I'm not one to share heartbreak stories, but in this case, I should probably share with you, why I've been—"

"Playing hard to get?" He couldn't hold back a smile.

"Yes. Only I'm not playing. I'm seriously not interested in getting involved with a man with so much…glitter."

"Glitter?" He laughed. "What's that?"

"You're always going to shine. No matter what." His smile faded. She was dead serious. "And any woman who gets involved with you, will be giving up her identity, her dreams, her heart, to someone who has pledged his life to his country."

"Who was he, Portia? Surely, someone has broken your heart."

"Yes, my heart was broken. I don't like talking about it, but since it's important to our conversation, I'll tell you about Travis Miles. He's like a king in America, a big time Hollywood celebrity."

Juan Carlos nodded. "Of course I know of him. I don't go in much for entertainment news, but he sure has quite a résumé."

"Travis knows everyone of substance in the country from sports figures and superstars to high-ranking politicians. We ran hot for a short time, and then...I became old news to him. He didn't have time for me and we began seeing less and less of each other. Shortly after, I found out he'd been cheating on me with a woman on the staff of his TV show for a long time. Seems that everyone knew about it but poor little gullible me. He'd made me out to be a fool and my career and credibility suffered. It's taken me three years to get my reputation back. Princess or not, I wasn't immune to the blonde-bimbo stigma and so now, I'm cautious. Which is why your royal status isn't a plus in my book."

He stood with hands on hips, silent, taking it all in. He understood her caution. The pain in her eyes, the tremor in her voice were telling, and his heart hurt hearing her confession. He should leave and let her resume her vacation. He shouldn't press her. But his feet were planted and they weren't moving. He couldn't face not seeing her again.

"If things were different, would you accept my offer?"

"Yes," she said, her eyes clear now. "I wouldn't hesitate. It sounds far too exciting to pass up."

"Then let's pretend that we've just met. There was no amazing kiss from before. We haven't danced and spent time together. This is a business meeting. And I promise to keep things completely professional between us."

"Why is it so important to you?" she asked.

"Because, I...I see how much you want to say yes. I see that you'd love to locate the secret artworks."

"And you promise that after we discover this wonderful treasure, we'll just be friends?"

He let a split second go by. He was a man of his word.

If he promised, he'd have to adhere to his vow, regardless of how much he wanted things to be different.

"I promise, Princess."

She nodded. "I know you mean what you say. So yes, I accept your offer."

The next morning, Portia informed the concierge that she'd be checking out earlier than expected from Villa Delgado and offered her thanks for his accommodations. He'd questioned her, hoping she hadn't been disappointed in her stay, and she assured him that was not the case. She'd been called away unexpectedly, she explained. And his brows arched as if he'd suspected King Montoro had something to do with her sudden departure.

And so, her adventure was beginning. Dressed for the search, wearing a pair of Gucci jeans and a red plaid shirt tucked in and belted at the waist, she swopped out her Bruno Magli shoes for tall leather boots and stood outside the villa at precisely eight o'clock. Sunglasses shielding her eyes, her bags packed and ready to go, she gave one last glance to the Atlantic shoreline and the clear azure waters lapping the sands. There would be no five-star accommodations where she was going. She was told to expect rustic and that was fine with her. She'd gone camping before; she knew how to rough it.

Sort of. Jasmine had convinced her once to rent a motor home and they'd trekked as far as Pismo Beach, California. They'd parked the giant thing facing the ocean, and then had gone out for lunch and dinner every night. They'd hit a few clubs, too, dancing until dawn. So maybe that wasn't roughing it per se.

But they had cooked their own breakfasts and hiked the beach in the mornings. Did that count?

One of Juan Carlos's bodyguards drove up in a black SUV, right on time. Poker-faced, he promptly opened the door for her and she got into the backseat as he hoisted her luggage into the cargo space.

As they drove off, she sat quietly in the car, enjoying the sounds of morning, excitement flowing through her veins.

She'd taken Juan Carlos at his word. He would treat her as a professional and so she had nothing to fear and everything to look forward to. Her little heartfelt speech seemed to convince him that she wasn't looking for romantic involvement. Surprisingly, it hadn't been hard admitting her failings to him. He'd put her at ease and that was saying something, since she didn't go around revealing her innermost feelings to anyone but her best friend.

They drove away from the shore, through the streets of Playa del Onda and onto a highway that led inland. "Excuse me. When will we be picking up King Montoro?" she asked Eduardo, the driver-slash-bodyguard.

"His Majesty will be meeting you there," he said.

Ah...discretion.

"Is it a long drive?"

"Not overly so. We should arrive in less than an hour. Is there anything you need, Princess?"

"No, no. I'm perfectly comfortable."

She gazed out the window taking in the scenery, where residential streets were soon replaced by more rural-looking spaces. As the minutes ticked by, the groomed vegetation bordering the road gave way to untamed brush and wildflowers. There was a certain neglected beauty to the land that inspired her. The road though was becoming less and less car friendly. The tires spit broken gravel as they traveled along a bumpy country road.

"Sorry, Princess," Eduardo said. "The road is washed out from here on."

"Is it much longer?"

"No, just another mile or two."

And shortly, he turned onto a path and drove through

wrought-iron gates clawed by fingers of dead branches
and vines. Weeds and overgrown scrub led to a two-story
house in desperate need of a good solid paint job. Banging
sounds reached her ears and she searched for the source
as the car came to a stop in front of the house. Juan Carlos
appeared on the porch holding a hammer, his shirt slung
open and sweat glistening on his beautiful bronzed chest.
His dark hair gleaming under the October sunshine, he
gave her a wide welcoming smile.

She sucked oxygen in. If she could slither away in a
trembling mass, she would. She could order Eduardo to
turn the car around, drive and keep on driving until she
forgot the exact chestnut color of Juan Carlos's eyes, the
deep dark shine of his hair and the powerful rock-solid
muscle of his body.

She bit her lower lip until it pained her.

As he made his approach, she bucked up and remembered why she was here, and the promise Juan Carlos had
made to her. Now, if she could get her heart to stop racing…

"Welcome," he said, opening the door wide for her. He
offered her his hand and helped her out of the car. Eyes
shining, his smile broadened. "I hope your trip wasn't too
uncomfortable."

"No, no. It was fine," she said, looking beyond him to
the house.

"Sorry about my appearance."

She nearly choked on her own saliva. Was he kidding?

"I found some loose planks on the porch. They could
be dangerous."

"You're handy with a hammer?"

"You sound surprised. Actually, I had a lot of odd jobs
in my younger days. My uncle believed in hard work and
I was always employed during my college years."

"Doing?"

"All sorts of things. Remind me to tell you about the time I worked at a strip club in Miami."

"You were a stripper?"

The image of him shedding his clothes made her mouth water.

"I didn't say that. But I sure got a quick education." Her eye fluttered and he squeezed her hand. "There's that wink again. I'm very happy you're here, Portia."

"It's not a wink," she assured him.

He smiled again and released her hand. Breath quietly swooshed out of her mouth.

"Let me assure you, the inside of the house is in better shape than the outside. Bella and James had two bedrooms renovated upstairs and my crew made sure the kitchen and living space are clean and functioning."

She flinched at the mention of the bedrooms and slid a glimpse at Eduardo, who was removing her luggage, appearing stoic as ever. "That's…fine."

She only wished that Juan Carlos would button his shirt so that she could breathe freely again.

Eduardo stopped at the steps with her two suitcases. "Just leave them. I'll take it from here," Juan Carlos said. "Thanks, Eduardo."

The man nodded, but it looked more like a bow. "Your Highness."

Juan Carlos rolled his eyes.

She chuckled. It would take him a while to get used to being royalty.

"Stop laughing," he whispered out of earshot of his bodyguard.

"I'll try," she whispered back. "Not promising anything."

He shook his head but grinned like a schoolboy.

She was up against massive charm and a killer body.

"Let me show you around." Juan Carlos took her arm and guided her inside.

The living room was cozy with a large brick fireplace and old wood floors that looked as though they'd been scoured and polished. A new patterned rug was laid down between two sofas covered with floral tapestry pillows. The smell of fresh drying paint filled the room.

"Come see the kitchen," he said, taking her hand. "It's rustic, but I didn't have the heart to replace everything. I'm assured the oven is in working order." The oven was indeed, quaint and lovely. She could tell it, too, had been scoured to a new brilliance, but it must date back to the 1940s. The refrigerator had been replaced, and the counters were chipped in places but the sink had passed the test of time. A kitchen table sat in front of windows overlooking the backyard grounds. Someone had recently plowed the area and planted a garden of fresh flowers and herbs so the immediate view was quite picturesque.

"It's charming the way it is."

"The refrigerator is stocked. Would you like a cold drink?"

"Sure."

He opened the door and peeked inside. "Lemonade, soda, orange juice and sparkling water."

"Lemonade sounds good. I'll get the glasses." She flipped open a few cupboards and found them. It was obvious the dinnerware and glassware were all new, or imported from the palace. "Here we go." She set two glasses in front of him on the counter and he filled them.

A cool, refreshing swallow quenched her thirst and as she sipped, she strolled through the kitchen, exploring. She passed a utility room and then entered a large bathroom. Juan Carlos was just steps behind her and prickles of awareness climbed up her spine. She felt his eyes on her and as she turned slowly, he didn't even try to look away. He was in the doorway, his arms braced on the doorjamb, his shirt hanging open loosely from his shoulders. All that pure masculinity in one man didn't seem fair.

He stared at her for long seconds, until regret seemed to dull the gleam in his eyes. She had the same regret. If only she was just a woman and he was just a man and they were here together, sharing a grand adventure.

She swiveled around, pretending interest in a claw-foot tub, running a finger along the porcelain edge. "Makes you wonder about what life was like here when the farm was active." She turned to him again. "Do you know if there were animals?"

"Hmm. I think so. There are many outer buildings on the acreage. Supply sheds, barns and feed shacks. They owned livestock. Probably sheep, maybe cattle, but definitely horses. Do you ride?"

"Horses? Yes, I do. I'm no expert but I know how to plant my butt in the saddle."

He smiled.

"Will we be riding?"

"Possibly. There's five thousand acres here to investigate. Between the Jeep and the horses, we should be able to scour the entire grounds. The horses will be here this afternoon."

"Did your family ever live here?"

"I don't think a Salazar ever lived here. But a Montoro must have at some point. This land is all part of the Montoro holdings."

"Do you have any idea where to start looking?"

"I'm thinking we should stick close to the house today and if we come up empty, we can venture out tomorrow."

"Sounds good. I have to admit, I'm eager to start."

"Okay, then I'll get your luggage. Your room is upstairs at the end of the hallway. It's been painted and furniture was brought in yesterday. Take some time to relax. I think you'll like the room, but if there's anything you need, just let me know."

"I'm sure it's fine." She'd roughed it with Jasmine, after

all. She really could handle her own luggage, but His Majesty would never allow that. His sense of gentlemanly duty would become tarnished. And darn, if she didn't find that amazingly appealing. "Thank you."

As she headed upstairs, a sigh escaped from her lips.

Juan Carlos was a big juicy ripe apple, dangling his unabashed charm and beautiful body in front of her.

And the wicked serpent in her head was daring her to take a bite.

Four

Portia's room was more than adequate. A queen-size bed, adorned with Egyptian cotton sheets, a snowy comforter and pale pink pillows took up most of the space. Southern light streamed into the room through twin windows with ruffled curtains and an exquisitely crafted armoire made of inlaid mahogany and cherrywood held the bulk of her clothes.

She glanced out one window to the unkempt grounds below. The Montoros owned all the land as far as her eyes could see. Would they find the hidden artwork somewhere out there? Her belly warmed to the idea. She was grateful for the opportunity to search for it.

And ready.

As she headed for the stairs, movement caught her eye from a room at the opposite end of the landing. Juan Carlos was in his bedroom, changing his shirt. Twenty feet separated them, and she immediately glanced away, but not before she caught sight of bare broad shoulders tapering down to a trim waist. She gulped and scurried down the stairs before she got caught ogling him.

She wandered outside into the yard. Birds flitted between tree branches and flew away. She knew the bodyguards were out here somewhere, watching over the place, but she'd yet to see anyone else since Eduardo had deposited her here this morning.

She heard the door open and close behind her and footsteps crunching the fallen leaves as Juan Carlos approached. "Where are they? I know they are out there somewhere," she said.

He chuckled. "Luis and Eduardo have orders not to disturb us unless there's danger. They're here, trust me."

"I'm not worried." She put on a pair of sunglasses.

"That's good. How do you like your room?" He sidled up next to her. Dressed in jeans and a chambray shirt, with a black felt hat shading his eyes, he looked like a modern-day Spanish vaquero.

"It's better than I imagined, considering the state of the grounds around us. I'm sure you had a hand in making it comfortable for me."

He shrugged. "If you're comfortable, that's all that matters. Let's check out what we can on foot. There's a stable and a few broken-down buildings nearby." He reached into his back pocket and came up with a pair of work gloves. "Here, put these on."

She slipped them on. "I'm ready." And off they went.

The stable was in ruins, like pretty much everything else on the property. As they entered, she spied a wagon wheel, some rusted harnesses and a stack of rotted grain bags. It didn't seem as though anything could be hidden in here, but Juan Carlos touched every wall, kicked clean every stall and scoured the entire area with assessing eyes.

She took his cue, and searched the outside perimeter of the building, looking for anything that could be used as a hiding place.

He met her outside. "Nothing here. I didn't think we'd find anything this close to the house, but we need to be thorough."

"Okay, where next?"

"There's some feed shacks farther out we should check. Are you up for a long walk?"

She stared into his eyes. "You know that pea under my mattress didn't ruin my sleep last night."

He gave her a look of mock concern. "There was a pea under your mattress, Princess? Twenty lashes for the chambermaid who made up your bed last night."

She grinned. "More like fifty lashes for the king who thinks I can't keep up with him."

"Okay, I get your point. You're not frail."

"Not one little bit. But I think your concern is sweet."

"And antiquated."

"That, too. But what woman doesn't dream of a knight in shining armor once in a while?"

He peered directly into her eyes. "Do you?"

"I'm...not going to tell."

With that, she dashed ahead of him and hoped she was heading in the right direction.

Juan Carlos's laughter reached her ears, but he hung back a little, watching her.

She came upon three outer buildings, each one fifty feet or so from the others. She was just about to enter one when Juan Carlos called out, "Portia, wait!"

She whirled around. He came marching toward her, making up their distance in long strides. "Let's do this together."

He was being overprotective again. "I don't see why I can't—"

"Humor me," he said, sweeping up her hand and tugging her inside with him.

The small shed was in better shape than the stable had been. Juan Carlos remarked on how it was a newer building, perhaps added on later as the farm prospered. The open door allowed a sliver of light inside the windowless and otherwise dark space. Juan Carlos released her hand and the tingles streaming down her arm finally eased.

He got down on his knees and scoured the floorboards, looking for a trap door while she tapped at the walls. She tugged at a splintered hoe leaning against the far wall, moving it out of her way. A deafening hiss broke the silence. She looked down and saw a snake coiling around her boot. Panicking, she gasped quietly.

Juan Carlos jumped up. "Don't move!"

She froze. Oh, God, no. "What should I do? What should I do?" The thing was moving up her leg.

"Hold still, sweetheart. Trust me."

Juan Carlos reached into his boot and a glint of silver caught her eye. A knife?

There was a flash of movement as he lunged forward, and she squeezed her eyes shut. He ripped the thing off her in seconds flat. When she opened her eyes, she saw that he'd slashed the snake's neck all the way through. Juan Carlos tossed the dead reptile, head and all, across the shed. It landed with a smack and her stomach recoiled.

She shook uncontrollably and Juan Carlos took her into his arms. "You're okay, Portia. You're okay, sweetheart."

Tears spilled from her eyes and she nodded.

"Let's get outside," he said softly.

"I don't know if I can move."

"You can. I'll help you."

She nodded. "Okay." She clung to him as he guided her into the daylight. Fresh air filled her lungs and helped with her shaking.

"I'm sorry," he said, over and over, kissing her forehead.

She held his neck tight. She'd never been so frightened in her life. It all happened so fast, but the thought of that thing crawling up her body would surely give her nightmares for days to come.

"No, she'll be fine. I've got this," he was saying to someone, shaking his head. Then he turned his attention back to her. "Sweetheart, we'll go back to the house now."

"Who were you talking to?" She glanced past his shoulders and caught Eduardo gazing at her for a second before he lowered his eyes.

"We can walk, unless you want Eduardo to drive us back to the house?"

"No." She clung to Juan Carlos tighter, still shocked. She wasn't ready to let go. "No, we have more to do."

He ran his hand over her ponytail, like a father would a child. "But not today, Portia." His voice was gentle. "Not if you're not up to it."

She glanced to where Eduardo had been standing. He'd disappeared.

"Just hold me a little longer, please."

"Of course." One hand ran comforting circles on her back.

"I...I guess you have your answer." She spoke into his shirt, still too freaked out to back away.

"What do you mean?"

"You're my knight in shining armor today."

"Just today?" There was amusement in his voice and Portia couldn't deny how safe she felt being in his protective arms.

"Hmm." To say more would be too revealing. She was vulnerable right now and had let her guard down with him. She didn't want to let go of him. She needed his strength. He bolstered her courage.

"I guess, I'll settle for that," he said.

She tipped her chin up and gazed into his eyes. It would be so easy to kiss him now, to thank him for saving her from that creature.

"Portia," he whispered. His gaze tumbled down to her lips and the longing in his voice tortured her.

Debating with herself, she closed her eyes.

She heard him sigh deeply as one hand gripped her shoulders. He gave a little shove and she stumbled back and then blinked. He'd set her away deliberately. She focused on the blade he still held in his other hand and the image of that snake's split body flashed again in her mind.

A tick worked at his jaw, beating an erratic rhythm. "You test my honor, Portia. I made you a promise."

"I…know."

He put his head down, not meeting her eyes, and then bent to wipe the blade clean on the grass. One, two, three slashes were all that he needed. Then he stood and sheathed the knife, placing it in his waistband. "Come," he said, reaching for her gloved hand. "We should go."

"Yes. I can make it to the other shacks now."

He nodded and led the way.

"Here." Juan Carlos set a glass of whiskey into her hand. "Take a few sips and drink slowly." She sat on the sofa near the fireplace and kept her eyes focused on the jumping blue-orange flames. They sizzled and popped and brought warmth to the cool evening. "You'll need it to calm down."

"I'm calm." She wasn't really. Her body still quaked inside even as she sipped the numbing whiskey. The thought of that snake wrapped around her made her stomach curl. Yuck, it was disgusting. And frightening. Juan Carlos had been wonderful. He'd stayed by her side and comforted her, and hadn't balked when she'd insisted on continuing on their search. Though he'd made a thorough check of the next two buildings for creatures before he allowed her to step foot inside. He'd told her he was proud of her. It hadn't been courage on her part, but rather sheer stubborn determination that made her put one foot in front of the other and kept her from running back to the house for refuge. They hadn't found a thing in those other sheds, not one clue as to the whereabouts of the treasure, and she'd been ridiculously happy to return to the house after they'd exhausted their foot search.

"How's that going down?" he asked.

"Smooth. I'm not usually a hard drinker."

"But you needed something tonight."

"I'm not usually such a wimp, either," she said, smiling awkwardly. She'd felt like an idiot for panicking after Juan Carlos explained that the snake probably wasn't poisonous or deadly, but her fear was real, and he'd understood that. Rather than take a chance, he'd done the manly thing. He'd killed the culprit. Her knight.

"You were very brave. You kept your cool."

"You mean I froze in panic?"

He stared at her from his perch atop the sofa arm. "I'm sorry you had to go through that. I promise nothing like that will ever happen to you again. I'm very cautious. I'll take care to secure the site before you go pouncing."

"I don't *pounce*," she said.

"Don't you?" He smiled over his glass and sipped whiskey. "I had to stop you from going inside by yourself."

"I didn't know there would be snakes."

He arched his brows. "All the more reason for us to stick closer together."

"Can't get much closer than this," she said, chuckling. Oh, but yes, they could, and Juan Carlos's arched brow, the amusement in his eyes, said he was thinking the same thing. The thought of sleeping just down the hall from him tonight killed her laughter. The alcohol was already affecting her brain, and her rational thinking. She set her glass down, looking into the amber liquid that remained. She needed her wits about her. It would be too easy to fall into lust with the king. "I think I'll be okay now. What's the plan for tomorrow?"

He thought about it a few seconds. "Tomorrow, we go out on horseback. There's some terrain I want to explore that we can't get to with the Jeep."

"Are the horses here?"

He nodded. "They arrived this afternoon. Eduardo and Luis have stabled them."

"You've thought of everything, Your Highness."

"Juan Carlos."

She grinned. "I'm sorry. Still can't get there."

He shrugged, and it dawned on her that she needed that wall of separation in order to remind herself who he was. She'd do better to think of him as a monarch, rather than a man.

"Are you getting hungry?" he asked, and she was glad he didn't press the issue.

"A little." It was after six and up until now, she hadn't thought about food.

"Wait here, I'll be right back."

He rose and entered the kitchen. She heard him rustling around in there, opening the refrigerator door and banging shut the cupboards. The dance of lights in the fireplace mesmerized her for the few minutes he was gone.

Juan Carlos returned with a plate of delicacy cheeses, a bunch of deep red grapes and a loaf of bread. "I hope this will satisfy your hunger. If not, I can cook a few steaks and bake some potatoes."

"No, this is perfect. I don't think I could eat much more."

"Want to sit in front of the fire?"

"Sure." She grabbed a fringy knit throw blanket hanging over the sofa and fanned it out in front of the fireplace. Juan Carlos waited for her to sit, and then handed her the plates before taking his seat facing her.

"This is nice, thank you." She arranged the plates in front of them.

The flickering flames cocooned them in a warm halo of light. She nibbled on the cheese and bread. Miles away from the city, she was at peace in this farmhouse.

She reached for a grape, and met with Juan Carlos's hand as he did the same. Their fingers touched and she lifted her eyes to him. He was staring at her, as if memorizing the way she looked right now. Her heart began to beat faster. Their gazes remained locked for a second, and then she tore a bunch of grapes off and popped one into her mouth.

Outside, breezes blew, making the windows rattle. The distant sound of horses whinnying carried on the wind and she pictured them in their stalls. How long had it been since there was life in those stalls? She hoped the winds wouldn't frighten the animals.

"What is it?" he asked.

"I'm just wondering if the horses are okay out there. The stable walls aren't solid anymore."

"I was going to check on them after you went to bed."

"I'd like to see them."

He pulled air into his lungs and nodded, as if convincing himself of his suggestion. "Then you'll join me."

Juan Carlos held a battery-powered lantern in one hand and Portia's hand in the other. He hadn't planned on spending more time with her tonight. Holding her shaking body and consoling her after the snake incident had stirred a possessive streak in him. He'd wanted to protect her from harm and keep her safe, but having her melt into him, her heartbreaking tears soaking his shirt, had sliced him up inside. He could have held her for hours and not tired of it, yet they'd continued on their search and he'd cursed that damn promise he'd made to her. He'd been desperate to get her to stay on in Alma. And he'd had to agree to her terms with a promise he hoped like hell he could uphold.

Tonight, he'd thought to escape her. Maybe he would have had a drink with Eduardo and Luis or taken a late-night ride, or simply waited until Portia was safely ensconced in her bedroom before making it up to his room. Yet he couldn't refuse Portia her request to join him in the stables.

So here he was, gritting his teeth as she walked beside him under the stars. The stables weren't far and he'd given the bodyguards strict orders to watch without being seen. They were out there somewhere.

The night air had grown cooler, and Portia wrapped both of her arms around herself despite her coat. She might've shivered once or twice.

"Cold?"

"Yes, but I'm okay. I have Scandinavian blood flowing through my veins. Cold weather doesn't bother me."

Juan Carlos hunkered down into his jacket. He'd lived in Miami most of his life. Neither Florida nor Alma got down into freezing temperatures very often. He could tolerate cold weather, but it wasn't his favorite thing. "This is about as cold as it gets here," he said. "At least that's what I'm told."

"It's mostly the wind I don't like."

Right on cue, a howling gust blew from the north. She shivered again and on impulse, he wrapped his free arm over her shoulder and drew her close.

She looked up at him.

"Thanks for keeping me warm," he said.

"Yes, Your Majesty. Anything for the king." A teasing smile played at her lips.

He laughed.

Before long they reached the stables.

"Want me to go in and check for snakes?"

She drew a breath and glanced around the property completely encased in darkness. "I have a feeling it's safer inside than out."

She had a point. There could be all manner of animals roaming the land. Wolves, wild boars and lynx were indigenous to the area. "Okay, then stick close to me."

"You still have your knife?"

"Of course."

"Then you won't be able to shake me."

"I wouldn't even try," he said, quite honestly.

A hum ran through her body. His subtle compliments did crazy things for her ego. After what she'd been through with Miles, that part of her brain had needed nourishment and was now being fed day in and day out by His Hunkiness the King.

She gasped.

"What is it?"

"Oh, nothing. I was just thinking." Jasmine would have a good laugh over this one. Portia was resorting to using terms from a romance novel to describe the handsome, honorable Juan Carlos Salazar II, King of Montoro.

He gripped her hand and led her into the stables. The protective way he held her was another turn-on.

The lantern lit up about five feet of the path in front of them. The place was dank and colder than she'd hoped for the animals. Juan Carlos lifted the lantern to his shoulder and illuminated the stalls. There were shuffling sounds, whinnies and snorts as all four horses came into view. Beauties.

They were curious enough to approach their individual gates. Though she'd been here earlier, Portia could see hints of work done today to make the stable more secure for the horses. The stalls had been shored up, and beds of straw had been laid down. Holes in the walls letting in cold air had been hastily boarded up. Juan Carlos knew how to get things done.

Her eyes darted to the animals' backs. "They're wearing blankets."

"To keep warm. I put Luis on it tonight. They seem comfortable enough, don't they?"

She smiled, relieved. "Yes, I feel better now. They are amazing creatures. Are they yours? I mean do they belong to the palace?"

"We haven't had time to build a remuda of horses for the palace. The transition takes time, but we will have a royal guard on horseback one day soon. These horses belong to me personally, as of two days ago. I have it on good authority they are gentle and trustworthy. I've yet to ride any of them. Tomorrow will be a good test."

"For them or for you?"

His brow arched. "Maybe for all of us."

"Maybe," she agreed. "I've never claimed to be an expert, but I do love animals. What are their names?"

"Come. Let me introduce you." Straw crunched underfoot as they made their way to the first stall. "This is Julio. He's a two-year-old gelding," Juan Carlos said. The sleek charcoal-colored horse had a thick black mane and tail. "He's an Andalusian."

"The horse of kings," she said.

"Yes, I've heard them referred to that way."

"Because they're powerful and sturdy?"

"Because they're intelligent and docile."

She eyed the commanding animal in front of her. He was gorgeous. "Docile?"

"Not as hot-blooded as a thoroughbred. He'll be my mount."

Julio was tall and grand. His curious ink-black eyes watched her. She lifted her hand to him cautiously and he edged closer. She took that as an invitation to stroke the side of his face. "That's it, boy. You and I are going to be good friends," she crooned. Back in Los Angeles, she volunteered at an animal rescue when she wasn't working. Her lifestyle and schedule didn't allow having a pet of her own and she enjoyed donating her time to animals in need.

"You're good with him."

She touched her cheek to Julio's cold nose and he nuzzled her throat eagerly. The force pushed her back a step and she righted herself and giggled. "Oh, he is sweet."

Juan Carlos's gaze touched upon her. Something flickered in his eyes. He swallowed and stroked his hand over his chin. He hadn't shaved today, and his stubble only added to his good looks.

With an inward sigh, she focused back on Julio, giving his mane a solid but loving stroke. She sensed that she had indeed made a new friend today.

Juan Carlos tugged her along to the next stall. "This is Sugar. She's an Arabian. Quick, sharp and good-natured. You'll ride her tomorrow."

"Hello, Sugar. You're a pretty one."

Sugar wasn't as tall or commanding as Julio, but was equally as stately. She had sensitive eyes and seemed friendly. Her chestnut coat glistened under the lantern light. "I'll see you in the morning, girl."

Juan Carlos showed her the other two horses, Arabians named Estrella and Manzana, who were presumably for Eduardo and Luis. Were the king's bodyguards good riders? Was that part of their job description?

New feedbags hung from nails in the walls, replacing the shredded ones from this morning, and a bag of carrots sat on a splintered bench. "Can we give them a treat?"

"Good idea." Juan Carlos went to retrieve the carrots. He dipped his hand inside the bag and came up with four. "One for each."

"Only one?"

"We don't want to spoil them."

"I bet you'd be a tough disciplinarian with your children."

At the mention of children his eyes twinkled and somehow the mischief seemed aimed directly at her. "I'm ready to find out."

Her blood warmed. She hadn't thought along those lines for herself. Parenthood was a long way off for her. But Juan Carlos seemed to know exactly what he wanted. He was resolute, an action taker and at times, he intimated her with his decisiveness. "You want a family one day?"

"Of course…I've lived my life without my parents. I have

no brothers or sisters, although I have my cousins and we have been on good terms. But to have a child of my own, to share that bond with someone I love…it's a dream of mine."

He handed her all four carrots and she walked the stalls, allowing Sugar to nibble at hers first.

"I would think being king would be your dream."

"It's my duty and a role I'm proud to uphold. But a man can have more than one dream, can't he?"

His eyes darkened, his gaze boring into her like a nail being hammered into the wall. He was too close, his expression telling her too much. She couldn't look at him and not see his life all planned out…with her beside him. Were the limited lighting and her silly imagination playing tricks on her?

She turned away from him, taking interest in the horses again. "I suppose." Three beggars were vying for her attention, shuffling their feet, bobbing their heads back and forth. She walked over to Julio next. "Here you go, boy."

Juan Carlos shadowed her to the next two stalls and watched her feed the other Arabians. "Do I make you nervous, Princess?"

Her eyes crinkled as she squeezed them closed. Why did he have to ask her that? She took a breath to steady her nerves and pivoted around. Her back to the stall door, the lie was ready to fall from her lips. Her one eye fluttered, like a wink, but certainly *not* a wink. Oh, boy. She wanted to sink into a black hole. "Y-yes." Damn her honesty. So much for pretending disinterest in him.

Juan Carlos gave her an approving smile as if he'd expected her answer. As if he was pleased with her honesty. "I promised not to pursue you, Portia. But I didn't say I would back off if you came to me. If you decided you wanted me, craved my body as I do yours, I would claim you in an instant and not feel I'd betrayed my vow to you."

He took her hand then, and led her out of the stable. "Come, it's time for bed."

Five

Sugar kept an even pace with Julio as they ambled farther out onto the property. The horse was gentle, took commands well and her sure-footed gait put Portia at ease. She gazed at the cloudless blue sky above. The warmth of the rising sun removed the bite of coolness in the morning air and made the ride pleasant.

Juan Carlos's felt hat shaded his eyes. Portia had put her hat on, too, one that Juan Carlos, who planned for everything, had given her to wear.

"How are you doing?" Juan Carlos asked after five minutes of silence.

"I have no complaints, Your Highness."

He paused. Gosh, why did she goad him? Oh, yeah, to put distance between them. "We've been riding a while now. Is your rear end sore?"

She chuckled. "A little, but I'll survive."

"You just let me know when you want to take a break."

Things had been a little weird between them since last night. Juan Carlos had put a bug in her ear. He'd given her an out. Up until then, her idea to keep their relationship strictly platonic had rested solely on Juan Carlos's shoulders. She'd made him promise to keep his distance. But now he'd tossed the ball into her court. And it had gotten her thinking. But it wasn't a good thing for a woman desperately attracted to a man who was all wrong for her to be given those options.

If you decided you wanted me, craved my body as I do yours...

Those hot words had thrown her. She'd thought of them, of him, all through the night. What would it be like to have Juan Carlos make love to her? What if, here, in this remote, private place, she gave in to temptation and spent the night touching him and being touched. Kissing his perfect mouth, running her cheek along that sexy stubble and nibbling on his throat? What would it be like to have him inside her, the steely velvet of his erection impaling her body?

She squirmed in the saddle, suddenly uncomfortable. Mentally, she forbade Juan Carlos to look over, to see her struggling with thoughts he'd planted inside her head. *Don't look at me. Don't see the expression on my face. Don't see me...wanting you.*

"Portia?"

Darn it. "I'm fine." She stared straight ahead. "Everything's good and dandy."

She sensed him studying her as they rode the length of five football fields until they came upon a graveyard surrounded by a run-down picket fence. The square of ground was full of weeds, unkempt. The neglect was almost sacrilegious. It was out in the middle of nowhere, a place long forgotten.

Juan Carlos slowed his gelding and she did the same. "We'll stop here," he said.

Her rear end rejoiced. She spotted trees that offered perfect shade just yards away. The horses moved toward an oak, massive in size, its roots splayed in all directions.

Juan Carlos dismounted quickly and strode to her. Sugar wasn't as tall as Julio, but Portia still needed help with her dismount. Either that, or run the risk of breaking an ankle when she tried to slide down the horse's left flank.

Juan Carlos's arms were up, reaching for her. She swung her leg over the saddle and his hands found her waist, securing her with a firm grip and guiding her down until her boots hit the ground. He held her for a few beats of time, with her back to his chest, his nose tickling her neck, breathing in her hair. "You smell delicious," he whispered, and then released her.

She sighed. If only she didn't miss his hold on her. Didn't enjoy having him touch her.

I would claim you in an instant and not feel I'd betrayed my vow to you.

He stood beside Julio, gazing at the graveyard as he unlatched a saddlebag and came up with a bottle of water. He walked over to her. "Here," he said. "Take a drink, you must be thirsty."

The water, cool and refreshing, slid down her throat. "That's good." She handed it back to him. His mouth clamped around the lip of the bottle and he tipped it back. He swallowed a big gulp, then another. A trickle of sweat ran down his forehead and he wiped it away.

Simple gestures. Yet her heart raced being near him, sharing water, doing natural things that seemed to bind them together.

"I'd like to check out the graveyard. You can stay here and rest. I'll put a blanket down. You'll be in the shade."

She shook her head. She was curious about the graveyard, too. "I'll come with you."

He nodded and began walking. She followed behind. Wind kicked up and almost blew her hat off. She grabbed it just in time and held it to her head as she approached a wooden gate. Overhead, tree branches made a makeshift archway, and scrolled in wood a sign read: Montoro Family Cemetery.

"So this is where the farm families ended up," she said.

Juan Carlos nodded. "They were probably distant cousins, relatives of my uncles. I'd bet Tantaberra made sure no one has ever come to honor their graves."

They walked through the battered gate. There were many headstones, maybe twenty-five in all. Portia stopped beside Juan Carlos as he bent his head in prayer over one after another. She sent up her own prayers for the lives forgotten here, stepping from one grave site to the next. "Do you know any of these names?" she asked.

"Some sound familiar," he said. The first and middle initials were etched on the headstones along with the last names. "Montoro, of course, and Olivio I've heard mentioned, but many I don't know. I will have this cemetery restored to honor their graves."

Juan Carlos insisted on clearing away the larger of the weeds that had overgrown the area. She bent to help him. "No, please. Your hands will be cut," he said.

"I'll be careful. I want to help." Her chin up, she was ready to do him battle.

He stared at her. "I forgot to bring you gloves." And then he warned, "See that you are careful, Princess."

She smiled and something tugged at her heart. He was angry with himself for the oversight. "I promise to be careful."

He began to pull away tumbleweeds clustered around the graves, staring at the names embedded on the stones as if embedding them into his brain. She, too, had little family. She could see the sadness and the loss in the contoured planes of his face, in the shadows of his dark eyes. The dictatorship had taken so much from his family.

"Let me see your hands," he said when they were all through. They'd cleared away as much as they possibly could. The wind was howling; breezes that had cooled the day's heat were swirling more rapidly now.

She turned her palms up.

Juan Carlos inspected her hands carefully, turning them one way then another.

"See. I'm not a wimpy princess."

He laughed, the shine returning to his eyes. "I'd never describe you that way. I'm grateful for your help."

"You're welcome. But there's one more thing to do."

His right eyebrow shot up. "What would that be?"

"I'll be right back. Don't follow me. I'll only be ten minutes."

She left him in the graveyard. This was something she wanted to do by herself. For his family. He leaned against the post outside the cemetery and watched her march into the fields. Every time she turned, his gaze was glued to her. He wouldn't let her out of his sight. She got that. He was a protector by nature. Gallant. He didn't interfere with her independence though and she appreciated that.

Ten minutes later, she returned to the Montoro family cemetery. Juan Carlos smiled broadly as he gazed at the large bunch of wildflowers she'd gathered in her hands. Some were probably classified as weeds, but they were indisputably pretty anyway. Bluebonnet blues, pale yellows, creamy whites and carnation pinks.

"Would you like to help me lay these down?"

He nodded, a play of deep emotion on his face.

They walked through the cemetery one last time, offering up the flowers to grave sites and headstones to tell the deceased that someone remembered them. Someone cared.

They left the place quietly, Juan Carlos taking her hand. It was a solemn moment, but a sweet one, too. Portia was moved by the care he'd taken with his distant relatives, the honor he'd bestowed upon them.

How many would have just ridden past? How many wouldn't have bothered to stop and clear up the neglect and mess?

This feeling she had for Juan Carlos wasn't going away. It grew stronger each moment she spent in his company.

The horses whinnied upon their return, huffing breaths and stomping hooves. Juan Carlos dipped into the saddlebag again, this time to offer the animals a handful of oats to keep them satisfied. "There, now. You two be quiet. No more complaining." He stroked Julio's head a few times and then turned to Portia. "Let's sit a minute. Take a rest."

"All right."

He grabbed a blanket and spread it out under the tree. The shade was no longer an issue; the weather had cooled and gray clouds were gathering in the skies. She shivered and walked to her saddlebag, picking out a jacket from the things she'd brought along.

"Cold?"

"A little bit."

"We can head back."

It was too early to return to the house. They had more ground to cover and she didn't want to delay their mission because of a little cold weather. Her family hailed from Scandinavia, where food was put out on windowsills to freeze quickly, where the elderly lived over one hundred years because germs couldn't survive the environment. She refused to slow Juan Carlos down.

"Ten minutes is all I need," she said.

She put on the jacket and sat down. He sat next to her and roped his arm around her. It seemed only natural to put her head on his shoulder.

"There is a giant rock formation about half an hour from here. The terrain is rough but these horses can make it up there. I found it on a GPS map of the area." His voice soothed her even as he spoke of a tough task. She closed her eyes. "I think it's a good hiding place for the artwork. I suspect caves have formed between the interlocking rocks. At least, that's what I'm hoping."

"Sounds reasonable. We'll check it out."

"Are you up for it? We can return tomorrow if you're not."

"I'm up for it," she said. "We're already halfway there, aren't we?"

"Yes, but the weather might be a problem."

"It won't be, Juan Carlos. I'm not a wimpy princess, remember?"

Laughter rumbled from his chest. "How can I forget? You keep reminding me."

"Good," she said, snuggling deeper into his arms.

The solid beats of his heart were like the revving of a powerful engine. It was dangerous and thrilling and though she hated to move, it was time to break this cozy moment with him. She slid away from his grip and rose to her feet. "I'm ready when you are."

He bounded up, regret in his eyes, as if she'd taken something precious from him.

From both of them.

The rocks were adobe-red, huge and intimidating. They were also beautiful against the landscape of gray skies and brown earth. The horses treaded with agility through the gravelly terrain, their sure-footed gait assuring her she would not fall to her death as they climbed a plateau that led to the face of the mountain. "This is amazing. It reminds me of Sedona back in the States. Have you ever been there?"

"In Arizona?" Juan Carlos gave his head a shake. "No, but I've seen pictures. It's an artist colony, isn't it?"

"Yes, among other things. There are some wonderful galleries and art exhibits in the area. I studied there one summer."

"Did you ever climb the rocks?"

She nibbled her lower lip. "I'd been tempted a few times, but no, I didn't climb the rocks. I was there for the art. Are we climbing rocks today?" she asked pointedly.

Juan Carlos spread his gaze over the entire mountainside, studying the terrain. "Just like back then, you came here for the art. So no. We don't have to climb the rocks.

The openings seem to be on the lower levels. We can reach them without climbing."

She released a tight breath. She didn't like heights and they didn't like her, so no rock climbing was a good thing. "I'm excited. I have a good feeling about this," she said. "I'm imagining the artwork tucked inside the mountain somewhere, deep inside a cave."

"Then let's go find it," he said.

He dismounted and strode over, lifting his hands to her waist again. Dust kicked up by the strong wind mingled with the potent scent of horseflesh and earth. More threatening clouds gathered above, and a shiver shook her shoulders as she slid into his arms. His hands steadied her until her boots hit the ground. Then he took the reins of both horses and they began walking toward a row of rocks, stacked neatly like building blocks five stories high.

He stopped at the base of a formation where two giant boulders separated and an opening appeared. It wasn't much wider than a double-door refrigerator, but large enough to allow a man to enter. "Wait here," he said. "Stay with the horses. I'll go inside and see if it goes anywhere. It might be a dead end. I'll be back in a minute." He pulled out a flashlight and turned to her. "Okay?"

She took the reins with one hand and stroked Sugar's nose with the other. Eyeing him, Portia confessed, "I'm not very patient."

A grin crossed his features, that gorgeous mouth of his lifting crookedly. "Good to know."

For real? The man had a one-track mind. "Come and get me, if you find anything."

"Will do. We're in this together," he said, and then disappeared into the gap.

Just then, the wind knocked her back against the rocks. It was fierce today. She huddled behind the horses, allowing them to block the sharp bite of cold. Her teeth chattered anyway. Goodness, it seemed as if Juan Carlos had already been gone for hours but it was more like a minute or two.

Then she heard his approach, his footfalls scraping the ground of the cave. Thank God. A thrill shimmied through her belly. She really wasn't patient, not when it came to this. If only they could find the artwork today.

When he emerged from the opening, she took one look at Juan Carlos's expression and her shoulders slumped. "You didn't find it?"

He shook his head. "Not in there." His eyes were solemn as they toured over her face and body. "You're freezing."

"I'm…not."

His lips twisted at her denial. Then he turned away from her and grappled with both of their saddlebags, freeing them from their fasteners and tossing them over his shoulder. "Come," he said, handing her their blankets. "It's warmer inside. Besides, there is something I want to show you."

"Really? What is it?"

"You'll see." He took her frigid hand and immediately the blood began pulsing more warmly through her veins. One would think he was a flaming hot furnace with how easily his touch could heat her up through and through.

He led her into the darkness. The flashlight illuminated the way and she squinted as her eyes adjusted. Around her, stone walls made up a cavelike space, tall enough for them to stand in and wide enough for an entire hunting party to take refuge. The air inside was cool, but without the outside wind gusts it was warmer by a dozen degrees. "You're right, it is warmer in here."

"Take a look at this," he said, aiming his flashlight at a far corner.

Eyes appeared first, round and frightened, and then the light followed the length of the animal, stretched out on the ground nursing her young. "Kittens!"

Five tiny bodies fought for a place at mama's table, eager for their meal. The mother cat, striped in reds, browns and grays, eyed both Juan Carlos and Portia warily. "She's scared," Portia said. "Poor mama." She'd had lots of experience with birthing pups and kittens at the rescue where she volunteered. "She might be feral, though I doubt it. She would've been hissing and scratching her way out of here by now. The babies look to be only a few weeks old."

"You think she's domestic?" he asked.

Portia crouched down, studying the cat from five feet away. "I think she's somewhere in between. She might've been abandoned. She's doing what comes natural and found this place to have her kittens. Cats like dark cool isolated places to give birth."

"Well, she found that," Juan Carlos said, keeping his voice soft. Both of them whispered now, so as not to startle the wary cat.

"I wonder if she's hungry. She looks pretty scrawny."

"About all we've got is water and sandwiches."

"Water, for sure. She'll need that. And we can pull out cheese and bits of meat from our sandwiches. If she's hungry enough, she'll eat it."

"Good idea. I'm getting hungry. Maybe we should stay inside and eat, too."

Portia kept her eyes fixed on the new little family. "I'd like that."

Outside the wind howled. The refuge they'd found would do for now until the weather let up. Portia worked with Juan Carlos to fix the mama cat a meal of beef and cheese, and laid it out on a cloth napkin. She was at a loss as to where to put the water. They had narrow-necked bottles and not much else that would work for a bowl.

"Here," Juan Carlos said, handing her his hat, tipped upside down in his palm. "She needs it more than I do."

Under the dim flashlight rays, his eyes were full of

compassion. He was a problem solver, but it was more than that. He was doing this as much for Portia's sake as he was for the sweet cat family. "You'll freeze your head off when we go back out there."

"Not if we stay here overnight."

Her heart skipped. To be alone with Juan Carlos all night? She couldn't possibly. He didn't mean it. It was hard enough knowing he was sleeping down the hallway at the farmhouse. "Surely, we can't."

His eyes twinkled. "It was a nice thought, though. Being trapped in here with you all night...*to watch over the kittens*."

Blood rushed to her cheeks. Suddenly, the cold dank cave sizzled with heat. She coughed, to cover errant thoughts of spending the night with Juan Carlos, of wearing nothing but a blanket to keep each other warm. His arms would wrap around her, and then their bare bodies would conform, mesh and he would nudge himself inside her.

"Are you okay, sweetheart?"

He knew. The sparkle in his eyes lit up even brighter.

"I'm fine."

"Are you sure?"

"Perfectly," she snapped. Goodness, she sounded like a witch.

He shrugged a shoulder, a smile teasing his lips as he handed her the cat's meal. "Do you want to take it to her?"

She nodded, recovering from the image that had sprung up in her head. "I'll try. I hope she doesn't run."

Portia took pained steps toward the cat, catching her eye and hoping her slow movements would show her she wasn't a threat. The cat's tail tensed and arched, her head came up and those tigerlike eyes watched her every move. Then she meowed.

"It's okay, sweet mama. I don't want to hurt you. Look, I have food. I hope you'll eat it."

The cat hissed, but she was just protecting her young. "This is as far as I'll go," Portia said softly. "See." She set down the napkin two feet from her and as soon as she backed away, the cat sniffed at it. "Put the hat down carefully," she said to Juan Carlos. He was only half a step behind and he set the water down next to the food. Then his hand clamped over her arm as he guided her several feet back, the beam of light dimming on the mama cat.

"Chances are, she won't eat or drink anything until she gives everything a complete smell test."

"We've done what we could for them," Juan Carlos said. "They are cute."

"Adorable," Portia said. The fuzzy fur babies were nestled against mama cat's underside, many of them satisfied and ready to nap.

Juan Carlos spread the blanket out and they began eating their sandwiches. Nibbling on her sliced steak sandwich sitting cross-legged, her eyes kept darting over to the cats.

"She'll eat eventually," Juan Carlos said.

"She's starving, but she won't make a move until we leave."

"Then we'll go as soon as we finish up here."

She nodded and within a few minutes, Portia was back atop Sugar, waiting for Juan Carlos to take his mount. She was torn about leaving the kittens in there, hoping the mama would survive the cold and be able to care for her young babes. How would she feed herself after the food they left behind was gone?

"Where to next?" Portia asked, blinking away tears, trying to distract herself from the sick feeling in her gut. She was a softie when it came to animals.

He stared into her eyes and smiled. "They'll survive. Don't worry."

He'd read her mind, but unlike most people, Portia didn't believe cats had nine lives. Sometimes, they couldn't beat the odds. If only this wasn't one of those times. She mustered a smile, but her heart wasn't in it.

"Since the wind has died down, I'd like to check out two of the nearby dwellings while we're here. If you stay put, I'll go in and be out quickly." He pointed north. "They aren't far. We'll get home before we lose light."

"I'm fine with that." She really was, though part of her wanted to stay behind and nurture the kittens. But that was impossible. Mama cat wanted no part of them right now. "I like the plan."

He nodded. "Let's go."

After showering and getting dressed, Portia marched downstairs in new jeans and a beige ribbed sweater to start dinner. She wasn't going to have Juan Carlos waiting on her. She planned to do her part. As she reached the bottom stair, she saw the fire crackling in the hearth and warmth settled around her. It was after seven; the darkened sky was lit with a scant few stars tonight. Her stomach grumbled, protesting over only having a light afternoon lunch. Thank God Juan Carlos wasn't around to hear the commotion her belly made.

The blaze in the front room beckoned. She could just as easily plop in a chair and watch the flickering fire, but she moved on and headed for the kitchen.

She found fresh tomatoes, whole garlic cloves, cans of tomato paste and packaged pasta in the cupboard. "Spaghetti it is." She wasn't a bad cook. She could crush tomatoes with the best of them.

Inside the fridge, she also found a covered dish of already cooked meatballs.

It seemed as though Juan Carlos had kitchen minions. She wasn't complaining.

She turned the stove on, grabbed a cast-iron pan, peeled and mashed two garlic cloves with a butcher knife and poured a little oil in the pan. Garlicky steam billowed up and pungent scents filled the room.

The back door opened and Juan Carlos walked in. "Mmm. Smells great in here."

"I hope you like spaghetti and meatballs."

"Who doesn't?" he said, coming to stand beside her.

"Hand me those tomatoes," she said, fully aware of his freshly groomed presence beside her.

Instead of walking to get them, he grabbed her waist with one hand from behind and stretched the other hand out as far as he could, snapping up three ripe tomatoes from the counter without leaving her side. "Here you go."

His touch sent heat spiraling through her body. "Into the pot with them, please."

"Like this?" He lowered them down gently, his face brushing against her hair.

He was a tease.

"Thank you."

"Don't you have to peel them?"

She shook her head. "The skin will peel off easily later from the heat. And then, you'll get to crush them."

"Me?"

"Yes, you. They need a manly crush."

"Well then, I'm your man."

She stopped and gazed into his eyes. Those words. They could be true. If she allowed it. Juan Carlos had owned up to his deal. He hadn't really come on to her, but every single second of every single minute of the day, he told her in his own silent, heart-melting way that he wanted her.

"Yes, well, uh…just let me get the meatballs."

How was that for a change of subject?

"I can crush those, too," he said.

She laughed. "I'm sure you can."

Dinner was half an hour later. They decided to eat in the kitchen this time, at a wooden table with inlaid painted tiles. One of the nearby windows faced the backyard garden, now bathed in starlight, and if she squinted she could see the plants. It was cozy and nice, and she'd put out a mason jar candle that cast a pretty glow over the room. Juan Carlos kept glancing at his watch as they forked spaghetti into their mouths and spoke of easy simple things. She refused to think any more about the snake with the severed head lying in that shack. Or the cemetery with so many families who'd lived here before.

After his eyes shifted to his watch once again, her curiosity got the better of her. "Am I keeping you from something?"

There was no television in the house. No important soccer games to watch. No distractions. Maybe he couldn't wait to get upstairs to finish the book he'd been reading.

He shook his head. "There's no place I'd rather be than right here."

Oh, she'd stepped into that one.

"The meal is delicious," he said.

"It was all that manly crushing," she remarked, and he put his fork down to grin at her.

She jingled in places that normally jangled. He turned her life upside down. She'd miss him when this adventure was over and she went back to LA.

She rose and grabbed up their empty plates. "Would you like another helping?"

He patted his flat, washboard stomach. "No, I'd better stop here."

"Then no cherry cobbler? It seems the kitchen minions made a trip to the bakery."

"Maybe later, Princess."

She washed dishes and he dried. It was all so domestic. Well, as domestic as she'd seen on the Hallmark Channel. Her life was hardly a typical American tale. What did one do after the dishes were cleaned and the night loomed ahead?

Her gaze slid to Juan Carlos, wiping his hands on a kitchen towel. He folded the towel neatly, set it on the counter and smoothed it out. With a slight tilt of his head, he sought her out, a question on his lips.

Before he could voice his thoughts, the purr of an engine reached her ears. Juan Carlos strode to the kitchen window that faced the side yard. "It's Eduardo. He ran an errand for me. Wait here, I'll be right back."

"Why?"

But he dashed out the door before giving her an answer.

She heard their voices and strained to hear what they were saying, but she couldn't make it out.

The back door opened with the slight kick of Juan Carlos's boot and he strode in holding a wire cage in both hands.

Meeeow.

The cats! Juan Carlos had the mama cat and her kittens.

Eduardo followed behind him, his hair rumpled, drops of blood staining his scratched hands. He looked almost as frazzled as the cat.

"Eduardo, you're bleeding!"

"Hazard of the job," he mumbled.

It took only a second for her to figure out what he'd done. What they'd both done. Juan Carlos had sent Eduardo on a mission to rescue mama cat and her babies.

"He wouldn't let me go," Juan Carlos was saying.

"My job is to protect you, Your Majesty."

"Not from cats." The king appeared annoyed at himself for allowing Eduardo to do the job he'd wanted to do. "I should've gone. Now look at you."

"Better me than you. They're nothing but a few scrapes. She put up a good fight." Eduardo grinned. "She is a feisty one."

Juan Carlos gritted his teeth. "Those injuries should've been on my hands."

"Stop arguing, you two," Portia said. "What you both did was very kind. Juan Carlos, take the cats in the living area. The room is dark and cozy. It might put mama at ease. Eduardo, come with me. I'll take care of your hands." She marched into the bathroom and heard footsteps behind her. Grateful that Eduardo had obeyed her order, she grabbed a washrag, filled a bowl of warm water and pointed for him to sit on the edge of the bathtub.

Goodness.

She sat, too, and took his big hands in hers, scouring over half a dozen scratch marks. "She must've been very frightened."

"That made two of us."

"Oh, Eduardo." She began dabbing at the wounds. He flinched, but took the pain. She dabbed a little more gently, cleansing and dressing his wounds. "There."

"The king is very angry with me. Luis and I both, we convinced him not to go. He wanted to do this thing… for you."

Portia closed her eyes. "I…know."

Her chest tightened. It was the sweetest gesture anyone had ever done for her. Or tried to do.

"He is a proud man. But don't worry, he won't be angry for long."

"He won't?"

"No. I think not. And thank you, Eduardo, for rescuing the animals."

She placed a chaste kiss on his cheek. He was large, built like a block of stone, but his expression softened and as he rose, he bowed to her with his eyes twinkling.

And she felt as though she'd made a new friend.

Six

"Do you think she'll try to escape if we open the cage?" Portia asked as she sat facing Juan Carlos on the floor beside the fire. The cage was between them. The leery mama cat's eyes were guarded and wide. Portia made a move to get a better look at the babies, and a mewling hiss, one born of fear more than anything else, pressed through the feline's tight lips.

Juan Carlos shrugged. "She has nowhere to go. The house is locked up and the doors to this room are closed. Right now, I think she needs to see us and know we won't harm her."

"I think you're right." Portia tilted her head to one side. "You're intuitive when it comes to animals."

While she had been bandaging up Eduardo, Juan Carlos had set out a bowl of water and a plate of leftover cheese bits for when they let the cat out later.

"At least she won't starve tonight," he said.

Outside the wind was howling again, even pushing through the flue of the fireplace. The flames scattered momentarily in the hearth, blazing wildly before returning to a normal easy burn again. "No, she won't starve and the kittens will thrive. Thanks to you."

He kept his eyes on the fire, not commenting, refusing to take any credit for the deed. It didn't matter. He couldn't hide his intentions from her.

"They're the cutest little things," she said, her voice squeaking. She couldn't help it. Babies in all forms brought her voice to a higher pitch. Who in the world didn't love furry new kittens? "I'm glad they're here."

She had a view of his profile, so sharp and defined. Firelight played across his face and when he turned to her, his expression softened. "Me, too."

"Why didn't you tell me your plan to rescue her?" It was what all his watch-glancing had been about. It made sense to her now and she was incredibly relieved to learn the reason for his impatience. "Was it a surprise?"

He nodded. "I didn't want you to be disappointed if Eduardo couldn't bring her back."

And there it was. On his face. Concern. Caring. Almost love.

Something shifted inside her. It wasn't a blunt move, but something that had been tilting and leaning gradually, like dominoes toppling in super slow motion. She could feel each one fall, until every shred of her defenses was being taken down by this good, kind, *sexy* man.

"It's late," he said.

No, it wasn't.

"We should unlatch the cage now and leave her, so she can eat."

"Okay," Portia said, sorely disappointed. She knew that meant saying good night to Juan Carlos and parting ways at the top of the stairs once again.

He sighed as he rose to his feet and strode to the fireplace to take up a metal poker. He slashed at the logs, until only simmering embers heated the brick floor inside.

Portia carefully unlatched the hook on the cage and flipped it away. The wire door swung open but the cat stayed put. "Here you go, Duchess. You're free now."

"Duchess?" Juan Carlos turned to her.

"She needs a name." She shrugged. "It seems fitting somehow."

He smiled, but his eyes remained hooded. "Duchess it is. What's one more royal around here, anyway? Well, I'll say good-night now. We have an early call tomorrow."

They did. They were going even farther out on the grounds in the Jeep.

"Are you coming up?" he asked. He had almost reached the hallway door.

She rose to her feet and stared at him from across the room. Words wouldn't come. Her heart was thumping, drowning out everything else in her world.

"Portia?"

"What if…?" A swallow stole her next words.

He waited, his face in the shadows so she couldn't see his expression.

"What if I said I was a w-wimpy princess, after all?"

He paused. "Would you rather not go out in the Jeep tomorrow?"

"No." She shook her head, her hair falling like a sheet around her shoulders. "Juan Carlos, it means I don't want you to go to bed…"

He stepped out of the shadows, his eyes dark, intense. Waiting.

She froze. Oh, God, she was breaking every rule she'd ever committed to.

"Say it."

The force of his command sent thrills careening through her body.

"Say it, Portia."

He wouldn't break his vow to her. She had to do it. He'd told her as much just the other day. His honor meant that much to him and he wouldn't have it any other way.

"Without me." She nodded, convincing herself. "I don't want you to go to bed without—"

And suddenly, he was there in front her, gazing into her eyes, cupping her head in his hands and brushing his lips over hers. Once. Twice. His hungry mouth devoured her over and over again. His arms wrapped around her, his hand brushing away her hair tenderly, his body trembling as he took her in kiss after kiss.

She was lost in the goodness of him, the thrill of his hands finally on her. The scent of his skin. The power of his body. Tears spilled down her cheeks at the clarity of this moment. She was his. He was hers. It was so easy, so simple. How had she managed to keep this amazing man at bay? How had she not realized earlier how perfect they would be for each other?

"Portia, don't cry," he was murmuring between kisses.

"I'm...happy, Juan Carlos."

"Oh, God. How I've waited for this. For *you*. Say my name again."

"Juan Carlos. Juan Carlos. Juan Carlos."

He grinned, a flash of white teeth in a broad happy smile that branded her heart. His gaze roved over her face and traveled the length of her body, his smile fading into something delicious. Something dangerous. And something she no longer feared. His eyes burned with want, the heat in them back full force. The man knew how to smolder.

"Portia." He breathed her name as if his life depended on it. "I need you."

"I need you, too," she admitted softly. She reached for the hem of his shirt, pushing the material up his torso.

"No," he said, taking her hands in his. "We'll do this right."

And in the next instant, he swooped her up into his arms. She wound her arms around his neck and as he headed upstairs, she pressed her lips to his, kissing him until they reached the threshold to his room.

"Here we are," he said, his voice reverent, as if the next step he took would be monumental. He carried her over the threshold with great ceremony and smiled at her. "I've wanted you since the moment I laid eyes on you."

"You have me," she said softly.

"God. I cannot wait much longer, but I will not rush with you." He lowered her down onto the bed. The mattress cushioned her body and then his hands were there, removing her sweater and unbuttoning her blouse, spreading it out so he could see her breasts. "You are beautiful," he said, planting both hands on the mattress beside her head, trapping her. She may never want to escape. His kiss was rough and hungry, and when she looked up, the sharp lines of his face tightened, a passionate preamble of what was to come. Her skin prickled in anticipation.

His fingertips grazed over her breasts lightly, hovering, teasing the sensitive tips. Hot liquid warmth pooled between her thighs. Then he wound his hands behind her back and she lifted herself up enough for him to unfasten her bra. With his help, she shrugged out of it and then lay back down.

"Fair is fair," he said, rising to grab the hem of his shirt. He pulled it up and over his head. Her mouth gaped open and she took a hard swallow, gazing at the tempting sculpted bronze chest.

"That is totally *unfair*," she whispered.

A smile spread across his face as he bent on his knees to remove her boots, her belt and then slowly, achingly moved the zipper of her pants down. Cool air hit her thighs, but she was too swamped already, too raggedly consumed by heat for that to have any lasting effect. He tugged at one pant leg and then the other, until she was free of them. All that was left on her body was a pair of teeny hot pink panties. "I like your style, Princess," he murmured, sliding up her thighs to hook the hem with his fingers.

"I like yours." She gulped.

He smiled again and dragged her panties down her legs.

Then the mattress dipped as he lowered down next to her. Immediately, his scent wafted to her nose: fresh soap and a hint of lime. She squeezed her eyes closed, breathing him in. He cupped her head and kissed her lips, her chin, her throat. "Let me explore you, Portia," he whispered.

She nodded. "If I can explore you."

"Be my guest," he said, his tone once again reverent. He fell back against the bed.

She rose up part of the way to lay a hand on his chest. Heat sizzled under her palm as she slid her fingers over tight skin and muscle. His chest was a work of art and as she continued to explore, he took sharp gasps of breath. Empowered now, she moved more confidently, her fingers flat over his nipples, weaving them through tiny chest hairs and reaching his broad shoulders. She nibbled on him there, nipping his hot skin and breathing the scent of raw sex emanating from his pores. "You are amazing, Juan Carlos," she said. And suddenly she was eager for him to explore her, to touch her in ways she'd secretly dreamed about. "Your turn."

She lay back on the bed and he rose over her to take a leisurely tour of her naked body, his eyes a beacon of light flowing over every inch of her. Then his hands began to trace the contours of her body, caressing her curves and moving effortlessly over her skin. He was thorough, leaving no part of her untouched. Goose bumps rose on her arms and legs, his precision and utmost sensitivity leaving her trembling in his wake.

Next, he covered her trembling body with his, wrapping her in his heat and claiming her with his presence. She bore his weight and peered up at him. He was amazing, so handsome, so incredibly virile. His hands cushioned her breasts, massaging them until the peaks were two sensitive tips. The pads of his thumbs flicked at them gently, and something powerful began to build and throb below her waist.

She had not been with a man in a long time. It felt so good. So right. Being with him.

He pressed her a little harder and she cried out. "Juan Carlos."

It seemed to satisfy him. He took her in an earth-shattering kiss, pressing her mouth open and sweeping into her. She moved under him, arching her hips, that feeling below her waist becoming stronger and stronger the longer the kiss went on.

His hand was moving again, leaving her full breasts and moving down her torso, past her navel and below her waist, where she ached and ached for him. "Trust me," he said.

All she could do was nod.

And his hands and mouth worked magic on her, shredding her into tiny pieces, squeezing tortured moans from her lips and making her squirm until she finally reached a fantastic, bone-melting orgasm.

"Juan Carlos," she breathed, lifting her head to find his eyes on her as he unbuckled his belt. He shucked out of his clothes quickly and sheathed himself, in all his naked glory, with a condom.

He touched her where she was most sensitive, lending her comfort and warmth in the aftermath of her pulsing release. She relaxed and eased back slowly, as another fire began to build. "I've waited for you all of my life, Portia. And now, you're mine."

She was ready for him when he entered her, wanting him this way, taking his weight and watching a fiery veil of passion burn in his eyes. He began to rock back and forth, each thrust a love note, a daring caress and sugary candy for her hungry body. "You are all I will ever need," he murmured.

She smiled as he pressed farther and farther inside her body. She was his. *He* was all she would ever need and as she met his driving rhythm, arching up and down, her breaths heavy, her body primed, she found solace and peace in his arms and lust and desire in his bed.

Juan Carlos drew a deep breath into his lungs. He'd often dreamed of waking up next to Portia, and now his very fantasy had come true. He turned his head and watched her chest rise and fall slowly. Her hair fanned across the pillow. He ached to touch it and sift the strands through his fingers. He wanted to kiss her awake and then make love to her again. But the sun had barely risen and the day would prove a long one. She needed her sleep. He'd worn her out last night. He shook his head at the thoughts running through his mind. He couldn't touch her again this morning and have her think he was lecherous, waking her with only one thing on his mind.

He smiled. He would come to her again sometime today. It would be hard to keep to the task at hand, but they were on a mission. Though a wicked part of him wanted to play hooky today. Why couldn't they just stay in bed all day? The States had snow days. Why couldn't he declare a Royal Day?

A little noise pressed through her lips, a moan that he'd come to know. Last night, she'd moaned plenty and turned his world on end.

She shifted toward him and one hand—warm, delicate and soft—flopped onto his cheek. He moved his head enough to press his lips there and kiss her.

"Hi," she said, smiling, though her eyes were still closed.

"Good morning, sweetheart."

"Is it time to get up?"

"You can stay in bed as long as you'd like."

"With you?"

"Yes, only with me."

Her eyes opened and he gazed into their sleep-hooded amazing blue depths. He could fall into those eyes and never want to return.

"Juan Carlos," she said, "last night was…"

"I know."

"I didn't know it could be that good."

He leaned in and kissed her tenderly. "I'm humbled to hear you say that."

"Humbled? Not over-the-moon, cocky and feeling proud of yourself?"

He chuckled. "Maybe that, too."

"I had…uh, you know. Three times. That's never happened before."

"Keep telling me things like that and we'll never get out of this bed."

She grinned and reached over to move a tendril of hair off his forehead, her delicate fingertips sliding down his cheek. He loved it when she touched him. "You know, that doesn't sound like a bad idea."

He caught her wrist and kissed her pulse point. "We can make that happen, sweetheart."

"If only," she said, sighing, her head falling back against the pillow. "But we need to finish what we started."

She would be leaving soon. She didn't have to say the words. He had only a few more days with her, before she would head back to the States. How quickly reality reared its ugly head. "We will finish it, one way or another."

"I hope we find something today," she said.

"We'll give it a good shot."

"I should get dressed. I'm anxious to see how our little family is doing."

She meant the cats. Juan Carlos had almost forgotten about them. "Right. Let's go check on them together."

She rose from the bed and turned away. As she fitted

her arms through the sleeves of his shirt, he glimpsed her lush blond hair falling down her back, the creamy texture of her skin, her rounded backside and the coltlike legs that had wrapped around him last night.

He sighed, enjoying the view and ignoring his body's immediate reaction to her. He threw on a pair of jeans and a T-shirt. Hand in hand, they strolled out of the bedroom and into the living area.

"Shhh," she said, spying the cat nursing her kittens outside the cage on a loop rug in front of the fireplace. "We don't want to startle her."

Duchess was resting with her head down, her eyes closed, allowing her five offspring to take their morning meal. Juan Carlos was moved by the sweet look on Portia's face as she silently watched mama and babies. He wrapped his arm around her shoulder and drew her closer, kissing the top of her head. How could he ever let this woman go? The answer was simple: he couldn't. It wouldn't be easy but he would convince her to stay. And marry him.

"Do you think Duchess will eat eggs?" she asked Juan Carlos as she scrambled four eggs in a cast-iron skillet. Morning sunshine brightened the kitchen, filling it with warmth. Bacon sizzled on the griddle and toast was cooking under the broiler. "I'll put a little cheese on them."

"You can try," he said, pouring two mugs of coffee. "She'll eat when she gets hungry enough. I'll send Eduardo out this morning for cat food."

She'd managed to get fresh water over to the cat without her running for cover. Duchess was still wary, but the kittens slowed her down or else she probably would've bolted when Portia set the bowl down. In time, Duchess would come to trust her. Sadly, she wouldn't be around long enough to see it.

She had work waiting for her in Los Angeles.

It was for the best that she leave Alma. She couldn't fall in love with Juan Carlos. He didn't fit into her plans for a quiet, unassuming life. Yet spending time with him had been magnificent.

He came up behind her, kissed the side of her throat and ran a hand up her thigh. She tensed in all the good places. He'd asked her not to dress yet, and now she knew why. She was only wearing his shirt, which gave him easy access to her body. Not that she minded. Heavens, no. She loved him touching her. "I'll be right back," he said. "Coffee's ready and on the table."

"Where are you going?" she asked.

"Don't be so nosy. I'll be back before you know it."

She smiled and turned, and his arms automatically wound around her. "See that you are. Breakfast is almost ready."

"Bossy, Princess," he said, staring at her mouth.

Her heart skipped a beat and a moment passed between them before he kissed the tip of her nose.

She shrugged a shoulder. "Kings."

He laughed and exited the back door.

Juan Carlos may have originally been a reluctant king, but there was no doubt in her mind that he was good for Alma and that he would put the country's welfare above all else. As it should be. Alma had been through tough times under a ruthless dictatorship. The country needed a strong man.

So do you.

No, she couldn't go there. The map was already drawn up for both of them, and after this little interlude, their paths wouldn't cross again.

After she set the table, Juan Carlos returned holding a bouquet of tall azure flowers. "For you," he said, handing her all but one stem. "Scilla hispanica."

"They're beautiful." She lifted them to her nose. "Are these from the garden?"

He nodded. "Spanish bluebells. They're almost a perfect match to your eyes, sweetheart." He pinched off the end of the one he still held and fitted it behind her right ear. "There. Now you're perfect."

"Hardly," she said.

"I think so."

"You think I'm bossy."

"Dressed like that, cooking my breakfast and wearing flowers in your hair? I can deal with a little bossiness."

She shook her head. "You're wicked." And so very thoughtful.

"So I'm told."

He took the flowers from her hands, snapped off the tips of the stems and arranged the bouquet in an old thick green glass bottle. After he filled it with water, he placed it on the table. "Have a seat, Princess," he said, pulling out a chair. "I'll serve you."

She had a protest on her lips, but Juan Carlos's expression wouldn't allow arguing. "Yes, Your Highness."

He smiled. "Good. I'm glad you know who the real boss is around here."

Portia's heart swelled. And as they sat down and ate, easy conversation flowed between them. Juan Carlos touched her hand often, as if needing the connection. She leaned over to brush hair from his forehead and he'd steal a kiss or two. They were in sync with each other; nothing had ever been as perfect as it was now, with the two of them doing ordinary everyday things, like cooking breakfast, sharing a meal and worrying over the cat family.

"So what will happen to Duchess and her babies when we have to leave here?" she asked.

"She'll become the official palace cat, of course."

"And the kittens?"

"We'll find them good homes, Portia. Don't worry."

Her eye twitched. "I know you're doing this for me." She covered his hand with hers. "Thank you."

The feelings between them were getting too heavy, too fast. She had no way of stopping it, short of leaving him right here and now. But she couldn't do that. Not only did she not want to, but she'd promised to spend a few days here helping with the search, and with the exception of a snake decapitation, she was having a wonderful time.

"You're welcome. Now, if you'll excuse me, I have to speak with Luis about a few matters."

Juan Carlos rose and began clearing the dishes. What a guy. She bounded up quickly and took the plates from his hands. "I'll take care of that," she said with enough authority to keep prison inmates in line.

"Okay," he said. "Thanks."

He bent his head and took her in a long amazing kiss. When their lips parted and he was through, her head spun. "That was…promising."

He grinned, shaking his head at her understatement. "Get ready. We'll be leaving in a little while. Unless you've changed your mind and want to play hooky today."

He was reaching inside her shirt. She slapped his hand away and pointed. "Go."

He went.

And Portia cleared the dishes and cleaned up the kitchen. She checked on Duchess and her brood; they were all sleeping. What a pretty serene picture they made, a mass of calico colors and balls of fluff all nestled together. She was grateful they'd have a home after they left the farmhouse. Her heart had never been so full.

Thirty minutes later, Portia climbed into the passenger side of the Jeep and Juan Carlos got behind the wheel. They said goodbye to Luis, though that didn't mean anything. He was sure to follow. Eduardo had gone into the local town on a cat food mission.

"All set?" Juan Carlos said, gunning the motor. "Strapped in?"

She nodded. The weather was glorious, the temperature in the mid-seventies with clear blue skies. She wore a lightweight white jacket that billowed in the breeze as Juan Carlos drove off and picked up speed.

"We're going out about five miles," he shouted over the engine's roar.

She sat back and relaxed, enjoying the scenery, excitement stirring her bones. Maybe today they'd find the art treasures.

For four hours they traveled at a snail's pace over lush lands, where wildflowers and lantana grew in abundance, the vista opening up to a prairie as they scoured the grounds looking for possible hiding places. They came upon another shack but after a thorough inspection, with Juan Carlos insisting on going inside first, they found absolutely nothing. Not even a snake.

"We have a little more land to cover before we head back," Juan Carlos said, and she heard the disappointment in his voice. She, too, was disappointed.

"Let's stop for lunch by that little lake we passed a few minutes ago." Maybe regrouping would give them a fresh perspective.

"It wasn't much of a lake," Juan Carlos said. "More like an oversize pond."

She entwined their fingers. "But it's pretty there and I'm getting hungry."

He smiled and gave her hand a squeeze. That was all it took for her heart to do a little flip. "Okay, we'll have a picnic." And he maneuvered the Jeep around, heading for the lake.

Warm breezes ruffled her hair and sweat beaded her

forehead as the sun climbed high overhead. She loved being outdoors. Much of her time in the States was spent indoors at art exhibits, galleries or simply poring over books and surfing the internet. She took a full breath of Alma air and vowed not to let disappointment ruin their day.

They'd packed a lunch and had a blanket. That was all they would need.

Juan Carlos braked the Jeep several yards from the water's edge. There were no shade trees so they used the vehicle to provide a bit of cover. From Luis. They were always being watched, but Portia was starting to get used to the idea and it wasn't as creepy as she'd once thought. Juan Carlos jumped down first as she gathered up the blanket. Then he reached for her and helped her down, crushing her body against his and taking her in a long, slow, deliberate kiss.

When he released her, her breathing sped up, coming in short clips. The blanket between them was her only salvation from being ravaged on the spot. She clung to it and backed away. "I should spread this out."

He backed off, too. "You do that," he said, his voice tight. "I'll get the cooler."

Once everything was in place, they sat down facing the water, their backs propped against the side of the Jeep. "The kitchen minions make great sandwiches," she said, taking a bite of chicken salad.

"I'll remember to thank them."

At some point during the day, either Luis or Eduardo would fill the refrigerator and cupboards with food, much of it readymade. She wasn't entirely sure it didn't come from the palace itself. The King of Montoro had a wonderful cook staff. But she decided the mystery was exciting and she didn't want to know how it magically appeared. She liked that it just did.

"What do we do now?" she asked, taking another bite.

Juan Carlos's throat worked, as he tipped a water bottle back and took a sip. He wiped the back of his hand across his mouth and turned to her, his eyes dark and searching. "I don't know. I think we've exhausted all possibilities. Where else is there to look?"

She had to agree. They'd searched the entire grounds—the prairies, the hills, the outer buildings—and found nothing. "The art could be anywhere and we'd never know it. There are no clues and sadly those secrets have been buried along with your family members."

He nodded. "At least the artwork didn't fall into the hands of the dictator, which was their main intent. I can't say I'm not disappointed. I thought we'd find something, a clue, some hint that would lead us to it. I can only hope it is found one day."

"I'm sorry, Juan Carlos." She set her sandwich down and brought her lips to his mouth. It was a chaste kiss, one of commiseration.

Instantly, his arms wound around her shoulders and he tugged, pulling her practically on top of him, deepening the kiss. "You're the only woman who can make me feel better," he murmured.

A pulse throbbed in her neck. She loved hearing his sweet words, even though they might be some of the last she'd hear from him. Soon, when the search was finally concluded, she'd have to say goodbye to him and all that they'd meant to each other in this short span of time. Yet, right now, she wanted to make him feel better—but she couldn't do it here. Out in the open. "We should go," she said. "Luis is watching."

He kissed her again, and then lifted himself up, pulling his phone out of his pocket. He spent a few seconds texting someone and then returned to her. "He's not watching anymore."

"Juan Carlos! What did you say to him?"

His lips twitched. "I told him to retreat one hundred yards and turn his head away from the Jeep for twenty minutes."

"You didn't!" Her face instantly burned. Her pride was stung. "He's going to know."

Juan Carlos touched her face gently, his fingertips on her cheeks, calming her. "Sweetheart, any man who sees how I look at you *knows*. Luis won't say a word."

"But I'll know he knows."

"It's beautiful here, Portia. And I need you. Do you not need me, too?"

His words worked magic on her. Yes, she needed him, too. She nodded. "But—"

He kissed away her doubts and then lowered her onto the blanket. His mouth was brutally tender, claiming her with each stroke of the tongue as soul-wrenching groans escaped his throat.

Thrills ran up and down her body as he exposed her to the sun's rays. The scent of fresh water and clear skies combined made her forget her inhibitions. She'd never made love outdoors and she only wanted to experience it with this one exciting man.

Firelight created jumping shadows across the living room walls. Juan Carlos sat with Portia beside him on the sofa as they watched Duchess bathe a kitten, her tongue taking long swipes across its furry body. The kitten took a playful swing or two at mama cat, but Duchess didn't relent. She used one paw to hold her charge down, determined to finish the job and lick away the grime of the day before moving on to her next one. She cleansed and fed her young diligently. Duchess, for all her wildness, was a good mama cat.

"You're quiet tonight," Portia said. "Still thinking about the missing art treasure?"

That was part of it. His failure to find it bothered him. He'd been so certain that there were clues here on the property and yet, he felt as if he was missing something important. He couldn't say what, but deep down in his bones he still believed the answers were here.

Yet most of his thoughts concerned Portia. They'd exhausted their search and there was nothing to keep them on the farm any longer. Tomorrow they would head back to Del Sol and then Portia would return to the States. Eventually. Unless he could convince her to stay.

"I'm thinking about us," he answered honestly.

Portia put her head on his shoulder. "What about us?" she asked, her smooth-as-velvet voice tapping into his heart. At least she didn't say, *there is no us*. She recognized that they were edging toward a precarious cliff.

Three sharp raps at the door interrupted their conversation. He gave it a glance and waited for the next two knocks, which would signal him that all was well. Those two knocks came and Juan Carlos rose, striding to the door. "It's either Luis or Eduardo," he said over his shoulder to reassure Portia, and then opened the door. "Eduardo. I trust everything is all right?"

"Yes. But I have something of interest I thought you would want to hear right now."

Eduardo glanced at Portia, who was now sitting on the edge of the sofa, her eyes round with curiosity. "Regarding?"

"Your search, Your Majesty."

Juan Carlos swung the door open wider. "Come in."

"Your Highness," he said to Portia as he made his way inside the room.

"Eduardo." She granted him a beautiful smile, most likely grateful it wasn't his counterpart, Luis, seeking them out. He could see the relief in her eyes. This afternoon, making love under blue skies behind the Jeep, Portia had let go her inhibitions and made a memory that would live forever in his mind. But afterward his Portia had gone on and on about Luis, asking how she could ever face him again.

Juan Carlos had succeeded in kissing away her worries.

"Would you like to sit down?" Portia asked.

"No, thank you. I didn't mean to interrupt." Eduardo regarded the kittens, his expression softening.

"Duchess is coming around," Portia said, her eyes glittering.

One look at Eduardo and the cat's back arched, and a low mewling hiss sprang from her mouth.

Portia rolled her eyes. "*Slowly* she's coming along. She should know better than to bite the hand that feeds her. Sorry, Eduardo. And how are your hands?"

He waved them in the air. "They are fine, Princess. No need to worry."

"What did you find out of interest, Eduardo?" he asked. "Something about the search?"

"Yes, Your Highness. You gave me the list of names on the graves at the Montoro family cemetery."

"Yes, I committed many of them to memory." He'd tasked Eduardo with contacting his uncle Rafe and alerting him about the cemetery. Juan Carlos wanted those family plots cleaned up and the headstones that were damaged beyond repair to be replaced as soon as possible.

"Yes, well, I spoke with your uncle, as you asked. He has no knowledge of those family members or that there even was a Montoro cemetery on the grounds. Not one name seemed to jar his memory."

"We didn't have first names. We only found initials on the headstones. It doesn't matter if he remembered the names or not. We will have that cemetery restored."

"There's more."

Juan Carlos nodded. "I'm listening."

"Your uncle claims that as a rite of passage, every Montoro had the privilege of being buried in the family mausoleum in Alma, whether rich or poor. If they were related to Montoro and had bloodlines, it was an honor to be buried there."

"Yes, I know that. But surely during Tantaberra's reign, that wouldn't hold true anymore. After the war, everything changed. I assumed those graves were there because Tantaberra controlled even where a person would lay to rest."

Portia walked up to take his hand. "But Juan Carlos, think about some of the dates on the headstones. Many were pre-Tantaberra."

He gave it a moment of thought, his mind clicking back to the headstones. "You're right. There were at least four that I remember that dated back to the 1920s and '30s. Before the war, before Tantaberra."

"Yes," Portia said, her voice reaching a higher pitch. "And those initials might've been used to throw people off. They'd have no real way of investigating who was laid to rest there."

"Hold on a second," Juan Carlos said, pulling out his phone. He clicked over to the list he'd brought with him of the known art pieces missing from the palace. His heart racing, he located the titles.

"*Joven Amelia.* J.A. were the initials on one of the headstones," he said. "It means Young Amelia. *Almas Iguales.* A.I. was another set of initials. The sculpture is called *Equal Souls* in English. And then there is *Dos Rios.*"

"D.R. I remember that one," Portia said. "I thought he was a doctor."

"There's a painting called *Dos Rios* that's missing," he said. "Portia, you said it yourself this afternoon, the secrets have been buried along with my family members.

But I don't think there are any family members buried in the cemetery."

"You think the artwork is buried there." Portia's voice was breathless and eager.

"It's a long shot, Princess. I think the cemetery is bogus. It was the family's way of protecting the art from Tanta-berra. We have to find out. Eduardo, get in touch with Luis. We'll need a bulldozer, but for now, round up shovels and some high-powered lights. I'm going tonight."

"Oh, Juan Carlos, do you really think you've found it?"

"*We* found it, Portia. You're as much a part of this as I am."

Portia nodded, an excited smile teasing her lips. "I'll go change my clothes."

"Portia," he said, "are you sure you want to go? If I'm wrong, it will be pretty gruesome."

"If you really want to see *gruesome* try and stop me, Your Highness."

He grinned. "That's right. You're not a wimpy princess."

He was glad. It wouldn't feel right going on this search without her by his side.

Whatever they found.

Seven

"I really know how to show a lady a good time, don't I?" With shovel in hand, Juan Carlos dug at the foot of a grave alongside Eduardo and Luis as the high beams of two cars cast the cemetery in an unearthly glow.

Dirt flew through the air and landed at the toes of her boots. If she weren't so excited, she'd be totally creeped out. "I can't think of anywhere else I'd rather be," she countered honestly.

Even her embarrassment with Luis had been forgotten.

"I can help out," she said, "when anyone wants to take a break."

Eduardo covered his laughter with a grunt.

Juan Carlos slanted her a be-serious look. "I'll keep that in mind, Princess."

Luis was too busy digging to look up.

She wrapped her arms around her sides as the night air became chillier. She'd refused Juan Carlos's suggestion to sit it out in the car and so she stood watching, waiting.

They were digging up the grave of J. A. Molina. The headstone dated the death to 1938.

After ten minutes of silent digging, she heard a thump. Eduardo's shovel smacked against something solid. Thump, thump. "I hit something, Your Highness," Eduardo said.

"Let's keep digging," Juan Carlos said. There was a

boyish tone to his excitement. "It shouldn't be long now before we know."

The men worked twice as fast now, focusing their efforts. The scraping sounds of shovels against wood filled the quiet night.

"Portia, will you get the flashlight and shine it down here."

The men were five feet below ground level now and working furiously.

She grabbed the biggest flashlight she could find and stood as close as possible over the grave site, sending beams of light down. Portia's heart sank. "It's a coffin, isn't it?"

"Maybe," Juan Carlos said. Under her flashlight, his eager eyes had lost some of their gleam. A layer of dirt remained on top of the box, and he used his gloved hands to swipe it off, searching for any hint of what lay inside. He found nothing written. "Let's bring it up."

It took some doing, but the three men hoisted the box up and set it on a patch of flat ground.

"Hand me the ax," Juan Carlos ordered. He made the sign of the cross over his chest. "And may God forgive us."

Luis handed Juan Carlos the tool and he carefully began to hack at the very edges of the coffin. Each blow of the ax brought the mystery closer and closer to an end. Eduardo used his shovel to help pry the lid of the box open.

It was time. Their work was nearly over. Juan Carlos hesitated a moment, drew breath into his lungs and then glanced at her. "Ready?"

She nodded.

"You might want to look away," he said.

"No, I will be fine with whatever we find." Her eye twitched, closing in a wink.

Juan Carlos stared at her. Perhaps he was equally as nervous as she was. With his gloved hands, he lifted the hacked lid. She beamed the flashlight on the contents, her heart thumping hard.

"There's no corpse." His voice elevated, he continued, "But there's something in here."

She held her breath, her pulse jumping in her veins. He unfolded a sheath, and found another box, no more than two by three feet, this one carved and quite ornate. He lifted it out and she shined the flashlight on it. *Joven Amelia* was etched in golden lettering on top.

Juan Carlos's hand shook. "It's here. Thank God," he said. Setting the box down on the ground, he kneeled, and she took a place beside him. He took great care to remove his filthy gloves and then opened the latch and lifted the lid.

Inside, surrounded by lush black velvet, there was a painting of a little girl, no more than ten years old, playing near the seashore with a much younger sister. The canvas was secured, not rolled up as one might expect, but mounted to a frame as if taken from the palace in a hurry. Portia would have to inspect it thoroughly and do some research, but she was almost certain that it was genuine, given the great pains the royal family had taken to hide the painting decades ago.

"It's beautiful," she said. "She is Young Amelia."

Tears welled in Juan Carlos's eyes. "We did it, Portia. We found the missing treasures."

"Yes," she breathed, her heart swelling. "Yes."

"Eduardo, Luis, come see."

Taking her hand, Juan Carlos rose and tugged her up with him. Once standing, he wrapped his arms around her waist and drew her close, so they were hip to hip. Joy beamed in her heart. It was a monumental occasion and she found no reason for pretense. As Juan Carlos had said, the way he looked at her left little room for doubt of his feelings, anyway. They were lovers. It was hard to disguise.

The bodyguards peered at the painting in its casing. Both seemed awed and a little surprised to be looking at a royal masterpiece lost for generations.

"Congratulations, Your Majesty," Eduardo said.

"Alma's precious treasures have been restored," Luis said.

The two men shook the king's hand. There was pride and resolve in all of their eyes.

Eduardo turned to her. "Princess Portia, congratulations to you, as well. It is a great find."

"Thank you, Eduardo. That's very kind of you to say." She stepped forward and placed a kiss on his cheek. "I'm thrilled to have helped in a small way."

Eduardo blushed, but gave no indication he was alarmed by her affectionate display. A smile tugged at his lips, bringing her a rush of friendly warmth inside.

Juan Carlos got right down to business again. "I would like you to secure the grounds tonight. When the bulldozers arrive, we will resume digging in the morning. Assemble a team. I would like to have all the art secured by the end of the day tomorrow, if possible."

"Yes, Your Highness," Luis said. "It will be done."

The men turned to do their tasks, and Juan Carlos took her hand and began dragging her away from the stream of lights. "Come with me, sweetheart," he said.

"Where are we going?"

"To bed, as soon as I can arrange it," he said. "But for now, this will have to do."

He pulled her behind the cars, out into the darkness under the stars. And the next thing she knew, Juan Carlos's hands were about her and she was flying, sailing through the air, spinning around and around. "We did it, Princess. We did it."

"Yes, yes, we did." Laughter spilled from her lips and a lightness of spirit filled her.

"This is an amazing moment. I'm glad to be sharing it with you," he said.

Her smile broadened. "I feel the same way, Juan Carlos. I'm bursting inside."

He brought her down to earth gently, her boots gracing the sacred grounds. And his lips sought hers instantly, kissing her mouth, chin, cheeks and forehead. His hands sifted through her hair and his dark, luscious eyes bored into her. "Do you have any idea how much I love you, Portia? I do. I love you, Princess. With all my heart."

"Oh, Juan Carlos, I love you, too." And there it was. Her truth. Her honest feelings poured out of her in this instant of happiness and joy. She could no longer hide away from the sensations rocking her from head to toe. The words she spoke were not damning, but blissful and joyous. She loved Juan Carlos Salazar II, King Montoro of Alma.

"You do? You love me?" His grin spoke to her heart in a language all its own. His was the sweetest of tones, as if he was in total awe of her love.

She nodded eagerly. "I love you."

He lifted her up and twirled her around once more before he set her down. His kiss this time made her dizzier than a dozen spins in his arms. His mouth claimed her, his lips demanding, his tongue penetrating through to sweep in and conquer. Her knees wobbled and she sought his sturdy shoulders for balance, her monumental declaration swaying both of them.

"Oh, Portia, my love. I cannot think of a life without you. Marry me. Be my wife. Be with me forever."

The words rang in her ears. It wasn't as if she hadn't expected them to come, but the surprise came only in her answer. "Yes, Juan Carlos. I will marry you."

The next morning, Portia woke in Juan Carlos's arms, opening her eyes to a face she had come to love. Handsome, breathtaking and dynamic. He was a man who got things done. He'd certainly pursued her to the point of her complete compliance. How could she not fall in love with this man?

"Good morning, fiancée," he said, kissing the tip of her nose.

"Hello, my love," she said.

They'd celebrated in this very bed well into the night. There was champagne and candles and bone-melting caresses.

As she plopped her head against the pillow, the sheets pulled away, exposing her bare shoulders. Her eyes lifted to the ceiling, focusing on tiles that were chipping away. The farmhouse, old and neglected as it was, had undeniable charm. She sighed. "Is this real?"

"So real," Juan Carlos said. "Here, feel my heart."

He grasped her hand and placed it on his chest. Under her fingertips, life-sustaining beats pulsed through his veins. "I am real. A man who loves a woman."

"But you are the king of Alma."

"And you are the princess of Samforstand...we are meant to be, sweetheart. Can you not see how perfect this is? Fate has stepped in and brought the two of us together. I can only marry a woman of royal blood. And that's you." He brought her hand to his lips and tenderly kissed one finger, then another and another. "When I became king, marrying was the last thing on my mind. But then I saw you at the coronation and all bets were off."

"And what if I weren't a princess? Then what would you have done?"

"I would have..." He hesitated and sighed, bringing her up and over his body so that she straddled his thighs. He nipped at her lips and wove his fingers through her hair, eyeing the locks as if they were made of gold. "Luckily, I don't have that burden."

"No, you don't," she said, taking his hand and placing it on her chest. The heat of his palm warmed her breast and she squeezed her hand over his. "Feel my heart."

His eyes filled with hunger and every cell in her body reacted to his sensual touch. "You are wicked, Princess."

She chuckled. "You bring it out in me."

"You see, we *are* a perfect match."

"Are we?" She nibbled on her lip. She'd disobeyed her hard and fast rule of not falling for a high-profile man. You couldn't get much higher than king. Was she destined to fame through association even though it's the last thing she wanted?

"Let me show you again, so that you will never doubt it."

His hands on her hips, he gently guided her over him and they welcomed the dawn with their bodies and hearts joined as one.

But her doubts remained, locked and hidden away, even as she agreed to marry him. Even as she claimed her love for him. Half an hour later, she was showered and dressed. She and Juan Carlos ate a quick breakfast of cereal and fruit, both anxious to get back to the cemetery site this morning. But Portia couldn't forget her six charges. She walked into the living area with bowls of water and cat food in her hands and set them down by the fireplace hearth, where Duchess had taken up residence. "Here you go, girl."

Duchess no longer looked at her with frightened eyes. She had at one time been domesticated, and she was beginning to remember her life before hunger and fear had changed her. Portia kneeled and watched the cat rise, stretch her neck and shake out her limbs, and then walk over to the water. She lapped furiously as five balls of fluff scrambled to be near her, one kitten losing his balance and plopping half his body into the bowl. He jumped back, as if hit by a jolt, and gave himself a few shakes. Tiny drops of water sprinkled Portia's clothes.

She giggled and pressed her hand to the top of the little one's head. Silky fur tickled her palm. "You are a feisty one."

Juan Carlos strode into the room. "Are you ready to go, sweetheart?"

She stood. "Yes. I can't wait to see what else we uncover."

According to Eduardo, two bulldozers and a full crew were working furiously this morning. In the middle of the night, he'd called upon and assembled a team of men he could trust with this secret. Soon, the entire country would know about the hidden artwork. What a story to tell.

Last night, Juan Carlos had shared his hopes of putting many of these treasures on display for Alma citizens as well as tourists who would come to view the find. It would be nothing short of a boon for the country. The restoration of the artwork would instill pride and honor in a country once diminished and downtrodden by a dictator. First, though, Portia, along with a Latin art specialist, would have to verify that the pieces were not fakes.

By the time they reached the site, half the graveyard was dug up. Dust swirled through the air from the many mounds of dirt dotting the cemetery. Ten men with shovels and axes were hoisting boxes up from the graves. Luis, with pen and pad in hand, was making an inventory list. As ordered, none of the boxes had been opened.

Juan Carlos helped her down from the Jeep. He took her hand and they walked to where Luis stood next to a gravestone marked with the initials P.P. Tasked with documenting and photographing each headstone before the box was brought up, Luis lifted his head to greet them.

"Your Highness, Princess," he said. "We have twelve boxes already accounted for. As you can see, we have more to do. We've placed them inside the tent over there," he said, pointing to a room-size tent set up outside the cemetery under guard by two men, "and they are ready for you to open."

"Thank you, Luis," Juan Carlos said. "Your men are working faster than I thought. Now, if you'll come with me, I'll need you to document what we find as I open the boxes."

"I'll take the photos," Portia said.

Luis handed over his digital camera and nodded. "Thank you, Your Highness."

Excitement stirred in her belly. To be a part of this find was a dream come true. How many dreams was one person allowed in a lifetime? All this joy in such a short span of time? She'd found adventure and love where she'd least expected it, in the arms of a king.

Inside the tent, Juan Carlos opened box after box, carefully removing the pieces for documentation. Oil paintings, sculptures, bronzed statues and the famed ancient Alma tiara had been locked away and hidden from the world for decades. Portia photographed everything, carefully making mental notes of the pieces she would research for authentication.

They worked alongside the men, until all the pieces were uncovered and the mock cemetery was emptied out. By late afternoon, they'd unearthed twenty-two boxes in all, the grave sites now nothing but pockmarks in the earth.

Juan Carlos climbed to the top of a pile of dirt in the center of the graveyard, his boots spread out, his voice booming to the loyal men who had labored here. As he spoke, shovels were held still, conversations died down. "The Montoro family cemetery has done its job to preserve what is sovereign to our country. You are all a part of Alma history now and I thank you for your hard work today. Until these items are authenticated, I would ask for your silence. Luis and Eduardo have assured me all of you can be trusted. The next step is to transport these pieces back to the palace in the trucks you arrived in. Again, thank you all for your diligence."

Juan Carlos jumped down from the dirt hill and once again, Portia was reminded of how well he fit the position of king. He was a true diplomat and leader. A man to be admired. Staunch in his beliefs and fair-minded…she was sure if the clocks were turned back in time to when Alma was last ruled by a king, he would have reigned over his people justly.

"What are you staring at?" he asked, approaching her.

She shook off her thoughts and smiled. "How handsome you are with dirt on your face."

He grinned. "I could say the same about you, Princess. The smudges on your face only make you more beautiful." He touched her nose, right cheek and forehead.

Goodness, she'd never considered what the hours of dust and grime had done to her fair complexion. "I must be a mess."

"Nothing a hot bubble bath wouldn't cure, and I'm volunteering to scrub your back," he whispered.

"I'll take you up on that, Your Highness."

And shortly after, they left the graveyard and returned to the farmhouse.

They had one night left to share here. And Portia was sure, Juan Carlos would make it memorable, bubble bath and all.

Portia was too much in love to think about her future and how marrying Juan Carlos would affect her life and her career. She had no details to cling to, only love, and it would have to see her through the tough decisions she would have to make. Now, as she sat at a long dressed table in the palace's elegant dining room, she gazed first at her secret fiancé seated at the helm. Dressed in a charcoal-black suit, he was beaming and full of determination. He appeared ready to make the announcement to his family. Rafe and Emily sat across from her with her friend Maria and Alex Ramon.

Gabriel and his wife, Serafia, sat to her left, along with Bella and James. James's little girl, Maisey, was holding tight to her chest a princess doll dressed in aqua-blue with hair the color of glistening snow.

"It's a lovely doll, Maisey," Portia commented, smiling at the child.

"She looks a lot like you, Portia," Bella commented. "I'm just noticing the likeness."

Maisey's curious eyes shifted to Portia and the girl giggled. It was true that she shared a resemblance with a famous cartoon character that all young girls seemed to love.

Juan Carlos covered Portia's hand, entwining their fingers. "Ah, but Portia is a one-of-a-kind princess."

All those close to Juan Carlos were here. He'd invited them for dinner tonight under the pretense of disclosing the facts around the graveyard find. Only he and Portia knew the truth.

"Before the meal is served, a toast is in order," he said. "We have much to celebrate tonight."

Waiters poured champagne into crystal flutes.

Once all the bubbles settled, Juan Carlos rose. "Thank you, cousins and friends, for joining me tonight. We all have much to be thankful for. As you know, with Portia's help, we have found the missing pieces of art at the Montoro family farm. Yes, it's true, we dug up mock graves to unearth the treasures. The finds are yet to be authenticated, but we are fairly certain our ancestors wouldn't have gone to such extreme measures to hide fake artwork. Portia will do the preliminary research on the items we've found and under her advisement we will also hire an expert to verify each piece.

"But that is not why I've called you here today. I have

something more personal to share with you." He turned to Portia, offering his hand. She took it and rose, warmth traveling up her cheeks. All eyes were on her and the king.

Juan Carlos went down on one knee, and gasps erupted from the diners at the table. She had no idea he would go traditional on her in front of his family. But how silly of her not to think it. Juan Carlos was a man of tradition and so as she gazed into his gleaming dark eyes, she began to tremble.

"Princess Portia, you know I love you with all of my heart. I have since the moment I laid eyes on you."

Tears wet her eyes.

"I have one precious thing left of my childhood and now, I am offering it to you." He reached into his jacket pocket and came up with a diamond ring, the stone so brilliant, it caught the chandelier light and virtually illuminated the room. "This was my mother's wedding ring," he said, his voice tight. "And here before our family and close friends, I ask you to wear it and become my wife. Portia, Princess of Samforstand, will you marry me?"

Not even a breath could be heard in the roomful of people.

Her cheeks were moist with tears as she nodded. "Yes, yes. Of course I'll marry you, Juan Carlos. I am honored to wear your mother's ring."

Her hand shook as he slid the ring that once belonged to his mother onto her finger. He stared at the ring, his eyes deeply reverent, and then grinned wide, looking foolishly happy. With the pads of his thumbs, he wiped at her tears and then took her in a kiss that nearly muffled the screams of delight and applause coming from behind her.

After the kiss, they were both swarmed with handshakes and hugs.

She was beside herself with happiness. The love and acceptance she experienced from his family and friends was more than she'd ever expected. There were no, *Are you sures?* or *This has happened so fasts*, but rather, "Congratulations" and "You two are perfect for each other."

After everyone returned to their seats, Juan Carlos lifted his glass of champagne. "Please join me in welcoming my fiancée, Portia, to our family. Today, she has made me the happiest man on earth."

Glasses clinked and sips were taken.

Portia's heart swelled. All doubts about her future were laid to rest. She and Juan Carlos would work things out. They would find a way to keep each other happy and not lose their own identity. She would be his wife in all ways. She would one day bear his child, an heir to the throne of Alma.

She locked the thought deep inside her heart and it filled her with joy.

"Jasmine, yes. It's true, it's true. I'm engaged to Juan Carlos. I wanted to tell you before news of our engagement reached the States. The king's assistant will be speaking to the media tomorrow to share our engagement news." Portia held the cell phone to her ear as she looked out the window of Juan Carlos's master suite in the palace. The king's room had a view of the gardens below, with its expertly groomed fall flowers.

"Congratulations, Portia. Wow. It's hard to believe. The king moves fast, doesn't he?" Jasmine asked, a little bit in awe.

"Yes, he does," she said softly, focusing on a row of red carnations growing in the garden. They were hardy this time of year. "He's quite persuasive when he wants something. That's why he'll be a great king and not just a figurehead. After news of our find comes out, the country will see how much Alma means to him. They'll rally behind him, and he'll be… Jas, forgive me, I'm rambling, aren't I?"

"Oh, my gosh, Portia. I hear it in your voice. You're really in love, aren't you?"

"He's amazing, Jas. And I resisted him as long as I could, but Juan Carlos…well, when you meet him, you'll see what I mean."

"I'm going to meet him?" She pictured her friend's eyes snapping to attention.

"Of course, silly. At the wedding. Jasmine, I want you by my side. I know it's a lot to ask, since the wedding will be held in Alma, but I'd be thrilled if you'd be my maid of honor."

"Portia…this is… Of course I'll be your maid of honor! I wish you could see me jumping up and down right now."

She chuckled. "I've got the image in my head. Just be careful. The last time you jumped for joy, you crashed into my dining table and nearly broke your leg."

"Okay, I've stopped jumping now," she said, out of breath. "This is all so very exciting."

"I can hardly believe it myself. Juan Carlos wants to be married, like, yesterday, so I think it's going to happen as soon as we can put all the pieces together."

"Count on me to help."

"Thank you. I was hoping you'd say that and I'm glad you're going to be in my wedding. Right now, I'm working on an art authentication project that will take me until the end of the week to finish. I should be home in three days. Then it'll be full steam ahead with wedding plans."

"I can't wait to see you. I have a million questions for you."

"And I don't have a million answers. But it'll work out," Portia said, taking a deep breath. "It has to. Have to run now. Love you, Jas."

"Love you, too," her assistant said, and then hung up.

"What don't you have a million answers to?" Juan Carlos was suddenly beside Portia at the window. His arms around her waist, he took the cell phone from her hand and turned her to face him. She looked into curious, warm dark eyes.

"All of this?" she said. She couldn't lie. The roller coaster was going fast and she was holding on for dear life. "I don't know how this will all work out. I have a career, a life and a job on both US coasts. As it is, I'm not home much."

He lifted her chin and tilted his head. She braced herself for the onslaught of his kiss. When he held her this way and gazed at her, she turned into a puddle of mush. The kiss was long and leisurely. He took his time with her and every bone in her body melted. Yes, her fiancé knew how to devastate.

"As long as we love each other," he said, "the obstacles won't be too great. I don't expect you to give up your work, Princess. I won't demand anything of you but your love."

When he spoke so sincerely, she believed him. She saw her future bright and clear. Nothing was more powerful than their shared love. "You have that, Your Highness."

His fingertips traced the outline of her lips. "I heard you say you'll be going in three days."

"Yes," she said. "When I'm through researching and authenticating what I can of the Montoro art collection, I'll head back to the States. I have appointments to keep."

"And you'll look into wedding protocols from your native Samforstand?"

"Yes, I know that's important to you. It is to me, too."

"Our union should reflect both of our heritages and royal traditions. The wedding must be a melding of both of our countries. The sooner, the better, my love. I can hardly stand the thought of you leaving." He sent her head swirling with another earth-shattering kiss.

"Well," she said, licking her lips. "We do have three

more days together. And nights." She arched her brows and slanted her head, playing coy.

Juan Carlos took the bait. With a growl, he lifted her up and carried her to the bed, unceremoniously dropping her so that she bounced on the mattress. A chuckle ripped from her lips. "Your Highness," she said, staring at the bulge growing in his pants. "It's half past eleven in the morning."

"Princess, I don't see a problem with that, do you?"

She shook her head, giggling. It didn't take much to tempt her new fiancé and she loved that about him.

He climbed onto the bed and Portia spent the next hour making up for the time she and Juan Carlos would be apart.

Eight

"Wow, Portia, you look beautiful in this dress. I think it's the one," Jasmine said, nodding her head in approval. Her friend was having a grand time getting her in and out of wedding dresses, much to the dismay of the shop owner who stood just outside the dressing room, hoping to be called in to aid and assist in the fitting.

Portia stood on a pedestal platform gazing at her reflection in the three-way mirror in the tiny wedding shop in Santa Monica. "You said that about the last three gowns I've tried on."

"I can't help it. They all look amazing on you. But this one with the ivory tulle and Swarovski crystals." Jasmine sighed. "It's heavenly."

"It is lovely," Portia said, admiring the lines of the dress. "It's such a big decision."

"I'll say. It's not every day a friend of mine marries a king. Princess or not."

Portia chuckled.

Once word of the new king of Alma's American fiancée had hit the Los Angeles newsstands, Portia had been inundated with offers of gown fittings, hair and makeup, photographers and wedding planners. She'd had requests for radio and television talk shows. She'd refused them all, trying to scale down the hoopla. She hadn't expected to be crowded at the airport by the paparazzi, or followed home for that matter. Once again, her personal life was under the spotlight.

None of it mattered, though. She was so deeply in love with Juan Carlos, the unwanted attention was manageable. On some level, she understood the public's desire for a fairy-tale love story. Ghastly news reports of wars, poverty and chilling murders needed some balance. The country craved something positive and lovely to grasp onto, and a newly crowned king marrying a princess, both of whom had lived in America, fit the bill.

Portia stepped out of the gown and redressed in her own clothes before letting Amelia of Amelia's Elegance into the dressing room. "Thank you for your time," Portia said to the shop owner. "I will keep this gown in mind. It's certainly beautiful."

Jasmine was careful handing the wedding dress over to Amelia. "This is my favorite, with the chapel length veil."

"I agree. It's certainly fitting for a princess," the shop owner said, nodding her head. "It's from a most talented designer. I shall put it on hold for you, if you'd like?"

Jasmine nodded. "Yes, the princess would like that."

Portia did a mental eye roll. Jasmine loved using the princess card for special favors.

"Your Highness, thank you for considering my shop for your wedding needs."

"You're welcome. I appreciate your time. You do have some stunning things here."

Amelia beamed with pride. "Thank you. We try to accommodate our clients with only the highest quality material and design."

"We have a few other stops to make, but I will personally call you when the princess makes up her mind," Jasmine said.

Amelia thanked them and walked them out the door.

"Did you love the dress?" Jasmine asked. "A bride has

to fall in love with her dress. They say as soon as she puts the right one on, she knows. Did you know?"

"Well, I did like it."

"But you didn't love it?"

Portia got into the front seat of Jasmine's car. "No, I didn't *love* it."

Luckily, no one had followed her to the dress shop. Jasmine got into the driver's seat and glanced around. "Did you hear? Rick Manning just got engaged to the daughter of a United States senator. It's all over the news. They claim to be crazy about each other."

Rick Manning, an A-list movie star, was dubbed the man least likely to ever marry. Handsome and charming and very much a ladies' man. "Yes, it was all over the news this morning. I've met Eliza Bennington. She's a nice person."

"Well, you can thank them both. Luckily, the tabloids have dropped you like a hot potato. At least, until more royal wedding news is announced. The dogs are on a different scent right now."

"I don't envy them. It's no fun having your every move analyzed."

"I hear you," Jasmine said, and pulled out of the parking spot. "Are you hungry?"

"Starving. Let's have lunch."

"Okay, but afterward, the great wedding dress search goes on."

Portia agreed to that plan and looked out the window. Jasmine was taking her maid of honor duties seriously. The truth was, Portia had a hundred loose ends to tie up before the wedding, and she missed Juan Carlos like crazy. They spoke at least twice a day since she'd left him at the airport in Alma.

"You are perfect for me, Princess. Always remember

that," were his last words to her as she boarded his private airplane.

It was after six in the evening when Jasmine dropped her off at home. She climbed the few steps of her one-level Brentwood condo, knowing she had another hunt on her hands. She'd promised Juan Carlos she'd look up royal wedding protocols from Samforstand. She'd been too busy with rescheduling her work appointments and dress shopping to dig into her old files until now.

She dropped her purse on the couch and then strode to the fridge and grabbed a Coke. Sipping from the can, she walked into her bedroom and pulled out the old cedar trunk from the back of her walk-in closet. The trunk held the few remaining things she had left of her parents.

Unlatching the lid, she found a massive amount of papers, deeds, bank account records and folders upon folders of news clippings about her parents when they were a young royal couple in exile. She lifted out an article written about them from the *New York Times*, just days before the tragic car accident that claimed their lives. Her eyes misted as she looked at a picture of the loving couple that accompanied the article. Her father was decked out in royal regalia with her mother by his side. They were young and happy and it hurt her heart still to look at them and think about all they had lost.

Her mother's wedding ring was in its original sapphire-blue velvet box, her father's tie clips and a gold wedding band were stored in a polished walnut case. She assumed most of their other possessions were sold to keep her comfortable and pay for her expenses. She'd been raised by her grandmother Joanna. But now all she had was her great-aunt, Margreta, who was a little senile. Portia paid for her care in a nursing home and visited her whenever she could.

As the evening wore on, she pored over every piece of paper in the trunk. She read every article and viewed every picture taken. Yet nowhere could she find any research that dated back to her great-grandparents' era of rule before they'd migrated to the United States after World War II. Surely, there had to be something? Having lost her parents early in life, she had only a fragmentary account of her heritage from her grandmother. Grandma Joanna hadn't liked to talk about the old days. It was too painful, a past wrought with the loss of her only son. Portia's questions about her parents were met with hushed tones and sadness and she'd never really learned much about them. She did remember her mother's bright smile and her father's light blue eyes. But even now, she wondered if those were true memories, or just recollections of the pictures she'd seen.

Her cell phone rang and a name popped up on the screen. She answered before the second ring. "Juan Carlos." She sighed.

His baritone voice drifted to her over thousands of miles. "Hello, Princess. I had to hear your voice once more before I started my day. I hope I didn't wake you."

She glanced at the clock. It was 8:00 a.m. in Alma. "No, not at all. I'm doing some research right now. I'm glad you called. How are you?"

"Besides missing you, I'm doing well. I'm scheduled to do a television interview later this morning. All of Alma is rejoicing over our art find, sweetheart. But I have a feeling the interviewer is more interested in our engagement. I'm sure I will be barraged with questions about our wedding."

"I'm sure you can handle it, Your Highness."

"What I can't handle is not being with my perfect princess. When will you be returning to me?"

"Give me a week, Juan Carlos," she said. "I need the time to get some things in order."

"Sounds like an eternity."

"For me, too, but I have a lot to accomplish. Jasmine

has been persistent. We are very close to choosing a wedding gown."

"I can't wait to see you in it. No matter which you choose you'll be beautiful. But what have you decided about your work?"

"I've managed to take a three months' leave of absence. I'm thinking of relocating to Europe. There are many American art collectors living abroad who might need my services. I...I don't have it all figured out yet."

"Take your time, sweetheart. I want you to be happy with whatever you choose."

"Okay. Thank you."

"I've been thinking. How does a Christmas wedding sound?"

"A Christmas wedding?" She pictured lush holly wreaths, bright red poinsettias and twinkling lights decorating the palace. "Sounds heavenly. But it's less than two months away."

Her fiancé was eager to make her his wife. She couldn't complain, yet her mind spun. She had so very much to do.

"We can make it work, Portia."

"Yes, yes. Okay," she said, smiling. The idea was too tempting to pass up. "Let's have a Christmas wedding."

There was a pause, and she pictured him smiling. "I love you, Portia."

"I love you, too, Juan Carlos."

The nursing home smelled of lye soap and disinfectant. Yet somehow the word *sterile* didn't come to mind as Portia walked the halls toward her great-aunt Margreta's room. Her aunt had once told her, "The odors of old age are too strong to conceal." Sharp old bird, Aunt Margreta was, back in the day. But Portia never knew what she'd find when she visited. Some days, her great-aunt was lucid, her wits about her. And some days, it was as if she'd fallen into a dark hole and didn't know how to get out.

This kind of aging was a slow, eternally sad process. Yet, as Portia popped her head into her aunt's room, she was greeted with cheery buttercup-colored walls and fresh flowers. Aunt Margreta sat in a chair, reading a crime thriller. A good sign.

"Hello, Auntie," Portia said. "It's me, Portia."

Her aunt looked over her thick eyeglasses and hesitated a moment. "Portia?"

Her voice was weak, her body frail and thin. "Yes, it's me."

The old woman smiled. "Come in, dear." She put the book down on her lap. "Nice of you to visit."

Thank heaven. Her aunt was having a good day. Maybe now, she could gather information about the Lindstrom monarchy that Portia hadn't been able to find anywhere else. She'd used up every one of her massive tools of research, including going through newspaper archives searching for an inkling about her family's rule and traditions carried out in Samforstand. She found nothing, which was very odd, and that lack of information brought her here today. Maybe Aunt Margreta could shed some light. She was her grandmother's sister and had lived in the homeland before the war.

Portia pulled up a chair and sat down beside her. "How are you, Auntie?"

"I can't complain. Well, I could, but it would do no good. I'm old, Portia. And you," she said, gazing over her glasses again. "You are as beautiful as I remember."

Portia took her hand and smiled. Aunt Margreta's hands were always soft, the skin loose and smooth over the aging bones. At ninety-three years old, she was as physically fit as one could expect, but for daily bouts of arthritis. But her mind wasn't holding up as well as her body and that worried Portia. "So are you, Aunt Margreta. You're a beautiful lady."

She'd always been a sweet woman, though as Portia remembered, she'd also been feisty in her day and not always in agreement with her sister, Joanna. The two would argue when they thought Portia couldn't hear. She never knew what they argued about, but as soon as Portia would step into the room, they'd shoot each other a glare and stop arguing, pretending things were all fine and dandy. Which they were, most of the time. Portia missed her parents, but she'd never discount the love Grandma Joanna and Great-Aunt Margreta bestowed upon her. It was the least she could do for her aunt to see to her care here at Somerset Village.

"Auntie, are they treating you well here?"

She nodded. "I'm fine, dear. The food's better now. We have a new chef and he doesn't cut corners. You'll see. You'll stay for lunch?"

"Of course I will. I'm looking forward to it."

"Then I'll get dressed up and we'll go to the dining room later."

"Okay. Auntie, I have good news." She lifted her left hand and wiggled her fingers. "I'm engaged."

Margreta squeezed her eyes closed. "Is it to Johnny Valente? That boy wouldn't leave you alone when you were younger. I never liked him. "

Johnny Valente? Portia used to play with him in grade school, two decades ago. He was a bully who'd called her Polar Bear Portia, because of her light hair and skin tone. "Gosh no, Auntie. I never liked him, either." She hoped her aunt wasn't digressing. "I'm engaged to…" How should she say this? "I met this wonderful man when I was visiting Alma."

"What's Alma?"

"It's this beautiful island country just off the coast of

Spain. I met him at his coronation. Auntie, he was just crowned king. His name is Juan Carlos Salazar, King Montoro of Alma."

Aunt Margreta put her head down. "I see."

Her aunt's odd reaction surprised her. "Do you like my ring?"

She gave Portia's left hand a glance. "It sparkles."

"Yes, it does."

"But it looks old."

"Yes, I suppose it's at least fifty years old. It was his mother's ring. He…lost his family at a young age also."

"In a car accident, just like your mother and father?"

"Yes, the same way. We have a lot in common."

Pain entered her aunt's eyes. "That's terribly sad, isn't it?" Her aunt made a move to get up from the chair. "Is it time for lunch yet, dear?"

Portia's eye twitched. "Not yet, Auntie."

Her aunt relaxed back into her seat.

"Auntie, I have a question to ask you. It's very important to me, so please try to concentrate. I will be marrying a king and, well, since I also have royal bloodlines, my fiancé wants very much for me to carry out the protocols of my homeland during our wedding. Do you know where I might find that information? I can't seem to find anything about our family's rule before World War II."

Aunt Margreta put her head down again.

"Auntie, please. Try to remember."

"There are no protocols from the family," she said stoically.

"But surely…there have to be. Have you forgotten?"

"No, my dear. I have not forgotten. Your grandmother and I never saw eye to eye about this."

"About what, Auntie?"

Margreta stilled. "Tell no one. Tell no one. Tell no one," she repeated.

"Not even me, Auntie? What is it you're not supposed to tell?"

Margreta looked straight ahead, as if Portia wasn't there. As if she was going back in time, remembering. "Don't tell Portia. She must never know the truth."

"What?" Portia absorbed her words, but they didn't make any sense. "What do you mean, I must never know the truth? What truth?" Portia grabbed her aunt's hand, gently squeezing. "Auntie, please. You have to tell me."

Her aunt turned to stare at her. "You are not a princess," she said. Her voice was sorrowful, etched in pain and Portia's heart sunk at her earnest tone. "Our family never ruled in Samforstand. Your mother wasn't royalty and neither was my sister, Joanna. It's all a lie."

Surely, the old woman was having a senile episode. "But, Auntie, of course Grandmother was queen. She raised me. I would know if she wasn't."

Silence.

"Aunt Margreta, please?"

"Yes, you're right, dear. You would know. Never mind."

Her aunt's quick compliance confused her even more. And she started thinking back about her life and how she'd never really seen any official documents regarding the Lindstrom monarchy. They'd been figureheads, holding no great power, yet she'd never known much about her homeland. It wasn't talked about. It seemed from her recent research the monarchy started to take shape in the United States, just after World War II.

"Oh, my God," she murmured. Her body began to tremble as tears stung her eyes. "You're telling the truth, aren't you? I'm not a princess."

Her aunt's eyes softened, dimmed by sorrow. "I'm sorry, Portia dear."

"But how can I believe that? How can that possibly be true?"

Could she take the word of an elderly senile woman who went in and out of coherency?

"There's a diary," her aunt said. "Joanna kept a secret diary."

"Where?" Now Portia would get to the truth. "Where's the diary?"

Aunt Margreta pointed to the bookshelf against the far wall overflowing with books. "Behind Agatha Christie."

Portia strode over to the bookshelf. Her hands were shaking as she parted half a dozen mystery novels. She lifted a weathered, navy blue soft-covered book from the shelf and brought it close to her chest. It had no title on the cover. Her heart racing, she took her seat next to Aunt Margreta and began reading the words that made a lie out of her entire life.

Portia lay quietly on her sofa, a cool towel on her forehead. She'd cried a river full of tears and every cell in her body was now drained. Princess Portia Lindstrom of Samforstand no longer existed. She never had. She was a fraud, a fake. An imposter. How could her family do this to her? How could they have perpetrated a lie that would affect her entire life?

How cruel.

How unjust.

Damn the circumstances behind their decisions right now. Their bold blatant betrayal was all that mattered to her. How dare they mislead her and let her believe in the fairy tale? She wasn't the snow queen. Hell, once the truth got out, she'd be deemed the black witch.

She'd been involved in one scandal already and it had taken years to live that down. But this? This was too much. The press would devour her. They'd make her out to be the villain, a lying deceiving bitch out to ensnare a wealthy king.

The humiliation alone would destroy all the positive good Juan Carlos had done for his country.

She muffled another sob. She didn't have it in her to shed more tears.

Feeling empty, she closed her swollen eyes, unable to rid herself of the thoughts plaguing her. The lies she'd been told, the deceptions perpetrated by her family. What of her career? Most importantly, what would she do about Juan Carlos? He was king, and as king he was pledged to only marry a woman of royal heritage. It was his destiny. It was what the citizens of Alma expected. Juan Carlos was the most dutiful man she'd ever known. This would destroy their relationship.

The towel was removed from her head. "Feeling better yet? Want to get up?" Jasmine asked.

"Nooooo. I don't want to ever get up."

Jas sat down on the floor beside the sofa. "Hey, that doesn't sound like the Portia I know. You've been wallowing for two hours."

"I'm not the Portia you know. I'm not… I don't know who I am. And I have a right to wallow."

"Yes, it sucks. But Portia, you are you, no matter if you have the title of princess or not."

"It's just…it's just so darn humiliating. I feel like a fool. I feel, well, I feel like everything's a lie. My childhood, my upbringing, my friends."

"Hey, watch it there."

"You know I don't mean you."

Jasmine reached for her hand and squeezed. "I know."

"All the doors that have opened for me because of my title, Jas… Those people will think the worst of me. They'll think I deliberately deceived them to get ahead in my career."

"When in truth, we know, they were using you. They

wanted to be associated with a princess. So it was a trade-off. You have nothing to be ashamed of."

"I'm ashamed of everything."

"And angry."

"Yes, of course. I'm spitting mad at my family."

"I'm not justifying what they've done, honey. But they came to the States after the war destitute, and like so many immigrant families, they didn't know how they'd survive here. And, well, pretending to be royalty from a tiny country…"

"It's far-fetched. Yet they got away with it."

"Yes, your grandmother speaks of it in the diary. How scared they were and how confused things were in Europe and Scandinavia after the war. There was a lot of rebuilding and restructuring and things just fell into place for them. Surprisingly, they weren't questioned. After all, we didn't have close ties to the monarchy of Samforstand the way we did England. Your grandmother speaks of Americans having much to deal with after the war. Hundreds of thousands of soldiers were coming home. Work and housing in our country was scarce. Things were chaotic."

"But others found a way to survive without deception. They worked hard and built honest, decent lives for themselves." Portia hinged her body up from her prone position and swiveled to plant her feet on the floor. Sitting upright, her head spun a little. "I don't know what I'd do without you, Jasmine. Honestly, you're the only person I can trust with this."

Jasmine rose from the floor and the sofa cushions dipped as she came to sit next to her. Her friend hung her arm around Portia's shoulder and they sat there like that for long minutes, quiet.

"I'm scared, Jas."

"I know."

"I don't know who I am. I can't expect you to understand fully how I'm feeling, but suddenly, I'm confused about everything. My heart is aching so badly right now."

"That's why I'm here, Portia. You're not alone."

She rested her head on Jasmine's shoulder. "Thank you."

The house telephone rang. "Want me to get it?"

"No," she said to Jasmine. "I can't talk to anyone right now."

Jas nodded.

Shortly after that, her cell phone began ringing and she knew both calls were from Juan Carlos.

They spoke every evening before she went to bed. Never fail.

Until tonight.

She couldn't speak to him and pretend everything was all right. She couldn't pretend that she was still a princess. She had a lot of thinking to do and she couldn't burden Jasmine any further in the decisions she'd have to make about her future.

Thoughts of Juan Carlos always squeezed her heart tight in a loving embrace.

This time, though, it was as if her heart was being strangled.

And the pain of losing Juan Carlos wouldn't go away anytime soon.

Portia sat in the throne room at the palace in Del Sol, her eyes closed, her heart pumping hard. Yesterday, she'd texted and emailed Juan Carlos one excuse after another as to why she wasn't answering his calls until she'd realized the only way to break it off with him was to face him in person. She'd flown half the night to get here. To see him one last time.

His family had been through a great deal to once and for all return the true and rightful heir to the Alma throne.

There'd been one debacle after another with his cousins, as they attempted to reinstate the monarchy, and the entire process had come under great scrutiny. All eyes were on Juan Carlos now and he'd made promises, staunch, determined promises to the citizenry that he would take his role seriously. By royal decree from decades ago, he was obligated to marry a woman of royal stature. The last thing he needed was to be made a fool of by marrying an imposter, a woman who hadn't a drop of royal blood flowing through her veins.

She wasn't his perfect princess any longer.

A tear dripped down her cheek. She wiped it away and steadied her shaky breathing. She glanced down at the engagement ring she wore. It was magnificent and maybe someday would belong to a woman worthy of wearing it and claiming a place beside Juan Carlos.

Her stomach ached at the notion of Juan Carlos living with and loving another woman. But it would happen one day. Rightfully so. She could only hope getting over him wouldn't destroy her.

She heard footsteps approaching along the corridor. She rose from her seat and mustered her courage. She'd never been much of an actress, but today she needed to provide an award-winning performance.

The door opened and there he stood, dressed in a crisp white shirt, sleeves rolled up—as if he'd been busy at work—and tucked into well-fitting black trousers. A lock of his neatly combed hair swept across his forehead and his tanned face showed a hint of stubble. Some days, when he wasn't going out in public, he didn't shave. She preferred him that way...a little rough around the edges. Tall, elegant, gorgeous.

Juan Carlos's gaze lit upon her and her heart tumbled. Oh, how she'd missed him.

"Portia, sweetheart. You're here." His warm winning

smile devastated her as he strode across the room. Genuine love entered his eyes. "I'm so glad to see you. You've come back to me early."

"Yes."

"I was worried when I couldn't reach you. But now I see, you wanted to surprise me."

He took her into his arms and heaven help her, she allowed him to kiss her.

His lips were warm, welcoming, filled with passion and beautifully familiar. She'd never been kissed the way Juan Carlos kissed her. She held her back stiff and didn't partake, but he was too caught up in the moment to notice her reluctance.

"We have much to talk about," he murmured, brushing his lips over hers again.

She stepped back and gazed into his dark gleaming eyes. "Yes, Juan Carlos. It's the reason I've come back to Del Sol so quickly."

He took her hand, covering it with his. "Come, let's sit then and catch up."

He began walking, tugging her along to the king and queen's thrones, two ornate tall chairs of plush red velvet and gilded carvings.

The irony of sitting upon that chair was too much. "I'd rather stand," she said.

"Okay." He looked at her oddly, but then nodded. "Would you like to take a walk? It might feel good to stretch your legs after the long plane ride. We can talk of the progress you've made with our wedding."

"No," she said. "No, Juan Carlos. I didn't come here early to discuss our wedding. I came to say that I can't go through with it."

"With what, sweetheart?" He blinked and appeared totally confused.

"The wedding. I can't marry you, Juan Carlos. I went home and really gave our situation some thought."

"Our situation?" He frowned. "You love me, I love you. That's our situation. We're engaged, Portia."

"No, as of today, we are not."

She inhaled and twisted the diamond ring off her finger. He was shaking his head, baffled. The gleam in his eyes dimmed. He almost appeared frightened. It killed her to wipe the joy from his face. "I'm terribly sorry."

"What is all this, Portia?"

She took his hand, spread open his palm and dropped his mother's wedding ring inside. "It's too much, Juan Carlos. We…we got caught up in the moment. Finding the art treasures put us both on a crazy romantic high and we took the little fling we had too far."

"Little fling?" he repeated, his voice hitching.

Oh, God, she'd hurt him. She knew she would, but she almost couldn't bear seeing that expression on his face. Better a small lie to save him, than the truth, which would make him look the fool in the eyes of his family and country. She loved him enough to suffer his anger and wrath. But the pain she'd inflicted would stay with her a long, long time.

"It happened so fast. You and I, we're different people. I love my job, Juan Carlos."

"You wouldn't have to give it up."

"Please understand," she said softly. "It isn't going to work out. I don't want to live here. I don't want to get married or have children right now."

His eyes snapped to hers. "I never rushed you about children, Portia."

"You'd expect it one day. And…and I'm afraid I'd disappoint you. I—I… It was a mistake to get engaged."

She backed up a step, putting distance between them. God should strike her dead for the lies she was telling. But it had to be done. Her sacrifice would make it easier on Juan Carlos in the long run. Yet her heart burned at the thought of leaving him forever.

"You're having cold feet. I hear it's common before a wedding."

"No, being away from here, from you, made it all clear to me, Juan Carlos. It's not cold feet, it's reality. I hope you'll understand and not make this harder on me than it already is."

He opened his palm to stare at the diamond ring. Then the sound of his deep wobbly sigh reached her ears. He was in pain. God, she hated this. "I love you, Portia," he said, searching her eyes.

Tears blurred her vision. Her throat constricted. She couldn't return his love. For his sake, she said nothing.

He gripped her forearms, gently shaking her. As if the impact would somehow clear her head of this nonsense. "Portia, you told me you loved me. You agreed to be my wife."

"I'm…I'm…" She took a swallow. Could she do this? Could she tell the biggest lie of all? She forced the words out. "I'm fond of you, Juan Carlos."

He dropped her arms. "Fond?"

She nodded.

"Then why are you crying, sweetheart?"

Her tears now were soaking her dress. She hated herself at the moment. "I don't like hurting you."

"Then don't. Stay and we'll talk this over. Give us time, Portia."

"I can't, Juan Carlos. It won't do any good. We're… over." She sobbed now, unable to hold back any longer. "I'm s-sorry."

He didn't reach for her. Thank goodness. If he touched her again, she'd melt into his arms. But he watched her carefully, as if trying to figure her out. Skepticism lingered in his eyes. He didn't believe her, but there was also resignation there and definite injury. She must have baffled him. He didn't know what to say to convince her she was wrong.

There wasn't anything he could say to her to change her mind. This was the hardest thing she'd ever had to do. She had to leave, to muster her strength and walk out the door. "I'll never forget the time I had with you… It was… *amazing*," she whispered.

He closed his eyes, shaking his head.

And that was her way out.

She turned her back on him and dashed away, leaving the palace and Juan Carlos and the love they'd shared behind.

Nine

"If you don't mind me saying so, Your Highness, you could use some sleep. Why not close your eyes while we travel," Eduardo said.

Juan Carlos sat facing his bodyguard in the reclining lounge chair on the palace's private plane. Under normal circumstances, Juan Carlos wouldn't travel so extravagantly; he wanted to be known as the king who flew coach. But it was imperative that this journey be kept secret and away from curious eyes. "Are you saying I look less than kingly, Eduardo?"

His bodyguard straightened in his seat. "No, I, uh, I know how hard this week has been on you, Your Highness."

"Eduardo, I'm in total agreement with you." Juan Carlos sighed. "I know I look like hell. I will fix that before we arrive in Los Angeles. The best I can, that is."

Eduardo's eyes softened. "Yes, Your Majesty."

Eduardo was quickly becoming his good friend and confidant. "Do you have a girl, Eduardo?"

"Yes, I do."

"Is it serious?"

Eduardo shook his head. "No, not really."

"Because of what you do for a living?"

"Yes. I cannot get serious with anyone while I'm away so much of the time. She understands."

"Ah, an understanding woman. It's lucky for me, not so fortunate for your girl."

"*Si*, that is true. But I am twenty-eight and not ready to settle down."

"I used to think that way. But sometimes fate steps in and knocks you over the head when a beautiful snow queen enters your path."

Eduardo chuckled. "Princess Portia."

"Yes, Princess Portia. And now I'm chasing her all over the globe."

"She is worth it, I would say, Your Majesty."

"*Si*, she is worth it."

He lifted the tumbler of bourbon he held in his hand and stared into the golden liquid. "I wish you could share a drink with me, Eduardo. We'll be in the air for five more hours. Surely the effects will have worn off by then."

"Thank you, Your Majesty, but no. I cannot drink while on duty."

Juan Carlos nodded. "Coffee then and a pastry?"

"I'd never refuse a pastry from Chef Andre, Your Highness. He showed me his creations before packing them up for this trip."

Juan Carlos pressed the button on the arm of his chair and ordered up coffee and pastries from his personal flight attendant. Then he rested back in his seat and sipped bourbon. Sleep was elusive lately and eating had become a chore. But he could tolerate a shot or two of bourbon when his mind wouldn't shut down. It helped blur the pain of losing Portia.

It had been one solid week since she'd left Alma and he hadn't heard from her since. What was she doing? Had she gone back to her work routine as if *they* hadn't happened? As if the time they'd shared together was nothing more than a passing fling?

He couldn't believe that. Something was up with her.

He felt it deep down in his soul that something had happened to Portia to make her deny their love and break off their engagement. Juan Carlos had waited patiently all week to hear from her, anticipating a call that had never come, and his patience was at an end. Now he was taking matters into his own hands. He knew enough about relationships to know women liked to be pursued. They liked to have men come after them. Maybe Portia was testing him? Maybe she'd expected him to come running and convince her she'd been wrong?

If only it would be that easy.

But he had to try.

Outside of his bodyguards, he hadn't told a soul of their breakup. He couldn't bring himself to share the news so soon after publicly announcing their happy engagement. He had hopes of winning Portia back, hopes of restoring their love. He'd vowed to bring honor and credibility back to the monarchy of Alma as well as to carry out his grandmother Isabella's dying wishes for the country. He wanted, needed Portia by his side. He and Portia belonged together. She was the love of his life.

Living without her would only be half a life.

Hours later, the plane touched down in Los Angeles, a place Juan Carlos had visited often. But this time, he had more than business to attend to—he had come to retrieve his woman. He'd managed to get a few winks of sleep, shaved and changed his crumpled clothes while they were in the air. Now he felt human again and more like himself, rather than the shell of the man he'd been this past week. Dressed in a slate-gray suit and neatly groomed, he planned on sweeping his princess off her feet again.

Returning home without her wasn't an option.

"Are you ready, Your Highness?" Eduardo asked, rising from his seat.

"Yes, and you have our little surprise all set?" he asked.

"I do. If it doesn't help your cause," Eduardo said, grinning, "nothing will."

Juan Carlos nodded. He couldn't disagree.

A frozen waffle popped up out of the toaster and Portia set it next to the scrambled eggs on her plate. She doused the waffle with maple syrup, grabbed a fork and took the plate over to the kitchen table. Breakfast for dinner was always an option when one didn't have the stomach to really cook. Or eat for that matter. Her belly squeezed tight as she looked at the food. She'd promised Jasmine she would eat something tonight.

Her friend had apologized profusely for breaking their dinner date. Jas had planned to cook a roast prime rib tonight, her specialty. They were going to do it up right with champagne and soufflé, and have a fun girls' night watching Turner Classic Movies on television. It was the only reason Portia had put on a dress, instead of wearing her usual comfy gray sweats. She didn't want to disappoint her friend.

"Poor Jas." She'd come down with a bug. Hopefully it wasn't the flu. Portia felt a little guilty about it, having dominated a lot of her time lately. Jasmine had been the best friend she could ever hope to have. Every day she'd come over to help Portia clean out her closets or rearrange furniture or cook a meal. Jasmine would bring in Mexican food on Taco Tuesdays and play card games with her until very late at night. She understood Portia needed to kill time so she didn't have to think too hard.

Now her friend was sick.

"For you, Jas, I'm going to eat this." She took a bite of her eggs and chewed and chewed. The eggs went down like rubber. She'd overcooked them again.

The waffle wasn't much better. It was still frozen in the center. Two bites later, she figured she'd fulfilled her promise and took her dish to the sink, dumping the contents down the garbage disposal.

Now what? She glanced around the condo. It was spotless. She'd been cleaning all week long. She had no official work to do. She hadn't been back to the office yet—they weren't expecting her anyway since she'd taken a three-month leave to deal with wedding plans and her new life as wife to a king.

She'd truly questioned whether to go back to her job. Could she continue with the pretense? How could she go back, when her friends and associates still believed her to be Princess Portia of Samforstand? Could she go about her life, living the lie? And what if she decided it was impossible to resume her life as usual? What if she revealed all the lies about herself and her family? What would that mean for Juan Carlos? His humiliation would be monumental. He would hate her. And appear a fool, a man easily duped.

She was at a crossroads in her life, and didn't know which way to proceed.

No one could possibly know how she felt right now. She was a phony, a fraud and an imposter. Jasmine kept telling her it wasn't her fault and no one would blame her if the truth got out. But Portia didn't know who she was anymore. Her life had been ripped out from under her. She felt at odds, lonely and bereft. Her emotions were all over the place. Anger took up residence, but sympathy crept in sometimes, as she imagined her family's plight after the war. Still, those emotions didn't come close to the emptiness she felt deep inside her heart. Because of something that had happened decades ago, she had had to give up the man she loved. The price was high, costing her her happiness.

The doorbell chimed and she jumped. "Who could that be?" she whispered. Surely, Jasmine wouldn't come out tonight. She was in bed with a fever.

Portia had a mind not to open the door, but the bell chimed once again and her curiosity had her heading to the front door.

She stuck her face up to the peephole and gazed out. "Eduardo?" What on earth was he doing here?

"*Si*, Princess, it's me."

She cringed at his reverent greeting. She didn't deserve to be called Princess. The chain lock allowed her to open the door three inches. She peered out and he smiled wide. "Hello."

Eduardo had become her friend. Seeing this solid block of a man on her doorstep was a welcome sight.

"Hi."

"Will you open the door for me?"

"Oh...of course." She undid the chain and opened the door.

Eduardo stood rooted to the spot. "Are you alone, Princess?"

"Yes, I am alone. Why?"

"I had to ask as it is my duty to protect the king. It's good to see you, but I am here on official bus—"

Juan Carlos stepped into her line of vision from a place on the porch that had concealed him. "Thank you, Eduardo. I'll take it from here."

Portia's mouth dropped open. She blinked and started trembling. "Juan Carlos."

He held a cat carrier in his hand. "Before you say anything, I brought you a gift. Well, two gifts. May I come in?"

With a lump in her throat, she looked away from Juan Carlos's face to the two kittens from Duchess's litter she'd appropriately named Mischief and Mallow. The kittens—one black and gray and mostly all trouble and the other almost all white with spots of caramel color here and there looking like a toasted marshmallow—were sleeping, curled up into little balls of fluff. Mallow's head rested on Mischief's body. Their sweetness brought a tear to her eye.

"Juan Carlos, you…you brought them," she said, touched by the thoughtful gesture. Words she wanted to say tightened in her throat and wouldn't come out. Initially, her heart had lurched when she spotted Juan Carlos, though he looked worn out. His eyes were rimmed with red—from sleepless nights? His handsome face looked haggard, as if he'd been through a war and his hair, while combed, needed a cut. She should have known he wouldn't take no very easily. He wasn't a man easily dissuaded. It was one of the qualities she loved most about him. "You didn't need to do that," she said, finally realizing she wasn't up to caring for pets. She'd barely been able to care for herself lately.

"I figured you might like the company. They are yours as much as they are mine."

She gazed into his solemn eyes. "Come in," she said.

She'd been engaged to a man who had never stepped foot into her home. How telling was that? An impetuous engagement, even though love was involved, wasn't an ideal way to start a relationship. She understood that now. During the coronation and then while living at the farmhouse searching for hidden treasures, they'd lived in a fantasy world, untouched by outside influences. It wasn't reality.

Juan Carlos stepped inside and glanced around, taking in the details of her home. "It's as beautiful as you are, Portia. I wouldn't expect any less."

"Thank you," she said. Her heart thumped hard in her chest. Thankfully, Eduardo's presence helped defuse the situation at the moment. She peered over Juan Carlos's shoulder. "Eduardo, would you like to come inside?"

She'd spent enough time with Juan Carlos and his bodyguards to know what Eduardo's answer had to be. He would be securing the premises and standing watch outside. "I wish I could, Your Highness," he said. "Thank you, but I will be right out here."

It was just as she'd suspected. "Okay, I understand." She turned to Juan Carlos and pasted on a false smile. "Surely, you and I both know that bringing me the kittens wasn't the reason you've come."

"But you're glad I did?"

She glanced at the sleeping kittens. "I'm glad to see them. They are sweet and I did…miss them." She cleared her throat. She couldn't admit she'd missed Juan Carlos also. "They've been weaned from Duchess, I'm assuming?"

He nodded. "Early this week. Where shall I put them?"

"A good question. If you'd called and asked me I would've told you not to bring them, Juan Carlos," she said softly. "I'm not equipped to care for them."

"I'll take them back to Alma with me, if you prefer." His back stiffened a little.

"No, no. Now that they're here, I can't turn them away. I… They're special to me."

Juan Carlos set the cat carrier down on the floor of the foyer. When he returned his gaze to hers, his eyes bored into her. "I had hoped you would say the same of me, sweetheart."

Her eyes closed at his hopeful plea. "You shouldn't have come, Juan Carlos."

"I couldn't stay away. It's not finished between us."

She sighed. "It has to be. We're not right for each other."

He approached her and heaven save her, her pulse accelerated as he laid his palm on her cheek. She lifted her eyes to his. His heavy expression softened, as if touching her made all the difference. As if a light inside him was turned back on. "Not true. We're good together. We're meant for each other. I am here. Don't turn me away, Portia. I would hope I am special to you, as well."

His gaze dipped to her mouth. She swallowed. Oh, God, the pull, the magnetic force of his love surrounded her like a protective shield. She didn't know where she found the will to back up a step, and then another. She couldn't hide her emotions or the passion he instilled and as she moved, he moved with her, thrusting his body against hers until her backside met with the wall.

"I've come a long way for you, Portia." His hands braced the wall, trapping her, so that she could only stare into his face and see his truth. "I've waited my entire life."

His sweet, sincere words stymied any defenses she could muster. She put her hands on his chest but instead of shoving him away as she'd planned, her fingertips clung onto his shirt and her palms flattened against him. His breath hitched from her touch, and his immediate reaction to her nearly buckled her knees. How could she not love this man? How could she turn him away now?

"I came here to talk to you, sweetheart."

She whispered, "Is that what you're doing to me? Talking?"

He flashed a charming, inescapable smile. "Maybe showing is better than telling, after all."

Then his mouth swooped over hers and claimed her in a breath-stealing kiss. His lips were rough but not unkind, wild but not crazy, sexy but not demanding. Caught up in the kiss, she couldn't think beyond the pleasure he evoked. The love she'd tried to bury was resurrected and she fell deeper in love with this man, this honorable king who had come for her.

She'd missed him and didn't know how much until this very second.

His tongue played over her lips and she opened for him. Sweeping inside her mouth, he kissed her again and again. A fire was building in her belly. She was past the point of refusal.

She was putty. He could do with her what he liked.

And she would enjoy every second.

She was lifted, floating on air now, held by two strong arms. She wrapped herself around his body, nestling her head into his chest. "Where's your bed, Portia?"

She pointed to the doorway down the hall.

His strides were long and determined and steady.

He continued to kiss her without missing a step.

Juan Carlos set Portia down on a ruffled lavender bedspread. Matching pillows, some big, some small, surrounded her head. He did a quick scan of her room decorated in soft whimsical colors. Wispy white curtains covered the windows and modern pieces of art, mostly pastels and some oils, adorned the walls. It was so Portia: soft, delicate, sweet.

God, he loved her.

And he wasn't going to leave here without her.

She was his prize, his love, the treasure he couldn't live without.

He unbuttoned his shirt, spread it wide across his chest and then gave it a toss. He kicked off his shoes and socks and gazed into her eyes as he unfastened his belt.

Her brows lifted, her lips parted slightly and a sharp breathy gasp escaped her lips. Her hungry expression softened his heart, but made every other part of his body hard. He had one night to change her mind. He wouldn't waste a minute. He took her hand and lifted her to her knees. "Come here, sweetheart," he demanded. "Touch me. Put your hands on my body."

Another gasp ripped from her lips and she moved to him. She wore a simple black dress with thin straps and short hemline. It adorned her breasts with just enough material to tempt him beyond belief. He ached to touch her, to shed her clothes and join their bodies, but first, he had to make her see how much she needed him, too. How perfect he was for her.

Her hands came to his torso and he gritted his teeth. She explored the breadth of him, tracing her fingertips over his chest, and then kissed everywhere her fingers had just touched. His body flamed; it was almost too much to bear. She was proving to him that they belonged together.

"Your touch is like no other, Portia. You know that. See what you do to me."

"We are good here, in bed, Juan Carlos," she whispered.

"We are good everywhere, sweetheart. Why do you fight me on this?"

She turned her face from him and disengaged, and he knew he'd pushed her too far. Something was eating at her. Something was making her hold back from him. "Don't retreat," he whispered. He couldn't let her think. Couldn't let whatever notions she had in her head continue to separate them.

He sank down on the bed beside her and unleashed his love for her, stripping down her defenses, loving her with everything he had inside. Holding her steady with one hand, he eased her dress off with the other, baring her upper body. He cupped her breasts, made love to them with his mouth and tongue and was rewarded with sighs of pleasure, little throaty moans of delight. Her throat, her chin, her lips. He devoured them all while covering her body with his. She arched her hips and they moved in the same unique rhythm, thrusting, aching, groaning until he couldn't take another second. He joined their bodies, pushing through her mental defenses and bringing them skin to skin.

Her eyes closed to the pleasure, her face beautifully masked in satisfaction. He thrust into her deep and long. It was hot and damp and sweaty and when he sensed her readiness, he called her name. "Portia." Her eyes snapped open. He stared into them and announced, "This is our place."

Connected by more than their bodies, she sighed and nodded her head.

Then he brought her home.

* * *

Early dawn broke through the curtains and Juan Carlos smiled in his drowsy state, his eyes still closed as images of making love to Portia flashed in his head. God, how he'd missed her. And now she was where she belonged. With him. After the night they'd shared, he hoped he'd convinced her that she loved him, he loved her and whatever was bothering her could be worked out and put to rest. It wasn't rocket science. Perhaps he'd pushed her too far early in their relationship. They'd only known each other for weeks. Not the months or years some take to cement their connection. She'd gotten cold feet. Any problems that arose could be dealt with. He couldn't see a reason why they shouldn't live their lives together. They'd made love twice during the night, and the second time had been even more thrilling and revelatory than the first. No one could tell him that Portia didn't love him. She'd displayed that in the way she'd taken the initiative, kissed him, touched him and made love to his body.

It was good, so good, between them. In all ways.

Juan Carlos rolled over to cradle her in his arms. They'd welcome the day together. But his hands hit upon cold sheets. He squeezed his eyes open. Portia was gone, her half of the bed empty. Was she always an early riser? He didn't know. They'd spent time together at the farmhouse in Alma on his schedule, not hers. There were still things they needed to learn about each other.

He hinged his body up, eager to see her. Eager to kiss her. Rising from the bed, he dressed in his trousers and shirt, ran a hand through his hair to comb down the spiky ends and then padded out of the room.

Halfway down the hallway of her modest three-bedroom condo, he halted, hearing mewling sounds coming from the living room. Of course, the kittens. Portia must have been anxious to see them this morning and tend to them the way she always had. Their carrier came equipped with kitty food, and water was their drink of choice. He grinned. He could almost picture her playing with them on the carpeted floor. Bringing them here had been a good plan to get his foot in the door and soften Portia's heart, but ultimately he'd done it to bring a smile to her face.

As he approached the sounds grew louder and no, they didn't appear to be coming from the kittens. It was a human sound, the heartbreaking echo of quiet crying. He stood on the threshold of the living room to find Portia, sitting up on the sofa, her arms around her legs, rocking back and forth with tears soaking her face.

The kittens were happily swatting at her feet, but it was as if they weren't there. Her sorrow was so deep she didn't hear him stride into the room. "Portia, sweetheart. What's wrong?"

She wiped her cheeks with the back of her hand, shaking her head. "You shouldn't have come, Juan Carlos," she whispered.

He narrowed his eyes. What on earth? Last night, they'd settled things. Maybe not verbally, but after the night they'd shared she had to recognize what they meant to each other. He'd come to retrieve her and bring her back to her rightful place, beside him on the throne of Alma. But now she was crying, looking so achingly sad. His gut clenched seeing her that way. "I don't understand."

He sat beside her and she unraveled her legs to face him, her eyes swollen from tears. "I can't be with you. I can't…"

"Sweetheart, my perfect princess, of course you belong with me. We don't have to rush into a wedding, if that's your concern. Whatever it is, we'll work it out. Just tell me. It kills me to see you in so much pain."

She rose then, yet her body slumped in defeat, her long hair falling onto her face. "That's just it, Juan Carlos," she said, shoving her hair aside. "I'm not your perfect princess.

I'm nobody's princess. I'm a fraud. I don't have an ounce of royal blood in my body. I cannot marry you. Ever."

Juan Carlos blinked several times, absorbing her words. He rose slowly, his heart pounding, his body shaking. "What you do mean you're not a princess?"

"I'm not. I never was. It's all a lie my family told after they migrated to the United States after World War II."

Portia spent the next few minutes explaining her family's duplicity to him. She gave him very little to hold on to as she presented the cold cruel facts that tore his life into shreds. Everything she told him made sense, yet nothing made sense. This couldn't be happening. Suddenly, he looked at Portia Lindstrom differently. She'd lied to him. Why? "How long have you known this?"

"I found out a little more than a week ago while researching our...my wedding rituals."

Juan Carlos stood ramrod stiff, his shoulders back and his heart breaking. "Yet you came to me and lied about the reasons for breaking it off between us. You told me you weren't ready to marry. You gave me excuses about your career and your love of the States. You knew, and yet you lied. How many other lies have you told me, Portia?"

"I didn't know what to do when I found out. Who to turn to. I'd just found out I'm...I'm an *imposter*." She spit the word out as if saying it stung her tongue. "I had trouble facing it, Juan Carlos."

His voice rose. "You should have trusted me with the truth. Or maybe you didn't want anyone to know the real truth? Maybe you wanted to keep on with the deception? Being of royal blood has its privileges. If I hadn't shown up here, what were you going to do? Live the lie forever?"

Her words from last week rang in his ears. *I'm fond of you. This isn't going to work. I don't want to get married. I don't want children.*

Had the woman he loved been nothing but a gold digger? Had her hard-to-get act been a ploy? All the warmth he had nestled inside evaporated. Last night had meant nothing to her. She'd deceived him over and over during the past few weeks. She'd broken off her engagement to him, but she hadn't revealed the truth to anyone. Of course, her precious career would suffer. She'd hidden the truth because she couldn't afford another scandal. She needed the art world to believe that she was a princess. So, of course, she had to come to him with lies about why she was breaking off their engagement in order to keep her secret.

"I took the bait and you reeled me in, didn't you, Portia? Then what happened? You ran scared when I offered marriage? Did you have a bout of conscience? Or did you finally realize you'd get caught if you didn't break it off with me? You couldn't marry me and risk being found out. Just think what would happen to your career if you were discovered to be a fraud. You'd never survive another scandal. Not professionally. No one in their right mind would hire you so you lied your way out of our engagement."

Her tears gone now, she squeezed her eyes closed for a second. As he waited, her breathing steadied and when she opened her eyes again, they were twin pinpoints of blue, focused on him. "You see things in black-and-white, Juan Carlos. There is no room for grays in your narrow line of vision. You only wanted me when I fit into your plans, but now you know the truth. I'm not royal. I'm flawed and can't be a part of your unblemished world."

His lips tightened. "You should've told me the truth, Portia."

"Another point against me. I'm human. I make mistakes." She folded her arms across her stomach. "Now that you have the truth, what are you going to do with it?"

He stared at her, wondering what had happened to the woman he'd fallen in love with. Thoughts clogged his head. She wasn't a princess. She had no royal blood flowing through her veins. She was an imposter. A fraud, as she put it. His shoulders dropped as he shook his head. He had no answer for her.

"You only loved the idea of me, Juan Carlos. You said it just a little while ago. You think of me as your perfect princess. But now you know I'm not perfect. Hardly that. And how can a man who demands perfection in everything and everyone want me? I was only good to you when I was Princess Portia of Samforstand."

He let that sink in. He loved her, wanted her as his wife. Now, nothing made sense, and blackness from deep in his soul overwhelmed him. His Portia, the woman he'd thought she was, was gone. She wasn't a princess, but a fraud. He couldn't marry Portia Lindstrom. According to royal decree he was obligated to marry royalty. She was once a part of everything good that had happened to him and now there was nothing left between them.

"We had a fling, and it's over," she whispered. "Let's let it go at that. I think you should leave. Go back to Del Sol, be the king you were meant to be. Give me some time, I'll make sure...no blame will come to you about this."

"Portia," he said. He couldn't bring himself to move.

"Go, please." Her quiet plea broke his heart. "You shouldn't have come back. Goodbye, Juan Carlos."

She picked up the kittens playing at her feet, hugged them to her chest and walked out of the room.

She was right. He should leave.

There wasn't anything left for him here.

"Mr. Tanaka, it was a pleasure seeing you again. I'll be in touch once I've found the right prints and antique paneled floor screens to separate your work spaces. You've given me a good idea what you are looking for. I promise you, you'll be happy with the collection I come up with for your magnificent new corporate offices."

"Thank you, Princess. I have faith in your abilities. Your recommendations for my home have worked out nicely. I'm grateful you would take time from your leave of absence to do this for me."

Portia shook hands with her client outside his private office, her belly squeezing tight every time he called her princess. The title she'd grown up with no longer rang true and his respectful use of it during their meeting reminded her constantly that she was a fraud. "Goodbye."

Mr. Tanaka, founder and president of a highly successful Japanese food chain, hadn't wanted to work with anyone else. He'd called her personally to request her expertise, offering a big bonus if she would consider advising him on the artwork for his new offices. She'd agreed without hesitation. Pining for Juan Carlos and what would never be had grown old. She couldn't cry herself to sleep any longer. Three days' worth of tears had exhausted her. But she was glad her secret was out. At least to him. Admitting the truth to Juan Carlos had been difficult, but it had also been liberating. There would be no more lies between them now.

He'd been angry with her when he'd left her condo the other day. She'd seen the pain in his eyes, too, and she'd shivered when he'd looked at her as if she were a stranger. It had been so very hard to hear him berate her. He hadn't believed her, and even thought so little of her that he'd accused her of putting her career above her love for him. His accusations had slashed through her body like a dagger. But ultimately, it was better to allow him to believe the worst about her. It was a clean break.

Still, the love she had for him would never die. It would be hard, if not impossible, to get over him. Even if he had believed her claims, he couldn't marry her. They would have no future. He lived by a stringent set of rules. He did everything by the book. It was a no-win situation. So she'd made the supreme sacrifice for his benefit. She'd dismissed him without defending herself. As if her life wouldn't be forever altered after knowing and loving him.

He would get over her. He had to. He had to go about his life as if they had never met. In the near future, she didn't know exactly when, she would quietly make an announcement that they'd broken off their engagement. Their whirlwind romance was over. And then at some later point, when it had all died down, she would admit to the world, or anyone who cared, that she wasn't of royal heritage.

She would not go on living a lie.

But for now her goal was to protect Juan Carlos from a scandal. She would not have him looked upon as a fool.

As she headed to the parking garage, her eyes clouded with tears. She was broken inside and there was no way to repair her. Taking on Mr. Tanaka's account would be a good distraction. She'd focus on work for the next few weeks and the terrible ache in the pit of her stomach would eventually go away.

She got in her car and glanced in the mirror. She looked a wreck. With the tips of her index fingers, she smoothed away moisture under her eyes. "No more," she whispered. She had to put on a happy face. It was Jasmine's birthday today and she was taking her to dinner to celebrate the big three-oh.

Ten

Juan Carlos ran a hand down his face. He stood at the bar in the study of his living quarters in the palace and poured himself a double whiskey, straight up. "It's impossible." He lifted the glass to his mouth and took a sip.

"What's impossible?"

He turned, a little shocked to find Maria standing beside him. He'd been so deep in thought, he'd almost forgotten about his dinner date with the Ramons tonight. Normally his senses were keen and no one could sneak up on him. Especially not a woman wearing a pretty dress and heels and smelling like something exotic. It served to show him how off he'd been lately.

"Sorry if I startled you. Your staff assured me I was expected."

"No, it's okay. You are." It was good to see a friendly face.

"Alex is running late. He's meeting me here."

Juan Carlos nodded. "That'll give us a chance to talk. Let me get you a drink. What would you like?"

"Just a soda, please."

He dropped two ice cubes into a tall glass and poured her a cola. "Here you go."

She took the offered glass and sipped. "So what were you mumbling about when I came in?"

The corner of his mouth crooked up. It was the best he could do. He didn't have a smile for anyone these days. "My life."

"Your life?" Maria's aqua eyes opened wider. "Your perfect, kingly, marrying-a-beautiful-princess life?"

He lifted his whiskey glass and pointed with his index finger to the bone leather sofa. "Have a seat. I have something to... I need some advice."

Maria arched an eyebrow. "Advice? About your wedding?"

He waited for her to sit and then planted himself on the other end of the sofa. "Maria, uh, there isn't going to be a wedding."

It was hard getting the words out, and seeing Maria's mouth drop open only added to his discomfort. "That's why I asked you here. I haven't told a soul yet. I can hardly believe it myself."

"But you and Portia seemed so perfect together. What happened?"

Perfect. He was beginning to really hate that word. Portia had accused him of demanding that everyone and everything around him be perfect. Was he guilty of that? Did he expect too much?

"We're not perfect. Far from it. We've broken up and I don't know what to think about it."

"Why? What happened, Your Majesty?"

"She came back to Del Sol almost two weeks ago to break it off. She claimed she didn't want to get married and move to Alma. She loved her career and didn't want it to end. She claimed all we had was a fling, and that she, we, were high on romance. Finding the hidden artwork and being on the adventure together made it all seem possible but when she got back home, she was hit with reality."

"Do you think she was running scared?"

He hung his head, staring at the ground. "Initially, that's what I thought. I believed I could convince her that we could work out logistics and that we belonged together."

He met with Maria's eyes. "I was fool enough to go after her. I was in love."

"Was?"

He shrugged. "From the day I met her, something inside me told me she was the one. I pursued her like crazy. She didn't make it easy and now that I'm home, putting the pieces together, I think I know why."

There was a beat of silence. Maria was waiting for him to continue. It was difficult to admit to anyone how wrong he'd been. "When I went to Los Angeles, we…connected again. And it was as it had always been—amazing. I thought I'd relieved her of her cold feet. But in the morning, I found her quietly crying. She said she wished that I hadn't come for her. I was confused and didn't know why she'd had a change of heart."

"Why did she?" Maria asked.

He shrugged and shook his head. "I think she was cornered and didn't see a way out, so she finally told me the truth. Portia is not who she says she is. She's not a princess. She never was. She claims she found out while trying to dig up protocols for our wedding. Her family fled to the United States right after World War II and assumed the role of royalty. They were impoverished and used their phony status to gain a leg up. Supposedly, Portia's great-aunt has a diary that confirms all this."

"Wow, this is…big. Poor Portia. She must've been devastated when she found out. I can only imagine how she feels right now."

He stared at her. "You mean you believe that she didn't know about this all along?"

"Why wouldn't I? More importantly, why wouldn't you?"

"I'll tell you why. When she came back to Del Sol a couple weeks ago she lied about her reasons for breaking it off. She made up one excuse after another and if I hadn't gone to LA, I would still believe those lies she'd told. Only when she couldn't get rid of me any other way, she was forced to reveal the truth."

"Oh, I don't know about that." Maria began shaking her head. "That doesn't sound like Portia. What did you say to her when you found out?"

"In the beginning I was shell-shocked. And then my methodical mind started working and I said some things out of anger. I practically accused her of being a gold digger. Now that I think back on it, she looked so...lost. She kept saying she was an imposter, and I couldn't sympathize with her. I wasn't in the frame of mind. I felt betrayed. She should have come to me with the truth from the beginning."

"It must've been a hard thing for her to admit. To herself, much less to the man she loved. Just think, everything she believed about herself and her life is a lie. If that were me, I wouldn't know what to do, who to turn to. I don't know if I'd have the courage to do what she did. It was a hard day for both of you."

He drew oxygen into his lungs. "I suppose. I still don't know what to think."

"What else did she say? How did you part?"

"She pretty much told me off. She said that I expected perfection in everything and that I only loved the idea of her." He stared into his tumbler at the last gulp of whiskey left. "That's not true."

"No?"

He gave Maria a glance. "No," he assured her. "I loved her."

"You still love her, Your Majesty. You can't shut down those emotions so quickly. And what if she still is that woman you fell in love with, without the title of princess in front of her name? What if Portia Lindstrom is the woman for you?"

"How can I believe that when she doesn't believe it? She

didn't try to defend herself against my accusations. She didn't try to convince me that I'd been wrong about her."

"Well, since you asked me for my advice, I'm going to give it to you. I know Portia a little bit, and I'm a pretty good judge of character. I have seen the way she looks at you. The eyes don't lie. She was deeply in love and happy."

A lump formed in his throat. In the short weeks that he and Portia had been together, they'd gotten to know each other pretty well. They'd shared an adventure or two, but it went deeper than that and he'd felt they were meant for each other from the very beginning. It was a sense he had, a feeling that clamped onto him and never let go. It wasn't an overreaction to her beauty or the fact that she was a princess. But that factored into the equation, at least a little bit, because her status meant he was free to seriously pursue her.

"I thought so, too," he said. "We were good together."

"Did you ever stop to think that she wasn't thinking about herself when she broke up with you? Maybe she loved you so much she didn't want you portrayed in a bad light. A hasty then broken engagement wouldn't instill much faith in the monarchy you are trying to reestablish. After the big splash announcing your engagement, how would King Juan Carlos appear to the country that trusted his honor? Wouldn't it make you seem frivolous? Or duped? Or worse yet, impetuous? Seems to me, if I was in that situation, I would do everything in my power to protect the man I loved from scorn and speculation."

He scrubbed his jaw and sighed. "The last thing she told me was that she would make sure no blame came to rest on my shoulders."

Maria smiled. "There, you see. Only a woman still in love would say that. She was shielding you from harm. I would bet on it."

"You would?"

"Yes, and you should, too, if you still love her."

"To what end? I can't change the future…"

"Who says you can't? You're the king."

"I'm not that kind of king. I don't want to break with tradition."

"No, you'd rather have your heart broken."

Juan Carlos sighed. She was right. He would never love another the way he loved Portia. Right now, he physically ached for her.

Maria continued, "Think of it this way. You'll rule with more clarity and fairness having Portia by your side. You won't be stung by bitterness and regret and live an empty life without her."

"But the people expect—"

"A ruler they can admire and look up to. If you make it clear to them that this is for the best, they will rally behind you, my friend. And as the newly reigning king of a lost monarchy you have the luxury of not needing a parliament to vote on changes you might want to make in your dynasty."

A slow smile spread across his face. "I hadn't thought of that." And just as the notion elevated his hope, another thought brought him down again. "No…it's too late after the way I walked out on Portia, without believing in her. She may not forgive me."

Maria scooted closer to him, the sparkle in her eyes grabbing his attention. "But she may. And I think she will. She sacrificed herself for you. Don't you think you owe your relationship one more chance? If you don't try, you'll always wonder and you'll live to regret it."

Did he still love Portia? Yes, very much, and the more he thought about Maria's argument, the more he began to believe she could be right. He couldn't throw away something so precious to him without giving it one more try.

A light flashed in his head as he began to formulate a

plan. Finally, after these past few days of living in a depressed stupor, he was waking up alert and seeing things much more clearly. He had the power of the throne behind him. He hoped it would be enough.

"Maria, I'm going to need your help."

"I'll give it gladly, Your Highness."

A knot formed in the pit of his stomach. "A lot will be riding on this," he warned.

"I know. But I have enough faith in love for both of us. Alex says I've taught him something about that."

Juan Carlos nodded. If only he had that same faith. He leaned forward to kiss Maria's cheek. "Thank you."

"What is it exactly that you've taught me, sweetheart?" Alex stood at the threshold of the study, catching Juan Carlos's lips leaving Maria's cheek.

"How important *trust* is, Alex," Maria said slowly, straightening her position on the sofa, "when it comes to matters of the heart."

Alex gave them a nod as he entered the room. "It's true...once upon a time my fist might've met with His Majesty's jaw seeing him kiss you. But now, I only see love shining in your eyes for me."

A chuckle rumbled from Juan Carlos's chest. It was a good sound. One he hoped to make more often, after Portia was back where she belonged.

The sound of her Nikes pounding against the treadmill echoed off the gym walls. Sweat beaded up on Portia's forehead as she gazed out the window of the high-rise. She was offered a view of distant mountains and below, a city waking just after dawn. It was a good time of day to work out, before the world came alive. She had about thirty minutes before the gym would crowd with businessmen and women coming for their daily fix. She'd be gone by then, away from any nosy members who'd try to talk to her, get to know her. Many people recognized her, but thankfully she was old news as the other royal couple— the Brits—were in town for a charity event and all eyes had turned to them.

It was a lucky break and she valued the bit of anonymity it afforded her.

"Oh…kay, Portia," Jasmine said, shutting down her machine. "I've had enough."

Portia continued running at a six-mile-per-hour pace. She had one more mile to go. "You've barely broken a sweat."

"You're insane this morning." Jas used her towel to wipe her face as droplets rained down from her eyebrows.

Portia slowed her pace, allowing her body to cool down. "I know. But this is the only time I have to work off my…"

"Sexual frustration."

Portia swiped at her friend's butt with her workout towel. "Shh…no. Stop that! Just frustration in general."

Jasmine reached over and pushed the Off button on Portia's machine. "You're done."

The treadmill's thrumming quieted as it shut down and Portia finally stood stationary facing Jas. "I know I am. So done." She sopped up her face and neck and allowed herself a moment of accomplishment. It had been a hearty workout.

"I meant on the machine, girl. You're being cryptic today. What's really bothering you?"

Aside from her broken heart? It was hard to put into words exactly but she tried to explain. "I'm almost finished with the Tanaka account, Jas. You've helped me so much this past week and we've been working at breakneck speed for long hours. When I'm through… I don't know how it will play out. I'm still officially on leave. I don't know what to do after this. I'm living a lie, but I can't do anything about it at the moment. I feel weird in my own skin right now."

"Wow, Portia, I'm sorry. Juan Carlos doesn't deserve you. You're hurting because of him."

"You got that backward. I don't deserve him."

"Oh, brother. Listen, I know it's going to take time getting over him, but you will, honey. I hate to stand by and see you beat yourself up over something out of your control."

"Thanks, Jas. It means a lot to know you have my back."

"I do."

They left the workout area and headed to the showers. After a quick rinse off, Portia dressed in her casual street clothes and combed her hair.

"Too bad we can't grab breakfast," Jas said, exchanging a look with Portia in the dressing room mirror as she slipped her long mane into a ponytail.

"Wish we could, but we've both got busy mornings. Sorry if I'm overworking you on this account."

"You're not at all. I was only looking for an excuse to have waffles and bacon this morning."

"And you wanted an accomplice, right?"

Jas nodded. "No fun eating alone."

"Another day, I promise."

"Okay, then I'll talk to you later. Oh, and thanks," she said, wrinkling her nose, "for dragging my butt in this morning." She pouted. "I ache all over and my legs feel like Jell-O."

"You'll thank me in twenty years when you're still hot and gorgeous."

"So I guess I'll have to be your friend forever now."

"BFFs. That's us."

"Yeah, that's us," Jas said, waving goodbye.

Portia rode the elevator down to the parking garage. Just as she was getting into her Volvo, her phone beeped. She glanced at the screen. Odd, she'd gotten a text from Maria Ramon.

I'm in town and would love to see you. Can you make
time for me today?

"No," she whispered. Any reminder of Juan Carlos right
now was hard to take. Seeing Maria would only bring
back memories of her time in Alma. She did have a terribly busy day. Hadn't she just turned down a breakfast
date with her best friend?

Another text came in. It's important that I see you.

Portia's breath caught in her throat. Her heart began to
pound. She couldn't refuse Maria. She was a friend and
more than that, Portia was curious as to what she wanted.
But that didn't stop her hands from trembling as she typed
her answer. Sure, would love to see you. Stop by this morning. She gave her the address and sighed, starting the car.
She planned on working from home this morning, anyway.

As it turned out, Portia couldn't concentrate when she
returned home. Those phone conversations could wait another day, she decided. She changed into a powder-blue
silk blouse and white slacks, and brushed her hair back
and clipped it on one side with a gemstone barrette à la
Gwen Stefani. She finished with a few flips of mascara to
her lashes and some pink lip gloss.

In the kitchen, she prepared coffee, arranged fresh pastries on a plate, and then brought it all to the dining table.
Mischief and Mallow played at her feet, swatting none too
gently at her toes. Before they destroyed her sandals, she
scooped them both up and carried them to the sofa. "Here,
let's cuddle," she said, laying them across her chest. They
obeyed, burrowing into the warmth of her body. The sound
of their purring brought a smile to her face. She stroked
the top of their soft downy heads. She loved the two fur
balls with all of her heart.

A few minutes later, the doorbell chimed and Portia
jerked up straight. The quick move sent the kittens tum-

bling to the floor. The little guys landed on their feet. Oh, to be a cat.

Portia rose and glanced at herself in the foyer mirror, checking hair and makeup. She approached the door, but her hand shook on the knob. She paused, took a deep breath. *Stay calm, Portia. Maria is a friend.*

She opened the door to find Maria smiling warmly, her pretty aqua eyes bright. A sharp twinge tightened Portia's belly. "Hi, Maria."

"Portia, it's good to see you."

She stepped forward to give Maria a hug. "I'm happy to see you, too. Please come in," she said, retreating as Maria made her way into the foyer.

She glanced around, noting the high-vaulted ceilings and the living and dining rooms. "It's a lovely place, Portia."

She shrugged. "Thanks. It's a rental. I travel back and forth from coast to coast a lot, so I have a small apartment in New York City, too. I haven't really made this place my own yet." She'd never felt settled enough in either place to put too much of herself into them. Aside from her treasured artwork on the walls, the rest of her furniture was simply… there. She had no emotional attachment to it, which had never really dawned on her before now. "It's not a big place. Would you like a tour?"

"Sure." Portia walked her through the condo, showing her the home office, the guest bedroom, her master suite and the kitchen. They stopped in the dining room. "Would you like coffee and a pastry?"

Maria's eyes darted to the dish of fresh pastries. They were impressive. Portia knew the pastry chef at the Beverly Hills Hotel and she'd made a call this morning to have them delivered. "I'd love some. Thank you. It's good seeing you in your own element here. This is very nice."

"Let's have a seat," Portia said. "Everything's ready." Maria sat down across the table and Portia poured them each a cup of coffee. "I was surprised, in a good way, to hear from you this morning. What brings you to California?"

Maria cradled the cup in her hands. "I, uh, I had no real business here, Portia. I came specifically to see you."

"Me?" Portia halted before the cup touched her lips. "Why?"

"Maybe because I'm a hopeless romantic. Maybe because I found the love of my life in Alex and want my friends to find that same kind of happiness. Don't get me wrong, Portia, I'm not here to meddle, but I do think Juan Carlos made a mistake with you."

"He told you?" Portia wasn't sure how she felt about that.

"Yes, I know you've broken the engagement."

"Who else knows?"

"No one. I don't think he's told his cousins yet."

Portia nodded. Her belly began to ache. "Do you know everything?"

Maria's expression softened. "I know you're not a princess, Portia. Juan Carlos told me the entire story. I'm so sorry you were misled all those years. It must have been extremely difficult finding out the way that you did."

Portia's eyes squeezed shut at the truth of those words. "Yes." Oh, God. This was so hard. If only she could blink this entire ordeal away. Too bad life wasn't that easy. Soon everyone would know her dirty little secret and they probably wouldn't be as kind as Maria. "It's been an adjustment. My whole life is a lie."

"Not all of it, Portia."

She snapped her eyes open, just as Maria's hand came to touch hers. She welcomed the warmth of her friend's gentle touch. "I can't possibly know exactly how you feel, but I do know you. Portia Lindstrom is a wonderful, sweet, caring woman. She's smart and funny and she's terribly in love with a good man."

Portia shook her head. "No. Juan Carlos...there's nothing left between us."

"There's love, Portia. Don't discount it. It makes the world go round, you know."

"Well, I'm spinning fast, Maria. And I'm about to fall off."

"No, you don't have to fall off. I know Juan Carlos still loves you. He's made a terrible mistake. He was in shock, I think, hearing the news about your identity, and he regrets how you two left off. He's sorry for how he treated you, Portia."

"I accept his apology. If that's what you came for, you can tell him not to worry about me. I'm...fine."

"That's not why I came. You love him very much, don't you?"

Portia sat silent.

"I know you're protecting him, Portia. I know, because if I were in your shoes, I'd do the same thing."

"You would?"

"Yes. Isn't it why you initially lied about the reason you broke off your engagement?"

"Maybe."

"Maybe yes?"

"Okay, yes. That's why I lied. It was inevitable that we had to break up, so why should both of us go down with the ship? I was to blame. It was my family's illicit behavior that put us in this position. Juan Carlos didn't need to suffer, too."

"I thought so." Maria selected a pastry and eased it onto her plate. "Juan Carlos is very lucky."

Portia scoffed. "Hardly. I'm a fraud."

"No, you're not, Portia. You may not be a princess, but that's not all you are. Juan Carlos believes in your love."

"Then why isn't he here? Never mind. I'm glad he's not. It was hard enough breaking it off with him the first and second time."

Maria chewed her raspberry cheese tart with a thoughtful expression on her face. "The third time's the charm,
they say. And he's not here, because well, he wants to
see you again. In fact, it's urgent that he see you. But he
wants you to come to Alma. What he has to say must be
said in Del Sol."

"Me? Go back to Alma? I couldn't possibly."

"I was afraid you'd say that. I'm not to leave here without you, but…I think I have something that will change
your mind."

"Nothing much could change my mind."

"Wait right here. I have something in my car. I'll only
be thirty seconds," Maria said, rising. "Don't you think
about putting those pastries away."

Portia smiled despite the mystery unfolding. What on
earth was Maria up to?

Just seconds later, Maria walked back into the dining
room holding a large package wrapped in brown paper.
The box was the size of a small television or a microwave.
Ridiculous.

"What do you have there?"

"Oh, no, I'm not telling. You have to open it. First read
the note."

"I don't see a note?"

"It's inside."

Portia stared at Maria and shook her head. Nothing
would get her to change her mind. But she had to admit,
she was intrigued. Her eye began to twitch. *Damn. Stop
it.* Okay, she was nervous.

"Go on," Maria said.

Portia dug her fingers into the wrapping and tore it
away. Paper flew in all directions. An envelope with her
name on it taped to the box popped into her line of vision.
She lifted it off, pulled the note out and read it silently.

Portia, sweetheart,
Give me another chance to prove my love.
This was to be my wedding gift to you.
I hope you will accept it and me back into your life.
It speaks for itself.
Juan Carlos

Tears trickled down her face. The note was short, but held the words that could make all things possible. She loved Juan Carlos. Would always love him. And now, dare she take a chance? What could he have possibly sent that would impact her more than those loving words?

"Open the box, Portia."

"I'm afraid to," she said, eyeing the lid, her body shaking so badly she could hardly move. "What if it isn't…"

"It is. Trust me," Maria said.

Portia pulled open the lid and found yet another box. She lifted it out and set it on the table, staring at the ornate workmanship on the box, the beautiful wood carvings of intricate design.

She undid the latch and slowly eased the lid open. She eyed her gift and a soft gasp rose up from the depths of her throat. This was amazing. Sweet. The gesture meant more to her than anything else she could imagine. Her lips began to quiver, her heart pounded and her tears fell like heavy rain.

"It's the s-statue. My favorite p-piece of the artwork we…" She gulped and whispered, "It's from the hidden treasure we uncovered." A man reaching his hand out for the woman he loves. *"Almas Iguales. Equal Souls."*

A royal chauffeur met her at the Del Sol airport terminal, grabbing up her suitcases and guiding her toward the limousine parked just outside the entrance. She was taking a giant leap of faith coming here, offering up her heart once again. But Juan Carlos had done the one thing, given her the one gift that could change her mind. His generous gesture told her he understood her, believed in her and wanted her back in his life. She didn't see how it was possible. She didn't know what terms Juan Carlos would dictate to her when she arrived. Could she bank on his integrity? Could she trust in him enough to believe there was a solution to their dilemma?

His gift had jarred her into believing the best was yet to come. But as the hours had worn on, she'd started to doubt again. It had taken Maria and Jasmine both to convince her that if she didn't travel to Del Sol and give it one last try, she would live to regret it.

"He's been solely devoted to you since the minute he set eyes on you," Maria had said.

"Think of your time at the farmhouse," Jasmine had prodded. "How many other men would rescue feral cats and give them a good home, much less a royal palace, to make you happy? And don't forget how he battled a snake to keep you safe. He's been there for you, Portia. And he'll be there for you again."

"Go, give your love another chance," they'd both chorused.

So here she was back in Del Sol where in less than an hour, Juan Carlos would address the citizens of his country in a speech that would set the tone for his rule.

The driver opened the limo door. "Thank you." She slid inside and immediately turned, startled to find Juan Carlos in the seat beside her.

"Hello, sweetheart."

The richness in his voice seeped into her soul. She faced the most handsome man she'd ever known. His eyes were deep dark shades of coffee and cocoa, flecked with hints of gold, and he was gazing at her in that intense way that made her heart soar. His smile was warm, welcoming and filled with the confidence she lacked at the moment. Oh, how she'd missed him. A whisper broke from her lips. "Juan Carlos."

"I am glad you came."

He didn't reach for her, didn't try to touch her, and she was glad. She had to catch her breath just from seeing him. Anything more would send her into a tailspin. "I, uh, I don't know why I'm here."

He sighed. "It's because you love me."

She couldn't deny it. "Yes."

"And I love you, above all else. I have misjudged you and I am truly sorry, my love. I hope your being here means you have forgiven me."

A lump formed in her throat. How could she explain the complexities of her feelings? "I do forgive you. Though it hurt, I realized you reacted as anyone might."

"But I am not just anyone, Portia. I am the man who loves you unconditionally. And I should have recognized that sooner. I should have believed in you."

"Yes. But that wouldn't have changed the outcome. Our situation is impossible, Juan Carlos."

He only smiled. "Did you like my gift?"

Tears welled in her eyes. "It's magnificent. I was truly surprised by the gesture."

"Not a gesture, sweetheart. It's a gift from my heart to yours. And I have another gift for you. One that will make all things possible. I am only asking for your trust. Do I have it?"

She hesitated for only a moment. And in that moment, she realized that yes, she trusted him with her life. She trusted him to make the right decision. She trusted him. With. Her. Heart. She nodded.

"Good."

He took her hand and lifted it to his lips, pressing the

softest, most reverent kiss there. The sweetness of the gesture left her floating on air. "I have missed you."

Their eyes met then. His were unflappable, determined, loving. She saw everything she needed in their brown depths. Then his hands were on her, cupping her face, his thumbs stroking her cheeks as his gaze flowed over her face. She was out of her depths now, living in the moment, heat crawling up from her belly to lick at her. When his lips rained down on hers, devouring her mouth in a kiss to beat all kisses, tremendous hunger swept her up and carried her away.

His groans matched her unbridled sighs. "I cannot live without you in my life," he murmured between kisses.

"I feel the same," she whispered, as he dragged her farther into his embrace. She was nearly atop him now. His hands were in her hair, his tongue sweeping through her mouth, their bodies trembling, aching.

"We have arrived, Your Highness," the driver announced through the speaker. They'd arrived? She didn't remember them taking off.

Juan Carlos stilled. "All right," he said to the chauffeur.

They had indeed arrived at a secluded private entrance in the west wing of the palace.

Juan Carlos sighed heavily and pulled away from her. "One day, we will finish this in the limo."

"I'll look forward to that." Her eyelid fluttered. Heavens, another unintended wink? She was hopeless.

Intense heat entered his eyes and a savage groan rumbled from his chest. "You are a temptation, Portia," he said. He took a second to smooth the hair he'd just mussed. The care with which he touched her and gently pulled tendrils away from her face sent shivers down her spine. Then he smiled wide and destroyed her for good. "You will attend my speech?"

"Yes." That was why she had come. His only request

was that she be in attendance when he spoke to the press and his fellow countrymen. Her flight had been delayed and there was a moment when she'd thought it an omen. A moment when she almost turned back. But Portia wasn't going to run from the truth any longer. No matter how bad. No matter that her life would be forever altered. She had gotten on the plane ready to hear what Juan Carlos seemed eager to say. He would be giving the speech very shortly. "I will be there."

He nodded, satisfied, and the door on his side of the car opened. The driver stood at attention waiting. "You'll be driven to the palace lawn now," he said to her. "I will see you very soon."

Then he climbed out of the car and was gone.

Juan Carlos stood tall and erect at the podium looking out at the crowd that had gathered on the palace lawn. Dressed regally in a dark suit and tie, he scanned his audience. Luis and Eduardo flanked him on either side, on the lookout for signs of danger. News crews from Del Sol's three television stations were in attendance, as well as reporters and journalists from far and wide. Portia saw Juan Carlos now, as the king surrounded by people who banked on his every word. He was a model citizen, handsome, refined, a man to be admired. He was the king of his people. The press loved him. Even more, they loved the idea of him *with Portia*. Who didn't love a good fairy tale?

Her stomach ached. She had no idea what he was going to say, but it was important to him that she hear him say it. There was no doubt she loved him. And she was fairly certain of his love for her. So she stood in the front row, but off to the side somewhat with Maria and Alex Ramon. Maria slid her hand over hers and squeezed gently. God, how Portia needed that show of support right now. Her legs were two rubber posts, holding her up only by sheer stubborn will. She swallowed as Juan Carlos tapped the mike, ready to begin his speech.

And when he spoke, his voice came across clear, strong and confident. Tears of pride pooled in her eyes. He addressed the crowd, garnering cheers as he began his speech. Then he graciously spoke of the future, of how he planned to work alongside the parliament to better the country. He spoke of helping the needy, working with charities and letting the people of Alma have a voice.

He seemed to seek her out of the crowd and as those gorgeous dark eyes landed on her, her breath caught in her throat. He trained that killer smile on her once again. How unfair of him to have such power over her, to stop her breathing with a look, a smile.

All eyes in the crowd seemed to turn her way. She was no stranger to the press, to having people recognize her, but today, she wanted no such attention. She'd rather be invisible.

Maria squeezed her hand again, giving her silent support. Portia inhaled and began breathing again.

"I have one more announcement to make," he continued to his audience. "Actually it is the reason I have called you here. I have made a decision that will change the ways of the monarchy for the better, I hope. For decades past, those in power, the honorable men and women who held the highest rule of the land, often did so out of duty. But with their duty often came great sacrifice." Juan Carlos glanced at Portia again briefly and then went on. "Many true loves went unheeded. Many of those loves were lost to baseless marriages, unions that held no great affection. The sacrifice was thought to keep the bloodlines pure. I have called you here today to say that my rule, this monarchy, is one that looks forward to the future, not backward at the past. It is time to bring the monarchy into the twenty-first century.

"As you know, Portia Lindstrom and I are to be married. Our engagement was swift, yes, but when it's right, you know it deep in your heart." His fist covered his heart and he awarded the crowd his beautiful smile. "And I am here to tell you it is right."

His eyes sparkled and he sent her a look filled with so much love, Portia's heart did somersaults. "Recently, it's come to light that Portia is not the true princess of Samforstand. In fact, she has no royal bloodlines at all. She came to me when she learned this news from an elder in her family. It seems there was much confusion about the legal heirs to the throne after the chaos and hardships of World War II.

"My family went through great hardships at that time, as well. Many of you here today know all about the recent trials and tribulations my family went through to find the true heir to the throne. Our great-grandmother's recently discovered letters proved to all of us the high price that was paid to keep to the letter of law when it came to royal protocol. In those letters we learned that her son, king Raphael Montoro II, and his direct descendants were not the rightful heirs to the throne, and thus am I standing before you today, a Salazar, as your king.

"Similarly, Portia has discovered the truth of her family's past and now needs to move forward with her life. But I will not allow mere decorum to once again steer the Montoros' destiny toward a tragic outcome. We will not let history repeat itself. We will not sacrifice our love in the name of an outdated custom. Portia Lindstrom is here today, as my fiancée, and princess or not, she is the love of my life and will become my wife."

Juan Carlos put out his hand. "Portia? Will you join me here? Be by my side."

The crowd was stunned into silence. Cameras angled her way, shots were snapped off by the dozens.

"Go," Maria whispered. "He is changing a centuries-old tradition for you. Don't leave him waiting."

She blinked, coming to grips with what had just happened. The depth of his commitment astonished her, delighted her and sent her hormones into a tizzy. She caught Eduardo giving her a smile and an encouraging nod from behind Juan Carlos. She smiled back.

Maria was right; she couldn't leave the king waiting. Not for another second. If he could do this for her, then she wouldn't hesitate to show him her love. With him by her side, she could conquer anything. She wasn't a wimpy princess. Well, she *wasn't* a princess at all, but she wasn't wimpy, either.

Her head held high, she stepped forward and made her way to the podium. As she reached it, she took Juan Carlos's outstretched hand and gazed into his eyes. In them, she saw her life, her future. The details were negotiable, but the love, that never wavered. She loved him. She would always love him. Thank God, King Montoro of Alma was a determined man.

Juan Carlos pulled her close and there before the world, bruised her lips in a kiss that left no one doubting their king's commitment. "Juan Carlos," she murmured. "Everyone's watching."

"Are they?"

Cameras clicked like crazy and she had no doubt this epic scene would go viral.

When Juan Carlos broke off the kiss, he nudged her tight to his side to present a united front and turned to the crowd. "Portia is a wonderful, bright, talented woman and in the days and years to come, you will all see in her what I see. I ask only that you welcome her today. Give her the same chance you gave me."

The crowd was silent and Portia's heart plummeted. And then a sole cheer rang out from a man shouting his support. And then another cheer went up and another, in a show of loyalty. And soon, the entire gathering displayed their acceptance as boisterous cheers and booming applause echoed against the palace walls, the citizens of Alma giving the king their allegiance.

They had accepted her.

Portia couldn't keep a wide, teary-eyed smile from spreading across her face. She was grateful for their support, but she was certain that even if the crowd had turned hostile, nothing would have deterred Juan Carlos. He had her back, and that was the best feeling in the world.

The speech over, Portia walked off with Juan Carlos. "I love you, you know," she said, winding her arm around his waist and leaning her head on his shoulder.

"I do know, but I think I'll need to hear you say it about a thousand times. Tonight?"

She nodded. "Tonight." She lifted her lips to his. "Do you think you can make me say it a thousand times?"

He laughed. "Oh, I know I can. Just let me alert the chauffeur we'll be needing the limo soon."

Her eyes went wide. "Juan Carlos, you don't play fair!"

"Sweetheart, I play for keeps. Princess or not, you're a royal temptation that I can't live without."

"So you're keeping me?"

"For as long as you'll have me."

"Forever, then. It's settled."

"Settled," he said, grinning as he picked her up and twirled her around and around.

She floated on air.

And her feet never did touch the ground again.

Epilogue

One month later

Juan Carlos couldn't stop grinning as he held Portia in his arms and danced to the royal orchestra's rendition of "Unforgettable" under hundreds of strung lights and a moonlit sky on the grounds of the newly restored farmhouse. This place that Bella and James would someday call home was where Juan Carlos and Portia had found love, too, and it seemed fitting to have a small intimate exchange of promised vows here in front of their close friends and family. His new bride dressed in satin and ivory lace, with his mother's diamond wedding ring sparkling on her finger, was the most beautiful woman on the planet.

"Are you happy?" he asked, fairly certain his answer was found in the sky-blue gleam in her eyes.

"I don't think I've ever been happier."

"That's how I want to keep it, sweetheart." He pressed her close and kissed her forehead, brushing his lips over her cheeks and nose and finally landing on her sweet mouth.

"I loved our sunset wedding," Portia said. "This is a special place."

Their first dance ended and Juan Carlos swung Portia to a stop in the center of the circle of their guests, who applauded them, their dance and their marriage. Portia's elegant grace, her help in discovering the hidden artworks and her work with local charities had endeared her to the country. Even the doubters had begun to come around as she constantly proved to them that she belonged at his side. It was a good thing, too, because Juan Carlos would rather give up the throne than live without Portia.

His cousins approached. "Welcome to the family, Portia," Rafe said, his very pregnant wife on his arm. "We couldn't be happier for you both."

"It was a lovely ceremony," Emily said.

"Thank you. I've heard all about your special ceremony, as well," Portia offered, glancing at Emily, Rafe, Gabe and Serafia. "I've never attended a double wedding before."

"We wish we would've known you then," Serafia added.

"Might've been a triple wedding, who knows?" Gabe said with a teasing smile.

Juan Carlos found it all amusing. His cousins had met their wives in uncanny ways and now every one of them was married. Rafe had resumed his position as head of Montoro Enterprises and the company was thriving. Good thing, too, because Rafe's father had decided to retire in Alma. After the ceremony he'd been the first to offer his congratulations, giving Portia a kiss on the cheek and wrapping Juan Carlos in a tight embrace. Juan Carlos owed a great deal to the man who had raised him from early childhood.

Gabe, the younger of his male cousins, had finally shed his bad boy ways and settled down with his lifelong friend and love, Serafia.

"I think I just felt something," Bella announced. She took James's hand and placed it on her small rounded belly. "Here, see if you can feel the baby."

James kept his hand there several seconds. "I'm not sure," he said softly, diplomatically. "It's early yet, isn't it, honey?"

"Maybe for you, but I think I felt it." Bella's eyes were two bright beams of light. She was carrying James's child.

James kissed her lips. "I can't wait to feel our baby, too."

Portia slipped her hand in Juan Carlos's and they watched the scene play out. James had one child already and Bella was proving to be a fantastic stepmother to one-year-old Maisey. And now, their family was expanding. Juan Carlos was glad that Bella and James had settled in Alma and James was back playing professional soccer—football as they called it here—and winning games for the home team. Things had been rough there for a while between James and his father, oil tycoon Patrick Rowling. Patrick had picked James's twin brother, Will, to marry Bella. The arranged marriage was an antiquated notion to say the least, and Bella was having none of it. James was the man for her. And then Will had also found love with Catalina Ibarra, his father's maid. The whole thing had sent Patrick into a nosedive but he was finally coming around and softening to the idea that perhaps his sons could make up their own minds about their love life and beyond.

"Now that we're all here together, I have good news to share with all of you," Juan Carlos said. He couldn't help his ever-present smile from intensifying. He had his family's attention now. "I'm told by Alex and the prime minister that Alma has never seen a better year. The country is well on its way to being financially solvent again. Thanks in part to our efforts here, I might add. With the discovery of the lost art treasure, tourism will climb, especially once we put those pieces on public display. We are working to that end. Since the state of Alma is now finally secure once again, a sizable portion of the Montoro fortune has been repatriated. It has been decided that the money will fund a new public school system named for my grandmother Isabella Salazar."

"That's wonderful," Bella said.

Rafe and Gabe slapped him on the back with congratulations.

"If it wasn't for Tia Isabella's determination to see the Montoros return to Alma in her lifetime—and those letters I discovered—none of this would even be possible," Bella said.

It was true. Juan Carlos wouldn't be king, he would never have met Portia and who knew what would have happened among his other family members. "We owe my grandmother quite a bit."

They took a solemn moment to give thanks to Isabella.

And then the orchestra music started up again.

Couples paired off and moved onto the dance floor.

Little Maisey Rowling had woken up from her nap. Wearing pink from head to toe, she was sitting on the front porch playing with the palace kittens alongside Portia's maids in attendance, Jasmine and Maria Ramon.

"I owe those two women a dance," Juan Carlos said to Portia. "If not for them, you may never have come back to Alma. Actually, I owe them much more than that."

"Yes, but first, my love, I have a wedding gift for you. I hope it will match the one you gave me. I cannot wait another second to give it to you."

"Okay," he said, eager to please her. "I'm yours."

She tugged him to the back of the house, to the garden area that was in full bloom, despite the late fall climate. Oh, the miracle of royalty that made all things possible. She sat him down on the white iron bench and then took a seat beside him.

"Juan Carlos," she began, taking his hands and holding them in her lap. "You have given me your love, a new family and a beautiful palace to live in."

"You deserve all those things, sweetheart."

"But there's one thing missing. One thing I want and hope you want, too."

He had no clue where she was going with this. He had everything he wanted. "Have you found another brood of cats to adopt?"

She shook her head and grinned, her eyes beaming with the same glow he'd seen in Bella's. His heart stopped beating. He gathered his thoughts and came to the only conclusion he could.

"You're not?"

She nodded now, bobbing her head up and down rapidly. "I am."

"We're going to have a baby?"

"Yes!"

A glance at her belly gave him no indication. "When?"

"Seven months from now."

Carefully, he pulled her onto his lap. "I'm…I'm…going to be a father."

"Yes, you are."

He curved his hand around her nape and brought his lips close to hers. "You're going to be a mother."

"Yes."

The idea filled him with pride. His Portia would give him a child. It was the best gift in the world. His mouth touched hers reverently and he tasted the sweetness of her lips. "I couldn't be happier, sweetheart."

"I'm glad. Our baby will grow up in a home filled with love. Neither one of us knew our parents for very long. But now, we will have a family of our own. It's quite unexpected…"

"It's all I've ever wanted, Portia. For us to be a family."

"Really?"

He nodded. His throat constricted. His emotions had finally caught up to him today. His life had come full circle—the orphaned boy who would be king, married to his heart's desire, was to have a family all his own now.

There was no better kingdom on earth than for a man to share his life with the woman he loved.

He and Portia were two of a kind.

Almas Iguales.

Equal souls.

* * * * *

DYNASTIES: THE MONTOROS
One royal family must choose between love and destiny!
Don't miss a single story!

MINDING HER BOSS'S BUSINESS
by Janice Maynard

CARRYING A KING'S CHILD
by Katherine Garbera

SEDUCED BY THE SPARE HEIR
by Andrea Laurence

THE PRINCESS AND THE PLAYER
by Kat Cantrell

MAID FOR A MAGNATE
by Jules Bennett

A ROYAL TEMPTATION
by Charlene Sands

MILLS & BOON®

Why shop at millsandboon.co.uk?

Each year, thousands of romance readers find their perfect read at millsandboon.co.uk. That's because we're passionate about bringing you the very best romantic fiction. Here are some of the advantages of shopping at www.millsandboon.co.uk:

✱ **Get new books first**—you'll be able to buy your favourite books one month before they hit the shops

✱ **Get exclusive discounts**—you'll also be able to buy our specially created monthly collections, with up to 50% off the RRP

✱ **Find your favourite authors**—latest news, interviews and new releases for all your favourite authors and series on our website, plus ideas for what to try next

✱ **Join in**—once you've bought your favourite books, don't forget to register with us to rate, review and join in the discussions

Visit **www.millsandboon.co.uk**
for all this and more today!